D1810451

GEO-POLITICAL CULTURAL STUDY OF PAKISTAN

Monawar Ali Syed
Ex-Chairman Geography & Pakistan studies
Aitchison College, Lahore, Pakistan
Faculty, Georgia Perimeter College, Atlanta, Georgia, USA

Adviser:
Dr. John Allensworth
Faculty, Georgia State University, Atlanta, Georgia, USA

Title   : Geo-Political Cultural Study of Pakistan

Author   : Monawar Ali Syed

Edition   : 2010

Copyrights : All rights reserved under the Copyright Act.

ISBN   : 9781439273265

Acknowledgements:

The author acknowledges with thanks the valuable guidance and encouragement extended to him by Dr. Walcott and Dr. John Allensworth of the Department of Geography Georgia State University Atlanta in compilation of the volume that without their help and assistance could not have accomplished. I am also indebted to Mr. Javed Abidi, a proficient publisher of Atlanta Georgia, to have edited and organized the script. Last not least I am thankful to Mr. Imran Ali serving as Director Foreign Affairs Islamabad to have initially suggested to undertake this venture, while he was posted in Pak Embassy Washington D.C., USA.

CONTENTS

LIST OF MAPS AND ILLUSTRATIONS

Preface

In compiling this book "Pakistan - A geopolitical and Cultural study" my aim has been to provide a handy work of reference to students of culture, Pak studies and common readers interested to be acquainted with history, geography, politics and strategic importance of this wonderful country. The changed scenario of present times - particularly the events after Nine Eleven, Seven Eleven, insurgency on a large scale, including assassination of chair person Benazir Bhutto that have brought a radical change in the geopolitics of the region, necessitated redrafting an earlier version of my book under the caption, Introduction to Pakistan Studies.

Efforts have been made through this volume to remove confusion created by exploiters, using religion to serve their political ends- resultant terrorism, suicide bombing and indiscriminate killing of innocent people including the political figure of international repute Mohtarma Benazir Bhutto, twice Prime Minister of Pakistan, a young charismatic lady, highly qualified, an excellent orator that attracted audience in hundreds of thousand, loved and respected, champion of democracy- had taken upon herself bidding farewell to her family to relieve her country men and women from the menace of military dictatorship.

Pakistan a member of O.I.C and a non-aligned country had to adopt a divergent policy in the present environment of terrorism perpetuated at home and abroad. Pakistan actively participated to fight global terrorism of which has herself been a victim in the shape of Sectarian killings, attacks on mosques and places of religious sanctities Sectarian differences are being used as a tool for achieving political ends. It is, therefore, considered imperative to equip our students and the readers with a true perception and understanding of the religion to dispel rumors designed to malign Islam and its followers. A considered endeavor has, therefore, been made in this volume for the purpose.

A commendable improvement in India- Pakistan relations had been possible with the untiring efforts of present and previous governments and so also due to the changed geopolitical situation in the region. A number of steps have been taken by both countries to sort out differences and to come closer to each other, giving up the policies of confrontation. Pledge of both the parties, to discuss and solve all disputes, including the main bone of contention, Kashmir problem, during SAARC conference held at Islamabad in January and subsequently in New York in Sept. 2004, is a welcome change and a step towards a bright future of the people of the region. Revival of cricket series and opening of Muzaffarabad Sirinagar route is another good gesture. There is need to maintain the good will that has been generated by the well- wishers of the poor masses particularly, the miserable people of Kashmir, who have been striving hard for their inherent rights since 1930s. Approach has been adopted to talk about such facts and events that can be instrumental in bridging differences and to bring the people of both India and Pakistan close to each other, to help put them on the path of harmony and understanding, giving up and forgetting bitterness that have prevailed since 1947. Religion strengthens relation of love and amity rather than dividing and inciting people against each other. Dr. Allama Iqbal the poet of the East in one of his famous poems addressing people of the sub-continent had said, "Religion does not teach to harbor enmity; same God, Allah, Parmatma is there and praised everywhere; in temples, churches, mosques and gurdwaras." He loves those who love their fellow beings.

Map study forms an essential feature in developing understanding of a region. A brief introduction of map study and various techniques of map making including GPS & GIS have also been included to cover this important skill that one ought to acquire to be able to locate and solve problems in practical life.

INTRODUCTION
GEOPOLITICAL IMPORTANCE

Pakistan is an important upcoming country of South Asia. Being a religious country has always looked to the west and all along been a reliable ally of USA and stood by her in the hour of need; in 1979 when USSR occupied Afghanistan a key region termed as the "HEART LAND" by Mackinder a British geographer, US approached China to help ousting the occupation as she maneuvered US exodus from Viet Nam. Lucrative offer for the job was made. In the first instance China accepted the offer but as a second thought and under threat from USSR declined it. It was then Pakistan's President General Zia- ul-Haq who not only accepted the challenge but also got the job done, that ultimately resulted in the disintegration of the rival world power. Pakistan's stance, in the recent years, to fight terrorism, and to be instrumental in the defeat of Taliban is a clear proof of her sincerity and ability to play an effective role in the region. Pakistan is a vital link in the new global order; deterrent against terrorism, ambassador of peace and harmony for the nations inhabiting the region in particular and the world in general.

Because of her strategic location; gateway to Central Asia adjacent to the Middle East, a Muslim bloc, where Pakistan is held in great respect, can help resolution of their problems instrumental in bridging differences with any member of the region. As an active member of SAARC Pakistan has been participating in the development and resolution of problems faced in the region and has displayed a commendable role during its 12th annual summit held in Islamabad on 3-6 January 2004 that was helpful in breaking the deadlock over Jammu and Kashmir issue with India hanging fire for the last more than 50 years and has been responsible of armed conflicts between the two neighbors a number of times.

Figure 1: Pakistan- Strategic- Location

Religion is an important factor that plays an effective role in the development of culture and civilization of a region. The sub-continent of India known as Hindustan, abode of people primarily practicing Hinduism, when under the influence of Muslim rulers and preachers- Sufis & Saints a large number converted to Islam, in the words of Quaid-e-Azam (Mohammad Ali Jinnah) the foundation of Pakistan was laid in India when a first Hindu accepted Islam. As the religion of Islam brings a radical change in the way of living, worship, food, clothing and the style of life gives rise to a different philosophy. As for instance Muslims worship God without seeing and making Idols. They slaughter and eat cow's meat whereas Hindus worship it as a sacred animal. Muslims bury their dead bodies. On the other hand Hindus burn them. In the same way there exist some social disparity; women following Islamic faith cover their body from head to foot and observe purdah (segregation) from males other than their family members. In Hindu society such restrictions do not prevail and are not observed by their womenfolk to that extent. As such the assumption of a separate nation by the Muslims was not out of place, as the two could not be governed by the same rule of law. When the British decided to liberate the sub-continent Muslims rightly claimed a separate homeland for them. In the beginning, however, all the Muslim leaders, Sir Syed Ahmad Khan, Allama Iqbal and Quaid-e-Azam tried to find an honorable and just position for the Muslims in a united India-but later all felt that a fair dealing from the Hindu majority once in power would be impossible. The Muslims wanted a way of life strictly according to the tenants of Islam and a state that provided them freedom to profess and practice their religion-the Ideology of Islam.

Pakistan emerged as a free independent state in South Asia on August 14, 1947. It was possible due to the aftermaths of World War II and decolonizing policy of England coupled with the efforts of the people of the sub-continent of getting freedom for them from the foreign rule. World War II ended in July 1945. British government decided to fulfill her promise to reward the people of the sub-continent for their support and active participation to help winning the war so also to shed the load of her responsibilities abroad.

Demand for Pakistan

Pakistan movement was launched under the banner of Muslim League, which was founded in 1906 to protect rights of Muslims of India. The slogan; "Pakistan Ka Matlab Kaya La Ilaha Illillaha' which meant land of the pure, where sovereignty of Allah would prevail, soon became very popular and Muslim students and youth chanted it all over in the streets in India.

Partition plan was approved by the British government on the demand of Muslim population who at long last were able to convince that Hindus and Muslims are two separate nations and as such could not coexist. Muslims, therefore, demanded a separate state consisting of Muslim majority provinces; Bengal, Balochistan, Punjab, Sindh and N.W.F.P. Hindus in the first instance opposed tooth and nail and tried to forestall the proposal with all the might at their disposal and tried to bring round Muslim leadership to the idea of united India and also threatened the use of force if not came to terms. A last minute attempt was made in 1946 through Gandhi Jinnah talks to reach a compromise to keep India together. Even that could not succeed for one reason or the other. Ultimately both Congress and Muslim League agreed on the partition of India, however, not on the original demand of the Muslim League but a truncated Pakistan with further bifurcation of the provinces of Bengal and Punjab.

Boundary commission, headed by Sir Red Cliff was constituted who was supposed to demarcate boundaries on the basis of population census of 1940 and to keeping in view the geographical factors involved. With limited time at his disposal for the tedious job, both India and Pakistan were made to commit that the verdict of the commission would be final and the parties would not have a right to appeal against the award. India taking advantage of the situation and her terms with Lord Mount Baton, who had already been nominated the first governor General of independent India, as such managed to exert pressure on the commission to favor them. Perusal of boundary commission file, available in the Board of Revenue office at Lahore clearly shows that certain last minute changes were affected out of the blue, most probably on the intervention of Lord Mount Baton, the then Governor general of India- the supreme authority. In this way India was given some areas from Amritsar and Gurdaspur districts with clear Muslim majority in the Punjab to provide India an access to Kashmir- valley. In the same way Calcutta, integral geographical part of Bengal delta, the only populous city and a natural harbor was included in India. The boundary commission award, although basically different from the agreed formula, but parties had no choice but to accept it as mentioned above. Quaid-e- Azam did not appreciate the verdict and remarked it as a last dagger pushed in their back and said, "what to talk of a crippled Pakistan, he was prepared to accept even a space to put his foot on to lay the foundation of a free Muslim state; an independent Pakistan".

HINDU MUSLIM RIOTS
It was contemplated by the leadership of both Congress and Muslim League that partition would not result in migration of population from one state to another and that people would continue wherever they were living and enjoy their rights- but no one speculated bloodshed, arson and looting at that scale. Unfortunately due mostly to the fiery speeches and utterances by some short sighted leaders from both sides, who incited masses for violence against one another and thus defeated the very purpose of freedom and particularly for the innocent men, women and children in millions, who were forced to leave their home and hearth amongst horror and fear had to pay a heavy price in the shape of their precious lives and belongings on an unprecedented large scale. The migration of population between India and Pakistan of 1947 was not only unprecedented but the highest of its kind in the world.

Beginning of Riots
On March 2nd, 1947 a public meeting of Congress was held at Kapoor Thalla ground Lahore. The Congress leader Mr. Patel addressing the same said," The nation who cannot handle 1 /5 minority has no right to exist." Master Tara Singh a Sikh leader in

the same meeting making a sentimental speech waved his naked sword to arouse the feelings of his followers present, against Muslims. Those irresponsible speeches and unscrupulous slogans resulted in bloody riots from the very next day. On March 3rd, 1947, students of D.A.V. College Lahore, a Hindu Institution, took out a big procession, carrying staffs in their hands, shouting slogans anti government and anti Muslim league entered Government college Lahore premises through its Katchery road entrance, and tried to persuade students to come out of the classes and join them. It was about 9 A.M. 2nd period and we were attending a class in Chemistry block located near the gate by which the mob entered. It was a timid first year class; no one dared join them when the lesson was in progress. The crowd then went towards the main building and left the College from the gate opposite district courts Lahore.

Incidentally there were some Burqa clad Muslim ladies riding a Tonga. These elements dragged those ladies to show their hatred towards Muslim community having been influenced by the speeches of their leaders the day before. Before general public or Muslim students intervened, police squads appeared and tried to disperse the mob-but the charged mob, armed with staffs and stones attacked the police squad and their vehicles, sounds of firing was heard. The mob was dispersed. Some miscreants were wounded and we saw their companions giving them first aid after dragging them in the Oval ground of the college. The news of the incident spread like a jungle fire and the entire city of Lahore was ceased with an atmosphere of awe and tension. By evening tempers went high and sense of insecurity prevailed everywhere. People surrounded by the members of opposite faith moved to places of safety. Several cases of stabbing and indiscriminate killing from both sides were reported. The state of affairs went on for about a fortnight before attaining normality. Similar riots had been reported earlier in Bengal, Noakhali and Calcutta, which left over 5000 dead due to similar incidents.

Implementation of partition plan took place on the mid night of August 14, when Quaid -e-Azam Mohammad Ali Jinnah assumed responsibility as first Governor General of Pakistan a newly born biggest Muslim state on the map of the world. In his maiden speech he congratulated the people on the birth of an independent state of Pakistan their cherished goal by the grace of Almighty Allah and advised the people to observe unity, faith and discipline and shoulder the task of building the newborn nation. He said," from today you are all members of one nation. There is no Punjabi, Balochi, Bengali Sindhi or Pathan but we are all Pakistanis." He expressed grief and sorrow for Hindus and Muslims who had been killed or had to face hardships in that long journey to freedom and advised both Indians and Pakistanis to remain calm and show perseverance. Jinnah along with Mahatma Gandhi made several such appeals to stop violence on either side of the border.

Initial Problems

The country was set rolling on the path to fulfill its objectives under the able leadership of the Quaid and his devoted associates overcoming and resolving problems and hardships the newborn state was faced with. The first and foremost one being the settlement of incessant large number of immigrants who had no shelter or food and the country did not have the resources to match with the enormous human problem. However, with the active participation of the people, government was able to overcome the situation through shear perseverance and intellect. Unfortunately Mohammad Ali Jinnah its founder could not live long and to witness the fruit of his efforts in a strong and prosperous Pakistan and breathed his last on September 11, 1948.

Thereafter his second in command Liaqat All Khan took upon to lead the nation but he also fell prey to a jealous unscrupulous group and was assassinated while he rose to address a public meeting at Rawalpindi on October 16, 1951. His assassin was killed on the spot and no clue of the group behind the crime could be found. After his murder no stable government could succeed and satisfy the masses. In the first instance, bureaucrats like Ghulam Mohammad and then Sikandar Mirza stood in the way of democracy and instead of letting politicians to undertake responsibility of running the affairs invited army to take over and thus abrogating the 1956 constitution Gen. Ayub Khan took over the reign of a newly established republic of Pakistan in October 1958. He remained in power for more than 10 years. No doubt his illegitimate tenure was a golden period of Pakistan when there was stability, agricultural reforms were introduced by reducing the limit of land holdings and thus dividing land to landless tenants on installments, Industries in both wings of Pakistan were encouraged and there was peace and prosperity. Militarily also the country was equipped with modern weapons and proved its mettle when India waged undeclared war in September 1965. India in spite of well equipped, 5 times bigger army could not contain a handful opponent and instead begged UNO and requested USA to intervene and help stop the trouble that she herself had invited.

SEPARATION OF THE EASTERN WING

Although Gen. Ayub Khan made great efforts to keep the eastern wing intact by giving them due share in the resources of Pakistan, dividing assets on equal basis and providing extra funds during natural disasters; floods and cyclones or a drought. But all this did not satisfy them. They wanted due representation in the Government, 1964 elections were held under Basic Democracy formula an indirect type of electorate. Begum Fatima Jinnah was contesting presidential elections against Gen. Ayub Khan who being in power was better placed to influence voters but it was a golden opportunity for the General to acquit himself honorably and in this way the spirit of united Pakistan amongst Bengalis, to chose Begum Fatima Jinnah as their candidate real sister of the Quaid would have maintained, the separation movements must have died or weakened and the masses could not have been easily led astray as it happened in case of denying their wish to elect a candidate- undoubtedly a symbol of unity of Pakistan.

Sheikh Mujeeb who was found involved in Aggartalla conspiracy, a puppet of India, had been allowed to pollute the minds *of* innocent masses. India, who was behind the separatists all along managed to bifurcate the country easily in a brief war in December 1971. Thus Bangladesh came into existence after remaining attached to its western wing for about 24 years. The debacle was primarily the result of keeping out politicians from the scene for such a long time. An army personnel however capable or upright may be cannot deliver what a politician can do; At Tashqand Gen. Ayub Khan, hero of '65 war lost at the table whereas Indian Prime Minister, Lal Bahadur Shastri, a politician, having lost the war in the battle field won it there. Similarly Pakistan lost the war on ground in 1971 but gained maximum on the negotiation table at Simla, through a politician of high caliber, Zulfiqar Ali Bhutto then president of Pakistan. He managed to retrieve about *90,000* POWs from India without paying any ransom or conceding any humiliating terms as against the Tashqand Accord where Pakistan was better placed.

Pakistan after 1971

With the separation of Bangladesh, its Eastern wing, Pakistan has now been left with an area of *307,000 sq.* miles, present population *160* million. Density *of* population is about 520 per sq. mile and annual growth of 2.85% and literacy 49%. More than 70% of its People live in rural areas, they are hard working, prudent and full of valor and strength and that is why most of the army of India before partition consisted of soldiers belonging to areas now included in Pakistan. Basically an agricultural country more than 80% of the people directly or indirectly engaged in agriculture. Most of the industries are based on agricultural raw materials. Pakistan is an important producer of cotton, wheat, rice, sugar cane, tobacco, fruits and oil seeds. There are hundreds of cotton ginning, spinning and weaving mills located all over the country with greater concentration in southern Punjab and Sindh cotton growing area. Flour mills, rice husking and polishing plants are located in the rice growing and sugar mills near sugar plantations; Punjab, Sindh and NWFP. Cigarette factories, oil mills, fruit packing and beverage industries are located in the areas of their cultivation. Pakistan after meeting her local needs has sufficient surplus for export.

PAKISTAN BECOMES NUCLEAR

After separation of the Eastern wing, Pakistan was greatly crippled and rendered incapacitated to face India, an unproportionally strong neighbor, who had invaded the country thrice lately in 1971. Kashmir life line of Pakistan, from where its rivers rise is forcibly held by India. It is the chief source of water supply and hydel power. In order to ensure water supply and energy vital for her existence, Pakistan needed to develop nuclear energy to make up and match with India so as not to be dictated or bullied by the big brother. Thus Pakistan with her indigenous technology, resources, with the due permission of USA and collaboration of France managed to set up a nuclear processing plant at Kahoota located in the northeastern mountainous region (1970's). The plant besides supplying fuel for atomic energy, in course of time, helped develop nukes that were tested in 1997, to make the country a nuclear state. Not only Pakistan has thus increased her defense potential considerably reduced possibility of any future armed conflict, but also created confidence in her leaders to talk to Indian counterpart boldly and settle issues on equal footing. Pakistan has also attained ability to produce fuel for generating power to meet her energy needs.

Nuclear capability of Pakistan is thus essential for the very existence of the country. It is not meant to be used for aggression against any country and is just like a bee's sting which it only uses as a last resort for its defense. Pakistan's nukes are in safe hands. They are not the property of any one individual. They are essentially for the protection and judicious economic use of the country- a national asset. There is no possibility of their landing in the hands of any extremist group. Pakistanis are responsible people and so far after seeking capability for over a decade haven't displayed any childish manifestation.

Legacy of Pakistani Culture

The area comprising Pakistan predominantly has the legacy of, Taxila, Harappa and Mohanjadaro civilizations, which existed here thousands of years ago. Taxila located in the northern area, its excavation reveals that it was a well planned city with developed housing plans, using granite and sandstone as building material, having a double storey resident university, coins seals ornaments made of metals are preserved in the Taxila museum. Harappa and Mohanjadaro are contemporary civilizations and depict similar construction and drainage patterns. Baked bricks and walls with crushed brick pieces as are used in construction these days in Pakistan, were in use. Harappa is located in Punjab near Sahiwal and Mohanjadaro in Sindh near Larkana.

Important Towns

Karachi is the largest metropolitan city and a port, with a population of 20 million, with its hinterland entire Pakistan, Afghanistan and Central Asia. It was the first capitol of Pakistan and now of the Sindh province. It is the center of trade, industry and educational center of the province. Sindh University, located at Karachi is an old recognized institution, over a hundred year old.

Islamabad-Rawalpindi twin cities: located in the north on the foothills of Himalayas, Islamabad is a newly constructed city and present capitol of Pakistan, inhabited by government officials, foreign embassy's staff or the people who have been attracted to the newly planned city, due to its moderate climate and beautiful environment and the city is fast growing. Rawalpindi is an old city of the Pothohar region located on the meeting of roads to Peshawar valley to northwest and to the valley of Kashmir to the northeast.

Lahore is an historical city with 60 million inhabitants, seat of the provincial government and center of trade and industry also called heart of Pakistan. Has been a center of political activities; Resolution of Pakistan was passed in a general meeting of Muslim League held at Minto Parks now called lqbal Parks in the year 1940 March 23. Other cities of historical and importance include Multan,

Quetta, Faislabad and we will discuss about them in greater detail in the forthcoming chapters.

Map is the laboratory of a geographer- a language of geography. Maps are equally important in war and peace. In order to equip the students with this important skill a chapter has been added in this volume, which should form an essential part of the curriculum.

Pakistan Studies as a compulsory subject was introduced after separation of its eastern wing, which served as an eye opener for the educationists, intelligentsias and well wishers of Pakistan who attributed the debacle towards lack of knowledge of Pakistani youths in the field of history and geography of their homeland, which form an important basis to promote patriotism. Thus mainly with the efforts and influence of Dr. Kaneez Yousuf Vice Chancellor Islamabad University the subject was introduced at all levels in Pakistan. I happen to be one of the pioneer members of her team. A more comprehensive-well thought syllabus of Pakistan studies was framed to include all aspects of history, geography and Islamic values to enable the students to develop sense of belonging and identity as Pakistani nationals. The subject replaced Social studies a superficial course, and introduced as a compulsory subject at High school and College levels in early 1970s. Later in 1980s it was also introduced in Cambridge and Oxford Universities as a compulsory subject for Pakistani candidates. I was the author of the first book, "Introduction to Pakistan Studies" in line with Cambridge syllabus and also appointed internal examiner of the subject in the Cambridge University.

CHAPTER I

PAKISTAN AN INDEPENDENT MUSLIM STATE

Pakistan means land of the Pure- a land where there is no exploitation-
where there is rule of justice- where there is protection for women,
children and the weaker ones- where everyone has shelter and provided
square meals- where there is no honor killings- where everyone is free to
follow and profess a religion of one's own choice- rights of minorities are
protected- in short a state where divine law- is supreme? Having been
attracted by those loud claims, majority of the Muslims of the sub-
continent voted in favor of the Muslim league, which under the dynamic
leadership of Quaid-e-Azam Mohammad Ali Jinnah turned that dream into
reality, within a matter of (8-10) years-but unfortunately did not live long
enough to fulfill the promises made out to the nation.

Pakistan is the first country, which has been created in the name of
religion. Thus Pakistan came into being to provide a home- land for the
Muslims of the sub continent on the basis of two-nation theory where
they could practice Islam freely. Mohammad Ali Jinnah was neither a
fundamentalist nor extremist and as such was in favor of a moderate and
progressive state where there would be freedom of religion, coupled with
tolerance and harmony between different sects, and linguistic groups.

Unfortunately the Quaid did not live long to see that the promises held
out to the nation were fulfilled, however, he set the ball rolling by
working day and night without caring of his ill health and left the new
born nation, just within a year of its creation, on Sept.11, 1948 It was a
moment of great grief and sorrow for the whole nation to have lost father
of the nation when he was most needed. Liaqat Ali Khan, second in
command also, did not live long and fell victim to a conspiracy to further
deprive the nation of its leadership when he was assassinated at Liaqat
Bagh Rawalpindi, as he rose to address a public meeting there in October
1951. Since then the country has been without a confided leadership and
the ill wishers of Pakistan got an opportunity to exploit the masses by
creating differences of which the father of the nation had already warned -
Eastern wing due to such exploitation, got separated, on linguistic bases,
from its western counterpart on December 18, 1971.

Mr. Zulfiqar Ali Bhutto, who had shown promise as a foreign minister in Gen. Ayub Khan's government was handed over charge of the truncated and broken Pakistan, after fall of Dacca, who with his untiring efforts, intellect and hard work, not only rebuilt the war torn country but also raised its status as one of the leading countries of South Asia and the Islamic world. In a short span of time he gave a workable unanimous constitution, got released about 90,000 POWs from India without paying any ransom, ensured an honorable living for the poor workers, and made them partners in businesses and industries owned by the tycoons of the country. He not only created jobs in the country but also opened opportunities for the surplus skilled and unskilled labor in foreign countries that helped enhancing foreign reserves and thus stabilized economy, introduced land reforms to provide land to the sitting tenants and landless peasants. He also brought reforms in bureaucracy and made them change their attitude to serve people, working under the elected members of the parliament. Then he also installed nuclear reprocessing plant at the cost of annoyance of world powers and thus increased defense potential of the country.

Mian Nawaz Sharif got Pakistan recognized as a nuclear state, improved communication and built motor ways to bring the country at par with the developed countries; Gen. Parvez Musharraf who took upon himself to cleanse the society of corruption and vices of sectarianism, stabilizing economy and has taken practical steps in that direction by banning extremist parties that were allowed to flourish during the past two decades, and also raised foreign exchange reserves of the country which was at the verge of bankruptcy-but in return, what these leaders and their families got — gallows — suicide bombing — imprisonment — exile! Gen, Parvez Musharraf has also faced some close attempts on his life.

Let us hope sanity prevails, both government, and the people develop understanding and work for the betterment of the country and learn to appreciate the efforts of the leaders who strive and work for the welfare of the nation. The policy of condemnation and revenge is contrary to the tradition of Quaid-e-Azam founder of the country, who did not take any revenge from the persons or parties who were opposed to the idea of the partition and creation of Pakistan. Digression from the tradition has not done any good to the nation so far.

Islam A Universal Religion

Pakistan has been achieved in the name of Islam it is, therefore, necessary that Pakistanis should have better understanding of the religion so as not to be exploited or led astray. Effort has been made to introduce the basic concepts derived from authentic documents: Quran, Sunnah and reliable known authors to remove misunderstandings in order to bridge differences between the factions.

Islam is the religion that Allah recognizes which has reached us after a great deal of hard work and sacrifices of His chosen ones. It is, therefore, incumbent on us to develop its true understanding and be its ambassador by setting personal example to convey the message to our children and the society in which we live.

Islam means submission before the will of God, to accept Him as the supreme authority. It is a constitution, a code that contains norms encompassing all spheres of life; moral, economic, social, political, cultural, in short a complete system -religion in all respects. One who says "La Ilaha Illillah" enters into peace or in other words comes under the protection of God Almighty as mentioned in Sura Al Hashar holy Quran I quote, "He is Allah, besides whom there is no god; the knower of the unseen and the seen; He is the Beneficent, the Merciful, the King, the Holy, the Giver of peace, the Granter of security, Guardian over all, the Mighty, the Supreme, the Possessor of every greatness; Glory be to Allah from what they set up with Him" unquote. A believer denies all other powers; only trusts and accepts His authority without having seen Him. Whatever is in the heavens and the earth declares His glory; and He is the Mighty, the Wise." He is remembered and bears 99 names; Allah, Rehman, Rahim, Karim, Ghaffar associated with his qualities mentioned in the holy Quran. He is flawless, creator of everything the earth, the heavens and whatever is there in between and under the earth.

REVEALED BOOKS

A believer has faith in divine authority, believes in all the holy books; revealed through His chosen apostles. The holy books contain directions, norms, and codes of conduct to make this life worth living and purposeful. Islam is a religion of peace and justice, also emphasizes constant struggle; jihad against evil that may lie within or without- with an added stress on self control- upholding and siding with truth any time. There is no contradiction in any of the revealed books and each ratifies the scriptures that preceded it. God's words and laws do not change nor become out dated. Holy Quran is the final and latest version- edition of the words of God as the holy Quran declares "This day have I perfected your religion and completed my favors on you and chosen Islam as your religion (Al Haj, 78) And strive hard in the way of Allah such a striving is due to Him.

He has chosen you and has not laid upon you any hardship in religion, the faith of your father Abraham (peace be upon him); He named you Muslims before and in this that the apostle may be a bearer of witness to you, and you may be bearer of witness to the people; therefore, keep up the prayers and pay the poor rate and hold fast by Allah; He is your Guardian, how excellent the Guardian and how excellent the Helper!

In Sura Aal-e- Imran, (19, 67) "surely the true religion with Allah is Islam; Abraham (PBUH) was neither a Jew nor a Christian but was an upright man, a Muslim and was not one of the poly theists."

Advice of Abraham (PBUH)): He advised his sons;"O my sons Allah has exalted the religion of Islam for you and do not die but as a Muslim".

Prayer of Yousuf (Joseph), (PBUH)), Sura Yousuf; My lord! Thou hast given me the kingdom and taught me of the interpretation of sayings; Originators of the heavens and the earth! Thou art my Guardian in this world and the hereafter! Make me die a Muslim and join me with the doers of good".

In the light of verses of the holy Quran quoted above it is evident that Islam is not a new religion, rather it is the religion preached and practiced by all the apostles: Abraham, Moses, the holy Christ, Mohammad (PBUH) and those preceded them.

When virgin Marry came to the people with a son in her arms, folks questioned her how come she got a son when she was unmarried"? Marry pointed towards the child, who spoke, that he was servant of God and had been blessed with the book- (Injeel). People believed him and thus not only exonerated the mother but also accepted holy Christ as an apostle of God and believed in the book. The Christ did not go to any school or university, yet he was knowledgeable, having been born with it. So also no prophet ever went to any place of learning in this world and was born knowledgeable, like the holy Christ. Those Christians are very close to

Muslims that do not indulge in polytheism and take Christ as Son of God; they are called 'Ahl-e-Kitab'.

ISLAM AND OTHER RELIGIONS

Besides the revealed religion Islam there are other religions, Buddhism, Hinduism, Jainism, and Sikhism practiced in the sub continent. All these religions have common base and roots in the basic divine laws; profess and believe in the sovereignty of God, Whom they call Bhagwan, Parmatama, Ishwar, Om, and they mean the same Supreme, as Muslims call Him by the names; Rehman, Rahim, Ghaffar, Razzaq. As long as they do not make idols of Him and start worshiping them as their creator-uphold sovereignty of one God, they are all believers and close to Islam. Their moral, social, economic laws have mostly roots in the divine laws incorporated in the revealed books. They believe in Dharma and Karma, which means faith, and actions; faith without actions i.e. believing without doing, is meaningless. The doer of good is compensated, in this world and earns a better living hereafter.

Man is composed of body, soul (conscious) and the spirit. Body is made of dust; "dust thou are to dust thy go", is a famous saying, that very well indicates the reality of this mortal and yet an immortal being. Body is mortal in the sense that it withers away after death whereas soul or conscious, which resides in this house i.e. body, and manages its affairs, is immortal after tasting death it remains and will be re-united with the body on the Day of Judgment (Altakvir 6, chapter 30). Spirit, however, is divine; it is a sort of energy and under His control (Bani Israel 84, chapter 15) which maintains connection between body and soul like a computer or any appliance, which does not operate without getting connected with energy.

Conscious is also called Nafs. It is of two kinds; Nafs-e- Lavama and Nafse Ammara. The first one is good natured and possesses strength to avoid evil (Alqiama 1, chapter 29), the second one Nafs-e-Ammara, incites, against it, to accept evil (Sura Yousuf 52, chapter 13). If one keeps control over one's conscious and avoids evil the Nafs-e-Lavama becomes strong and one cannot be easily led astray, like a strong healthy person who develops resistance against diseases. On the other hand if one loses control over self and is given to petty temptations Nafse Ammara gets strong at the expanse of Lavama. Yet another name mentioned in chapter 30, Wal Asar, Holy Quran, is Nafse Mutmainna; one that has a complete control over Nafse Ammara and avoids evil any time.

In order to remain physically healthy we do physical exercise, play games, go to gyms, in the same way for the health of the conscious we must also practice good things; read holy books, pray and observe fast, sit in the company of learned and pious people as bad company weakens the resistance to avoid evil and renders us mentally sick. It is, therefore, the duty of parent, school and the society to take equally effective measures to develop and maintain health of the conscious as is done for physical health. Sleep or slumber is a temporary death when spirit goes off the body and while asleep one loses cognizance of one's surroundings, holy Quran also upholds this anomaly; "He it is who takes away spirits when you go to sleep and returns of those He wishes to keep alive and stops ones who are destined to die."

Krishna in his message to Arjuna has also expressed such views. He also believes that it is the conscious that is responsible for whatever one does. A doer of good would earn a better place in the heavens and an evil- doer would be punished by transformation of his soul in some hateful creature that keeps wandering here in distress.

There exists cast system amongst Hindus alone which is nonexistent with Sikhs and Buddhists, the cast system was introduced and imposed by Arians who were invaders from central Asia and to dominate the original inhabitants (Dravidians) assigned them lower casts and retained higher positions in order to humiliate and perpetuate their authority and hegemony to get all the dirty work done by them. That is why the lower casts have never been happy, and changed their religion and accepted Christianity, Islam or Sikhism without much speculation where they did not face such humiliation and discrimination.

Most of the Muslims in the sub-continent are converts and that is why similarity in customs, rituals and traditions particularly on occasions of marriages and death is observed. Simply by change of faith the culture does not undergo a radical change, however, some philosophical changes do occur; Muslims bury their dead bodies, realizing that the body has been the house of the conscious which does not leave the body even after death when the spirit goes out of it, death is a sort of paralysis, when the body stops obeying the mind. Medical science has also revealed that certain functions of the body; hair growth and other metabolisms though slowed continue for quite some time after death and that is why body parts can be used for transplantation in another body within that time. A dead person feels the presence of people around and hears them but due to paralysis cannot move turn its eyes or speak. We some time have this type of experience while half sleep — a sort of nightmare.

The dead is at the mercy of the living who are supposed to treat the dead with utmost respect and care, wash, clean and cover the body with a neat dress and lay him/her softly in the grave and pray to God for granting forgiveness and a better place in the world here after, which has been a practice amongst believers since inception of life from Adam (PBUH) onwards.

Hindus and Sikhs burn the dead bodies out of ignorance; the founder of Sikh religion BABA GURU NANAK, who was born in a Hindu family, learnt holy Quran from a Muslim theologian, performed Haj and visited Medina to pay homage to the holy prophet Mohammad (PBUH) was also greatly influenced by Sufis and Saints and had been a regular visitor to the shrine of Hazrat Bahlul Dana (A.R.) in Baghdad, Iraq, where he had his seat (bathak) and meditated there. The verses inscribed by him on the walls of the shrine indicate that he believed in Tauheed and prophet hood of Mohammad peace is upon him, had accepted Islam, and was not one of the polytheists. But his family might not have accepted his change of faith. That is why when he died, it is commonly believed, the Hindus wanted to cremate his dead body, while the Muslims considering him as one of them wanted to burry, either to end the dispute or to rescue him from the torture of burning, the body disappeared and that is why the place of burial or cremation of Guru Nanak is not known and remains a mystery. The Sikh religion, in its present form, is not as practiced and professed by its founder - but has been introduced by a subsequent chain of his followers, not originally taught and endorsed by Baba Ji himself.

Figure 2: Guru Nanak

Shrine of Hazrat Bahlul and seat of Guru Nanak, Baghdad

Buddhists, Janis and most of the Hindus are vegetarians; some do not eat meat thinking that to kill animals for food is a sin and some even go to the extent and do not eat eggs- the potential chicken. This again is due to lack of concept about life; there are three forms of His creations; stones, plants and animals; stones also have life they hear and speak; they join in prayer of Almighty stated by David (PBUH) holy Quran. Once holy Christ while passing by a mountain tract observed the mountain trembling with fear, he enquired about that, the mountain replied; they had heard that stones would form fuel of the fire of hell. At this the prophet of God, Christ (PBUH) replied rest assured there would be some other stones, not from them! At this the mountain stopped trembling (holy Quran).

One form of life sacrifices in favor of the other and become part of a superior being; stones disintegrate by the agents of change, weathering to form soil, plants and crops grow using vitality of the soil, most animals feed on plants crops, while there are flesh eaters amongst them. Man uses plants and animals as food, and there is guidance in the revealed books about the animals that can be killed for the purpose; mainly the grazing animals, goats, deer, cow, buffaloes, camels, some birds, fish that provide concentrated proteins, most needed for growing children and during convalescence. It is a matter of concern that those who consider it a sin to slaughter animals, having been prohibited in their religion, kill human beings at their will. We are all creation of God, Who loves those who love their fellow beings. Killing a human being is highly disliked by our Creator; "one who kills another without any justification is as if he killed the entire humanity and one who saves one is like who saved all human beings"(holy Quran). Hindu Muslim unity existed in the sub-continent in spite of religious differences; they would join in the festivals of one another, and there existed a healthy spirit of co-existence! Why can't that kind of attitude and spirit be revived?

Liquor or wine is not permitted in any religion; neither in Hinduism, Muslims nor Christianity or Judaism and those who use that do so against moral and social laws. Men and women dress alike in the subcontinent according to weather conditions prevalent in different seasons and there is not much difference; women cover their entire body with 'Saree' or a pair of clothes, Shalwar, Kameez and Dupatta. Before partition, even Hindu women covered their faces, like Muslim women considering it an act of modesty. In case of men Muslims and Hindus both wear shirt and pajamas, with slight difference in their style and tailoring. Both wear cap or a turban with a slight difference in shape, which is considered a part of a dignified dress.

India and Pakistan, Estranged Neighbors

People of India and Pakistan got freedom from a foreign rule after a long united struggle for which they put in concerted efforts. Both Hindus and Muslims belong to the same soil and have common problems of poverty, deprivation, poor health and lack of resources but instead of helping each other and solving problems of the masses that send their leaders to the Assemblies for that purpose they waste their time and resources - making weapons of destruction rather than construction, resultantly with the exception of a small lucky ones that number- not more than 5-10%, the rest of the masses on either side of the border keep suffering and have not been able to taste the fruit of freedom for which they had to bear great hardships; they are now being victimized by bureaucrats, land lords, industrialists, business men or the parliamentarians. It is high time that the leadership on both sides takes practical steps to bridge differences and make joint efforts to change the fate of the masses by spending their meager resources on the welfare of the poor needy people. That is the true religion, a true faith, source of earning pleasure of the Al mighty and earning a better place in the world hereafter.

However, after the 12th SAARC meet held at Islamabad, Feb. 2004, a beginning has been made, which is seen in restoration of rail and road traffic links and resumption of cricket series that remained suspended for a long period of time, frequency in cultural visits, restoration of dialogues on disputes including Kashmir. With opening of Rail Road links in Kashmir, Punjab and Sindh, it is hoped that these jesters would help bringing the people of both countries closer to each other, and develop a better atmosphere of understanding and co-existence that prevailed in the past.

ISLAM AND TERRORISM

Islam is a universal faith and belief as has been explained above: which is the religion named and practiced by Abraham and the apostles that came after or before him. The fault, therefore, does not lie with the religion but it lies with those that under the cover of religion exploit and use innocent people for their selfish motives. Such individuals or organizations in fact have no religion and bring a bad name to a discipline, which they do not practice. Islam is against self-emulations, which is a great sin. Islam does not allow wasting this invaluable life except in the name of God and teaches its followers to address their problems with intellect and mutual understanding acting under the frame work of Islamic law or Shari' a.

Islamic Militants in fact is a political group organized and developed in 1980s with the collaboration of the west particularly US to combat Russian occupational forces in Afghanistan, which also included volunteers from Pakistan and Afghanistan to wage Jihad. Recruiting and training centers for the jihadis were opened where they got the requisite training by Pakistani and US army personnel. After a successful venture the Islamic militants were encouraged, established themselves in Afghanistan, then turned their guns on them who handed it in their hands- started creating trouble in Pakistan and other countries; Nine eleven attacks in US, subway train blasts in U.K, Iraq and Egypt are alleged to be acts of that or any other militant group whose motto may be anything but Islam.

The holy prophet and so also those preceded him never invaded countries for territorial gains; loot or plunder — but only fought battles in defense. Islam teaches to win hearts through education and not by physical possession or steel. The example of grandson of the holy prophet, Hussain (A.S), who tried to evade conflict, bloodshed and ultimately laid down his life and those of his companions to protect the teachings of Islam; he thus conquered hearts and won appreciation instead of gaining power and possession. His glorious sacrifice was the result of the teachings and training of the prophet of Islam - a clear proof of Islam being a non-terrorist religion. Allama Iqbal appreciating his action has said, When he took out sword against the tyrant rule - drained off evil blood from the veins of liars and hypocrites-plunged in the pool of blood for the sake of maintenance of truth; in other words Allama approves of the action of the Imam and considers it in line with the injunctions of the holy Quran.

Role of United Nations

The people in the position of authority, the world powers, are required to change their conduct and behavior, towards weaker nations, who are crying hoarse, demonstrating and offering sacrifices to attain their legitimate rights: in Palestine, Chechnya, Bosnia, Kashmir and elsewhere who then out of desperation, to invite attention of the world, resort to violence and acts of immolation. Unfortunately U.N.O has also become in effective and the world powers do not take any notice of its Resolutions. Justice is being impaired; atrocities are being allowed, discrimination is

the order of the day. Neither the world powers nor the people who resort
to violence follow Islam and yet blame the religion and label it as such.

JIHAD (Holy war)

Jihad is mostly miss understood; during the time of the holy prophet
there used to be no regular army and whenever there was an emergency or
invasion on the sovereignty then jihad was proclaimed meaning thereby
that all able bodied individuals (male only) were supposed to come out to
defend the country and when the emergency was over the people would go
back to their normal day to day work. The bounty was evenly distributed
amongst the participants and even non-participants would get their share.
These days almost all the countries have regular armies for their defense,
which get compensation for their services from the state. However, a state
can declare jihad to obtain the services of volunteers from the people to
defend the country in case of an emergency. Jihad, therefore, does not
mean to invade other lands for killing and gaining supremacy over them
but largely for the purpose of defense and help restoring law and order if
required and assist administration in case of emergency like flood,
earthquake etc.

Sectarian Problem

Religion is a great force and religious leaders, pundits, mullahs exercise
great control over the masses; marriages, social or political matters cannot
be resolved without their consent. There are two main factions of Islam;
Sunni and Shi' a, that worship one god, read and follow the same book,
during the life- time of the holy prophet, Mohammad, (peace be upon
him,) there was only one version of Islam and even until the fourth
caliph Ali (K.W)), who was unanimously elected after the assassination
of the third caliph Osman (R.A), there was no bifurcation. However, there
existed some difference over the institution of Caliphate; some believed
that appointment of the Caliph is from God and base their point of view on
the revelation of holy Quran; alBaqra 29, while the second school of
thought considered it the right of the people to select/elect their leader to
run the affairs of the state-but there were no sects, like Sunni or Shia.

Origin of Sects in Islam

As soon as Ali (K.W) assumed title of Caliph (head of the Islamic state),
Emir Muavia fearing that Ali might remove him from the governorship of
Syria, because of his un Islamic ways of life, revolted against the caliphate
and managed to raise a sizeable group to fight and create unrest by
spreading rumors; leveling unfounded charges of assassination of the

former caliph Osman (R.A), against Ali (K.W)). Although Emir Muavia could not gain supremacy in any of the battles he fought against Ali (K.W) yet continued his opposition and thus managed to keep control of Syria.

After Ali's assassination by a kharji Abdul Rehman s/o Muljim, people elected his son Imam Hasan (A S). But Emir Muavia started fighting against him as well for the same purpose i.e. to perpetuate his rule of Syria and then also to assume control of the entire Islamic state. This time using the slogan that from both sides Muslims were being killed so why not to decide the matter through a dialogue? He also offered a white paper and asked Imam Hasan to include conditions of his choice that he would abide by (Emir Muavia). Imam Hasan in the first instance tried to convince the people that he was only playing a trick to assume power and did not mean it- but later, under the pressure of misguided people, accepted truce offer and stepped down on 14 clear written conditions that are on record, inclusive that Emir Muavia will not appoint his successor and after his death the control of the state would revert to the Umma (the people) who would decide about the successor. In this way he tactfully took control of the entire Islamic state and soon after that changed Caliphate into monarchy so that he might not be answerable to the people as was required in the caliphate- a form of democracy in which consultation and adherence to Quran and tradition was the practice. It was this white paper that Quaid-e-Azam had referred to when Mohan Lal Gandhi made a similar offer and remarked, "Such a document was offered in the past and a part of history when even the written agreement was never acted upon once the power was assumed".

Emir Muavia also started Sahaba versus Ahlul Bait controversy; exalted himself as a reverend Sahabi to equate himself with Ahlul Bait who do not necessarily consist of the members of the family of the prophet but to be one of them is a unique honor and a qualification bestowed on those who exercise TAQWA, fear of Allah, as is evident from the famous saying of the prophet, Al Salman O Minna Ahlul Bait; that Salman (R.A) a sahabi, is included in the stream of Ahlul Bait, because of his piety and fear of Allah. Those are the ones on whom Allah and his angels send darood and Salam and all the believers are ordained to join in this prayer with them. (Holy Quran).

After assuming power and control Emir Muavia did not honor any of the terms of the agreement which he enacted before taking over as head of the Islamic state nor did he ever bothered to take revenge from the killers of

Osman (R.A) that he trumpeted a lot before and in clear violation of the agreement, appointed his son Yazid as his successor- and not only that he also won over and got allegiance in favor of his son from prominent tribal chiefs and those who did not agree were persecuted or put in jail. He thus laid the foundation of a state of his dynasty; Umayyad in place of an Islamic state, which was founded by the holy prophet and consolidated by the four rightful Caliphs of Islam. He, however, could not purchase or win over Banu Hashim and some of their loyalists during his life- time.

After his father's death Yazid took over as the head of the Islamic state and demanded allegiance from Imam Hussain (A.S) the grandson of the holy prophet, whom he considered a great hurdle towards establishing an empire of his family. Imam refused to accept his ascendance to that position and told him that according to the terms of the agreement settled and signed between Emir Muavia and his brother, Imam Hasan (A.S) it was his right which he had usurped. He further said," A person like Hussain cannot accept authority or pay allegiance to a person like Yazid." On refusal to comply with his demand untold atrocities were let loose on the Imam and his family to cow them down. They had to leave Medina and then even Mecca and surrounded in the desert of Karbla in Iraq where he and his kiths and kins including loyalists, that totaled 72, laid down their lives. Thus Yazid could not succeed in his mission to achieve certificate - an approval in favor of his rule from the grandson of the prophet; as a Sufi poet Khawja Moin-ud-Din Chishty Ajmeri (A.R) has said," He gave his head and not his hand in the hand of Yazid; thus emerged as a symbol of La Ilaha Illillah- Hussain (A.S) is indeed the king of kings". Allama Iqbal has also paid rich tributes to Imam and his companions who for the sake of maintaining original version of Islam and Islamic values laid down their lives and strengthened foundations of La Ilaha Illillah.

Most of the followers of Islam and loyalists of the family of the holy prophet opposed these tactics of Emir Muavia and subsequently massacre of the grandson of the prophet by Yazid while certain weak people kept quiet. They, however, remained loyal and practiced original version of Islam introduced by the holy prophet. These followers are the loyalists; Sunnis and Shi'as. They are the ones who follow the book and tradition of the holy prophet and hold his family, Ahlulbait and Sahaba kiram in respect and denounce the politics and ways used for establishing a tyrant kingdom of Umayyads.

In Saudi Arabia the rulers, who mostly follow Imam Hambal's version of Islam, prohibit holding Majalis to revive the tragedy of Karbala or taking out processions in protest as is done in other parts of the world, do so not to cover the crime of Yazid but to save their monarchy, as the protest and sacrifice of Imam and his companions was not against Yazid alone but against the system which was opposed to Islam- considering it may have bearing on their masses, who may demand a democratic regime there as well-but nowadays have relaxed the restrictions to a great deal.

Imam Shafi (R.A) a famous scholar has said, O Ahlul Bait, Is this not a sufficient proof of your greatness and reverence that our prayers are not accepted unless we recite Salawat (darood) on you? History is like fragrance, which cannot be contained. Every Muslim respects and holds in highest esteem, the Ahlul Bait and Sahaba Kiram who have been near and dear to the holy prophet. This is what the holy prophet has professed and practiced. We are all Muslims who have been named by the father Abraham and no one has the right and authority to change the name given by the father; we are not Sunni or Shi' a but Muslims. It was what Quaid-e-Azam in his maiden address to the nation had emphasized and Allama Iqbal had professed. We should, therefore, be mindful of the enemies of Islam who create differences to weaken Muslim Umma to serve their selfish political goals, use violence and incite innocent uncouth to kill each other. They do no service to Islam and rather tarnish its image and defame the religion of God and yet claim themselves as the true followers of the holy prophet (peace is on him) - this dualism must be guarded against- not alone by the government but by all faithful followers of Islam; Shi'as and Sunnis.

Before partition in the sub-continent and up to 1980s in Pakistan, harmony prevailed between the two sects and they celebrated all religious functions; Moharram, Milad un Nabi, Meraj Sharif, Shab-I- Brat, Ramadan and Eids together with grace and mutual understanding —but then coming into existence of extremist groups; Sipah Sahaba and Sipah Mohammad, to serve their political ends, fundamentalism replaced mutual love and understanding, so much so that even prayers in mosques these days are held under protection of police. Was this Islam and Islamic state demanded and dreamt by its founders? It is this weakness that opponents exploit and laugh at. Present regime has taken practical steps to revive old atmosphere and has already banned the above- mentioned extremist organizations. Now it is the duty of educationists, scholars, poets, and writers to develop and inculcate tolerance and respect for each faction's rituals and customs through education to help restore, the same atmosphere of understanding that existed, not in the distant past.

Teachings of Islam conveyed to us by scholarly works of Sufis, and Saints like Shah Waliullah, Hazrat Nizam-ud-Din Aulia, and their contemporaries, and also Allama Iqbal who have emphasized to foster cohesion and unity between Muslims to put an end to the menace of sectarianism; havoc in Iraq should be an eye opener for everyone, where these sectarian differences are being exploited and even after the end of the tyrant rule of Saddam Hussain and formation of an elected government the killing of innocent people is order of the day and hundreds and thousands have been massacred and the horror continues in spite of the fact that both Sunnis and Shia's time and again have openly declared that there exists no conflict among them and nor it existed in the past and the differences are being politically played upon by the ill wishers of Muslim Umma.

Five Fundamentals of Islam

Whereas prayer (namaz), Fasting (Roza), Haj (pilgrim to Mekka), and Zakat (tax) are among pillars of Islam, the fundamentals narrated below are basic beliefs that every Muslim bears in mind without which our faith remains incomplete:

1. TAUHEED (Oneness of God)

God is one. He does not take partners. Allah is He, Whom all depend; He begets not, nor is He begotten. No one is like Him. Polytheism is the greatest of sins. His is the kingdom of heavens and the earth and He does not take to Himself any son and has no associate in the kingdom; He created everything and then ordained for its measure. (Sura Akhlas, Al Furqan-2)

2. ADAL (Equity and Justice)

Allah is just and likes justice to be done, to one self and others. He is the Master of the Day of Judgment when everyone would receive justice without discrimination. He rewards those that avoid evil, and punishes the wrong doers - those who do wrong and then realize and repent should not get disappointed Allah is most gracious and most merciful and may forgive whom He pleases. So besides avoiding evil we should always be hopeful of His forgiveness and mercy.

3." NABUWAT"(Prophet Hood)

In order to get Him introduced amongst; men and Jins He sent 124,000 apostles to convey His message to the communities of men and the Jins. He has exalted some of His apostles over the others Out of them there are 313 `Rasools (messengers)` seven of them are the chosen ones: Adam, Noah, Abraham, Moses, David, Christ, and Mohammad (P.B.U.H) blessed with books- guidance for men and the jins. He it is who raised among the illiterates an apostle from among them-selves, who recites to them His communications and purifies them, and teaches them the book and the wisdom, although they were before in clear error (holy Quran, Sura Jumma). Although the holy prophet said that he is a creation like us with the difference that Allah communicates with him. The prophet however did not say that we are like him. It would be, therefore, wrong to infer from his humble statement that man or Jins can equate with the apostles of God. Apostles are like a kettle, which absorbs heat from fire and passes it on to the container-.the container cannot get heat directly from fire without the help of the medium. Hence prophets in spite of looking like us are a different creation-the exalted ones, who directly get guidance from God and then pass that on to us.

4. IMAMAT (The Apostolically Succession)

The spiritual life the prophet had infused into his people did not end with his life. The two great sects into which Islam became divided at an early stage are agreed that the religious efficacy of the rites and the duties prescribed by the law (Shariat) depends on the existence of the vicegerent and representative of the prophet, who, as such, is the religious Head (Imam) of the Faith and the Faithful.(Sura Bani Israil-71) `Remember the Day when we will call every one with their Imam; who so ever is given his book in his right hand shall rejoice its reading And they shall not be dealt with slightest of injustice" Adherents of the apostolically Imams Shi' a have a philosophy of their own quite distinct from the followers of the traditions. According to them the Imamate descends by divine appointment in the apostolic line, who must be sinless or immaculate (masoom), and that must be knowledgeable the excellent (Afzal) of mankind and support their version on revelation of holy Quran; 'alBaqra' 124 and "Yasin", 12.

Further they say that the spiritual heritage bequeathed by the prophet devolved on Ali and his descendents by Fatima, the prophet's daughter. They consider that Ali, who was indicated by the prophet as his successor returning from his last pilgrimage at Ghadir- e- Khum, is the first Imam and Caliph of the Faithful, and that after his assassination the spiritual leadership descended in succession to his and Fatima's posterity in the direct male line until it came to Imam Hasan Askari , eleventh in descent, upon his death in the year 874 A.D. or 260 Hijra the Imamate devolved upon his son Mohammad, surnamed al Mahdi the last Imam who is living but (ghaib) and is awaited.

According to the followers of the tradition, who regard the pontificate of Abu Bakr, Omar and Osman and then Ali as rightful Caliph and Imam; they believe that Imam Mahdi is still to be born while Shi' a hold that he is already born and is awaited; they also call him as Imam-al- Muntazar. The Philosophical student of religions will not fail to observe the strange similarity of the Shia and the Sunni beliefs that a divinely appointed Savior, named al Mahdi would reappear from Mecca who is to save the world from evil and oppression. This belief bears similarity with the Jews who believe that the Messiah is yet to come. Christian believe that the Messiah has come and gone, and will come again.

Shia believe that Imam is born knowledgeable, having 'Ilm-e-ladunni'- does not learn from any worldly scholar or a teacher. On the other hand the followers of the tradition are of the view that an Imam learns in this world, has teachers and acquires knowledge 'Ilm-e-kasabi'. Imam Abu Hanifa, Imam Shafi, Imam Humbal and Imam Maalik are highly respected with large following are their prominent Imams.

According to the saying (prophecy) of the holy prophet (PBUH), the awaited Imam will appear at a time when there will be wars and bloodshed all over, Muslims will be in a miserable plight. Al Mahdi the awaited Imam would then come to their rescue. Holy Christ will also descend and join him. They will then establish a true Islamic rule and the world would be freed from all sorts of injustices and evils. It would happen before the Dooms day.

Allama Iqbal's view in this context can be judged from the following verse:" Kabhi Aye Haqiqat-i-Muntazar, Nazar Aa Libas-i-Majaz Meyn, Keh Hazaron Sijde Tarrap Rehe Hain, Meri Jabeen-i- Niaz Meyn; Tujhe Yunhi Sadiyan guzar gain issi purdai hijab mein; Kabhi aye haqiqati muntazar nazar aa libas-e- majaz mein. As is depicted from the verse Iqbal believes that Mahdi (A.S.) is living - but a hidden Imam, who is vehemently awaited.

5. DAY OF JUDGEMENT

We all believe that there is a Day of Judgment its time is only known to the Almighty and none else (Alnaziaat 41-43, chapter 30). It will, however, take place as per prophecy of the holy prophet (PBUH), after a while of the re-appearance of Imam Mahdi and descending of the holy Christ when the mountains will move and be leveled, and all whoever is born in this world be raised from their graves and assembled and tried for their deeds. Those declared successful would enjoy the bounties in the paradise prepared for those who avoided evil and followed the right path and those pronounced unsuccessful because of their wrongs will be thrown in the burning fire prepared for the evildoers. All the apostles and messengers of Allah have been reminding about the Day. So one should take full advantage of this remission- an opportunity, never to come again, and try to do as much good to deserve a better place in the heavens, world hereafter. Sheikh Saadi Shirazi in this context has said, "Aye Fullan Khaire Kun wa Ghanimat Shumar Umr Zan Paishtar Keh Bang Bar Ayad Fullan Namand". Addressing men he advised to do as much good as possible and consider this life an opportunity before the last bell tolls and this remission will be over once for all.

Chapter II
SPREAD OF ISLAM

It is not true to believe that Islam was introduced in the sub-continent during or after appearance of the holy prophet Mohammad (P.B.H)- But the religion of Islam existed in India much before as is evident from the excavations of Harrappa (Punjab) and Mohanjdaro (Sindh) in the pre historic time. The study of ruins proves that the religion of Islam was known and practiced there from times immemorial; as is depicted from the excavations of these extinct towns. At Harappa (Punjab) location of a cemetery and the skeletons of men, women and children found and preserved in the museum at site is a clear indication of the fact that the people buried their dead bodies which has been a practice in Muslims and not amongst Hindus.

Moreover there exist traces of catastrophes subjected in succession: there are layers of ashes result of huge fires, pebbles because of divine stoning, sediments caused by high floods, toppled walls, houses due to severe earth quakes. All that happened in considerable intervals of time; presumably a generation who lived there and in spite of untiring efforts of an apostle of God did not obey the Lord and belied his teachings who would recommend their destruction and as such one after the other the punishments became their destiny. God does not punish a nation unless He sends any warner for the people before (holy Quran). Since all the apostles professed only one religion, it can be assumed that Islam was also practiced in India and the Indus valley civilization is legacy of the same culture.

Role of Traders
Undertaking sea voyage and going out of the boundaries of India was prohibited in Hindu faith in those days and who so ever broke that restriction had to pay a heavy fine. Therefore, all the foreign trade was in the hands of Muslim traders who would deal in such trade with the people of the sub-continent enroot to china and the Far East. These traders because of their honesty fair dealings and good manners won their hearts and thus proved to be good ambassadors of Islam.

Role of Sufis and Saints

A Sufi is one who rejects all worldly desires and adopts a simple living strictly according to Sharia; and even voluntarily gives up legitimate comforts to get nearer to Almighty Allah and devotes his time in service of His creation the needy ones. Sufism roots from Ali (K.W) who said "Oh the world I have divorced you thrice and therefore, I can no more revert to thee go and entice someone, other than me". In spite of being a caliph of Islamic State, he wore rough dress and his food was dry bread of barley. Allama Iqbal has mentioned it in his poetry saying that the secret of the invincible strength and power of Ali (K.W) was the barley bread and not the rich foods. All Qutubs, Walis acknowledge and bow before the Willayat of Ali (K.W) without which no one attains that rank, is a well-known concept in the realm of Sufia Kiram.

Sufis of high caliber endowed with inner light established their seats of learning to spread the teachings of Islam in different places in the sub continent. They were knowledgeable, and possessed of high moral values; so that people were attracted to wards them. They would selflessly help solve their multifarious problems and in this way were successful in spreading the message of Islam far and wide even before any Muslim ruler established its rule in the sub continent. Eminent dedicated ones amongst others are: Khawja Moeen-ud-ud-Din Chishty, Hazrat Data Ganj Bakhsh, Sheikh Bahau-ud-Din Zakria, Khawja Bakhtiar Kaki, Baba Farid-ud-Din Shakar Ganj, Hazrat Nizam-ud Din Aulia, Shah Wali Ullah, Shaikh Ahmad of Sarhind, Lal Shahbaz Qalandar, who rendered invaluable services in the spread of Islam in the sub-continent.

Sultan Mahmud Ghaznvi invaded India seventeen times and after each venture he left behind a trail of saints and scholars to do the job of winning over hearts of the people, instead of extending his empire. If he had established his regime and himself invited to accept the religion of Islam, then it would have been labeled a religion spread at the head of sword and the result would not be different from what happened in Spain. The credit of winning over large number of enlightened followers of Islam in the sub-continent, therefore, goes to the wisdom and farsightedness of Sultan Mahmood Ghaznavi.

Khawja Mueen-ud Din Chishty (R.A)

The small town of Ajmer, 400 kilometers south and west of Delhi, is unremarkable to the eye at first glance. However, on closer inspection, one beholds the reason that it stands out, pilgrims-thousands upon thousands they come, Muslim, Hindu, Buddhist, of all nationalities; raising their voices in celebration and prayer, in praise and remembrance of one of the greatest saints ever produced in the long and illustrious history of Islam. The deservedly titled Sultan of India, the Qutub or spiritual axis of the eastern Islamic world; he is the fountain from whose spiritual light have sprung all the beautiful, mighty saints of the Chishtiyya Silsila: Hazrat Khawja Muin-ud-din Hasan Chishty Gharib-un-Nawaz Ajmeri (R.A).

The chieftain and founder of the Chishtiyya Silsila, one of the four great orders that radiate throughout the world, Khawja Gharib-un-Nawaz (R.A)) is one of the most respected and universally recognized figures in Sufism and Islam. He stands tall as a great spiritual leader; a reformer and purifier of hearts at the most turbulent of times. Most of the saints before his time had been concentrated around the lands of the Middle East, but he was a pioneer, a missionary who was responsible for spreading the Sufi and Islamic sphere of influence to the remotest regions of polytheistic India.

His pious character was a true picture of Islam; his practice exactly in accordance with the dictates of the holy Quran and Sunnah, and his teachings beautiful lessons in godliness, truthfulness, and equality which enlightened the hearts of multitudes. Authentic estimates place the number of people he guided to the path of Islam is nine million. It is a historical fact that his Chishtiyya Silsila wielded a direct and crucial influence on the course of Indian history, the development of the embryonic Bhagti Movement of Hinduism, and modern (pantheistic) Buddhism.

Khawja Muin-ud-din Chishty (R.A) was born in the year 536AH in Sijistan, the son of Khawja Ghyasuddin Chishty, a pious and influential man of what is now Iran. He was a direct descendant through both his parents of Hazrat Ali (K.W)). It was a time of chaos and great upheavals in both India and the Muslim Empire as a whole. In the year of his birth, Sultan Sanjari was finally defeated before the implacable advance of the Mughal, spelling the beginning of the end of the Sultanate; and in Khurasan, where, religious sects and barbarism had laid waste a once civilized country. He was orphaned at the tender age of fourteen and was thus raised in the same condition as our holy prophet (P.B.U.H). Social evils, moral degradations and personal tragedy stirred something deep within the young man, and he began to turn towards the spiritual life. Once when watering his father's garden, he came across a dervish, Hazrat Ibrahim Qanduzi (radiallahu anha) He was deeply affected by the saint's holy manner, and Hazrat Ibrahim (R.A) for his part transformed Khawja Muin-ud-din Chishty (R.A)'s inner being. His eyes became opened to the ultimate realities of the spiritual world. Renouncing all material things, he sold his father's garden all his possessions and distributed the money among the poor and set out for the service of mankind.

SHAH WALI ULLAH

Shah Wali Ullah, a great saint, scholar and reformer, was born in a religious family in Delhi, 1703. He was educated at Madrasa-i-Rahimiyah founded by his father, Shah Abdul Rahim. After finishing his education, he went for pilgrimage to Saudi Arabia. On his return to India he tried to revive Islamic spirit amongst the Muslims who were heading towards a social disaster- having been given to sectarianism and un-Islamic practices.

Shah Wali Ullah persuaded the Muslims to follow in the footsteps of the Holy Prophet (Peace be upon him) and introduced the basic tenets of Islam to the people. He advocated the education of Quran for the welfare and benefits of the Muslims and asked them to abandon un-Islamic habits and customs. He urged the people to live simple life and avoid involvement in the luxuries of the world.

Shah Wali Ullah's singular and most important act was his translation and commentary of the holy Quran in simple Persian, the language of the land so that the people of the sub-continent could understand and follow it. He studied the writings of each school of thought to understand their point of view, before compiling comprehensive volumes about what is fair and just in the light of teachings of Islam. He worked out a system of thought, beliefs, and values, on which all but the extremists could agree. He thus provided a spiritual basis for national cohesion. He also wrote many books, which included `Hujjatullah-ul-Balighah' and `Izalat-al-Akhfa' as the most famous works of Islam, Fiqah and Hadith.

Apart from imparting religious education to the Muslims, Shah Wali Ullah also led the Muslims to wage struggle for their political rights. He came to guide them in a meritorious manner to create political awakening in the Muslims of India. After the death of Emperor Aurangzeb, the political unity and stability of the Muslims began to show signs of decadence. The Mughal Empire began to crack and crumble as it fell into the hands of most incapable successors. The Mughal rulers were no more in a position to withhold the supremacy of the Muslim rule, which was gravely jeopardized by the emergence of the Sikhs, Marhatas and other non-Muslim forces. Shah Wali Ullah came forward to tackle this precarious situation. He brought the Muslim nobles together and asked for the military assistance from them against Marhatas. He then persuaded the great Afghan ruler Ahmed Shah Abdali to retrieve Muslim rule in India. Ahmed Shah Abdali, on the call of Shah Wali Ullah proceeded to India and engaged in battle with Marhatas at Panipat in 1761. The victory of Ahmed Shah Abdali at Panipat blasted the Marhatas' might and paved way for the revival of Islam in India to a greater extent.

Shah Wali Ullah emphasized on the rulers to enforce Islamic laws and to mould their lives according to the Islamic way. He clarified the importance of `Jihad' to the soldiers and urged them to fight for the glorification of Islam. He asked the traders to adopt the fair principles of trade and wished them to refrain from accumulating wealth by unfair means. After his death, his sons Shah Abdul Aziz, Shah Abdul Ghani, Shah Rafi-ud-Din and Shah Abdul Qadir carried out the noble mission of the religious education and Islamic preaching at Madderesa-e- Rahimiyya founded by their great father.

HAZRAT NIZAM-UD DIN AULIA (R.A)

Muhammad by name son of Syed Ahmad and his grandfather Syed Ali of Bokhara were well known Syeds and traced their lineage to Hazrat Ali (K.W.). He was called by various titles, like Mehbob-i-Elahi, Sultan-ul-Aulia, Sultan-ul- Mashaikh and Sultan-ul- Salateen. He was one of such Saints who illuminated the nooks and corners of India with the divine light of the Din-e- Islam. He was born in 636 Hijra at Badaiyoun in India and after learning the holy Quran learnt different subjects from well-known scholars and obtained the degree of Mashariqul Anwar at Delhi.

Search for the Teacher; He later set out in search of a teacher and guide who could lead to spiritual and intrinsic learning. At Badaiyoun he was informally introduced to Baba Farid Gunj-e- Shaker through Abu Bakar Qawwal and came to have faith in him and longed to see him. Baba Farid's younger brother was his neighbor in Delhi that helped him to reach his cherished teacher and guide. Baba Farid was extremely pleased to see him and removing his cap from his head placed it on his head and seeing symptoms of fear in him said," Welcome! God willing, you will find bounties of this world as well as of Din." Baba Farid also gave him his robe, sandals, prayer mat and staff etc.

Hazrat Nizam-ud-din pledged obedience to Baba Farid on Rajab 15, 655 Hijri and stayed at his service up to 3, Rabiul Awwal 656 Hijri. And engaged in prayer and meditation under his guidance and soon attained proficiency in conduct and divinity. Baba Farid then sent him to Delhi laden with divine and spiritual conduct.

He selected Ghayaspur for his stay at Delhi where he started meditation and prayers renounced material things and kept fast regularly. He continued this practice and led a life of resignation and renunciation. In the morning he would discuss religion and associated problems with scholars and saints, at mid day he talked to the students and seekers of knowledge and spent his nights in prayers.

He spent early days of his stay in Delhi in extreme poverty. He often observed fast continuously for three days. When he had nothing to eat his mother would say," We are Allah's guests today." He drew much taste from his mother's statement. But later by the grace of Allah and prayer of his teacher Baba Farid he got so much that his kitchen was never closed and thousands of needy and beggars ate from it. Many people drew sustenance and numerous students and Hafiz were given help.

He laid his life on 18, Rabi-us-sani 725 A.H (1324 A.D), when he anticipated his death he gave his special robe, a turban, and prayer mat to Maulana Burhanuddin Gharib and ordered him to go to Deccan and gave the same things to Maulana Yaqoob and asked him to go to Gujarat. The next day he then called Maulana Nasiruddin and entrusted to him staff and robe, and other sacred relics of Baba Farid and said," You will have to bear the tribulations of the people and stay here in Delhi." His tomb stands in Nizam-Ud-din Basti and attracts thousands of Hindus, Sikhs and Muslim pilgrims every day.

SHEIKH ALI HAJWERI (popularly known as Data Ganj Bakhsh)
Along with Muslim warriors came saints and Sufis, who promulgated Islam in India. The most important amongst them was Sheikh Ali Hajweri. He was a renowned Sufi who not only spread the message of Allah in Lahore, but also in other parts of Punjab. His book titled Kashaful-Mahjub, in Persian is an authentic book on Sufism. Thousands of pilgrims from all parts of Punjab come to pay homage to the saint and Almighty Allah fulfills their wishes that they may have and that is why his title as Data. Langar of Data Ganj Bakhsh remains open 24 hours and all needy, poor homeless, travelers get food and shelter in the compounds of

shrine of the saint. Urs Data Ganj Bakhsh is a largely attended ceremony of the city of Lahore, which is attended by hundreds and thousands of his faithfulls.

SHEIKH AHMAD SARHINDI (known as Mujadad Alf-i-sani)
He was born at Sirhind in A.H. 971 June 14, 1564 and was the fourth child of his father Sheikh Abdul Ahad. He went to Agra to begin his preaching of Islam in the royal court of Mughal Emperor Akbar. From Agra he was called back by his father and given education in the mystical knowledge. After the death of his father he set out for Haj but changed his mind at Delhi and became a disciple of Baqi Billah. A few years of stay with Baqi Billah, he returned to Sirhind and began preaching of Islam and emphasized the concept of Tauheed. Akbar the Mughal emperor had introduced a religious philosophy known as Din-i-Ilahi, Shaikh Ahmad exposed its fallacies and termed it opposed to Islam and openly refuted it that made him popular with the Muslims.

He continued preaching after Akbar in Jahangir's rule as well and his popularity aroused jealousy of the superficial Ulema of the court. They conspired against him and complained to Emperor Jahangir that his popularity was harmful for the throne. Jahangir summoned Sheikh Ahmed to the court- but he did not perform the act of `Prostration' and declared that prostration could only be offered to the God Almighty and none else. He was imprisoned. He did not stop the sacred task of preaching Islam even in prison. After two years of imprisonment emperor Jahangir, having realized, set him free and venerated him as a saint and scholar. Although Sheikh Ahmad was popularly known as Mujadid but it may be clarified that Islam has since been completed and there is no room for any Mujadid or Reformer; the supreme court of Pakistan in its verdict in Qadianis case has upheld the above version- Sheikh Ahmad displayed courage before Emperor Akbar and Jahangir. No doubt it is commendable, but in so doing he did not create any new tradition and acted as a true Muslim. We should, therefore, be cautious in using such words as Mujadid or Reformer when Islam has been completed and Risalat has been sealed.

LAL SHAHBAZ QALANDAR (R.A)
The real name of `Lal Shahbaz Qalandar' was Syed Muhammad Usman who was born in 1177 AD in Marwand, Iran. His father, Syed Ibrahim Karim-ud-din, was a pious dervaish, and his mother was a high-ranking princess. His ancestors migrated from Iraq and settled in Meshed from where they again migrated to Marwand. During those days Meshed and its

surrounding cities were renowned centers of learning. Even as a young boy, Shahbaz Qalandar showed strong religious leanings. He learnt the holy Quran by heart at the age of seven and at the age of twenty embraced the Qalandar order of Sufism. Qalandar is a type of dervaish who clothes in rags, likes poverty and austerity and has no permanent dwelling. Lal Shahbaz Qalandar wandered throughout Middle East and came to Sindh from Baghdad via Dasht-i-Makran. In 1263, he arrived in Multan, which at that time was at the height of its glory and splendor. People welcomed him and requested him to stay at Multan but he continued his journey southward and eventually settled down at Sehwan, which was a famous center of learning and a popular place of worship for Hindus, where he lived under the trunk of a tree, out skirts of the town, for six years. During this period he disseminated the light of Islam, providing guidance to thousands of people.

Sehwan rises on the top of a conical hill, overlooking ruins of a huge fort founded by Alexander the great. Sehwan was the capitol of the rulers of Gupta dynasty in 400 AD. Mohammad bin Qasim, an Arab, passed from here in 712 AD en route to Multan.
Because of its location that commands routes from the lower Indus to the upper Indus Sehwan has been very important in the history of Sindh.

Lal Shahbaz Qalandar is an overwhelmingly popular saint, cherished and adored alike by Hindus and Muslims of Sindh. He was a great missionary, mystic, scholar and a poet. He has been author of several books in Persian and Arabic on philology and poetry. He was called: Lal because of his (red) attire, Shahbaz for his noble and exalted divine spirit, Qalandar due to his Qalandria order of Sufism, exalted and intoxicated with love for eternal being of God.

He died after living a good span for 97 years. His tomb built in1356, gives a dazzling look with its Sindhi kashi tiles, mirror work and two gold plated doors, one donated by Shah of Iran and the other by late Zulfiqar Ali Bhutto. The inner sanctum is about 100yards square with the silver canopied grave in the middle. The Hindus regarded him as the incarnation of Bhartihari, the saintly brother of the king Vikramaditya, who believed to have worshiped Shiva at the venue where Lal Shahbaz shrine is situated. Thousands of devotees visit the shrine every day while on Thursdays the number is multiplied. Especially at the time of his death anniversary, `Urs' celebrated every year on 18th of Sha' ban when Sehwan springs to life and the number of devotees exceed half a million from all over Pakistan. The narrow lanes of Sehwan are packed to capacity with thousands and thousands pilgrims and fakirs make to the shrine to commune with the saint, offer their tributes and make a wish, garlands and green chadars with Quranic inscriptions are presented by the devotees. A devotional dance known, as `dhammal' is a special ritual performed at the rhythmic beat of the drum. A record number of seven hundred thousand pilgrims visited the shrine in 2002.

SYED AHMAD SHAHEED BRAILVI

The name of Syed Ahmad Shaheed carries immense importance with regard to the struggle for revival of Muslim rule in the history of the sub-continent. He picked up a vigorous- two-pronged struggle aimed at the purification of the Muslim society and gaining freedom from the non-Muslim forces; Sikhs and the British.

Syed Ahmad was born at Rai Braily in 1786. He was greatly influenced by the preaching of Shah Wali Ullah and was extremely dismayed over the decline of the Muslims and earnestly desired to see the restoration of their supremacy in India. The main purpose of Syed Ahmad and his followers was to establish a Muslim state in India. In his time Punjab was under the Sikh's regime ruled by Raja Ranjeet Singh known all over India for his tyrannies. Muslims suffered heavily under his rule and were denied freedom to profess their religion; so much so that they were stopped from giving call for prayers. N.W.F.P. had also fallen to the Sikhs. Syed Ahmad was of the opinion that if Punjab and N.W.F.P. were liberated of the Sikh domination, the Muslims would regain their old position.

JIHAD MOVEMENT

Syed Ahmad picked up N.W.F.P. to launch his movement for the eradication of the non -Islamic regimes. He invited people to join him in the holy war to save the Muslims from the Sikh domination. Shah Ismail Shaheed, a saint son of Shah Waliullah, joined Syed Ahmad along with his followers. Syed Ahmad directed Shah Ismail to march from Rai Baraily with a force of six thousand Mujahideen and he himself proceeded from other parts of Punjab and Delhi where he was joined by many other followers possessed with the spirit of jihad. Syed Ahmad reached Nowshera in December 1826 and established his headquarter there. He sent a message to Ranjeet Singh to embrace Islam or be ready to face the Mujahideen in the battlefield. Ranjeet Singh turned down the offer of Syed Ahmad in a most scornful manner.

The first battle against the Sikhs was fought at Akora Khatak on 21st December 1826 in which the Sikhs were defeated. The Muslims were successful in the second encounter as well which was fought at Hazro. The immediate and astonishing success of Mujahideen in the two clashes against Sikhs spurred the popularity of the jihad movement and of Syed Ahmad. Many people including the famous Pathan tribes joined Syed Ahmad in the struggle. Yar Muhammad Khan and Pir Hakman Khan joined with their followers and by that time the number of Muslim fighters rose to 80,000.

Jihad Movement swiftly passed through the early stages of struggle with amazing success. A conspiracy was hatched against the movement and an attempt was made on the life of Syed Ahmad by poisoning him, which he survived. Sardar Yar Muhammad was bribed to betray Syed Ahmad and join the Sikhs against Mujahideen.

Syed Ahmad now set out for Peshawar and Kashmir to wage his struggle against the Sikhs afresh and captured Peshawar. A clash took place between Mujahideen and Pathan tribes who had defected Syed Ahmad. Sultan Khan, brother of Yar Muhammad Khan was leading the Pathan forces. Sultan Khan was arrested after his defeat. Syed Ahmad pardoned him but he did not join the Muslim forces and was killed while fighting against them.

Syed Ahmad shifted his headquarter to Balakot in 1830, to begin his Jihad movement from Rajauri to annex Kashmir. While Syed Ahmad had camped at Balakot in the valley of River Kunhar, situated on the cross routes to Kaghan valley in the north, Mansehra in the south and Muzaffrabad in the east, Sikh forces from an adjacent hill top from the south, which was left unguarded, launched an attack with a big force which caught the Mujahideen in surprise. A fierce battle was fought between Sikh and Muslim armies. The Mujahideen fought valiantly but they could not stand the well-planned surprise attack of the Sikh forces. The Muslims were defeated; Syed Ahmad and Shah Ismail laid their lives fighting for the cause of Islam. The graves of both the Shaheeds are prominent, located near the bridge on river Kunhar at Balakot.

With the defeat of Mujahiden at Balakot and loss of their leaders the Jihad movement fell in disarray and could not be carried out with the old fervor and enthusiasm. The Jihad movement, however, is regarded as the forerunner of the Pakistan Movement in the history of the sub-continent.

AILAMA IQBAL (1877- 1937)

A great poet-philosopher, political leader, who was more of a Qalandar than an aristocrat; he undoubtedly was the poet-thinker of the 20th century, born at Sialkot, Punjab, in 1877. He belonged to a family of Kashmiri Brahmins, who embraced Islam about 300 years ago. He received his early education in the traditional Maktab and later joined Mission School from where he passed his matriculation examination securing first position and setting a record in the 'University of the Punjab.

In 1897 he obtained his Bachelor of Arts degree/from Government College, Lahore. After two years he got Masters in Philosophy and was appointed in the Oriental College, Lahore as a lecturer. He later proceeded to England for higher studies. After having obtained a degree at Cambridge, he secured his doctorate at Munich and then finally qualified as a Barrister.

He returned to India in 1908. Besides teaching and practicing law, he continued to write poetry and in 1911, resigned from the government job and wholeheartedly took up the task of individual thinking and inspiring depressed Muslim nation through his poetry. Allama Iqbal wrote both in Urdu and Persian languages; he however, seemed to have greater liking for Persian and there he is known to be influenced by Maulana Rumi a scholar of a high order. Yet there was another scholar, Allama Hirvi from Iran, not much heard of, who would visit Lahore and addressed religious congregations in Persian at Mubarik Haveli and other places, particularly on the occasion of Muharram. Iqbal a lover of the Persian language and having thirst for knowledge regularly attended his addresses and followed him on his bike, wherever he went to address a Majlis.

Besides eloquence of language he was much impressed by his scholarly vision of Islam and according to a contemporary of Iqbal, Mirza Ahmad Ali, one day when Allama Hirvi got down from the stage after finishing his address at Nawazish Haveli, Mochi gate Lahore, Iqbal started kissing his hands and touching his feet- having been overwhelmed by his clarity and depth of knowledge; Mirza Ahmad Ali who was a witness to the incidence among others, further related that some of his acquaintances present tried to dissuade him by conveying in their colloquial Punjabi, " Rafzi Oh Rafzi" meaning thereby that Allama Hirvi belonged to Shi'a sect, his action, therefore, was uncalled for - but Allama Iqbal without paying any attention to their exuberance continued to appreciate and showing respect to the Allama the way he liked. It clearly shows that Allama Iqbal was above sectarianism and did not appreciate any division or bifurcation in the followers of Islam - who time and again stressed on the unity of Muslim Umma. When united they achieved Pakistan and divided they lost its eastern wing and if do not learn a lesson from their mistakes are warned in these words; *NA SAMJHO GEY TO MIT JAO GEY AYE GHAFIL MUSALMANO- TUMHARI DASTAAN BHI NA HO GI DAASTANO'N MEY*. Mirza Ahmad Ali an Accounts officer by profession an admirer of Allama, a good orator, also issued a periodical, Khair-ul-Amal which his son, Dr. Askari Mirza, a medical practitioner, main market, Samnabad Lahore, now issues in which he is believed to have given more details about the life of Allama Iqbal based on his personal observations. The views and ideas of both Maulana Rumi and Maulana Hirvi are, greatly reflected in Allama Iqbal's poetry.

1. **RAMZ-E-QURAN AZ HUSSAIN AMOKHTAM AZ AATISH-E-OO SHULAHA ANDUKHTAM**. Allama admits that he got guidance and grasped understanding of Quran from Hussain (A.S) And picked up a few drops from his vast sea of knowledge. He has also mentioned him in his poetry as **HAQQA KEH BINAI LA ILAH AST HUSSAIN**. It was he who practically taught us the meaning of **La Illaha Illil Lah**.

2. *ISLAM KE DAMAN MEY BUS ISKE SIWA KAYA HEY, IK ZARBI YADULLHI IK SAJDA-I- SHABBIRI*. There is not much for the Muslims to boast of, except the might of Yadullah, Ali (K.W.) or the grand sacrifice of Hussain (A. S).

3. *AJIB SADA 0 RANGEEN HAI DASTAN-I-HARRAM – NAHAYAT ISKI HAIN HUSSAIN IBTIDA HAI ISMAIL* The story of Islam starts from the obedience of Ismail (A.S) and culminates in the patience of Hussain (A.S)

4. *YEH FAIZAN-i-KARAM THA YA KEH MAKTAB KI KARAMAT THI SIKHAI KIS NE ISMAIL KO ADABI FARZANDI*. It was spiritual guidance or the teaching of Islam that helped Ismail (A.S) to display the remarkable respect to his father!

5. *BAI DHRAK KOOD PARA AATISHI NAMRUD MEIN ISHQ AQAL HAI MAHVAI TAMASHAI LABI BAM ABHI*. It was

complete faith and maddening love for his creator that made Abraham to plunge in the burning fire – a feat unconceivable and beyond rationality.

6. ***SIDQE KHALIL BHI HAI ISHQ SABRE HUSSAIN BHI HAI ISHQ- IS MARKAI WAJUD MAIN BADRO HUNAIN BHI HAI ISHQ.*** Sincerity of Abraham as depicted by his determination to offer sacrifice of his beloved son and that of Hussain (A. S) to lay down his life and those of his kiths and kins is nothing but Ishq; a highest degree of love for the Almighty and in the same way participation in the battles of Badar and Hunain where a paltry force of Islam fought against large well equipped armies was out of similar spirit and zeal.

As stated above Allama Iqbal was an exponent of unity and against any division-sectarianism and purporting hatred towards one another- Muslims or non-Muslims.

He liked to be associated with Qalandars, lovers of simple life, having been impressed with their ways as is depicted from the following verses;

Neither the power of crowns and kings,
Nor the might of armies equals the might of a Qalandar.
People have been impressed by his simplicity (Qalandari)
Otherwise Iqbal cannot boast of his poetic qualifications.
Qalandar, whose heart is the abode of God, looks magnanimous!
Compared to any Emperor with all his sovereignty, splendor, and stateliness that is why Iqbal liked and has professed simple living;
Try to gain fame in adversary and lack of resources, and do not run after abundance as the divine power (QUWATI HAIDRI) is hidden in dry bread of barley.

It was this Qalandar in Iqbal who pondered and found a way to revive the lost honor and prestige of Muslims of the sub-continent. It was Iqbal who persuaded Jinnah to lead the nation and get a place of refuge where they could live honorably and peacefully. The nation forgot the message of the great man who wanted them to be united and be a part of great Muslim Umma right from the shores of Nile to Kashghar the lands of central Asia.

Muslims give lot of respect to the poet- philosopher and in Pakistan his birth and death anniversaries are celebrated; armed personnel are posted on his grave-but his teachings; message of unity and acquiring knowledge and wisdom have not been given due wait age with the result the nation has been given to linguistic, sectarian and different grouping, jeopardizing the spirit and purpose of an Islamic sovereign state that the poet philosopher had aimed.

HAKIM UL UMMAT AND IWAN-I-IQBAL

The scholars and writers besides writing novels, dramas and plays that are displayed on television and cinema screens and watched eagerly by young and old should also further Iqbal's mission. Alhamra theatre, located close to Iwan-i-Iqbal, remains abounded with people who go there for relaxation and enjoyment, whereas Iwan-i-lqbal remains secluded and devoid of much activity that should have been used as a full fledge academy, to design and teach comprehensive and crash courses on the teachings of Allama Iqbal in various fields; Philosophy, Islam, democracy, nationalism, moralities at different levels of achievement recognized by boards and universities where students, service men, bureaucrats, parliamentarians may undergo condensed relevant courses for each category. Pakistani nation is ailing and suffering from various viruses: sectarian, linguistic, tribal, provincialism and moral degeneration and needs to be treated and cured which can be best administered in the shape of teachings of Allama Iqbal-Hakim ul ummat.

IQBAL AND ELECTORAL

Pakistani nation needs an educational revolution and not an 'askari' or any other type. Present government in the light of the teachings of Allama Iqbal, has already fixed minimum qualification for an electorate but this change is also required in the qualification of the voter who is supposed to use the discretion to chose the electorate; if the required qualification of an electorate is graduation there ought to have been some basic qualification for the voter as well- at least Matriculation; possessed with awareness of social, economic and political needs of the country to be able to cast his vote sensibly. In this regard Allama Iqbal has very rightly said, Keep away from democracy and accept obedience of a wise dictator; because 200 donkeys cannot have the wisdom of a human being'. In another verse he has remarked about western democracy, 'it is a way of election where heads are counted and not the brains.'

If the above basic qualifications already introduced and suggested in respect of voters and members of the parliament are introduced- would usher an educational revolution in the country which would not only bring maturity in the parliaments but also be helpful in eradicating fundamentalism and other social and moral vices that are the result of ignorance and lack of desire to learn.

ALLAMA IQBAL AND ISLAM
TUO AGAR KHWHI MUSALMAN ZISTAN- HATCH MUMKIN NIEST BA QURAN ZISTAN

Iqbal in an unequivocal term says that if you want to be a Muslim it is possible only through grasping Quran and molding one's life accordingly. Quran is the basic document and code of conduct for a Muslim, He further says that they could build a mosque over night but their hearts, given to petty weaknesses, do not make them acquire essence of the prayer; and addressing himself says; *JO MAIN SIR BASIJDA HUA KABHI TUO ZAMIN SE AANE LAGI SADA TERA DIL TUO HAI SAN AM ASHNA TUJHE KAYA MILE GA NAMAZ MEIN*;

Whenever, I prostrate hear a voice of the heart saying," what shall you gain out of that Hippocratic act when he was not involved in it"? He, therefore, stresses on the purity of heart, which is the very purpose of prayers. He, however, does not stop from saying prayers or going to the mosque but expects from the worshippers to exercise and display the qualities the prayer generates: honesty, devotion to duty, hard work and loyalty in their practical lives. The nations, who have practiced these values, today are at the top and those who ought to have been leading, are at their lowest ebb because of being unmindful of their commitments.

ALLAMA GAINED ETERNAL LIFE
Allama Iqbal died and met his Creator in 1938, at the age of 61 years and is buried on the side of Lahore Shahi Mosque built by Emperor Aurangzeb. A dignified mausoleum has been built under which the great poet philosopher rests. A number of visitors and dignitaries come to pay homage at the grave. A squad consisting of men in uniform, from all the three forces posted in turn, remain there as a mark of respect to the late hero of the nation, who still lives in the heart of millions of lovers and admirers and according to the holy Quran and a famous hadith; a Momin does not die but gains eternal life of which you do not have the cognizance.

CHAPTER III
HISTORY OF PAKISTAN MOVEMENT

Hindus always desired to crush the Muslims as a nation and ultimately to merge them into Hindu society. Several attempts were made by the Hindus to erase the Muslim culture and civilization. Hindi-Urdu controversy, Shuddhi, Bande Matram, Wardha and Widdia mandar schemes to converting non Hindus to Hinduism were the glaring examples of the ignoble Hindu mentality. These attempts were aimed at the total elimination of Muslim culture in order to merge it into Hindu Culture and Nationalism.

One of the great objectives of the Pakistan movement was the protection of Muslim culture and to save it from Hindu domination. The Muslims were not prepared to accept Hindu superiority over them. They were very much alive to their sense of supremacy as a separate and distinct nation. In fact this feeling of separateness was motivating element of the Pakistan movement. The Muslims wanted to give stability to their nationhood, which was not possible in the United India under the Hindu hegemony. The Muslims, therefore, decided to separate themselves from the Hindus in order to safeguard their cultural values.

TWO-NATION THEORY

The entire freedom movement revolved around Two-Nation Theory, which became the basis of demand for Pakistan. It meant that the Muslims were a separate nation with their distinct culture, civilization, literature, history religion and social values. Islam, the religion of the Muslims, was based on the concept of Tauheed and, therefore, could not be assimilated in any other system or religion.

Sir Syed Ahmed Khan was the first Muslim leader who propounded this theory. In the beginning he was a staunch advocate of Hindu-Muslim unity. Later on while observing the prejudiced Hindu and Congress attitude toward the Muslims, he came forward with his Two-Nation concept and declared that the Muslims were a separate nation having their own culture and civilization.

The establishment of Pakistan further strengthened the Two-Nation concept, which meant that Pakistan would be a country where Islamic principles would be followed. With the creation of Pakistan it became possible for the Muslims to mould their lives according to the principles of Islam.

EMANCIPATION FROM THE PREJUDICIAL HINDU MAJORITY

The Muslims came to India with conquering armies and permanently settled there in the Indian society, though maintaining their separate identity. The conversion of Hindus to Islam, in the later stages, caused the population of India to undergo a gradual change. With lapse of time the Muslims came to form one-fourth of the total population of India.

The Muslims belonged to all walks of life and understandably dominated in all spheres of social life during their rule. The Arab conquest was a blessing for the sub-continent, which attained maximum economic prosperity during Muslim rule. The Muslim domination aroused Hindu jealousy that had to live under the Muslim hegemony in spite of their numerical majority.

With the advent of the British rule the Muslims lost their empire and political supremacy. The British extended favors to the Hindus in view of their numerical strength in order to win their co-operation. The Hindus, who were eagerly looking for an opportunity to settle their old score with the Muslims, were very happy on the turn of the events. They quickly snatched the golden opportunity, offered to them by their new masters, and joined hands with the new rulers of India for the elimination of the Muslims from the Indian society.

The British and the Hindus adopted a cruel policy of mass elimination against the Muslims in order to erase them as a nation and subsequently merge them in the Hindu nationalism. That policy of the British created great difficulties for the Muslims to maintain their national integrity. The Congress ministries further strengthened their suspicions, which were now fully convinced that there was no other way than separating themselves from the Hindus in order to avoid total elimination. The demand for Pakistan was based on this very feeling that the Muslims should be emancipated from the clutches of the eternal Hindu domination.

ESTABLISHMENT OF A BALANCED ECONOMIC SYSTEM

The economic condition of the Muslims, before partition, was deplorable. The Hindus had monopolized commerce and trade. The Muslims were not in a position to enter in the business and trade because of biased policy of government. After the war of Independence of 1857, the British Government had banned Muslims entry into government service. All high civil and military positions were reserved for the Hindus. The Muslims were considered eligible only for peons and low ranking jobs. The Government had confiscated estates and properties of the Muslims to punish them for their involvement in the war of independence. The Hindus who fully exploited the Muslim cultivators mostly owned the agricultural land. The Government policy provided no shelter to the Muslims for earning their sustenance in a respectable manner.

The Muslims also lagged behind in the field of education. The Hindus on the other hand had advanced in modern knowledge and were in a better position. The ignorance in education also played havoc with the economic condition of the Muslims, as they were not capable of getting any reasonable job.

These measures and biased policies of the government badly affected the condition of the Muslims. Their future as a nation was in a shamble and they reached at the lowest ebb of their social and economic life in India. The inexorable economic exploitation of the Muslims at the hands of the British and Hindus compelled them to think about a separate homeland for their economic security. They wanted a country where they could erect a social and economic system free of exploitation and which could pull them out of despair to show them a new horizon of life.

The major objective of the creation of Pakistan was the establishment of a balanced economic system based on the economic principles of Islam, which could ensure a happy and stable economic life to every individual. The demand for Pakistan was motivated by the desire of Muslims to have a homeland of their own where everyone had enough opportunities to earn his sustenance and where every individual was self-sufficient in his economic matters.

The economic system of Islam is based on the balanced principles, which do not permit an individual to keep wealth and economic resources more than one's needs and requirements. By the systems of Zakat and Ushr, extra wealth is extracted from the people and distributed amongst the poor and needy persons of the society to maintain economic balance. Quaid-e-Azam, while inaugurating the State Bank of Pakistan on 1st July 1948, said, "The bank symbolized the sovereignty of our people in the financial sphere. The Western economic system has created many problems for humanity. The Western economic system would not help us in setting up a workable economic order. We should evolve an economic system based on Islamic concept of justice and equality."

IDEOLOGY OF PAKISTAN AND ALLAMA IQBAL
Allama Iqbal was a great philosopher poet. He had acquired countrywide fame and recognition as a thinker. He received his education from the Government College, Lahore and later on went to England to pursue studies in Law. He got his Ph.D. in Philosophy from a German University. Allama Iqbal taught for few years at the Government College, Lahore. He had studied Islam deeply and had a profound liking for the Islamic principles and its tenets. He compared the Western culture with Islam and reached at the conclusion that mankind's emancipation and welfare lay in the adoption of Islam as a way of life. Basically Allama Iqbal was a poet, teacher and thinker. However, he had to come in the political field in order to safeguard the interests of the Muslims of the sub-continent. His entry into politics was greatly welcomed by the Muslims where a trustworthy companion of the Quaid-e-Azam was badly needed.

Allama Iqbal proved a great political leader and a reliable companion of the Quaid-e-Azam. He awakened the Muslims of the sub-continent with his stirring verses to demand a separate homeland. He led the Muslims at every step and rendered great services in the accomplishment of Pakistan. Allama Iqbal considered Islam as a complete code of life. He said that I am fully convinced that the Muslims of India will ultimately have to establish a separate homeland, as they cannot live with Hindus in the United India. He advised the Muslims to understand their real position and shed away their mental confusion and narrow approach to life. He clarified the glorious image of the Muslim Umma.

Allama Iqbal openly negated the concept of One-Nation of India and emphasized on the separate and distinct national image of the Muslims. He considered the establishment of Pakistan very essential and vital for the restoration of national and religious identity of the Muslims. His poetry reflects his love for the nation and country. He produced a large number of poems, which indicate his immense love for his homeland.

He said that Islam guides the mankind in every aspect of worldly life and, therefore, must be enforced in an Islamic State as a code of life. He based the foundation of homeland on the religion, which later on became the ideology and basis of Pakistan. He said that Islam strengthens the life by infusing spiritual unity. He said that in Islam the Almighty 'God and Universe' the 'soul and matter' are the different part of One Whole'. He did not believe in any system separated from religion and declared that religion and politics are not separated from each other in Islam.

Allama Iqbal firmly believed in the separate identity of the Muslims as a 'Nation'. He said that I am fully convinced that the Muslims of India will ultimately have to establish a separate homeland, as they cannot live with Hindus in the United India. He said that there would be no possibility of peace in the country unless and until the Muslims are recognized as a separate nation, as they had their own cultural values, which they must preserve and maintain. He declared, "India is a continent of Human beings belonging to different languages and professing different religions. To base a constitution on the conception of homogeneous India is to prepare her for civil war. I, therefore, demand the formation of a consolidated Muslim State in the best interest of the Muslims of India and Islam. The formation of a consolidated Muslim North-West Indian State appears to be the final destiny of the Muslims, at least of North-West India".

Allama Iqbal believed in the federal system and thought it as an ideal system for India in the prevailing conditions. He emphasized on introduction of the federal system to bring unity and solidarity to the country. He also believed that the federal system would promote unity amongst various factions of the society, which would help in defense of the country.

"A unitary form of Government is inconceivable for India. The residuary powers must be left to the self-governing units. I would never like the Muslims of India to agree on a system, which negates the principles of a true Federation or fails to distinguish them as a separate political unit. In this way only the Muslims of India will have maximum opportunities of development and in return would be able to render best services for the defense of the country against foreign invasion, be that invasion one of ideas or of Guns and bayonets."

The Allahbad address of Allama Iqbal carries great importance and significance in the freedom struggle of the Muslims of India. The

Presidential Address at Allah bad in fact, molded the destinies of the Muslims of the sub-continent and put their endeavors in right direction. Presidential address of Allama Iqbal further clarified the Two-Nation Theory and demanded a separate homeland for the Muslims. He said "I have been a staunch advocate of putting an end to religion's prejudices and distinctions from the country. But now I believe that the protection of separate national identity is in the best interests of both Hindus and the Muslims." He further said that 'It was the prime duty of all civilized nations to show utmost regard and reverence for the religious principles, cultural and social values of other nations. Since the Muslims are a separate nation with their distinct cultural values and religious trends, and they want to have a system of their own liking, they should be allowed to live under such system considering their separate religious and cultural identity".

Allama Iqbal expressed the Muslims sentiments and ideas in true spirit by defining them as a separate nation with their distinct national image. His presidential address washed away all the confusions from the Muslim minds and showed them new dimensions in their struggle for freedom. It later on enabled the Muslim masses to determine their line of action and work out a clear-cut and definite program in order to accomplish their goal *of a separate* homeland. The spirit which Allama Iqbal infused in the Muslims by his presidential address developed into an ideological basis for the Pakistan movement. The famous Pakistan Resolution, passed on 23rd March, 1940 at Lahore was in fact based on Allama Iqbal's presidential address of Allahbad.

Allama Iqbal joined Muslim League and rendered services for the safeguard of Muslims interests. He was on the delegation, which represented the Muslims in the Second and Third Round Table *Conferences in* 1931 and 1932. In these *Conferences he very* ably advocated the Muslim cause and vehemently opposed all such schemes, which in *any way* jeopardized the Muslim interests.

Allama Iqbal infused a spirit of nationalism amongst Muslims with his stirring and thought-provoking poetry. He preached an idea of nationalism based on Islamic unity and brotherhood. He was of the opinion that the individual is not linked with *the* geographical boundaries but with a spiritual relationship. He negated the concept of territorial nationalism and brought to light its adverse affects and influence on the Muslim.

Allama Iqbal's *writings, poetry* and sayings kindled a new light, aroused a sense of respect, self-realization and determination in the Muslim masses. The new Muslim generation particularly responded vigorously to Allama Iqbal's call and took active part in the freedom struggle for the creation of Pakistan.

QUAID-E-AZAM'S ROLE IN THE FREEDOM MOVEMENT

CREATION OF PAKISTAN

PERSONAL LIFE

Muhammad Ali Jinnah, also known as the Quaid-e-Azam, was born in Karachi on December 25th, 1876. He was sent to the Sindh Hadassah High School in 1887. He then joined the Mission High School, Bombay from where he passed his matriculation examination.

His father decided to send him to England to acquire some business experience. Jinnah, however, had made up his mind to receive education in Law. He joined Lincoln's Inn, one of the legal societies of England, which prepared students for Bar. In 1895, at the age of 19, he was called to the Bar. He successfully completed his studies and also watched closely the British political and parliamentary system. He used to visit the British House of Commons to study its working and system.
During his stay in England Jinnah took keen interest in the Indian affairs. He took active part in the election campaign of Dadabhai Noroji, a leading Indian nationalist, when he ran for the membership of the British parliament. Dadabhai Noroji won the election to become the first ever Indian to be elected to the House of Commons.
Jinnah returned to Karachi in 1896. By that time there was nothing for him in his father's business. He decided to become a lawyer and started legal practice in Bombay, where he had to work day and night to establish himself as a first rate lawyer.

ENTRY INTO POLITICS

Jinnah first entered politics in 1906 by taking part in the Calcutta session of the All India National Congress. Jinnah joined Congress because it aimed at securing self-Government by adopting constitutional means. Four years later Jinnah was elected to the Imperial Legislative Council.

It was the beginning of a long and distinguished political/parliamentary career for Jinnah.

POLITICAL ROLE ACIV1TIES OF M. A. JINNAH

In politics, MA Jinnah was greatly impressed by Krishna Gopal Gokhale, an eminent Congress nationalist leader. Jinnah, being highly inspired by Gokhale, aspired to become 'a Muslim Gokhale'. Jinnah also greatly admired the British political pattern. He eagerly desired to raise the status of India in the international community and to develop a sense of Indian nationalism among the people of India. By that time he also looked after the Muslim interests.

By 1906, the Muslims of the sub-continent became conscious of their separate identity; therefore, All India Muslim League was formed with the prime objective of protecting Muslims' interests. Quaid-e-Azam did not involve in the League's politics and kept away from it. Quaid-e-Azam joined Muslim League in 1913 only after being assured that the Muslim League, too, was committed to the Indian freedom and self-rule.

AMBASSADOR OF HINDU-MUSLIM UNITY

The Quaid-e-Azam was a great Advocate of Hindu-Muslim Unity. He was of the opinion that both Hindus and Muslims should make joint efforts to get rid of the British rule. He did lot of work to bring both Hindus and Muslims closer. It was mainly through his efforts that Muslim League and congress began to hold their annual meetings jointly to facilitate mutual consultation and participation. In 1915 the two organizations held their meetings in Bombay and in 1916 in Lucknow where the Lucknow pact was concluded. Under the terms of the pact the two organizations gave their approval to a scheme of constitutional reforms. Both Muslim League and the Congress demonstrated a large heartedness. Muslim League agreed to Hindu demands of representation while Congress agreed to Muslim participation in the legislative bodies according to their strength. Congress also accepted Muslims' demand of separate electorate. Mr. Jinnah's endeavors to bring about political union of Hindus and Muslims earned him the title of 'best ambassador of Hindu-Muslim Unity'.

By 1920 Gandhi had emerged as a strong political leader. He managed to control both the congress and Home Rule League. Gandhi was basically an extremist Hindu politician with highly pro-Hindu approach to politics. Due to Gandhi's non-cooperation movement Quaid-e-Azam resigned from the Congress in 1920. For a few years he kept himself away from active politics. After leaving the Congress he used the Muslim League platform for the projection of his political views. But during 1920s the Muslim league and the Quaid-e-Azam were over-shadowed by the Congress and the Khilafat leaders.

The post Khilafat period saw the rise of Jinnah as a leader of the Muslims. Before that, and even in 1916 when he as the president of the League, was instrumental in bringing about the Lucknow Pact, Jinnah was a thoroughgoing nationalist. But since the mid twenties he increasingly identified himself with Muslims and the Muslim League, and re-entered active politics in 1924. He believed in the constitutional progress in the country, which he thought could be built on the bedrock of Hindu-Muslim unity.

A split emerged in the Muslim League over the acceptance of the Simon Commission with Jinnah acting in opposition to the group led by Sir Shafi and joining hands with the Congress in boycotting the Simon Commission. His sincere endeavors to build Hindu Muslim unity were blatantly foiled by the publication of Nehru Report (1928) which forced him to part ways with the Congress, never to seek unity with them again. Before parting ways he passionately tried to convince the Congress to incorporate his amendments in the Nehru Report at the National Convention (1928) convened by the Congress at Calcutta that went unheeded and was booed by the Congress participants. As the Nehru Report failed to offer adequate safeguards to the Muslims, Mr. Jinnah had to come up with his famous 14 points (1929), which was ratified by the Muslims as the basis of future Muslim demands.

Mr. Jinnah's failure to bring about even minor changes in the Nehru Report over the question of separate electorate and seats for the Muslims in the legislatures disappointed him greatly. The Muslim League was a divided house at this moment and the Punjab League repudiated Jinnah's leadership and organized itself separately under the leadership of Sir Muhammad Shafi. Feeling peeved and disgusted Jinnah decided to leave India and settle in England. From 1930 to 1935 he remained in England. During this period he devoted himself to legal practice appearing before the Privy Council. He also represented the Muslims in Round Table Conferences (1930-32). He was, however, persuaded to return to India when the constitutional changes were introduced. He returned to India in the beginning of 1935.

When Mr. Jinnah returned to India, Congress was a far better organization than Muslim League. Provincial elections under the Act of 1935 were held in 1937. The Quaid-e-Azam was still thinking in terms of cooperation between Congress and the Muslim League. The elections of 1937 proved to be a turning point in the relations between the two organizations. The Congress obtained clear majority in six provinces. When the Muslim League desired to form coalition government with Congress, the Congress refused unless the Muslim League subscribed to its creed. As a consequence the relations between the Congress and the Muslim league started to deteriorate and soon Muslim discontent and disillusionment became boundless.

At this moment the Muslim India were a disunited, disgruntled and despaired mass of men and women. The Congress decision of eliminating the Muslim League from the ministries widened the gap between the Muslims and the Hindus. Quaid-e-Azam was extremely pained to find Congress acting in a highly anti-Muslim behavior. He had to change his views about Hindu - Muslim unity and repudiated his belief that India was a homogeneous country. He declared, "Muslims can expect neither justice nor fairly treatment under Congress Government".

From then onwards MR. Jinnah re-organized the Muslim League from being a debating party for Muslim landed aristocracy and went to the masses for support. Within a brief period of four years Jinnah awakened the slumbering Muslim masses, brought them on platform and less than one banner and gave coherence to their innermost but vague urges and aspirations. The sincere and dauntless leadership of Mr. Jinnah stirred Muslim consciousness and a hundred million people discovered their soul and destiny. They shed their minority complex and developed a national consciousness of their own. Thus Jinnah became the unquestioned leader of the Muslim community and was elected each year as President of the Muslim League. The bulk of Muslims from all over India supported the Muslim League. They assembled under the flag of the Muslim League like a united whole and extended their full support to Jinnah. And it was out of sheer gratitude for the stunning discovery of Muslim nationhood that the Muslim India hailed Jinnah as the 'Quaid-e-Azam'. Jinnah became the great leader of the Muslim India to take them to their destiny of Pakistan.

QUAID-E-AZAM, CREATOR OF PAKISTAN

By 1939 the Quaid-e-Azam had emerged as undisputed leader of the Muslims who had embarked upon a new line of action; soon after the resignation of the Congress ministries, the Quaid-e-Azam gave a call to his Muslim brethren on December 29, 1939, to observe the Day of Deliverance and thanks giving. The call was widely supported. Three months later on 22-24th March 1940, the Muslim League in its annual meeting at Lahore passed the famous Lahore Resolution for a separate homeland for the Muslims of India. The Congress opposed the idea of Pakistan. The Muslim League under the dynamic leadership of the Quaid-e-Azam strove very hard to accomplish Pakistan by August 14, 1947.

TWO NATION THEORY AND QUAID-E-AZAM

Quaid-e-Azam was a staunch believer of Two Nation Theory and considered the Muslims a separate and distinct nation. He said, "Pakistan was created the day the first Indian national entered the fold of Islam". He further said, "The Muslims are a nation by every definition of the word nation. They have every right to establish their separate homeland. They can adopt any mean to promote and protect their economic, social, political and cultural interests".

Quaid-e-Azam laid great stress on the Islamic Ideology as being the basis of the struggle for Pakistan because he believed that Islam was the only unifying force of the Muslim Millat. He said, "What relationship knits the Muslims into one whole, which is the formidable rock on which the Muslim edifice has been erected, which is the sheet anchor provides base to the Muslim Millat, that relationship, the sheet anchor and the rock is the Holy Quran". In 1946, addressing a gathering at Islamia College, Peshawar, he said, "We did not demand Pakistan simply to have a piece of land but we wanted a laboratory where we could experiment on Islamic Principles, which was to put an end to the Muslim isolation and exploitation.

SYED AHMED SHAHEED BARAILVI

The name of Syed Ahmed Shaheed carries immense importance with regard to the revival of Islam in the history of the sub-continent. Syed Ahmed Shaheed picked up the course of a vigorous two pronged struggle aimed at the purification of the Muslim society and the destruction of the British power in India. His approach to freedom was based on the armed struggle and confrontation against the foreign and non-Muslim forces.

Syed Ahmed Shaheed was horn at Rai Baraily in 1786. He was greatly influenced by the preaching of Shah Wali Ullah and was a staunch follower of his son Shah Abdul Aziz. Syed Ahmed was extremely dismayed over the decline of the Muslims and earnestly desired to see the restoration of Islamic supremacy in India.

The purpose of Syed Ahmed's life and struggle was not only confined to the spread of Islam by preaching and persuasion but he believed in taking practical steps for this purpose. The main purpose before Syed Ahmed and his followers was the establishment *of a state, which was based on the* Islamic principles.

In the time of Syed Ahmed, Punjab was under the Sikh regime of Ranjeet Singh who was widely known all over India for his oppressive and tyrannical rule. The Muslims suffered heavily under his rule and were denied liberty and freedom to profess and practice their religion. The N.W.F.P. had also fallen to the Sikh domination and was included in the Sikh regime. The Sikhs, however, had not been able to establish a stable Government in N.W.F.P.

Syed Ahmed was of the opinion that if Punjab and N.W.F.P. were liberated of the Sikh domination, the Muslims would regain their old position. He picked up Punjab to begin his Jihad against Sikhs and selected N.W.F.P. to launch his movement for the eradication of the non-Islamic forces. Syed Ahmed invited the people to join him in Jihad against the un-Islamic regime to save the Muslims of the Sikh domination. Shah Ismail Shaheed, a great Muslim saint and a grandson of Shah Wall Ullah, joined Syed Ahmed along with his followers. Syed Ahmed directed Shah Ismail Shaheed to march with a party of six thousand followers from Rai Baraily. He himself proceeded from other parts of Punjab and Delhi where he was joined by many other followers in the noble task.

Syed Ahmed reached Nowshera in December 1826 and established his headquarter. He sent a message to Ranjeet Singh to embrace Islam or be ready to face the Mujahideen in the battlefield. Ranjeet Singh turned down the offer of Syed Ahmed in a most scornful manner and demonstrated a high degree of disdain for Islam and Muslims.

The first battle against the Sikhs was fought at Akora on 21st December 1826 in which the Sikhs were defeated. The Muslims were successful in the second encounter as well which was fought at Hazro. The immediate and astonishing success of the Mujahideen in two clashes spurred the popularity of the Jihad movement and Syed Ahmed. Many people including the famous Pathan tribes joined Syed Ahmed in the struggle. The Pathan leaders Yar Muhammad Khan and Pir Hakman Khan joined Syed Ahmed with their followers. With the time the number of the Muslim forces rose to 80,000.

The Jihad movement swiftly passed through the early stages of struggle with amazing success. A conspiracy was hatched against the movement and an attempt was made on the life of Syed Ahmed by poisoning him, which he survived. Sardar Yar Muhammad was bribed to betray Syed Ahmed and join the Sikhs against Mujahideen.

Syed Ahmed now set out for Kashmir and Peshawar to wage his struggle against the Sikhs afresh and captured Peshawar. A clash took place between the Mujahideen and Pathan tribes who had defected Syed Ahmed. Sultan Khan, the brother of Yar Muhammad Khan was leading the Pathan forces. Sultan Khan was arrested after his forces were defeated. Syed Ahmed pardoned him but he did not join the Muslim forces and was killed while fighting against them.

Syed Ahmed shifted his headquarter to Balakot and began his Jihad movement from Rajauri in 1830. A fierce battle was fought between the Sikh and Muslim armies. The Mujahideen fought valiantly but they could not stand the much stronger and superior forces. The Muslims were defeated after a fierce battle in which Syed Ahmed and Shah Ismail laid their lives while fighting for the cause of Islam. With the death of Syed Ahmed the Jihad movement fell *in disarray and* could *not he carried out with the* old fervor and enthusiasm. The Jihad movement is regarded as the forerunner of the Pakistan Movement in the history of the sub-continent.

FRAIZI MOVEMENT

The Muslim Sufis and mystics spread the light of Islam in Bengal in the 13th and 14th centuries. In the beginning Bengal was very much receptive to the call of Islam but thereafter there had been a strong Hindu revival, which immensely infused a new religious spirit among the Hindus. This Hindu revival converted many areas to Hinduism and also made its impact on the Muslim society. Serious impediments were observed in the spread of Islam as the Muslim missionaries had discontinued their efforts. There was wide-scale ignorance prevalent among the Muslim masses about Islam resulting in the emergence of Hindu beliefs and practices in the society.

Haji Shariat Ullah

The person who came forward to stir the dormant faith of the Bengali Muslims was Haji Shariat Ullah who was born in 1781 in the village of Shamail in the Faridpur District. After receiving his early education Haji Shariat Ullah left for Hijaz in 1799 in a very young age. After a long stay of twenty years he returned from Mecca in 1820. During his stay in Arabia he was greatly impressed by the doctrines of Sheikh Muhammad Abdul Wahab who had initiated Wahabi movement in Arabia.

Haji Shariat Ullah began his reform movement known as Fraizi *Movement* in the center of Bengal. The Muslim revivalism in Bengal began in the 19th century to the anti-Muslim policy of the British. The Fraizi movement based on and emphasized the performing *of* Fraiz/duties imposed by the God and His Prophet (peace he upon him). The followers of Haji Shariat Ullah are known as Fraizis for their insistence on the fulfillment of the religious obligations. Haji Shariat Ullah was extremely dismayed to see deplorable condition of the Muslims who have been crushed by the East India Company. The Zamindars who were mostly non-Muslims, were exploiting the Muslim cultivators by denying the due share of their toil.

Haji Shariat Ullah was deadly against the false and superstitious beliefs, which had arisen, in the Muslim society due to long contact with the Hindus. He utterly disliked the expressions of Pir (master) and Murid (disciple) and desired them to be replaced with the title of Ustad (teacher) and Shagird (student). He believed that these titles signified a complete submission by relationship between Ustad and Shagird. He strongly forbade the laying on of hands at the time *of* accepting a person into discipleship, which had crept into Muslim society. He required from his followers Tauba as a manifestation of repentance for all past sins and a pledge to lead a righteous and God-fearing life in future. His followers as already mentioned, were known as Fraizis but they preferred to call themselves as Tauba Muslims. His movement brought the Muslim peasantry together against the cruel exploitation by the Hindu zamindars.

Haji Shariat Ullah was a pious man who lived a simple life. He *won* deep loyalty and confidence of the people by *his utmost* Sincerity and devotion. His disciples and followers blindly took him as competent and able to pull them out of crisis and despair. He was to provide consolation to the people in their time of adversity and affliction. He declared Jihad against the infidels as inevitable and termed the sub-continent as Dar-ul-Harb where the offering of Friday prayers was unlawful.

The Fraizi movement of Haji Shariat Ullah injected a great deal of confidence among the Muslim masses that were awakened from their slumber. It infused spirit among the Muslim peasants who got together for the protection of their rights. Haji Shariat Ullah became the center of a great spiritual revival of the Muslims and laid the foundation for his successors to continue their struggle.

Haji Sahib invited opposition of the Hindu zamindars who were perturbed on the unity of the Muslim peasantry. They started harassing him by instituting false cases against him. Ultimately he was forced to leave Najabari in the district of Dacca, a place where he had settled after his return from Arabia. He returned to his birthplace in Faridpur district, where he continued his religious preaching and fighting against *the* non-Islamic *forces till his death in* 1840.

DUDU MIYAN

Haji Shariat Ullah succeeded by his son Mohsin-ud-Din Ahmed (popularly known as Dudu Miyan). He became very popular in the districts of Dacca, Faridpur, Pabna, Bakarganj and Noakhali. He was born in 1819 and went to Arabia in his early age.

Dudu- Miyan assumed the leadership of Fraizi Movement left by his father. He divided the whole of Bengal into circles and appointed a Khalifa to look after his followers in each circle. He introduced a political tinge in the movement, which became the symbol of the resistance of the Muslim peasantry of Eastern Bengal against Hindu Landlords. Dudu Miyan vehemently opposed the levying of taxes by landlords. In those days the Muslim peasants were required to contribute towards the decoration of Hindu goddess, Durga or towards the support of any of the idolatrous rituals of his Hindu landlord. Dudu Miyan strongly resented this practice and considered it a highly oppressive measure to crush the Muslim peasantry. He declared that the earth belonged to the Almighty God and that no one could inherit it or to impose taxes upon it. Dudu Miyan believed in equality and considered the richest and the poorest as equally important. He preached that whenever a brother was in distress it was the duty of his comrades to help him.

Dudu Miyan in order to save the Muslim peasantry from illegal taxes asked them to occupy the Khas Mahal land, which was directly managed by the Government. He allowed the peasants to refuse paying the taxes except the revenue tax, which was imposed by the Government.

Dudu Miyan believed in taking practical steps for the amelioration of the Muslim peasantry. For this purpose he had established his own State where he used to administer justice by settling disputes and by punishing the wrongdoers. He was particularly very strict in punishing those landlords who preferred to go to a court of law for the recovery of debts instead of coming to him for redress. The Hindu zamindars dreaded him most and conspired to check the spread of his movement. The landlords and European planters retaliated with their usual tactics of instituting false criminal cases against him. He was harassed all his life and was put in jail time and again on frivolous charges.

Dudu Miyan died on September 24, 1862 at Bahdurpur in the district of Dacca. The Fraizi movement under Haji Shariat Ullah and Dudu Miyan cultivated a great deal of political awareness among the Muslims of Bengal and particularly among the Muslim peasantry who put a formidable resistance against the Hindu landlords and the British rulers.

TITU MIR

Mir Nasir Ali, popularly known as Titu Mir was an important leader of the Muslim peasantry of Bengal. He diligently worked for the independence and renaissance of the Muslims of Bengal. He was born in 1782 and belonged to a noble family. From his early age he began to take interest in the political affairs of the country. Though he did not belong to the group of Haji Shariat

Ullah but he had similar views on the political, religious, social and economic objectives of the Muslims of Bengal. He earnestly desired to revive the past glory of the Muslims and Islam.

Titu Mir went to Mecca in 1819 for performing Haj where he came into contact with Syed Ahmed Shaheed Brailvi, who extremely inspired him with his spiritual insight. After his return from Mecca, Titu Mir began preaching the poor classes of Jessore and Nadiya in Central Bengal. Soon he formed a sect known as Maulvis among his followers.

Titu Mir finally stood against the Hindu customs and practices. The main objective of his movement was the elimination of Hindu rituals, which invited Hindu antagonism. The Hindu Zamindars instituted false cases against the Maulvis in the courts where fines were levied against the Maulvis. Kishan Rai, a notorious Hindu zamindar imposed a tax on his Muslim tenants who professed to be a Wahabi. The tax was called as the Beard Tax because the Wahabis did not shave according to their school of thought. Titu Mir protested against this inhuman tax and physically resisted the tax collectors sent by the zamindars. The Government ordered action against Titu Mir, and a strong military contingent was sent to crush him. A fierce encounter took place between the Government forces and the followers of Titu Mir on November 18, 1831. Titu Mir was killed in action. His followers were arrested and his movement extinguished in course of time.

WAR OF INDEPENDENCE 1857, MAJOR CAUSES

After the death of Aurangzeb, the Mughal Empire crumbled because of the shortcomings of the incapable successors. The British, who had come to India for the purposes of trade, immediately noticed the signs of decadence in the Mughal Empire. They began to indulge in the political affairs of the country and very, soon acquired considerable control in the policy matters of the Government. In fact they were now planning to stay in India as its rulers and to snatch away the political reign from the Muslims.

The Muslims who had been rulers of India before the advent of the British came to India as a conquering force and settled here and entered every walk of life. They were administrators, soldiers, traders, peasants, scholars and artisans. They dominated every walk of life but did not monopolize as the Hindus were also represented in every aspect of society.

Despite living with the Hindus, the Muslims maintained their distinct religious and socio-political identity. In spite of differences of culture, civilization, history and thinking, between the two nations Hindu and Muslim families, lived in the same neighborhoods for generations. They mixed co-existed but maintained their cultural identity.

The British quickly~ realized that it would be to their own advantage to play up these differences between the two major nations of the sub-continent. They considered the Muslims to be a great threat to their existence in the sub-continent and, therefore, outlined a plan to subdue the Muslims. They tried to undermine the role and influence of the Muslims and patronized the Hindus to reduce the Muslims to inferior level in the society. In order to please the Hindu majority, a fake attempt was made to rewrite the Indian history to show the Muslims as oppressors and persecutors. The Hindus welcomed the change with amazing pleasure and extended their allegiance to the new rulers. For them it merely meant *'Changing of Masters,* coming under the subjugation of a new ruler and being relieved of the yoke of the Muslim rule.

The British, with the connivance of Hindus, took a number of actions to crush the Muslims completely. There was first of all, the reservation of all higher civil, judicial and military appointments for the British. The economic welfare of the Muslims mainly depended on the Government service without which they neither had the social status nor bread and butter to exist. The positions left open, were given to the Hindus and the Muslims were debarred from all high positions.

Persian was the official language during the Muslim *rule.* In 1835 the British replaced Persian with English as the official language and decided to use it in the higher courts of law. To the Hindus it was a mere replacement of one foreign language with another and they took to English readily. For the Muslims the decision was of greater consequences. It was a deliberate attempt by the British to diffuse the Muslim culture and to contaminate the religion of Islam. The Muslims did not learn English language, which resulted in their ineligibility for Government service.

The existing educational system, which reflected Islamic tinge, was replaced by the educational system evolved by Lord Macaulay entitled as 'Minute on Education'. The new system aimed at producing a class of persons, who *were* Indians in blood and color but British *in taste,* opinion, morals and intellect. The major aim of this system was to erase the Muslim culture and civilization and to *infect* Islam with alien concepts and philosophy.

As a result of this policy the Muslims suffered heavily in social and economic fields. Their position abruptly changed from that of a ruler to the most oppressed and dominated subjects. The British had acquired complete control over the country and the Hindus were blindly obeying the new rulers. The Muslims were heading towards social disaster and a respectable life had become unthinkable for them.

The British did not stop there. They used their power to crush the Muslims still further. In 1850 a bill was passed by which the right of inheritance of those Indians was accepted who entered the fold of Christianity. Many other facilities were offered to attract the Indians to defect their religions and accept Christianity. When these methods proved unsuccessful, attempts were made to convert the Muslims into Christians by force. Indians were compelled to send their children to co-educational institutions and forced to abandon purdha. The estates of the princes were confiscated and their privileges were withdrawn. All high positions in the army were assigned to the British officers.

The Indian army, which mainly contained Indian soldiers, was supplied with such cartridges, which were folded in cow and pig fat. These cartridges had to be unfolded by chewing with teeth before using them in the guns. The Indian soldiers were compelled to chew the fat of cow and pig with their teeth to use the cartridges. These highly unethical acts of the Government created a great deal of unrest amongst the Indian soldiers as the pig fat was forbidden for the Muslims and cow was a sacred animal for the Hindus.

By these methods the British Government, in fact, desired to establish their command on every Indian national. Naturally an unbridgeable gulf was created between the people and the British Government. They saw in these laws and policies the complete elimination of their culture and image as a nation. The deplorable economic conditions of the Indians added fuel to the fire and there was a strong wave of unrest in the country.

The people were fed up of the tyrannical rule of the British and wanted to get rid of it at all costs. The Indian army, which included both Hindus and Muslims soldiers revolted against the Government in 1857 to wage a struggle for freedom from the oppressive regime. The Mughal Emperor Bahadur Shah Zafar was made the supreme commander of the freedom fighters, which contained a large number of Muslims.

The war of Independence of 1857 ended in disaster for the Muslims. The British army soon brought the war under their complete control and the Indians' attempt to dislodge the British failed. The Mughal Empire was liquidated and the direct British rule was established over the sub-continent. Mughal Emperor Bahadur Shah Zafar, along with his entire family was arrested and put in jail and exiled to Rangoon (Burma), where he died. The Muslim nobility and middle classes were ruined. Although Hindus and other nations also took part in the war, yet only the Muslims had to bear the brunt of the British re-action who put the whole responsibility of war on the Muslims. The British carried out a large-scale massacre of the Muslims after the war and did everything to completely obliterate them from the society. The Muslims at the brink of social and economic disaster and were presenting a pathetic and gloomy picture when a courageous leader in Sir Syed Ahmed Khan emerged to their rescue.

SIR SYED AHMED KHAN

HIS SERVICES FOR THE MUSLIMS OF THE SUB-CONTINENT

PERSONAL LIFE

Sir Syed Ahmed Khan was a great Muslim scholar and reformer. He came forward to guide the Muslims who were destined to be ruined and eliminated from the Indian society as a result of Hindu and British domination. Sir Syed awakened the Muslims from their slumber to put up a struggle for the revival of their past position of eminence.

Sir Syed Ahmed Khan was born in a noble family on 17th October, 1817 in Delhi. He got his primary education from his maternal grandfather which included the study of Holy Quran, Arabic and Persian literature. He also acquired excellence in history, mathematics and medicine.

After completing his education, Sir Syed joined Government service in 1837 and was posted as Naib Munshi in Commissioner's office in Agra. He served in different capacities in Fatehpur Sikri and Mainpuri before he was elevated to the position of Chief Judge in 1846. He was posted as Chief Judge at Delhi where he wrote his famous book *"Asar* us Sanadred".

ALIGARH MOVEMENT

Sir Syed always felt aggrieved over the deplorable social and economic condition of the Muslims of India. He desired to see them (Muslims) at a respectable position in society and decided to guide them in their struggle for the revival of their past position of glory and eminence. The services, which Sir Syed rendered for the renaissance of the Muslims, are known as the Aligarh Movement in the history of Muslims of India.

He was conscious of the miserable state into which the Muslims had fallen over the years. He also realized that the present deplorable condition of the Muslims was partly because of their own extremist and conservative attitude. The Indian Muslims had always considered the British as their enemies and avoided any social interaction with them, which created a great deal of misunderstanding amongst the British about the Muslims. Sir Syed very rightly observed that the pitiable condition of the Muslims should not improve unless the Muslims changed their behavior towards the British. He was of the opinion that the British were the rulers of the country and the Muslims attitude towards them was undesirable. Sir Syed felt that the Muslims should extend co-operation to the British because they (British) were the rulers and likely to stay in country for many years. He was also of the opinion that Hindus would get closer to the British if the Muslims continued with their policy of hatred towards the British rulers. He emphasized on the Muslims to change their policy of keeping away from the British and come closer to them because only then they would be able to counter the Hindu and Congress propaganda to win back their position in society.

EFFORTS TO REMOVE MISUNDERSTANDING BETWEEN THE MUSLIMS AND THE BRITISH

Sir Syed believed that the first essential step towards the betterment of the Muslims was to restore mutual trust between the Muslims and the British. Without it, he felt, any plan for the renaissance of the Muslims would be useless. He wrote a pamphlet on the causes of the Indian revolt in order to remove misunderstanding amongst the British about the Muslims. The British had put the entire responsibility of war of Independence on the Muslims and considered them as their greatest enemies. When the war ended the British adopted a policy of mass extermination against the Muslims to punish them for their involvement in the war. The Hindus and other nations, who were equally responsible for the war were forgiven and ignored.

PAMPHLAT EXPLAINING CAUSES OF INDIAN REVOLT

Sir *Syed* explained the real causes of the war in this pamphlet and said that the Muslims were as much responsible for the war as were the other nations. He wrote that the Muslims were dragged into the war and it was unworthy to blame the Muslims alone for the war. He put the responsibility of the war on the Government and declared that the dictatorial and oppressive policies of the Government contributed a great deal towards out-break of the uprising against the Government in 1857.

He pointed out in the pamphlet that as there was no link between the rulers and the ruled, the Government could not know the grievances of the people, which resulted in the hatred and misunderstanding between the people and the government. He wrote that because of the ignorance and oppressive policies of the government, the embers of discontent continued to smolder resulting in the armed clash with the government. The armed rebellion, Sir Syed wrote, was in fact the manifestation of the discontentment found amongst the people about the tyrannical rule of the British. He said that in these circumstances, to hold the Muslims responsible for the war was unjustifiable, as they were dragged into the war along with other nations.

Sir Syed Ahmed Khan attributed the following reasons to the outbreak of war of Independence. According to him the major causes of the war were:

Non-representation of the Indians in the legislative councils,

Forcible conversion of Indian people to Christianity,

Mismanagement of Indian army,

Other ill-advised measures of the government, which created large, scale dissatisfaction amongst the various classes of society.

Sir Syed translated the pamphlet in English language and dispatched copies to the high officials of the government and the members of the royal family so that the British government should come to know the real causes of the revolt.

Sir Syed gave explanation of the word *'Nadarath'* in a magazine to remove the misunderstanding of the British about the Muslims. The British were annoyed with the Muslims because they (Muslims) used the word *'Nadarath'* for the British, which they felt degrading and contemptuous for themselves. Sir Syed clarified that the Muslims did not use this word for the British to degrade them. He gave the meaning of the word *'Nadarath'* and *wrote that the word has been* taken *from the* Arabic *word 'Nasar'* which meant benefactor or helper. The Muslims, therefore, Sir Syed explained, used this word for the British because they considered them as their helper and benefactor. Sir Syed said that the Muslims of India had always held their British rulers in the highest esteem and veneration.

He wrote the philosophical explanation of Bible entitled as *'Tabacen al Kalant'. In this work Sir Syed pointed out the* similarities between Islam and Christianity. He wrote 'Loyal *Mohammedans of India'* in which he gave a detailed account of the services, which the Muslims had rendered to the British rulers.

EDUCATIONAL SERVICES

Sir Syed's Aligarh movement was based on a two-fold program for the Muslims renaissance, which included modern education for the Muslims and co-operation with the British government. He persisted to it even in the face of extreme opposition from the conservative elements. The next vital step for the uplift of the Muslims, he considered, was the acquisition of modern knowledge by the Muslims of India to prepare them for taking due place in new society. Modern education, he felt, was very essential to equip the Muslims to compete with the Hindus. He was of the opinion that the present deplorable state of the Muslims was mainly because they lagged behind in the modern and English education. The Muslims could not compete with the Hindus because they did not acquire English education out of extreme hatred for the British. He clearly told the Muslims if they did not acquire English and modern education they would not be able to get their due status in the society and would be ruined forever. He told the people that Hindus progressed because they were well advanced in education. Sir Syed removed the misunderstanding of the people, created by the orthodox and conservative ulema, and said that it was not against Islam to acquire English education.

Sir Syed took practical steps for the improvement of educational standard of the Muslims. In 1859 he opened a school at Muradabad where Persian was taught. He established another school at Ghazipur in 1864 and founded a scientific society at Ghazipur in 1864. The scientific society translated the modern works in Urdu for the benefit and convenience of the people. The scientific society issued a journal in 1866 entitled as *'Aligarh* Institute Gazette' published in English and Urdu languages. The main purpose of this journal was to arouse the sentiments of goodwill amongst the British for the Muslims. In 1866 Sir Syed founded the British Indian Association, which worked for the safeguard of the rights of the Indian people.

Sir Syed went to England in 1869 with his son Syed Mahmood who was given a scholarship for higher studies in England. Sir Syed observed the educational set up of British educational institutions and was greatly impressed by the systems of Oxford and Cambridge Universities. He made up his mind to set up an educational institution in India on the pattern of Oxford and Cambridge. He countered the allegations leveled against the Holy Prophet (Peace be upon him) in the book *'The Life of Muhammad* written by Sir William Muir.

MOHAMMEDAN EDUCATIONAL CONFERENCE
In 1866, he established Mohammedan Educational Conference, which was to take steps for the educational uplift of the Muslims of India. The conference held its meetings at various places and established its sub-committees at other places in India.

MOHAMMEDAN ANGLO ORIENTAL COLLEGE

The establishment of M.A.O. College at Aligarh in 1877 was the great achievement of Sir Syed Ahmed Khan with regard to the educational services for the Muslims of India.

During his stay in England Sir Syed decided to set up an educational institution in India on the pattern of Oxford and Cambridge Universities. When he returned to India he set up a committee which was to explore the possibilities of the establishment of a college for the educational advancement of the Muslims of India, A fund committee was also set up which was to collect funds for the college. The committee toured whole of India to collect funds for the establishment of the college. A request for financial assistance was also made to the government.

On 24th May, 1874, M.A.D. High School was established at Aligarh where modern and eastern education was imparted. Sir Syed worked very hard to raise the school to the college level. In 1877 the school was upgraded to the status of a college and inaugurated by Lord Lytton. It was a residential campus and offered both western and eastern learning. Islamic education was also given to the students. The college was open for both Muslim and non-Muslim students. Sir Syed earnestly desired to see the college raised to the level of a University, which was fulfilled after his death in 1920 when the college was made a university.

The college at Aligarh was more than an educational institution. It was a symbol of a broad movement affecting every phase of Muslim life. The actions taken by Sir Syed Ahmed Khan for the educational uplift of the Muslims left a far-reaching impact on the social, economic, political and religious aspects of the Muslims. His precepts and examples revived hope and self-confidence, showed new ways to progress and opened the doors to modern education and economic prosperity for the Muslims of the sub-continent.

POLITICAL SERVICES

The Indian National Congress came into existence in 1885 on the initiative of a retired British civil servant Allan Octavian Hume. Indian National Congress which gradually grew to be the most powerful political organization in India was originally intended to provide a forum for the Indian politicians to meet yearly and point out to the government in what respects the administration was faulty and how it could be improved. It had claimed at the time of its inception that it would strive for the safeguard of the interests of all the communities in India irrespective of their religion or political tendencies. For some time in the beginning, Congress did adhere to its promise and displayed a posture of a national organization. But with the time it turned into a pure Hindu body working for the safeguard of the interests of the Hindus only. The demands, which were projected from the Congress platform, appeared very innocent and democratic but actually were aimed at the complete elimination of the Muslims from the Indian society.

The first demand, which came from the Congress, was the introduction of representative democracy on the lines and patterns of Britain. Sir Syed vehemently objected to this demand and said that western democracy could not be introduced in India as India was inhibited by many nations whose thinking, way of life, culture and history was different from each other.

Congress made another demand for the appointments in the government service on the basis of competitive examination. By making this demand the Congress, in fact, wanted to oust the Muslims from the government service. The acceptance of this demand would have rendered the Muslims economically destroyed and ruined. Sir Syed Ahmed opposed this demand and said that the Muslims could not compete with the Hindus who were better educated. He demanded equal opportunities for the Muslims for the enhancement of their educational standard before they could be asked to compete with the Hindus in the competitive examinations.

The attitude of Congress greatly perturbed Sir Syed Ahmed Khan who advised the Muslims not to join it. Sir Syed's opposition to Congress was based on his view that the Congress was a Hindu organization. The Hindus had advanced in education, wealth and political consciousness to dominate Congress to use it for voicing demands, which would suit them and were against the Muslim interest. Sir Syed felt that the Muslims should concentrate for some time on the acquisition of education and economic rehabilitation before competing with the Hindus in the political field. He firmly believed that political *activities* would divert their (Muslims) attention from the constructive tasks and would revive British mistrust, which had been removed to a greater extent by that time. He, therefore, emphasized on the Muslims to fully concentrate on the acquisition of knowledge and equip themselves with the modern techniques of politics, and only then they should embark upon the political participation.

Sir Syed Ahmed Khan took several steps for the revival and betterment of the Muslims in the sub-continent. He published the most influential magazine *'Tahzib-ul-Akhlaq'* in which he described ethical aspects of the Muslim culture. In this magazine he criticized the conservative attitude of the Muslims and urged them to adopt new trends of life. He worked diligently for the promotion of Urdu, which was the language of the Muslims, and gave new tone and color to the Urdu literature. He founded 'Anjuman-e-Tariki-e-Urdu' which worked for the protection of Urdu as the language of the Muslims. He wrote another magazine as 'Ahkam-e-Ta'am-e-Ahle-Kitab' in which the Islamic principles and etiquettes of eating and dinning were discussed. In this magazine Sir Syed wrote that it was not against Islam to eat with the Christians on the same table. He gave references from the Holy Quran and proved that it was not un-Islamic to eat with a nation who was the bearer of a Holy book.

Sir Syed Ahmed Khan died on 27th March, 1898 after rendering invaluable services for the Muslim cause in India. He laid the foundation stone for a movement, which turned into the Pakistan Movement in the later stages.

TWO NATION THEORY

The entire freedom movement revolved around the two-nation theory, which was introduced by Sir Syed Ahmed Khan. Sir Syed Ahmed was an open minded and a large hearted person. He was a staunch patriot and loved India very much because it was his beloved country. He considered all those who lived in India as one nation and was a great advocate of Hindu-Muslim unity. Speaking at the meeting of Indian Association he said,

"I look to both Hindus and Muslims with the same eyes and consider them as my own eyes. By the word 'Nation" I mean only Hindus and Muslims and nothing else. We, Hindus and Muslims, live together on the same soil under the same government. I consider the two factions as one nation.'

The attitude of Hindus and Congress, however, compelled Sir Syed Ahmed Khan to re-shape his ideas about one nation. He was extremely hurt to see both Congress and Hindus working against the interests of the Muslims. Congress had turned into a pure Hindu body and was working on the lines, which would have erased the Muslims completely from the Indian society as a nation. Sir Syed always advocated Hindu-Muslim unity and made every effort to bring them closer on one single platform. For this purpose the membership of British Indian Association was kept open for the Hindus and Muslims. In spite of the sincere efforts by Sir Syed Ahmed Khan to create an atmosphere of amity and brotherhood, the Hindus never came forward with open mind and always adopted a policy to damage the Muslim cause.

HINDI - URDU CONTROVERSY

In 1867 the Hindus demanded that Hindi should be made an official language in place of Urdu. They launched an intense and aggressive agitation to press for their demand of making Hindi as the official language. The government surrendered and declared Hindi as the official language in place of Urdu, which was the language of the Muslims. Sir Syed felt sorry that the Hindus were asking for the replacement of Urdu with Hindi as official language. He was now convinced that the Hindus would never be friendly with the Muslims.

Sir Syed expressed his views about Hindus and Muslims as two separate nations for the first time in 1868 while speaking to Mr. Shakespeare, the Governor of Benaras for the Muslims only. Mr. Shakespeare was surprised to see Sir Syed speaking about the Muslims only, and inquired as to why he was referring to the Muslims alone today. Sir Syed replied with noticeable grief and sorrow, *'I am convinced now* that Hindus and Muslin's *could never* become *one nation as* their *religions and* ways *of life were quite* distinct *from each other.'* Sir Syed declared the Muslims as a nation and Hindus and Muslims as two separate nations because their religion, history, culture and civilization were different from each other.

FREEDOM STRUGGLE IN THE PROVINCES

In the time of the Mughal Emperor Jahangir, the British, in view of the stable economic conditions of India, expressed their desire of developing trade relations with India. The Government of India accepted their request and allowed them to set up a trade company known as the 'East India *Company'* for the sole purpose of trade.

The British, soon after their arrival in India, began taking interest in the political affairs of the country. The Mughal rulers, after the death of Emperor Aurangzeb, proved inefficient, corrupt and incapable of holding the vast Empire together which gave an incentive to the British traders to interfere in the governmental affairs. Seven centuries Muslim rule, with manifest decadence, finally crumbled after the war of 1857, with the British proudly ascending the throne, which they had always cherished.

The Muslims, however, could not reconcile with their subjugated position in the society and waged intensive struggle for their revival to the old position of glory. The Muslims had to take up arms even on different occasions against *the* usurpers *for* their restoration. They also adopted constitutional means under the leadership of their dedicated leaders for the protection of their rights and interests. Details of the Muslim struggle for freedom in different provinces, before independence are given below:

1. FREEDOM STRUGGLE IN N.W.F.P.
The province of N.W.F.P. is the home of the valiant *'Pathans* who launched their struggle for freedom, first against the oppressive rule of the 'Sikhs' and then against the British. In 1927 the Muslim League had demanded that constitutional reforms should be introduced in the province, which initiated the political awakening amongst the ignorant people. In response to the demand by the Muslim League, reforms were introduced. The people of N.W.F.P. at the time of Lahore Resolution openly supported the resolution in favor of Pakistan in 1940. Sardar Aurangzeb Khan represented the province to support Pakistan Resolution.

ORGANIZATION OF LEAGUE IN THE PROVINCES
As the Congress had a strong hold on the political developments of N.W.F.P, the Muslim League could not be organized on stable footings until 1945. Congress openly opposed the freedom movement in the N.W.F.P. and its provincial ministry, set up after 1945 elections, and oppressed the freedom-loving people. False cases were initiated against freedom fighters that were put into jails to suffer the most inhuman torture for their desire for

freedom, Congress, through its Muslim members, did its best to curb the freedom movement in order to keep the strategic and sensitive province of N.W.F.P, out of Pakistan. Huge sums of money were spent to bribe the people who refused to kneel down before Congress tactics and gave their verdict in favor of Pakistan.

In 1945, with the great efforts of the Quaid-e-Azam, the Muslim League was re-organized on stable foundations and rendered invaluable services during independence movement. Muslim League brought new dimensions to the movement and continued its efforts in spite of sheer opposition by the Congress. A daily 'Sada-i-Pakistan' was published secretly and a radio station was set up to relay instructions to the freedom fighters.

ROLE OF ULEMA STUDENTS AND LADIES
The religious leaders, Ulema and Mushaikh also came forward with their spiritual might to guide the people of N.W.F.P. in the freedom struggle. They played important role in organizing the freedom movement in the province. They spread the message of freedom throughout the province and won great deal of public support for Muslim League. The religious leaders, with their preaching managed to bring the scattered people together on one platform. The students of Islamia College, Peshawar and Edward College, Peshawar took active part in the movement. The ladies of the province did not lag behind in giving sacrifices for the independence. They organized the women wing of Muslim League and did a lot of work in organizing the movement.

2. FREEDOM STRUGGLE IN BALOCHISTAN
Balochistan was backward and under-developed region before partition. The British Government did not bother to take developmental steps in this area. As a result of negligence on the part of government, Balochistan remained an under-developed province lacking in facilities of social life. In 1927 Muslim League had demanded that reforms should be introduced in Balochistan as had been introduced in other provinces. The government did not pay any heed to demands by the Muslim league.

Muslim League began its struggle for the safeguard of the interests of the Muslims of Balochistan by setting up a branch of Muslim League in the province. Qazi Muhammad Issa rendered invaluable services in organizing Muslim League during its infancy in Balochistan. It was solely because of

Qazi Issa's sincere efforts that the Muslim League was able to launch its freedom struggle effectively in the province. In 1940 Qazi Muhammad Issa represented the people of Balochsitan to support Pakistan Resolution at the famous meeting at Lahore. On 23rd March, 1941 Pakistan Day was observed in Quetta. A big meeting was held on this occasion under the hectic supervision of Qazi Muhammad Issa. Resolutions in favor of Pakistan were unanimously passed which amply reflected the feelings of the people of Balochistan. The people pledged their unflinching support to Muslim League and came forward with every sacrifice for the accomplishment of the noble objective.

The students of Balochistan, too, took part in the freedom movement. Muslim Student Federation was set up in Balochistan in 1943, which provided young and energetic leadership to the freedom struggle.

In 1947, at the time of partition, it was decided that a royal *'Jirga'* would decide the accession of Balochistan with either India or Pakistan. Congress left no stone unturned to convince the Jirga to accede to India but its efforts failed and the Jirga announced its decision in favor of Pakistan. Nawab Muhammad Khan Jogezai performed pivotal role in Balochistan accession to Pakistan.

3. FREEDOM MOVEMENT IN THE PROVINCE OF SINDH

The province of Sindh holds immense importance in the history because Islam entered the sub-continent through this province. It is because of this fact that the province of Sindh is known in the history as 'Bab-ul-Islam' (gate of Islam). Sindh was a Muslim majority area at the time of partition. The British in order to eliminate the influence of Muslim majority had attached it with the province of Bombay. Muslim League demanded the separation of Sindh from Bombay, which was accepted under the Government of India Act, 1935 and it became an independent province.

The freedom struggle in the province began at a very early stage. The first session of Muslim League was held in the famous city of Karachi, which was the capital of the province. This meeting was of great historical significance with regard to the Muslim League in the province of Sindh. The provincial branch of Muslim League passed its resolution in favor of Pakistan in 1938. It was demanded through this resolution that the Muslims should be allowed to form their own government in those areas of the sub-continent where they (Muslims) were in majority. The foundation of the famous Pakistan Resolution, passed in 1940, was in fact based on this particular resolution passed by Sindh Muslim League in 1938. The Muslims of Sindh extended their full support for Pakistan Resolution in 1940. Sir Abdullah Haroon, representing the people of Sindh, expressed his utmost support to Pakistan Resolution at Lahore in 1940.

The Quaid-e-Azam set up a committee for the re-organization of Muslim League in Sindh, which adopted important measures to make Sindh Muslim League an effective political party in the province. The Muslim League ministry was set up in the province, which is considered as the first Muslim ministry of the sub-continent. The Sindh Provincial Assembly unanimously passed a resolution in favor of Pakistan in 1943. Muslim League by now had been established on stable footings, which enabled it to win the 1945-46 elections with majority.

Pir Sibgatullah of Pagaro was a great spiritual leader of Sindh whose services for the cause of independence cannot be forgotten. He rendered great services for organizing the freedom movement in the province. Pir Sibghat Ullah challenged the British rulers and refused to surrender before their ruthless rule. The followers of Pir Sibghat Ullah are known as 'Hur' and are famous for their bravery and staunch loyalty to their leader. They fought the battle for freedom with utmost bravery and courage along with their great leader. Pir Sahib of Pagaro began his armed struggle against the British after the Second World War and inflicted heavy losses on the British. His brave and valiant Hur followers fought by the side of their leader and laid down their lives for the cause of independence. Pir sahib of Pagaro was killed while fighting against the British and attained the status of a great *'Shaheed'* in the history. The Hur followers of Pir sahib continued with their struggle even after the Shahdat of their spiritual leader.

ROLE OF ULEMA, STUDENTS AND LADIES

The contribution made by the Ulema and religious leaders of Sindh in the freedom movement carries great significance in the history. Jamiat Al Mushaikh was set up in Sindh, which openly supported Muslim League and helped in organizing it on firm grounds. The student community of Sindh, too, came forward with their energetic support to the Muslim League in its struggle for independence. The students of Sindh Madrassa Karachi worked day and night for the movement. The Muslim Student Federation became an active party and worked meritoriously for organizing the students in Sindh. The ladies of Sindh, too, came forward and worked with sincerity for Pakistan.

4. FREEDOM STRUGGLE IN THE PROVINCE OF PUNJAB

The Punjab province was a big area before partition with regard to population and territory. It comprised of two geographical zones known as Eastern and Western Punjab. The Western Punjab consisted of the areas, which fell in present Pakistan after partition while the Eastern Punjab went to India. The inhabitants of this province were known for their valor, bravery, love and respect for their land. It had a rich soil and comparatively more developed industry and agriculture in comparison to the other areas of the United India.

The contribution made by this province in the freedom movement is not less than any other province of the United India. The people of this province gave every sacrifice for independence for achieving Pakistan. At the time of partition, Punjab was not the only province, which had to be divided into two parts. Its boundaries were such altered that a large number of its inhabitants were made to leave their homes and ancestral places. The Muslim refugees were mercilessly slaughtered while migrating to Pakistan. The history is full of the horrifying tales of atrocities, which were inflicted on the poor Muslim refugees who came to Pakistan. The sacrifices, which the province *of* Punjab made for independence, were really tremendous.

The importance of the Punjab in the history of freedom movement is even greater because the famous Pakistan Resolution was passed in Punjab's big city *of* Lahore. The passage of Lahore Resolution brought the entire Muslim community together under the banner of Muslim League. The moment the Pakistan Resolution was passed, the Muslim *of* India made it clear that no other solution, except Pakistan, was acceptable to them. A countrywide movement was launched to prepare the Muslim League for the coming elections of 1945-46. The Muslim League won these elections with great majority to prove its stand for the partition of India.

Religious leaders, Ulema and Mushaikh belonging to Punjab also took part in the freedom struggle. They prepared the people to fight the war for independence by injecting fervor amongst them with their speeches and preaching. The people of Punjab stirred by these speeches worked day and night in spreading the message of independence to every corner of the province.

ROLE OF STUDENTS
The students of Punjab were very active during the freedom movement. They were the devoted and dedicated workers of Muslim League and strenuously worked to make Muslim League an active and stable political party in the province. The students of Lahore and other cities scattered throughout the province to win support in favor of Muslim League. They undertook intensive tours of various cities of the province and raised slogans in favor of Pakistan in every street. The Punjab Muslim Students Federation proved an effective organization of students, which had demanded a separate homeland for the Muslim of India in 1937. The students of Islamia College, Lahore took part in the freedom struggle as the dedicated workers of Muslim League and Quaid-e-Azam. Pakistan Conference was held on the historic grounds of Islamia College, Lahore under the President ship of the Quaid-e-Azam. The students of Punjab sustained hardships and tortures in the jails for the national cause of independence.

ROLE OF LADIES IN FREEDOM STRUGGLE
Freedom movement in the province of Punjab also owes much to the ladies of Punjab who took great pains in organizing the membership of Muslim League and promoting its women wing. The ladies in Punjab courageously took part in the civil disobedience movement and extended utmost co-operation to Muslim League to make the movement a complete success. It was a brave woman of Punjab who threw away the Union Jack from the Punjab Secretariat building and unfurled Muslim League's flag in its place.

5. FREEDOM STRUGGLE IN THE MUSLIM MINORITY PROVINCES
There were many provinces in the United India where Muslims were in minority. The Muslim population of these provinces had to bear atrocities of the Hindu majority before the establishment of Pakistan. The Congress ministries of 1937 of these provinces dealt grievous blows to their Muslim subjects during two and a half years of their rule.

The Muslims of the minority provinces took active part in the freedom struggle by the side of other provinces. They proved to be the vanguard of the movement by initiating the struggle for freedom. They invited the annoyance and opposition of hostile Hindu majority by openly supporting the demand for Pakistan knowing the fact that their areas would not be included in Pakistan.

Chaudhri Khaliq-uz-Zaman was the first Muslim leader of U.P. who declared his support for the Lahore Resolution in 1940. Besides U.P. the Muslim leaders from Bihar, C.P., Madras and Mumbai, too, supported the demand for Pakistan and extended their sincere co-operation to Muslim League for passing the Lahore Resolution. Muslim League won the elections of 1945-46 in the Muslim minority provinces, which is an ample proof of the staunch support and loyalty of the Muslims of these provinces.

ULEMA'S ROLE
The Ulema and Mushaikh of the Muslim minority provinces also had their share in the freedom movement. They played a pivotal role in making the annual meeting of Muslim League at Lucknow a success in 1937. The Mushaikh Conference held in Banaras in 1946 declared its support for Muslim League in its struggle for freedom.

THE CONSTITUTIONAL STRUGGLE OF MUSLIM LEAGUE
The All India Congress, as already mentioned, turned into a pure Hindu organization, promoting and voicing the Hindu cause from its platform. As long as effective authority remained in the hands of the British, the conflicts between Hindus and Muslims were confined to cultural and social matters. With the introduction of representative institutions, political interests came to occupy the center of attention, which the Muslims could no longer ignore. The Hindus, because of their superior education, wealth and influence were in a far better position to extract benefits out of the new situation. Moreover Congress, as an effective political organization was also there to get more privileges for the Hindus than the Muslims. The Muslims greatly lagged behind than the Hindus in every field of social and economic endeavor, and the Hindus had come to regard this state of inequality as their birthright, which they were determined to maintain by means of political power. Prospects of democracy thus intensified the struggle between Hindus and Muslims.

The Muslims had no political organization of their own which could counter the influence of Congress and Hindus. The Muslims also lacked in political maneuvering and direly needed a platform from which they could voice their political grievances. The Hindi-Urdu controversy brought the Muslims on their alert about Hindu and Congress designs. The demands, projected from the Congress platform developed suspicion amongst the Muslims and they were extremely perturbed about their future in India.

PARTITION OF BENGAL

Bengal was an unwieldy province with a population of 78 million people. Viceroy Curzon divided it into two provinces in 1905. By combining its eastern part with Assam, a new province of Eastern Bengal and Assam was created. The majority of population in the new province was Muslim who was now in a dominant position with chances of progress and development at their doors. The Bengali Hindus, who had progressed on the toil of the Muslim peasants of Eastern Bengal, found this partition a grave threat to their cultural, economic and political domination and were not prepared to see the Muslims in a superior position. The Hindus and Congress launched a violent agitation for the annulment of the partition of Bengal.

Mass meetings and protest marches were organized. The movement for the boycott of the British goods was started. There was an outburst of terrorist activities. Religious and nationalist color was given to this movement. The Muslims because of their backwardness in education, wealth and modern means of publicity, could not counter the Hindu and Congress propaganda. They relied on the promises of the government and were soon disillusioned. The British government yielded to the Hindu agitation and in 1911 the partition of Bengal was canceled to the great dismay of the Muslims of Eastern Bengal who reverted to their previous position of subservience to the Hindus.

SIMLA DEPUTATION

Lord Minto, who was known for his administrative qualities, came to India in 1905 as Viceroy. With his arrival in India, it was felt that some constitutional reforms would he introduced in India. The Muslim leaders decided to avail the opportunity and decided to meet the Viceroy in order to apprise him of the Muslims' demands.

The Viceroy was vacationing at Simla where a delegation of Muslim leaders, led by Sir Agha Khan, called upon him in 1906. The deputation, who came to be known as Simla Deputation in the history of freedom movement, included some eminent leaders of the Muslims from all over the country.

The deputation apprised the Viceroy of the Muslims demands and asked that the representation of the Muslims should be commensurate not merely with their numerical strength but also with their political importance and the value of contribution, which they made to the defense of the empire. The deputation demanded seats in the legislatures, quota in government services and seats of judges in the courts for the Muslims. The deputation also demanded separate electorate for the Muslims with separate constituencies, which meant that the Muslim voters should vote for the Muslim candidates only.

Lord Minto gave a patient hearing to the demands of the Muslims presented by the Simla Deputation. He promised to give sympathetic consideration to the demands and assured the deputation that he would do all what was possible to accept the demands.

It was a great achievement of the Simla Deputation to have convinced the Viceroy about the genuineness of the Muslims demands. The Muslims were now convinced that organized efforts were always essential to press for the acceptance of the demands. At this time the Muslims had left the Congress and had no organization of their own to project their demands. They *badly* needed a forum for the projection and safeguard of their interests to counter the false propaganda of Congress.

FORMATION OF ALL INDIA MUSLIM LEAGUE

Congress was propagating its own concept of nationalism and claiming to have represented all communities of India. It was striving very hard to project the image of United India, which was actually aimed at the extermination of the Muslims from the Indian society. The politics of Congress was extremely detrimental to the cause of the Muslims and a dire need was felt for a political organization of the Muslims to counter the injurious propaganda of Congress.

On December 30, 1906, the annual meeting of the Muslim League Educational Conference was held at the residence of Nawab Salim Ullah Khan of Dacca. The Muslim leaders from all over the country attended this meeting. Nawab Salim Ullah Khan convened a meeting of the Muslim leaders after the meeting of the Educational Conference to discuss the possibilities of a Muslim political organization in India. Nawab Viqar-ul-Mulk presided over the meeting in which the participants stressed upon the need of a political organization for the Muslims of India, which could project and safeguard the interests of the Muslims in the sub-continent. Nawab Salim Ullah Khan presented a resolution for the formation of a political party for the Muslims and suggested the name of All India Muslim Confederacy for the organization. Hakim Ajmal Khan and Maulana Zafar All Khan supported the resolution and on 30th December, 1906 All India Muslin League was formed. Nawab Viqar-ul-Mulk was appointed as the President of the newly born organization and Nawab Mohsin-ul-Mulk as the General Secretary. A constitution committee was set up to draft the constitution of the Muslim League.

The first session of the All India Muslim League was held on 29th and 30th December, 1907 in Karachi under the Chairman-ship of Sir Adamjee Pirbhai. The constitution of the League was presented in this session and approved with unanimity.

The next session was held at Aligarh on March 18th, 1908 which was presided over by Justice Shah Din. By this time Nawab Viqar-ul-Mulk had died and Nawab Mohsin-ul-Mulk had been appointed as the Secretary of the Aligarh College. Sir Agha Khan was, therefore, appointed the President of the Muslim League and Husain Bilgrami as the Secretary. It was decided in this session that the branches of the League would be opened in other parts of the country. Syed Amir Ali established Mohammedan Association in London, which was turned into a London branch of the Muslim League.

AIMS AND OBJECTS OF THE MUSLIM LEAGUE

The main purpose of the formation of the Muslim League was the safeguard of the interests and rights of the Muslims and their political training to equip them with the basic political knowledge so that they (Muslims) should be able to face the Congress propaganda and counter it effectively. The main purposes of the Muslim League were as follows:-

- To safeguard and protect the interests of the Muslims of the sub-continent and to convey their demands to the government.

- To create feelings of goodwill and respect for the government amongst the Muslims and to remove all sort of misunderstanding about any action of the government.

- To bring all nations of India closer and together without doing harm to the above purposes of the Muslim League.

The Muslim League met with immediate success and its demand for the separate electorate was accepted by the government and incorporated in the Minto-Morley Reforms of 1909. The demand for the appointment of Muslims to the posts of judges of the courts was also accepted and many Muslims rose to the judgeship of higher courts. Muslim League managed to get the Auqaf Bill passed by which the management of Auqafs in the country was taken over by the government.

AN EVALUATION OF THE STRUGGLE OF MUSLIM LEAGUE

Muslim League rendered invaluable services to the cause of the Muslims of the sub-continent. It was under the banner of the Muslim League that the Muslims of India were at last able to re-establish their lost importance in the Indian society and they finally succeeded in achieving Pakistan as a separate homeland. The formation of the Muslim League and its subsequent struggle was the continuation of the Aligarh Movement, which Sir Syed Ahmed Khan could not complete in his life.

However, after creation of Pakistan its cherished goal, the party got divided and the politicians used its different versions: Mamdot league, counsel league, Pagara league, Quaid-e-Azam league, Nawaz league, Chattha league and so on. In short the parent league gave birth to a number of rightist parties. On the other hand out of the leftist group People's party emerged in 1960s organized by late Zulfiqar Ali Bhutto that soon gained popularity with the poor masses and the leftist groups. People's party won general elections in 1971 and in 1988 and ruled the country twice. It is still a strong national party with its representation in all the provinces. Jamaat-e-Islami is an old established national party having representation in all the provinces. Being primarily a religious party could not find much favor as it believes in strict Islamic rule and thus could not be popular with the masses except lately when People's party and the Nawaz league leadership, Benazir Bhutto and Nawaz Sharif is out of the country, could win sizeable seats in the national and provincial Assemblies in the last general elections held in 2003 and thus has been able to form a coalition government in two provinces: Balochistan and the N.W.F.P.

There is yet another party, M.Q.M., formed in 1980s with its leader and founder Mr. Altaf Hussain. It basically represents a particular linguistic group, Urdu speaking in the province of Sindh, that consists of mainly the youths born in Pakistan but label them as 'Mahajirs' (immigrants) and the party is based and popular in the urban areas of Sindh province only. Their leader remains in self-exile and keeps contact with his followers regularly on telephone. Gen. Parvez Musharraf who himself is an immigrant Urdu speaking, has patronized and given due representation to the party in the provincial Sindh government.

Hence Muslim league the party who led the Muslims of the sub-continent and helped achieving an independent country having been divided and sub divided is no more that effective and popular enough to form its sole independent government at national or provincial levels.

MINTO-MORELY REFORMS

Three years after the formation of the Muslim League, Minto-Morley reforms were introduced in 1909, which contained the most important demand of the Muslim League, the right of separate electorate for the Muslims. The acceptance of separate electorate and separate constituencies enhanced the political position of the Muslims in the sub-continent. They were now in a position to elect the members of their own choice who would protect their rights in the legislatures and would convey their grievances to the government. The acceptance of these demands was a great achievement of the Muslim League as it had effectively countered the harmful propaganda of Congress. Meanwhile an extremist Hindu organization 'Hindu *Mahasbha'* had also come into existence, which contained the extremely narrow minded and prejudiced Hindu elements. The Hindu Mahasbha aimed at the elimination of the Muslims from the Indian society, and suffered by an immensely prejudicial concept of the political position of the Muslims. The Muslim League now stood exposed to the exploitation of both Congress and Hindu Mahasabha and was at the most perilous brink of its struggle. The two Hindu organizations were determined to destroy the national character of the Muslims to dominate and subjugate them perpetually. In these critical circumstances the presence of the Muslim League was really a blessing, which was striving hard to restore the image and national character of the Muslims in the sub-continent.

MUSLIM LEAGUE CHANGES ITS COURSE
Muslim League had observed that the Government always responded to the harsh and hostile manner and yielded only to pressure. Because of this reason Congress made the government to accede to its demands at will. On the other hand the Muslim League, in the beginning, had to adopt a humble and courteous posture to present its demands as it was going through the period of its infancy. Muslim League had to accept whatever was offered to it because it was a new organization, but Congress, on the other hand, was in a position to dictate its terms, as it was an organized party.

Muslim League decided to change its line of action in the wake of government attitude and came out with a new course towards the Hindu-Muslim unity. The Muslim League adopted new political strategy to put greater pressure on the government as it had come to realize that unity between Hindus and Muslims would compel the government to kneel down and accept the demands of the Indian people. In view of the new development the Muslim League had to change its policy and included, in its demands, the introduction of self-rule for India. A resolution was passed from the platform of the Muslim League in which the Hindu-Muslim unity was stressed in order to achieve progress and prosperity for the Indian people. It was also decided that the leaders of both Hindus and Muslims would sit together to chalk out program to accomplish Hindu-Muslim unity in the shortest possible time.

LUCKNOW PACT 1916
The Indian political scene took a new turn in 1913, when the Muslim League adopted the principle of self-rule for India as its

goal, which brought the Congress and the Muslim League closer to each other. The leaders of both parties agreed that they should co-operate with each other to bring the government around to accept the demands. The purpose could be achieved only, if they agreed, the two major communities of India forget their differences on petty issues and come closer to each other to see eye to eye on important national issues. Quaid-e-Azam was greatly respected in both Congress and Muslim League, under whose guidance, efforts for the Hindu-Muslim unity, was launched.

In December 1916 the Muslim League and Congress, for the first time in the history of India, held their sessions in Lucknow. The Muslim League session was presided over by the Quaid-e-Azam while Ambeka Charan Maujamdar presided over the Congress session. Mainly due to the efforts of the Quaid-e-Azam, who was hailed as ambassador of Hindu-Muslim unity, an agreement on a scheme of constitutional reforms was reached between Congress and Muslim League known as 'Lucknow Pact'.

The agreement conceded separate electorate to the Muslims and provided for elections of central and provincial councils and responsibility of the executive to the legislature. They agreed to the principle of separate electorate and reservation of 1/3rd seats in the Central Legislature for the Muslims. The Muslim representation was fixed at 33 1/3% of the elected members for Central Government, 50% and 40% respectively for Punjab and Bengal and 33, 30, 25, 15 and 15% respectively for Bombay, U.P., Bihar, C.P. and Madras.

It was also decided that the members of assemblies should have the right to present adjournment motion. Provincial autonomy shall be given to the provinces, and the communal problems shall be solved. Seats shall be reserved for the Muslims in those provinces in which they are in minority and protection shall be given to the Hindus in Muslim majority provinces. No resolution or motion shall be presented in the assembly, which may be affecting the interests of any of the two communities without the approval of the concerned group.

The Lucknow Pact was a great achievement of the Hindu and Muslim leaders and particularly of the Quaid-e-Azam who had always been a staunch advocate of Hindu-Muslim unity. The main characteristic of the pact was that the Hindus, for the first time, acknowledged the

Muslims as a separate nation and accepted their right to the separate electorate.

MONTAGUE CHELMSFORD REFORMS 1919

The country was going through the most critical period of its history. The British Government now felt it necessary to respond to the aspirations of the Indian people. On August 20, 1917 Edwin Montague, the Secretary of State for India, made an announcement of the British policy in the House of Commons. The announcement declared: *The policy of His Majesty's* Government with *which the Government of* India *is* in *complete* accord, is that *of the* increasing association *of* Indians in every *branch of* administration *and the gradual development of self-governing* institutions *with a view to the progressive* realization *of responsible government* in India as an integral part *of the* British Empire.

In the middle of 1919 Edwin Montague and the Viceroy Lord Chelmsford, published a report on Indian constitutional reforms, which formed the basis of the government of India Act of 1919. The report was sent to the Government for approval and was enforced in 1919 which is known as 'Montague *Chelmsford Reforms* 1919'.

The Act of 1919 established legislative councils in the provinces with a system of Diarchy. Under this system anything relating to *'Law and Order'* was to be administered by Executive Councilors responsible to the Governors. The main recommendations of the Act of 1919 were as follows:-

- Bicameral legislature was established in the Center. The Upper House consisted of 60 members and the Lower House of 145 members. The tenure of the Upper House was to be five years and that of the Lower House to be three years.

- Separate electorate was kept for the Muslims and the Sikhs were also given the right of separate electorate.

- System of Diarchy was introduced in the provinces by which the law enforcing and few other departments were put under the direct control of the Governor and the remaining departments were assigned to the Executive Council. The new system of Diarchy gave authority to the Central Government to interfere in the provincial matters.

- Out of 103 seats of the Imperial Legislative Council 30 seats were reserved for the Muslims.
- More constitutional reforms shall be introduced after ten years.

The political circles in the country were not happy with the reforms of 1919 and declared them as inadequate and unsatisfactory. Congress split into two factions over the question of accepting the reforms. Muslim League, too, was not very optimistic about the proposals, as they did not contain any concrete suggestion about the introduction of self-rule. Congress, however, accepted the proposals after passing a resolution to condemn them. Muslim League also extended its approval to the proposals, and decided to intensify its political struggle for the constitutional reforms.

KHILAFAT MOVEMENT

The political situation of the country, at this juncture was extremely unhappy and ridden with political turmoil. Before the constitutional reforms of 1919 could be introduced the sub-continent experienced a political storm of unprecedented severity, which was to leave its mark on all subsequent events.

The First World War had come to an end and the victorious allied countries were bent upon demolishing the Ottoman Caliphate of Turkey, which fought by the side of Germany. The Indian Muslims were greatly perturbed over the fate of Turkey and desired that a respectable rapprochement be concluded between the British and Turkey. The results of the war had placed the Indian Muslims in an extremely awkward situation. They were not prepared to see any humiliation of the Caliphate and at the same time could not afford to pick up confrontation with the government.

When the war ended it was felt that Turkey, which fought against the allied countries, would be dismembered and distributed amongst the victorious allied countries. The Indian Muslims, because of their emotional attachment with the Caliph, had always held the institution of Caliphate of Turkey in the highest esteem and veneration. They were not prepared to see the dismemberment of Turkey at any cost and, therefore, informed the Government about their sentiments. The Indian Muslims made it clear to the Government that they would not, in any circumstances, tolerate the humiliation of the Caliph and of the sacred places in Turkey. They urged the Government to give an assurance that the institution of Caliphate would not be demolished and that due respect would be shown for the sacred places of the Muslims in Turkey. The British Government promised that the feelings of the Indian Muslims shall be given due consideration and that no harm shall be done to the Caliphate and the sacred places of the Muslims.

The war concluded by the *Treaty of Sevres,* which shocked the Indian Muslims. The harsh terms of the treaty made it clear to the Indian Muslims that the victorious allies were not content with the dismemberment of the Ottoman Empire, but were determined to destroy even the Turkish homeland. To Indian Muslims the treaty appeared to be a deliberate attempt by the Christian community to exterminate forever the political power of Islam as symbolized by the Khilafat.

KHILAFAT COMMITTEE

The Indian Muslims, to their utter disappointment, found that Turkey has been divided and distributed amongst the victorious allies as the war bounty. With the dismemberment of Turkey, the institution of Caliphate was also to be demolished. The Muslims were not happy over the development in Turkey and were particularly saddened over the naked betrayal by the Government. The Muslims of India decided to launch a movement for the safeguard of the institution of Caliphate and to manifest their resentment over the actions the allies had taken in Turkey. *A Khilafat Committee* was set up to conduct and organize the movement with Maulana Shaukat Ali as its Secretary. The first meeting of the Committee was held on 23rd November, 1919 under the President ship of Maulana Fazal-ul-Haq.

THE NON-COOPERATION MOVEMENT

The Hindus, under the leadership of Mahatma Gandhi came forward with their full support for the movement. Gandhi being a shrewd politician had planned to use the Khilafat agitation to pressurize the Government to come to terms for Indian Independence. Whether the Muslims won or lost on Khilafat issue was immaterial to Gandhi, what mattered was the purpose the movement could be made to serve. He, therefore, advocated full support by the entire Indian nation of the Muslims demands and outlined a program of non-cooperation for the achievement of dual objective of Indian Independence and restoration of the Caliphate.

The plan was to paralyze the administration by a complete boycott of British institutions and goods. Indians were asked to give up government service, renounce titles, boycott courts of *law,* walk *out of schools* and colleges *and take* no part in elections, which were to be held under Montague-Chelmsford Reforms of 1919. Gandhi assured the people that if they carried out his program of non-cooperation in a united, disciplined and non-violent fashion; they would attain *Swaraj* - self-rule - within a year.

Gandhi's personality greatly appealed to the Hindu sentiments. They came together under his leadership. The enthusiasm of the Muslims were already in a state of agitated mind due to the treatment extended to Caliphate in Turkey and the decision of the Khilafat Committee to launch agitation in India. Congress at a special session adopted the non-cooperation program of Gandhi and later reaffirmed it at its Nagpur session in December 1920. The Quaid-e-Azam, however, was not in favor of Gandhi's non-cooperation program as to him the plan was bound to invite violence and would lead to disastrous confusion. He resigned from the Congress party in 1920.

KHILAFAT DELEGATION

The Khilafat Committee decided to send a delegation under the leadership of Maulana Mohammad Ali Jauhar to England to apprise the Government of the sentiments *of the* people. The Khilafat delegation left for England in March 1919 and met the Prime Minister Lloyd George who was known for his anti-Muslim thinking. The delegation reminded the Prime Minister of *the* promises the Government had made with the Indian people about the Caliphate in Turkey. The Prime Minister refused to accept any argument extended by the Khilafat delegation. The delegation returned without achieving its purpose.

The political scene in India, after launching the non-cooperation movement, abruptly changed. For some time in the beginning, the Hindus and Muslims forgot their long-standing suspicion and animosities. The prolific leadership of Ali brothers carried *the message of* unity everywhere. Everything foreign was rejected, the foreign cloth was burnt and Khadar became the dress of even the most westernized society. The charkha or spinning wheel became the symbol of the Indian freedom.

The Muslims carried out the program with Zealous endeavors. The ulema pronounced service under the British Government as un-Islamic. The Ali brothers laid a siege around the Muslim University at Aligarh to carry out the educational boycott.

CHAURI CHAURA INCIDENT

However, the atmosphere of co-operation between the Muslims and the Hindus could not last long. The non-cooperation movement, as had been foreseen by the Quaid-e-Azam, was leading to violence and losing its momentum. In February 1922, at Chauri Chaura, a village in the United Province, a trouble erupted between the police and the demonstrating procession. The hostile mob set fire to the police station where twenty-two policemen were burnt alive. Gandhi and Ali brothers were in jail at this moment. Gandhi was so upset at this act of violence that he immediately and unilaterally called off the non-cooperation movement doing great deal of damage to the entire Khilafat movement. The sudden reversal produced bewilderment amongst the dismayed Muslim masses and leaders. The people generally felt, if the non-cooperation movement had been allowed to continue, despite the Chauri Chaura incident, the British Government would have been compelled to make major concessions.

END OF MOVEMENT

The reaction amongst the Muslims was bitter and strongest. They felt betrayed on the eve of victory. But there were still bigger shocks for them to come. The institution of Caliphate, for which they had struggled so sincerely, was demolished not by the enemies but by a Muslim hero, Mustafa Kamal Ataturk who established a nationalist Government in Turkey. The Indian Muslims were stunned on this action of Ataturk under whose leadership the Turks decided to make a new start. The movement was in disarray and the people did not know what to do. The sacrifices of the people were doomed and appeared to have been in vain.

The Khilafat movement ended without achieving its goal. The Indian politics had entered into a new era and was presenting a shabby scene. The Hindu-Muslim unity and brotherhood were the things of the past and people, once again, were moving within their traditionally narrow mindedness. Some Hindu leaders had started a movement for converting the Muslims to Hinduism, which provided a new cause of bitterness. Over the next few years Hindu-Muslim riots erupted at a number of places. The political climate in the country was that of a general apathy.

HIJRAT MOVEMENT

When Maulana Muhammad Ali Jauhar and other leaders were released from jail in 1924, they stepped into a different world. The country presented a most horrible picture. Maulana Muhammad Ali

Jauhar was greatly disappointed and pained to see the awful state of Indian society and declared India as *'Dar-ul-Harb', 'Home of War',* and urged the Muslims to migrate to a place where their religion and national image was safe. On his call nearly eighteen thousand Muslims left hearth and home and migrated to Afghanistan in religious protest against British policy towards the Caliphate. The Afghan Government welcomed the migrants in the beginning but refused to accept them when the number increased later. The people who migrated to Afghanistan faced many difficulties and a large number of them perished in the way. Those who were refused entry in Afghanistan had to return back to India to find them homeless and doomed forever. The migration to Afghanistan is known as the *'Hijrat Movement'* in the history of India.

The Khilafat movement failed and the Muslims were left in the lurch. Once again the Muslims *were* at the brink of disaster and facing the Hindu contempt and hatred. In this gloomy period, the Muslim League, under the fearless and infallible leadership of the Quaid-e-Azam, came forward to pull the Muslims out of darkness.

SIMON COMMISSION
At the time of introducing the Montague-Chelmsford Reforms of 1919, the British Government had declared, that a Commission would be sent to India after ten years to examine the effects and operation of the constitutional reforms and to suggest more reforms for India. In November, 1927, the British Government appointed a Commission under the Chairmanship of Sir John Simon to report on India's constitutional progress for introducing constitutional reforms as had been promised. The major task of the Commission was to examine the political conditions of India for the introduction of constitutional reforms. Since the Commission had no Indian member, the Congress and a section of Muslim League, under the leadership of Quaid-e-Azam, decided to boycott the Commission. The other group of Muslim League, led by Sir Muhammad Shafi, was in favor of co-operating with the Commission.

There were large-scale agitations against the Simon Commission in India. The Commission was received in the midst of hostile demonstration. The people welcomed the Commission with the slogans, Simon go *back,* Simon *go* back.' In spite of non-cooperation from the Indian political leaders, the Commission set out with its task and prepared a detailed report for constitutional reforms in India. The report was sent to the Government for approval who prepared a plan of constitutional reforms on the basis of the Commission's report. The Congress and the Muslim League both refused to accept the recommendations made by the Simon Commission.

NEHRU REPORT

When the report of the Simon Commission was presented in the Parliament in October 1927, for approval, India was going through a political turmoil. The Congress and the Muslim League had already rejected the recommendations of the Simon Commission which made Lord Birkenhead, the Secretary of State for India to declare in the Parliament, "The Indians *are so divided, opposed and fed up of* each *other* that *they are* unable to *produce a* unanimously *accepted constitution."* The Indian leaders accepted the challenge and convened an All Parties Conference in February 1928 to prepare a draft for the constitutional reforms. The Conference appointed a Committee under the Chairmanship of Moti Lal Nehru to identify the principles for India's future constitution.

The other members of the Committee were Sir Tej Bahdur Sapru, G.R. Pardhan, M.R. Jaikar, N.A. Joshi, Sir Ali Imam and Shoiab Qureshi (Muslim members). The representation of the Muslims on the Committee was of an insignificant nature. The Muslim members attended only one meeting of the Committee and put their signatures when the report was ready. The report submitted by the Committee is known *as 'Nehru* Report' which contained the following major recommendations:--

- Full responsible government on the model of self-governing dominions to be introduced in the sub-continent.

- Separate electorate should be replaced with the joint electorate with reservation of seats for the minorities in proportion to their population.

- The foreign affairs, army and defense should be placed under the control of parliament and Viceroy.

- Sindh should be separated *from* Bombay to form a new *province if it were* capable *of* bearing its expenditure.

- Full provincial status is given to N.W.F.P. and Balochistan.

- Hindi should be made official language.

The Nehru Report clearly reflected the Hindu mind and was based on anti-Muslim and anti-Islam sentiments. An All Parties National Conference was convened in Calcutta in December 1928 to consider the Nehru Report.

Quaid-e-Azam proposed three amendments in the Nehru Report which were as follows:-

- 1/3rd representation for the Muslims in the Central Legislature.

- Muslim representation in the Punjab and Bengal on the basis of population.

- Residuary powers should be given to provinces instead of Central Government.

The amendments proposed by the Quaid-e-Azam were very reasonable and did not reflect a sharp contrast of ideas and point of view. Dr. Ambedekar *says, "These* amendments show, *that the* gulf *between* the Hindus *and* Muslims *was* not in any way a wide one. Yet *there was no desire to bridge the same"*. The Hindu majority rejected all these amendments, when put to vote. The Quaid-e-Azam declared, *The Nehru Committee* has *adopted a narrow-minded policy to* ruin *the* political *future of the* Muslims. *I regret to declare that the report is extremely* ambiguous *and* does *not deserve to be implemented'*.

FOURTEEN POINTS OF QUAID-E-AZAM

Quaid-e-Azam decided to give his own formula for the constitutional reforms in reply to the Nehru Report. He convened the meeting of the Muslim League in 1929 in Delhi and gave his famous Fourteen Points Formula. While delivering his Presidential address, the Quaid-e-Azam declared that no constitution shall be accepted by the Muslims of India without the Fourteen Points which were as follows:-

1. The form of the future constitution should be federal with the residuary powers vested in the provinces.

2. A uniform measure of autonomy shall be granted to all provinces.

3. All legislatures in the country and other elected bodies shall be constituted on the definite principle of adequate and effective representation of minorities in every province without reducing the majority in any province to a minority or even equality.

4. In the central legislature Muslim representation shall not be less than one third.

5. Representation of communal groups shall continue to be by separate electorates, provided that it shall be open to any community, at any time, to abandon its separate electorate in favor of joint electorate.

6. Any territorial redistribution that might at any time be necessary shall not in any way affect the Muslim majority in the Punjab, Bengal and N.W.F.P.

7. Full religious liberty, that is, liberty of belief, worship and observance, propaganda, association and education shall be guaranteed to all communities.

8. No bill or resolution or any part thereof shall be passed in any legislature or any other elected body if three fourths of the members of any community in that particular body oppose it as being injurious to the interests of that community.

9. Sindh should be separated from the Bombay.

10. Reforms should be introduced in the N.W.F.P. and Balochistan on the same footings as in the other provinces.

11. Muslims should be given adequate share along with other Indians in the services of the State.

12. The constitution should embody adequate safeguard for the protection of Muslim culture and for the promotion of Muslim education, language, religion and civilization.

13.   No cabinet, either Central or Provincial, should be formed
      without at least 1/3rd of the Muslim Ministers.

14.   The Central Legislature except shall make no change in the
      constitution with the concurrence of the States constituting the
      Indian Federation.

The reasonable and moderate demands, contained in the Fourteen Points,
were rejected by the Hindu leaders, which further widened the gulf
between the two communities. Meanwhile the Congress made an abrupt
demand that new constitution must be given to India by 31st December,
1929. The Government turned down this demand and the Viceroy Lord
Irwin, in October 1929, made a two-fold declaration. The first part related
to the constitution. He said, "I *am authorized by His Majesty's
Government to state clearly that in their judgment it is implicit in the
Declaration of 1917 that the natural issue of India's constitutional
progress, as they're contemplated is the attainment of Dominion Status.*"
The second was the announcement of a Round Table Conference at which
the British Government would meet the representatives of British Ind'a
and the princely states for the purpose of seeking the greatest possible
measures of agreement on constitutional proposals.

With the rejection of Fourteen Points by the Congress and other Hindu
leaders, the Nehru Report was also doomed. The Nehru Report created
great deal of suspicion in the Muslims who were now seriously thinking
for the attainment of a separate homeland for themselves.

ALLAMA IQBAL'S PRESIDENTIAL ADDRESS AT
ALLAHABAD 1930

The Fourteen Points of the Quaid-e-Azam had infused a new political
insight in the Indian Muslims. These points created great confidence .
amongst the Muslims, gathered behind their leader. The Muslims of the
sub-continent were now fully aware of their distinct national character
and identity. They were convinced that the Hindus and Muslims were
two separate nations, which could not be welded together by any
political system.

The annual session of the All India Muslim League was held at Allahbad
in 1930, which was presided over by Allama Iqbal. Allama Iqbal was a
poet, philosopher and thinker who had gained countrywide fame and
recognition by 1930. He awakened the Muslims of the sub-continent to

demand a separate homeland. He had deeply studied Islam as a religion and system of life and believed that Hindus and Muslims were two separate and distinct nations who could never become one nation. He expressed his views while delivering his presidential address at Allahbad in 1930.

In his address Allama Iqbal discussed the political situation of the sub-continent at large. His address is regarded as an authentic document on Islam as a system of life. The address is a great asset of the Muslim history of the sub-continent with regard to their struggle for independence.

He declared Islam as a complete code of life and gave very sound and strong arguments in support of his views. He said that Islam guides the people with respect to every aspect of life. He said that I am fully convinced that the Muslims of India will ultimately have to establish a separate homeland, as they cannot live with Hindus in the United India. Allama Iqbal was of the view that Punjab, Sindh, Balochistan and N.W.F.P. should be grouped together to make a separate state, which should be given dominion status within or outside the British Empire. He declared, *"India is a continent of human beings belonging to different languages and professing different religions. To base a constitution on the conception of homogeneous India is to prepare her for civil war. I, therefore, demand the formation of a consolidated Muslim State in the best interests of the Muslims of India and Islam. The formation of a consolidated North-West Indian Muslim State appears to be the final destiny of the Muslims, at least of Northwest India'.*

Allama Iqbal's presidential address further clarified the Two Nation Theory and demanded a separate homeland for the Muslims. It was the first occasion when a demand for a separate homeland was made from the Muslim League platform. The Lahore Resolution passed in 1940 was in *fact* based on this historic address of Allama Iqbal.

ROUND TABLE CONFERENCES
The Simon Commission report was published in March 1930, which invited criticism, as anticipated, from the political parties. Congress in its annual meeting at Lahore of December 1929 had authorized its Working Committee to start a civil disobedience movement when it felt necessary. The Working Committee of the Congress accordingly launched its movement under Gandhi's leadership in April 1930. The movement was

declared as illegal and Gandhi and Nehru were arrested. The Muslims reserved their decision knowing that the report was not final. The political situation had become tense in the country.

The Government, however, did not want to confront the political parties and decided to hold a Round Table Conference in which all parties were to be invited to present their point of view.

The 1st session of the Round Table Conference began in London on 12th November, 1930. All the parties were represented except the Congress, which had given the ultimatum that unless the Nehru Report was enforced completely as the constitution of India it would have nothing to do with the future constitutional discussions. Since the Muslims had separated themselves from the civil disobedience movement of the Congress they decided to attend the Conference in spite of Congress boycott. The Muslim delegation included Agha Khan, Maulana Muhammad Ali Jauhar, Quaid-e-Azam, Maulvi Fazal-ul-Haq, Sir Muhammad Shafi, Sir Shah Nawaz, Chaudhry Zafar Ullah and Ghulam Husain Hidayat Ullah.

The most important decision taken at the Conference was the approval of a federal system for India. The princely states declared that they would extend maximum co-operation to form an All India Federation. There was unanimous agreement on all points. Muslims favored Sapru's proposal for dominion status and responsible government at Center by scraping the system of Diarchy in the provinces. The delegates also agreed on giving Sindh a separate identity and for establishing a responsible government in the province.

Eight sub-committees were formed to deal with different matters, i.e. federal structure, provincial constitution, franchise, province of Sindh, the N.W.F.P, defense services and minorities. There was a deadlock on the question of the distribution of subjects in the federal system. The deliberations of the minority's sub-committee, too, could not reach a conclusion. The Muslim delegation declared in the end that in those circumstances the only course was to repeat our claim that no advance is possible without sufficient safeguard for the Muslims of India.

The 1st Round Table Conference finished on 19th January, 1931. The British Prime Minister issued a statement that the government had accepted the proposals for full responsible government in the provinces and a federal system in the Center.

GANDHI - IRWIN PACT

The Congress was repenting on its decision of boycotting the 1st Round Table Conference. The civil disobedience movement had failed which exposed the Congress position. Congress now wanted to wriggle out of this situation in a dignified manner. They were looking for an opportunity to come to terms with the government. On the other hand the government too was desirous of Congress's participation in the Second Round Table Conference. The government had realized the importance of Congress and understood that without Congress, any solution for constitutional reforms would be difficult to implement. The government, therefore, decided to make peace with the Congress.

Lord Irwin extended invitation to Gandhi for talks. Gandhi agreed to call off the civil disobedience without laying down any pre-conditions. The talks between Gandhi and Irwin continued from 17th February, 1931 to 19th February, 1931. The agreement between Gandhi and Irwin was signed on 5th March, 1931. Following were the salient proposals of the Gandhi-Irwin Pact:-

- The congress will end its civil disobedience movement.
- The Congress will attend the Second Round Table Conference.
- The government will withdraw all ordinances to curb the Congress.
- The government would withdraw all notifications! Enactments relating to offences not involving violence.
- The government would release all persons detained during civil disobedience movement.

Accordingly, the government released all the persons detained during the civil disobedience movement launched by the Congress. On the other hand, the Congress, as decided by the Gandhi-Irwin Pact, set out to attend the Second Round Table Conference.

SECOND ROUND TABLE CONFERENCE

The Second Round Table Conference opened on 7th September, 1931 in London and lasted till 1st December, 1931. Gandhi was there as the sole representative of the Congress. Maulana Muhammad Ali Jauhar had died by the time the Second Round Table Conference began. The Muslim delegation in the Second Round Table Conference included an important personality, Allama Muhammad Iqbal, who had gained immense importance and fame as a poet, thinker, philosopher and politician in India.

Two committees were set up to carry out the work of the Conference on Federal structure and minorities. The most sensitive issue before the Conference was the Hindu-Muslim relationship. Gandhi was the member of the two committees.

Gandhi adopted a stubborn and childish attitude on all matters in the beginning. When the minority issue was presented in the Conference Gandhi refused to accept any rights of the minorities and demanded that the minority committee should be disbanded. He claimed that he being the sole representative of the Congress represented the Indian people. He refused to accept the representative character of other delegates, as they did not belong to the Congress. After adopting the stiff attitude Gandhi sat back to quietly observe the proceedings of the committee. He did not at all give any practical suggestions of his own for bringing a settlement.

Gandhi did his best to prove India as one nation and nationality so that he could claim to represent the Indian people alone. When the communal problem came for discussion, a great difficulty was faced in convincing Gandhi who had rejected the presence of any other community except the Hindus in India. Gandhi insisted that there was only one nation in India, which was Hindus. But the Quaid-e-Azam replied that Indian Muslims were also a separate nation of India, which had its own interests.

During the proceedings of the Conference Gandhi continued with his resolute and stubborn attitude and demanded that the work of constitution making be started by putting aside the minority's issue. Sir Shafi did not agree to this proposal and insisted that minority's issue must be resolved before taking up constitution making. Sir Shafi also demanded that the Fourteen Points of the Quaid-e-Azam should be incorporated in the future constitution of India which Gandhi refused to accept.

No settlement of minorities issue could be reached because of Gandhi's rigid behavior. Gandhi put forward his own scheme to resolve the minority's issue, which was based on the recommendations of the Nehru Committee. The minorities, therefore, adopted a more stiff approach for the solution of their problems. As a counter to Gandhi's scheme the minorities presented a joint statement of claims. All minorities entered into an agreement on their demands and insisted on its acceptance as a whole. Gandhi refused to accept this settlement. The Second Round Table Conference, therefore, ended without reaching at any conclusion mainly because of the rigid attitude of Gandhi.

THIRD ROUND TABLE CONFERENCE

The Third Round Table Conference began on 17th November, 1932 and ended on 24th November, 1932. The Congress once again abstained from the conference because Gandhi had started his civil disobedience movement. Quaid-e-Azam did not take part in this conference. In his absence Sir Agha Khan led the Muslim delegation.

The Third Round Table Conference could not solve the long standing Hindu-Muslim problem and proved a mere formality. There was an unbridgeable gulf between the ideas of the two major communities of India. Gandhi, Nehru and other prominent leaders of the Congress were in jail. The conference, therefore, ended after few meetings without achieving anything.

COMMUNAL AWARD

The British government gave enough time and chance to the Indian leaders to come with a workable constitutional set up. However, after vainly waiting for some mutual settlement among the Indian themselves, the British government published their own scheme known as 'Communal *Award*' in August 1932. It retained separate electorate for the Muslims and for all other minorities. But the Muslim majorities in Punjab and Bengal were reduced to minorities.

The Indian political parties rejected the award. Gandhi, however, managed to win over Dr. Ambedkar to renounce the award for the untouchables. The Muslims, too, were not happy with the award as it reduced their majorities in few provinces.

GOVERNMENT OF INDIA ACT 1935

The Round Table Conferences could not achieve anything in spite of their best efforts to solve the constitutional problem of India. However, there was one important factor in the holding of these conferences that they amply projected the public opinion to enable the government to fully understand the problems and to take some concrete steps to solve them.

The recommendations of the Round Table Conferences were contained in a white paper, which was published in 1933 and discussed in the parliament. A committee was set up under the chairmanship of Lord Linlithgow, the Viceroy of India, to consider the recommendations of the white paper. The other members of the committee were the Agha Khan, Muhammad Zafar Ullah Khan, Shafaat Ahmad Khan, Abdur Rahim and A.H. Ghaznvi.

The report of the committee was published in 1934, which was contained in a Bill of Law. The report along with the Bill was presented in the British Parliament for approval. The parliament passed the Bill which after the Royal assent on 24th July, 1935 was enforced in the country as *Government of India Act,* 1935.

IMPORTANT REFORMS OF THE ACT OF 1935

The Act contained 14 parts and 10 schedules and consisted of two parts. Part I pertained to provincial subjects while Part II contained federal list of subjects. The Act came into operation on 1st April, 1937 except Part II, which could not be enforced until a specific number of princely states acceded to the Indian Federation. The Act introduced federal system in the center. The provincial reforms were as follows:

- The provinces were given more authority and powers and for the first time the provinces were made the separate entities.

- The system of 'Diarchy' was scrapped in the provinces and introduced in the center.

- Three subjects were drawn up: the federal list, the provincial list, and the concurrent list.

- The provincial legislatures were given powers of legislation on provincial and concurrent subjects.
- The provincial executive was handed over to the representatives of the people who were accountable before the provincial legislatures.

- The country was divided into 11 provinces.
- Responsible parliamentary system was introduced in the provinces. The provinces were given complete autonomy. The ministers were to be chosen from the representatives of the people.
- Every province was given a council of ministers whose advice was binding on the governor. However, in the discharge of his responsibilities the governor was to act under the general control of the Governor General.

- Special powers were given to the governors for the protection of the rights of the minorities.

A BRIEF EVALUATION OF THE ACT OF 1935

The Act of 1935 failed to win appreciation from various sectors. The political leaders of India rejected it for it failed to meet the demands of the different political factions. Quaid-e-Azam declared it as a 'defective document'. Rajgopalachria declared it as worst than the system of Diarchy.

The federal system introduced by the Act of *1935* was defective in many ways. There was no guarantee of individual liberties neither it could give a workable dominion status. The people were not given their rights. All authority was vested in the parliament, which was a British institution.

The system of Diarchy, which had failed in the provinces, was introduced in the center without any hopeful results. Vast authority was given to the Governors in the provinces and to the Viceroy in the Center, which was against the principle of democracy and provincial autonomy. The Minister of State could interfere in the government services without any cogent reasons.

The central part of the Act could not be enforced and was suspended for some time. However, the provincial part of the Act was enforced under which the elections were held in the country.

CONGRESS MINISTRIES

Elections under Act of 1935: As already mentioned the Act of 1935 could not be enforced completely. There were some differences with regard to the central part of the Act due to which the Part II of the Act could not come into operation. However, the Part I (Provincial Part) of the Act came into operation on 1st April, 1937 and the holding of the elections under this part was announced.

The government announced to hold elections to the provincial legislative assemblies in 1936-37. There were 1771 seats of the provincial assemblies to be filled by these elections. Although both Muslim League and the Congress had rejected the Act of 1935, yet they decided to contest the elections.

Both Muslim League and the Congress issued their manifestoes. The Muslim League laid down two main principles on which its elected representatives would work:-

- The present provincial constitution and proposed central constitution should be replaced by a system of self-government.

- In the meantime the representatives of the Muslim League would sincerely work to get the maximum benefits out of the present constitution.

The Congress, too, came forward with somewhat the similar slogans of public welfare, freedom and liberty and for the release of the political prisoners.

The results of the elections were shocking for the Muslims of India and the Muslim League, which could not get mentionable support from the voters. Congress achieved a big victory and managed to get clear majority in five provinces. It, however, maneuvered to form coalition in few other provinces to form its ministries in eight provinces. Congress got clear majority in Madras, Bihar, Orissa, United Provinces and Central Provinces. In Bombay, the Congress won some independent groups to form a coalition ministry. The Muslim League failed to win considerable support. It managed to get a few seats in the Muslim minority provinces but failed in the Muslim majority areas.

FORMATION OF MINISTRIES

The Congress adopted a rigid attitude after winning the elections in majority. The Congress leaders behaved in a dictatorial manner and imposed their own will. On 1st April, 1937 the governors of Bombay, Madras, Central Provinces, United Provinces, Orssia and Bihar invited the leaders of the Congress parliamentary groups in their respective provinces to form ministries. In reply to these invitations the Congress leaders put a condition on the government to give assurance that the governors would not use their special powers of interference granted by the constitution for the protection of the minorities' rights. This otherwise meant asking the government functionaries not to perform their duties. The government clearly expressed their inability to give such an assurance. However, Lord Linlithgow, the Viceroy, issued a statement on 31st June, 1937 in which he clarified that the governors would use their special powers in matters of utmost urgency and that the ministers would be allowed to perform their jobs freely. After this statement the Congress Working Committee on 7th July, 1937 passed a resolution permitting the Congress to accept the office.

The Congress took office in eight provinces. In Punjab the Unionist Party of Sir Sikander Hayat formed ministry. Muslim ministry was formed in Sindh, which was dissolved because of the Congress conspiracies. A coalition was formed in Bengal with Maulvi Fazal-ul-Haq of Krishak Praja Party as the leader of the coalition. Muslim League could not form ministry in any province. Congress formed its ministry in N.W.F.P. as well which brought the number of Congress ruled provinces to six. In Bombay and Bengal the Congress formed coalitions with other groups.

As Muslim League had got sizable success in the Muslim minority provinces, it was hoped that the Congress would include Muslim League in the government in the Muslim minority provinces. But the Congress was reluctant in sharing the power with the Muslim League and laid down degrading conditions for the Muslim League to be included in the Ministry. Discussions were held between the Congress and Muslim League leaders. Maulana Abu-al-Kalam Azad, a member of the Congress high command communicated to Chaudhry Khaliq-uz-Zaman, the leader of the Muslim League, the following terms on which the Congress was prepared to let the Muslim League enter the provincial government:-

- The Muslim League group in the U.P. legislative assembly shall be dissolved.
- The members of the Muslim League in the U.P. assembly shall join the Congress and would come under the party discipline.

- The Muslim League members who will join the Congress shall carry out the instructions issued by the Congress party leaders pertaining to their work in the assemblies.

- The Muslim League parliamentary Board shall be dissolved.

The above conditions/terms proposed by the Congress amply manifest the rigid and dictatorial attitude, which the Congress had adopted after winning the elections. No party with a slightest feeling of self-respect would have accepted these degrading conditions. The Muslim League, therefore, rejected these terms and a pure Congress ministry was formed in the United Provinces.

CONGRESS ATROCITIES ON THE MUSLIMS

Congress had formed its ministries in the eight provinces. The Muslims living *in these provinces* under Congress *rule were* subjected to most inhuman treatment and made to bear the oppressive and tyrannical *rule of* the Congress for two and a half years. The Congress adopted every mean to completely erase the Muslim population of the provinces under its rule.

Congress had adopted an unconstitutional method to rule the provinces and its administration did not conform *to the* parliamentary system as laid down in the Act of 1935. The Congress ministries were not accountable to the parliament. They received all instructions from the Congress High Command for all matters. The Congress High Command appointed and removed the ministers. A parliamentary sub-committee was set up by the Congress to deal with the work of legislatures in all provinces. This committee was to guide and advise the legislatures in their functions. It consisted of Maulana Abu-al-Kalam Azad, Rajendra Prasad and Sardar Vallabhai Patel. The provinces were distributed amongst the three members of the committee. Maulana Azad was given the charge of Bengal, United Provinces, the Punjab and the N.W.F.P. Rejendra Prasad got Bihar, Orissa and Assam. Vallabhai Patel was allotted Bombay, Madras, *the* Central provinces and Sindh. This sub-committee *was given vast authority to deal with* all matters in the Congress provinces. The Congress regime was an absolutist rule and in fact an oligarchy dominated by Mr. Gandhi.

With the installation of Congress ministries the Hindus came out to impose Hindu Nationalism on the Muslims. The Congress began its rule by imposing its will on the Muslim minorities in the provinces under its rule. The Muslims were forbidden to eat beef. Severe punishments were awarded to those who slaughtered the *'Mother Cow'*. Every effort was made to humble and humiliate *'Islam'* the religion of the Muslims. A systematic policy was framed by the Congress to stamp out the Muslim culture. Hindi was enforced as the official language in all the provinces under the Congress rule. Azan was forbidden and planned attacks were made on the Muslim worshippers busy in the mosques. Intentionally, noisy processions passed near the mosques at prayer times. If a Muslim had to kill a cow for sacrifice, hundreds of Muslims including their children and women were to be killed in retaliation. Pigs were pushed into the mosques and 'Azan' was frequently interrupted.

Hindu-Muslim riots occurred under Congress supervision in various places to make a pretext for severe action against the Muslims. The Muslims were openly and freely mauled and molested. The government agencies offered no protection to the Muslims who were subjected to the Hindu domination and high handedness. If the Muslims lodged complaints with the authorities the decisions were always against the Muslims.

BANDE MATRAM

Bande Matram was a song in which degrading remarks were used against the Muslims and their religion Islam. The song was written by a Bengali novelist Bankim Chatterjee in his novel *'Anadamath'* and urged all the non-Muslims to wage war against the Muslims in order to expel them from 'Hindustan', which was meant for the Hindus only. In order to strengthen the Hindu nationalism, the Congress members in the assemblies, under the instruction from the Congress High Command, insisted on commencing the days' beginnings by the recitation of the song Bande Matram. Bande Matram was also adopted as national anthem and was to be recited before the start of official business every day.

WIDDIA MANDER SCHEME

Another attempt was made to erase the Muslim culture by introducing a new educational system. The education policy was known as *'Widdia Mander Scheme'* and aimed at converting the non-Hindus to Hinduism. It was introduced in all schools.

MUSLIM MASS CONTACT CAMPAIGN

The Congress started a Muslim mass contact campaign. The main objective of this campaign was to crush the popularity of the Muslim League amongst the Muslims. It was Nehru's imagination to destroy the Muslim League as the only representative party of the Muslims. The campaign began by directly contacting the Muslim masses with a view to win them over to the Congress.

MUSLIM LEAGUE'S ROLE DURING CONGRESS RULE

The Muslim League remained very active during the atrocious rule of the Congress. It continued drawing attention, through its resolutions, to anti-Muslim policies of the Congress and appealing to the Congress to change its biased attitude towards the Muslims. The Muslim League protested against anti-Muslim policies of the Congress and openly condemned its various steps like the recitation of 'Bande Matram' as the national anthem, Wardha scheme, Widdia Mander scheme and Congress attitude against Islam. The Muslim League expressed its grave concern over the communal riots in the United Provinces, Bihar, the Central Provinces and Bombay. Quaid-e-Azam bitterly criticized the Congress rule and declared it as Hindu Raj, which worked and existed to annihilate every other community. He said that the Congress rule was a fascist and authoritarian set up which uprooted all norms of democracy.

END OF THE CONGRESS RULE

The Second World War began in 1939. Britain declared war against Germany. The government appealed to all political parties for help and assistance in this hour of need.

Congress convened its meeting to consider government's appeal and put the following conditions for assistance in war:

- The British government should explain the objective of the war.

- The government should announce that the elected legislature would draft the constitution of India.

- The members of the Viceroy's Executive Council should be those only who enjoy the support of the Central Assembly.

The acceptance of these demands would have meant the transfer of power to the Congress as these demands clearly proved that the Congress was asking for the right of constitution making. The government could not accede to these demands, as it wanted to pacify both Congress and the Muslim League. Viceroy declared that due consideration would be given to the point of view of every party and that dominion status would be given to India after the war.

The Congress did not believe in the promises of the government. The Congress leaders expressed their utter disappointment on the decision of the government. The Congress with a view to putting more pressure on the government refused to extend co-operation to the government in the war *activities* and announced to resign from the ministry. The Congress High Command asked its ministers to tender resignations in protest against the decision of the government. In November 1939 the Congress ministries resigned from *their office.* The poor Muslim population took a sigh of relief, as they have *been* relieved of the most tyrannical and oppressive *rule of* the Congress.

DAY OF DELIVERANCE

With the resignation of the Congress ministries the Muslims of India were relieved of the most dreadful domination of the Congress and Hindu majority. The two and a half years of the Congress rule was an extremely hard and grievous experience *for* the Muslims of India who had *seen* the real face of the Hindu mentality. The Quaid-e-Azam appealed to the people to observe *the Day of Deliverance on* 22nd December, 1939 and bow their heads before Almighty Allah Who relieved them of the clutches of the Congress. The Quaid-e-Azam appealed that the day should be observed with peace. The Muslims of India, in accordance with the appeal of the Quaid-e-Azam celebrated the day with acclaim. Public meetings *were* held and thanks giving prayers were offered in token of relief from the tyranny, oppression and high handedness of the Congress regime.

THE PAKISTAN RESOLUTION

The Muslim League held its annual session in Lahore on 21-24th March, 1940. It was a historic meeting as the Muslims of India took a decision, which left its deep impact on the freedom struggle of the Muslims of the sub-continent. In his presidential address, The Quaid-e-Azam declared, "It has *always* been *taken for granted* mistakenly *that* the Musalmans *are* a *minority. The* Musalmans *are not a minority. The* Musalmans *are a* nation *by any definition. What the* unitary *government of* India *for 150 years has failed to achieve cannot be realized by* imposition *of a* Central *Federal Government except by means of armed force.* The problem in India is *not of an* inter-*communal character but manifestly of* an *international one, and* it must *be treated* as such. *The* Hindus *and Muslims* belong to *two different civilizations, which are based* mainly *on conflicting ideas and conceptions.* To *yoke together two such* nations *under a* single *State, one as a numerical minority and the other* as *a majority,* must *lead to growing discontent and final destruction of any fabric* that *may be so* built *up for the Government of* such *a State."*

The Indian Muslims had a distinctive national identity of their own which they wanted to preserve and promote at all cost. All the Muslim leaders from Sir Syed Ahmad Khan to the Quaid-e-Azam struggled hard for the protection and safeguard of this very national identity of the Muslims and the demand, for Pakistan was, in fact, made in 1940 for the protection and safeguard of the national character of the Muslims of India. Sir Syed Ahmed Khan, who was the greatest advocate of the Hindu-Muslim unity, was ultimately convinced that the future of the Indian Muslims was not safe in the United India. Sir Syed Ahmed Khan, therefore, pronounced his famous two-nation theory and laid down a foundation on which the Quaid-e-Azam and Allama Iqbal erected the glorious edifice of Two Nation Theory in the later stages.

This was the famous two-nation theory, which aroused so much controversy. The Congress leaders indignantly rejected it, although Savarkar, the President of Hindu Mahasabha, had frequently referred to Hindus and Muslims as two nations. The facts on which the Two Nation Theory was based were well known to everyone including the British. The Joint Committee of Parliament on Indian constitutional reforms had stated in 1934: *India is inhabited by many races, often as distinct from one another in origin, tradition and manner of life as are the nations of Europe. Two-thirds of its inhabitant professes Hinduism, over 77 million are follower of Islam and the difference between the two is not only of religion in the stricter sense but also of law and culture. They may be said, indeed, to represent two distinct and separate civilizations.'*

By 1937 the Muslim political leaders were compelled to give serious consideration to the partition of India. The atrocious Congress rule had intensified the suspicions amongst the Muslims who dreaded the Hindu domination in the event of the British leaving the country. The Muslims, therefore, decided to demand the partition of India in the presence of the British so that the Muslims could be saved of the Hindu domination.

The historic session of the Muslim League began on 21st March, 1940, at Lahore under the Chairmanship of Quaid-e-Azam.

On 23rd March, 1940, the famous resolution, which came to be known as *'Pakistan Resolution'* was moved and passed unanimously. The Bengal Chief Minister Maulvi Fazal-ul-Haq, known as 'Sher-e-Bengal' and seconded by Chaudhri Khaliq-uz-Zaman and others, moved the resolution. The resolution stated that: *no constitutional plan would be workable in this country or acceptable to the Muslims unless it is designed on the following basic principles, namely, that the geographically contiguous units are demarcated into regions which should be so constituted, with such territorial readjustments as may be necessary that the areas in which the Muslims are in a majority as in the North-Western and Eastern zones* of India *should be grouped to constitute independent states in which the constituent units shall be autonomous and sovereign. Adequate, effective and mandatory safeguards should be specifically provided in the constitution for minorities for the protection of their religious, cultural, economic, political, administrative and other rights.*

The Pakistan (Lahore) Resolution was unanimously accepted by the participants of the Muslim League session from all over the country. The Muslims responded to it enthusiastically while the Hindus condemned it roundly. The denunciation by the Hindu leaders who referred to partition as 'vivisection of mother India', were calculated to arouse Hindu religious feelings. Gandhi called it a moral wrong and a sin to which he would never be a party. The Quaid-e-Azam replied to Gandhi and said, "We maintain *and hold that the* Muslims *and Hindus are two major* nations by *any* definition and *test of a* nation. *We are a* nation *of 100* million and what is *more, we are a* nation with *our own* distinct *culture and civilization by all canons of international law we are a nation".*

The words and contents of the Pakistan Resolution clearly show that the proposal for the partition of the sub-continent was passed on the theory that there were two major nations in the sub-continent. The acceptance of the Lahore Resolution gave impetus to the freedom movement. The Muslims gathered under the dynamic leadership of the Quaid-e-Azam who gave new meaning and shape to their quest for independence. The Muslims began to acquire a new hope and confidence in their destiny, the moment they were convinced that there was no other solution to the Indian constitutional problem except the creation of two separate and sovereign states of Hindustan and Pakistan. The Muslims demanded Pakistan because they failed, in spite of their sincere efforts and wishes to live in peace and amity with the Hindus. They were tormented by the fear that being Muslims they would never be acceptable to the Hindus in the United India. Pakistan, therefore, was not demanded on the philosophy of hatred for the Hindus but for the protection of the Muslim civilization and culture.

PARTITION PROPOSALS

In fact the idea of the Indian partition was not a new one. In 1920, Muhammad Abdul Qadir Bilgrami had advocated the division of the sub-continent between the Hindus and Muslims giving a list of districts, which was almost identical to the present boundaries of East and West Pakistan. Three years later in 1923, in his evidence before the Frontier Enquiry Committee, Sardar Gul Muhammad Khan of Dera Ismail Khan had proposed a partition of India by which the Muslims were to get *the* area from Peshawar to Agra. In 1934 Lala Rajpat Rai, one of the founders of Mahasabha, had suggested the partition of India between Hindus and Muslims. Allama Iqbal, while delivering his Presidential address at the Annual Session of the Muslim League at Allah bad in December 1930 said, "He *would like to see Punjab, N.W.F.P., Sindh and Balochsitan amalgamated into a single State. Self-government within the British Empire, the phonation of a consolidated North-East Indian Muslim State appears to me to b e t h e final destiny of the Muslims, at least of North-West India."*

These proposals, however, could not attract desired attention until a concrete scheme for the establishment of a Muslim State, came for the first time from a person of high intellectual stature and prestige. *Ch. Rehmat Ali,* a student at the University of Cambridge, England, coined the word *'Pakistan' in* which P stands for Punjab, A for Afghania (NWFP), K for Kashmir, S for Sindh and Tan for Balochsitan. The word itself means the *'land of the pure.'* It gave concise and comprehensive expression to Iqbal's idea, contained in his Presidential address at Muslim League Session of Allah bad in *1930,* and was both a symbol and slogan.

Muslim League set up a Committee to examine the partition proposals and submit a detailed report highlighting the possibilities of a separate homeland for the Muslims of India. The Committee included Quaid-e-Azam (Chairman), Liaqat Ali Khan (Convener), Sir Sikander Hayat Khan, Nawab Ismail Khan and Syed Abdul Aziz.

Meanwhile the Muslim League branches of Sindh and U.P. passed resolutions demanding separate homeland for the Muslims of India. All the resolutions were dispatched to the Central offices of the Muslim League, which set out with the preparation to put forward the demand for Pakistan in its next annual session of 1940.

CRIPPS MISSION

Germany achieved amazing victories in the Second World War to pose difficulties for the British who stood alone with the fall of France. The results of war in North Africa and South East Asia were discouraging and humiliating. The Japanese forces, which were fighting by the side of Germany, had entered Singapore on 15th January, 1942. It appeared to many in India that the Japanese could overrun India with the same ease with which they had conquered South East Asia. The security of the sub-continent was gravely threatened which created great concern for the British Government.

The sudden revelation of British weakness produced shock and surprise in India. The British Government was faced with a number of problems and wanted to win the co-operation of the Indian people and political parties to cope with the war requirements. On August 8, 1940, the Viceroy, Lord Linlithgow, made an offer on behalf of the British Government to expand the Executive Council by including the representatives of the political parties and to set up a War Advisory Council comprising representatives of Indian States and of other interests. After the war, an Indian constitution making body would be set up to devise a new constitution with due regard for the minorities. Large and powerful sections in India's national life directly denied the British Government, however, made it clear that they could not think of transfer of power to any party, at present. Nor could they be a party in suppressing those elements to install a government. They hoped that co-operative endeavor for victory in war would pave the way towards the attainment by India of that free and equal partnership in the British Commonwealth which remains the proclaimed and accepted goal of Imperial Crown of the British Parliament.

The Muslim League and Congress both rejected the offer made by the Viceroy. Congress wanted the transfer of power at all costs, while the Muslim League rejected it because it promised inadequate representation to the Muslims in the Government. In fact the British wanted to win the war first and transfer of power afterwards. The Congress demanded power at once, and a Hindu-Muslim settlement afterwards. The Muslim League insisted on Hindu-Muslim settlement first. The two communities Hindus and Muslims stood at daggers drawn to further pollute the political climate of the country. The people were not prepared to cooperate with the government in war without getting a positive assurance from the government about their demands. The government was unable to cope with the war without the co-operation of the people. Prime Minister, Mr. Churchill announced that the government had chalked out a program for the welfare of the people of India. Mr. Churchill declared that a responsible delegation would soon be sent to India for talks with Indian leaders to suggest recommendations for the constitutional reforms in India.

The British Government appointed a delegation under the (Chairmanship of Sir Stafford Cripps, a prominent member of the War Cabinet of England. The Cripps Mission reached New Delhi on March 23, 1942 to hold discussion with Indian leaders. The Cripps Mission could not hold talks with the Indian leaders because of non-cooperation by the Indian leaders and left after a fortnight. The Cripps Mission, however, submitted its own suggestions to the Government in April 1942 for constitutional reforms which were as follows:-

1. A Constituent Assembly consisting of elected representatives from the provinces and nominated representatives from the States shall be formed immediately upon the cessation of hostilities to frame the future constitution of India.

2. The constitution framed by the Constituent Assembly shall have to be accepted on the following grounds:-

   - Any province or state would be free either to adhere or not to adhere to the new constitution.
   - Meanwhile the British Government would retain the control of the defense of India.

   - A fresh agreement would have to be concluded between the constituent assembly and the British Government to settle the issues pertaining to the transfer of power.

   - The Government of India Act, 1935 shall remain in force until the cessation of war.

   - The C-in-C (Mil Commander in chief) and Finance Minister shall be British nationals.

3. The suggestions are to be accepted or rejected completely and there shall be no amendments.

4. The recommendations would be implemented only if both Muslim League and Congress accept them unanimously.

Congress rejected the Cripps proposals on the advice of Gandhi who regarded it as *'a post dated check'* on a failing bank. The Muslim League also rejected them because the proposals did not concede Pakistan unequivocally. Gandhi now began to press for an immediate withdrawal of the British from India and the transfer of power to the Congress without any prior settlement with any party.

GANDHI - JINNAH TALKS

Gandhi - Jinnah talks occupy a significant position with regard to the political problems of India and Pakistan Movement. The talks began between two great leaders of the sub-continent in response to a general public desire for a settlement of Hindu-Muslim differences.

Gandhi wrote to the Quaid-e-Azam on 17th July, 1944 in which he expressed his desire of meeting the Quaid-e-Azam. The Quaid-e-Azam asked for permission of meeting Mr. Gandhi from the Muslim League, which was duly accorded.

Gandhi-Jinnah talks began on 19th September, 1944 in Bombay and lasted up to 24th September, 1944. The talks were *sometime* held directly and sometime through correspondence. Gandhi told the Quaid-e-Azam that he had come in his personal capacity and was not representing the Hindus or Congress.

Gandhi's real concern was to extract from Jinnah's mouth that the whole of Pakistan proposition was absurd. Quaid-e-Azam pains-taxingly explained the basis for the demand of Pakistan. *"We* maintain' he wrote to Gandhi 'That Muslims and Hindus *are two major* nations by *any* definition *or* test *of a* nation. We *are a* nation *of* hundred million. *We have* our own *distinctive outlook on* life. *By all the* cannons *of* international law, *we* are a *nation."* He added that he was, "convinced *that the true welfare not only of* the Muslims *but of the rest of India lies in the* division *of India as proposed in the Lahore* Resolution"

Gandhi on the other hand maintained that India was one nation and saw in the Pakistan Resolution "Nothing but ruin *for* the *whole of India."* If, *however,* Pakistan *had to be conceded, a Commission approved by both the Congress and Muslim League should demarcate the areas in which the*

Muslims are in an absolute majority. The *wishes of the people of these areas will be* obtained through Referendum. *These* areas shall *form* a separate State as soon *as* possible *after* India is *free from foreign domination. There shall be a* treaty of separation which *should also provide for the efficient and* satisfactory administration *of foreign affairs, defense, internal* communication, custom *and the like which* must necessarily continue to *be the matters of common interest between the* contracting countries.

This meant, *in effect, that power over* whole *of* India should first be transferred to Congress, which thereafter would allow Muslim majority areas that voted for separation to be constituted, not as independent sovereign state, but as part of an Indian Federation. Gandhi contended that his offer gave the substance of the Lahore Resolution. The Quaid-e-Azam did not agree to the proposal and the talks ended.

SIMLA CONFERENCE 1945
Lord Wavell succeeded Lord Linlithgow as Viceroy of India in 1943. Lord Wavell was a reputed military Commander and had commanded the British armies in the Second World War. Before coming to India he was the C-in-C of the British forces, which were fighting in North African against German forces. Being a military commander Lord Wavell possessed great administrative experience. When he *took over as Viceroy, the* tide of the Second World War was turning in favor of the allies. Lord Wavell declared that the British Government wanted to see India as an independent and prosperous country.

When the war ended in August 1945, Viceroy Lord Wavell decided to hold a political conference to which he invited Muslim League and Congress representatives. The conference began in Simla on 24th June, 1945 and lasted till 14th July, 1945. Muslim League was represented by the Quaid-e-Azam, Liaqat All Khan, Khawja Nazim-ud-Din, Ghulam Husain Hidayat Ullah, Sir Muhammad Asad Ullah and Hussain Imam. Maulana Abu-al-Kalam Azad, Khizar Hayat Tiwana, Dr. Khan sahib and some other leaders, represented the Congress.

The Viceroy proposed an Interim Central Government in which all the portfolios except that of war would be given to Indians. There was to be parity of representation between the Muslims and caste Hindus. There was a deadlock over the Muslim League's demand that all five Muslim members of the Executive Council should be the nominees of the

Muslim League. The Viceroy was of the opinion that four members should be taken from the Muslim League while the fifth member should be a Punjabi Muslim who did not belong to the Muslim League. The Viceroy's insistence on having a non-leaguer in the Executive Council was in accordance with the advice given by British and Hindu officials to support Khizar Hayat Tiwana in his stand against the Muslim League. Khizar Hayat Tiwana, Chief Minister of Punjab had demanded that one seat of the Executive Council, out of Muslim quota, should be given to his Unionist party which was happily accepted by the Viceroy. The Congress also supported Khizar Hayat in his stand against Muslim League. The Congress denied the Muslim League's claim of being the sole representative of the Indian Muslims. The Quaid-e-Azam took a strong stand on these two issues and the conference failed to achieve anything and finally ended on 14th July, 1945.

ELECTIONS 1945-46

The Second World War finally came to an end in August 1945. Labor Party returned to power with clear majority in the general elections in England in July 1945. The Congress leaders, who had cultivated close relations with the leaders of Labor Party, felt elated at this unexpected turn of events. The Congress leaders expected support from the Labor Party because the Labor Party had favored the maintenance of India as a single administrative and political entity. It was the main cause of dispute between the Congress and the Muslim League.

The General elections to the Provincial and Central Legislatures were held in India in 1945-46. Both Congress and Muslim League contested these elections with utmost efforts, because on the results of" these elections depended the constitutional future of India. The results showed a decisive victory for Pakistan. The Muslim League won all the Muslim seats in the Central Assembly and 446 out of 495 Muslim seats in the Provincial Assemblies. The Congress won a similar victory in the Hindu constituencies and came to power in all the provinces with Hindu majority. In Bengal the Muslim League won 113 out of *119* Muslim seats and was able to form ministry with H.S. Suharwady as Chief Minister. In Punjab the Muslim League got *79* out of 86 Muslim seats. In Sindh Muslim League ministry was formed. In N.W.F.P. the Muslim League could not get majority and won only 17 out of 36 Muslim seats. The Congress formed a ministry in the N.W.F.P. with Dr. Khan Sahib as the Chief Minister.

The elections of 1945-46 proved that the Muslim League alone represented the Muslims of India. The sweeping majority of the Muslim League enhanced Congress hostility towards Muslim League. Instead of acknowledging the undeniable majority of Muslim League and coming to terms to it, Congress persisted with its policy of dividing the Muslims and denying political power to the representatives of the Muslim-community even in the provinces where the Muslims were in majority. In this way Congress deepened Muslim suspicion, intensified communal discord and made an amicable settlement impossible.

CABINET MISSION PLAN

The new British Government headed by Prime Minister Lord Attlee announced on February 19, 1946 that a special Mission consisting of three cabinet Ministers would be sent to India to discuss the constitutional issues with the Viceroy and the Indian political Leaders lord Attlee, during a debate in the House Commons on March 15, 1946, on the visit of Cabinet Mission to India said, *"l am well aware that I speak of a country containing congeries of races, religions and languages, and I know well the* difficulties *thereby created but the Indians can only overcome these difficulties. We are* mindful *of the rights of the minorities. On the other* hand *we cannot allow a minority to place a veto on the advance of a majority."*

Attlee's words visibly pleased Congress and caused concern in Muslim League circles. Quaid-e-Azam said, 'we *acknowledge the Hindu majority of India, but the Muslims are a separate* nation and *they must have the* right of *self-determination."*

The Cabinet Mission, which consisted of Lord Patrice Lawrence, the Secretary of State of India, Sir Stafford Cripps, the President of the Board of Trade and Mr. A.V. Alexander the first Lord of the Admiralty, arrived in India on March 24, 1946. There was a great deal of unrest and political activity in India as to the future of the sub-continent and the people looked towards the Mission with expectation and hope. Freedom was in sight, but the hands that reached out for it grappled with each other in conflict. Strife between the two major communities Hindus and Muslims was mounting day by day. The country's political and economic conditions were deteriorating and becoming unstable every day. The war had come to an end and the bulk of men, recruited during the war, had to be reabsorbed into the civil life. The inflationary conditions that prevailed during the war strained the economy almost to the breaking point. The specter of unemployment was rising.

Quaid-e-Azam made it clear to the Mission that the Muslim majority areas should be grouped together to make a sovereign and independent Pakistan. He said, "India has *never been* a symbol *of* unity *of Hindu-Muslim civilizations. It is not possible for the British* Government *to create homogeneity* between *Hindu and* Muslim cultures *and civilizations* as the two systems *are* distinctively opposed to *each other. There* is *no way other* than *the partition of India."*

The most active member of the Mission was Sir Stafford Cripps who openly sympathized with the Congress. The Mission held negotiations with the top leaders of the Congress and Muslim League and arranged a joint conference in Simla. Maulana Abu-al Kalam Azad, Jawaharlal Lal Nehru, Vallabhai Patel and Abdul Ghaffar Khan represented the Congress. The Quaid-e-Azam, Nawabzada Liaqat All Khan, Nawab Ismail and Sardar Abdur Rab Nishtar represented Muslim League.

Congress party insisted on a single Constituent Assembly to make the Constitution for All India Federal Government. It also wanted to have a Legislature dealing with foreign affairs, defense, communications, fundamental rights, currency, customs and planning and power to raise revenues by taxation. The remaining powers were to be vested in the provinces or units. Groups of provinces may be formed and such groups may determine the provincial subjects, which they desire to have in common.

On the other hand on April 9, 1946, the Muslim League's Central and Provincial Legislators, had demanded through a resolution that the six provinces of Bengal, and Assam in the North East and the Punjab, N.W.F.P., Sindh and Balochistan in the North West be constituted into a sovereign and independent State of Pakistan and that two separate constitution making bodies be set up by the people of Pakistan and Hindustan for framing the respective constitutions. In the light of this resolution the Muslim League proposed to the Cabinet Mission that two Constitution making bodies, one for the six provinces in the Pakistan group and the other for the group of six Hindu provinces be set up.

There was a deadlock as neither party could accept the proposals of the other. The fundamental issue was that whether there should be one sovereign state for the whole sub-continent or two independent states. The mediation of the Cabinet Mission could not bridge the gulf between the Congress and Muslim League.

On May 1946, the Cabinet Mission and the Viceroy published a statement containing their own solution of the constitutional problem. The focal point of their plan was the preservation of a single federal system for India, which the British had labored to build up. On economic, administrative and military grounds, they rejected the proposal of two independent sovereign states. The Mission was, however, of the opinion that the Muslim culture might become submerged in a purely unitary India dominated by Hindus. These considerations led them to formulate a three tier constitutional plan which was as follows:-

1. *There should be a union of India embracing both British India and States which should deal with the subjects of foreign affairs, defense* and *communications and have power to raise necessary finances.*

2. *There should be three groups of provinces; Group A comprising the six Hindu majority provinces; Group B, the provinces of the Punjab,* N. W.F.P., *Sindh and Balochistan and Group C, the provinces of Bengal and Assam.*

3. *The provinces and States* should *be the basic units. All subjects other than the union subjects and all residuary powers would vest in the provinces; the States would retain all subjects and powers other than those ceded to them.*

The plan also proposed that in the constituent assembly each province should have seats in proportion to its population. Each of the three groups, A, B, and C of the constituent assembly should settle the Constitution for the provinces included in each group. The new legislature of any province shall be free to opt out of the group. The Mission also proposed of setting up of an interim Central Government in which the Indian nationals shall hold all portfolios.

Gandhi criticized the plan and made his own interpretations. He maintained that the plan was *'an appeal* and an *advice'* and that the constituent assembly as, a sovereign body, could vary the plan. The

Congress Working Committee, in its resolution of May 24th, 1946 followed the line given by Gandhi and demanded transfer of power to Hindu dominated legislature.

The Muslim League Council met on 3rd June, 1946 and deliberated for three days. The Muslim League after weighing the pros and cons, decided on June 6, 1946 to accept both the long term and short-term plan of the Cabinet Mission. The Muslim League Council affirmed that the Muslim League would join the constitution making body. With regard to the proposed Interim Government, it authorized its President to negotiate with the Government.

Negotiations for the formation of Interim Government proved difficult beyond expectations. The Congress refused to accept Viceroy's proposal to include Muslim League in the Interim Government. The Congress wanted to include the Muslim League in the Interim Government with lesser seats and objected to giving equal number of seats to the Muslim League. The Viceroy distributed twelve seats of Government, five Congress, Muslim League five, one Sikh and one Christian. Congress refused to accept this arrangement and demanded that one seat out of Muslim League share should be given to a non-leaguer Muslim appointed by the Congress. The Viceroy again proposed that there should be 13 seats, six Congress, five Muslim League and two representatives of the minorities. Congress did not agree to this proposal too.

The Viceroy then issued invitations to 14 persons at his own to join the Interim Government. The list included the name of the Quaid-e-Azam who declined to join. The Viceroy also declared that it was the intention of the Government to proceed with the formation of the Interim Government even if any of the two major parties refused to join. The Viceroy declared that in the event of any major party refusing to join the Government, the Interim Government would be formed with the party willing to join.

A secret agreement was concluded between Gandhi, Patel and Cabinet Mission. Gandhi was given assurance if Congress refused to join the Interim Government; Muslim League would not be invited to join the Government alone. In keeping with the understanding reached between Gandhi and Cabinet Mission the Congress refused to join the Interim

Government but accepted the Long Term Plan of the Cabinet Mission about constitution making.

Immediately following the rejection by the Congress, the Muslim League passed a resolution agreeing to join the Interim Government on the basis of Viceroy's and Cabinet Mission statement. In terms of that statement the Viceroy should have called upon the Muslim League to form the Government along with others willing to join the Government. But despite Quaid-e-Azam's reminders the Viceroy formed Caretaker Government of permanent officials. Quaid-e-Azam said, "I maintain that the Cabinet Mission and Viceroy *have* gone back on *their words* within ten *days of the publication of their* final proposal in not implementing their *statement, statesmen should not eat* their *words.'*

The Muslim League, betrayed by the Viceroy and the Cabinet Mission, decided to take direct action and withdrew its approval of the short term and long-term plan of the Cabinet Mission. Congress immediately, on Muslim League's decision at withdrawing its approval of the Cabinet Mission plan, announced its acceptance to join the Interim Government. The Viceroy gave invitation to the Muslim League to join the Government, which the Muslim League accepted in the larger interest of the Muslims of India.

JUNE 3 PLAN

Prime Minister Attlee declared in Parliament that India would be freed by 20th of February 1948. He said in the House of Commons, *if* is a mission, it is a mission *of fulfillment."*

Lord Mountbatten had been appointed as the last Viceroy of India who was to replace Lord Wavell. Lord Mountbatten arrived in India on March 22, 1947. He came charged with the mission to make a peaceful transfer of power from British to Indian hands by June 1948.

Lord Mountbatten was told by the Prime Minister Attlee to hand over the power to the Indian by 1st June, 1948. The Prime Minister in a letter directed the Viceroy to do his utmost to keep the unity of India. The Prime Minister wrote that it was the definite objective of His Majesty's Government to obtain a unitary Government for British India in accordance with the Cabinet Mission Plan.

Upon his arrival in India, Lord Mountbatten had to face many problems regarding a peaceful transfer of power. Muslim League was demanding partition of India and was not prepared to accept anything less of Pakistan. On the other hand Congress was pressing hard for the transfer of power to the Hindu dominated Constituent Assembly. Another set of problem was created by the choice of June 1948, as the effective date for the transfer of power. The fifteen months were too short a period for the innumerable political, constitutional and administrative decisions involved.

Lord Mountbatten soon began negotiations with the political leaders of India. Having successfully completed his task Mountbatten entered into discussions with Indian leaders on the constitutional problems. After prolonged talks, Mountbatten had worked out a partition plan by the middle of April 1947. It was felt if the partition came it should be the responsibility of the Indians.

The Working Committee of Congress met on May 1, *1947* and gave its acceptance of the partition plan. Muslim League also gave its approval to the final draft of the partition plan.

Mountbatten went to England to seek the approval of the British Government, which was duly accorded. The plan was issued on June 3rd, 1947 and is known as *June 3* Plan. The main characteristics of the plan are as follows:-
The Legislatures of the Punjab and Bengal shall decide whether the provinces should be divided or not.

- The Indian people shall make the Constitution of India. This Constitution shall not be applicable to those areas whose people reject it.
- Referendum shall be held in N.W.F.P.

- Province of Balochistan shall adopt appropriate way to decide its future.

- States shall be free and independent to join one or the other country.

- A Boundary Commission shall be set up after partition, which will demarcate the boundaries of the two countries.

- Both countries shall have their own Governor Generals who will be the Executive Heads of their respective countries.

- Military assets shall be divided amongst two countries after partition.

RADCLIFF AWARD

It was provided in June 3 Plan that as soon as the Legislatures of Punjab and Bengal decided in favor of partition, a Boundary Commission should be set up to demarcate the boundaries. Since the Legislatures of Bengal and Punjab voted in favor of partition, Boundary Commissions were set up for Punjab and Bengal under the Chairmanship of Sir Cyril Radcliff, an eminent lawyer of London. Each Boundary Commission was to consist of an equal number of representatives of India and Pakistan and one or more impartial members. The claims of India and Pakistan were bound to conflict and there was little chance that the representatives of India and Pakistan on the Boundary Commission would reach any agreement among themselves. There was a proposal to put the problem of boundary demarcation into the hands of UNO, which Nehru refused to accept. The Quaid-e-Azam wanted three law Lords from the United Kingdom to be appointed to the boundary Commission as impartial members. Mountbatten insisted on Radcliff who would have the power to make the award in case of a deadlock. The members of the Punjab Boundary Commission were Justice Din Muhammad and Justice Munir on behalf of Pakistan and Justice Mehr Chand Mahajan and Justice Tej Singh on behalf of India. The members of the Bengal Boundary Commission were Justice Abu Saleh Muhammad, Justice M. Akram and Justice S.A. Rahman on behalf of Pakistan, and Justice C.C. Biswas and Justice BB.K. Mukerjee, on behalf of India.

The Commission was set up by the end of June 1947. Radcliff arrived in India on July 8, 1947. The two Commissions were assigned the responsibility of demarcating the boundaries of the two parts of the Punjab and Bengal on the basis of the contiguous majority areas of Muslims and non-Muslims.

India and Pakistan agreed to accept the award of the Boundary Commission and to take proper measures to enforce it. Radcliff did not take part in the public sittings of the Commission, in which arguments were presented by the Muslim League, the Congress, the Sikhs and other interested parties. He studied the record and proceedings of the meetings and held discussions with other members of the Commission. As expected the members of the Boundary Commission were unable to reach agreement on the boundaries. Lord Radcliff, as the Chairman, gave his award.

The Radcliff award was unfair to Pakistan because it awarded many Muslim majority areas in the Punjab and Bengal to India. In Bengal, the great city of Calcutta occupied immense importance. It was the capital of the province, its only major port and the biggest industrial commerce and educational center. Being the center of all activities Calcutta was the most developed area of the province. The entire development of Calcutta was mostly based on the toil of Muslim peasantry of Bengal. East Bengal produced most of the raw material which had to be sent to Calcutta because all the factories and mills were in or around Calcutta. Wi'hout Calcutta Eastern Bengal would prove to be a rural slump. For Pakistan, separated by one, thousand miles of Indian Territory, the importance of sea communications and hence of Calcutta could not be ignored. For that very reason the Congress leaders were determined to deny Calcutta to Pakistan and insisted on retaining it in India. Mount batten was in favor of giving Calcutta to India. Radcliff, in accordance with the desires of Mount batten, awarded Calcutta to India in spite of the Muslim claim to it.

Although the Muslims formed only a quarter of the population of Calcutta, yet the hinterland on which the life of Calcutta depended was a Muslim majority area. Calcutta had been built mainly on the resources of East Bengal. Pakistan, therefore, had a strong claim upon Calcutta and its environs. Mount batten had entered into a secret agreement with the Congress leaders to get Calcutta for India. Sardar Patel declared in a speech in Calcutta on January 5, 1950: *We made a condition that we could only agree to partition if we did not lose* Calcutta. If Calcutta is *gone* then India is *gone.'*

In case of Punjab the award was again partial and against Pakistan. The award that Radcliff gave in the Punjab chopped off a number of contiguous Muslim majority areas from Pakistan. In case of India not a single non-Muslim area was taken away from her. In Gurdaspur district two contiguous Muslim majority tehsils of Gurdaspur and Balata were given to India along with Pathankot tehsil to provide a link between India and the State of Jammu and Kashmir. The Muslim majority tehsil of Ajnala, in the Amritsar district was also handed over to India. In Jullander district the Muslim majority areas of Zira and Ferozepur in the Ferozpur district, were also given to India. All of these areas were contiguous to the Western Punjab.

Commenting on Radcliff's award in a radio speech, the Quaid-e-Azam said, *the division of India is now finally* and *irrevocably effected. No doubt we feel the carving out of this great* independent *Muslim State has suffered* injustices. *We* have been squeezed *in as* much *as* it was possible, *and the latest* blow *that we have received* was the *award of Boundary Commission.* It may *be wrong,* unjust and *perverse;* and it *may* not be a judicial *but* a political *award, but we have agreed to abide by it and* it is *binding* upon us. *As honorable people we* must *abide by it. It may be our misfortune but* we must *bear up this one more blow with fortitude, courage and hope."*

INDEPENDENCE ACT 1947

On July 4, 1947, the Viceroy announced the Partition Plan on radio. According *to* this Plan, India was divided into two sovereign -States of Pakistan and India and the British control over India would come to an on 15th August, 1947. The princely States were given the option to join one or the other country. They were also authorized to have their independent legislatures, constitutions and other administrative departments. The Act of 1935 was to remain in force until both countries drafted their own Constitutions. Both countries would have right to remain in the British Commonwealth if they so desired. The agreements between the princely States and the British Government would come to an end with the end of British control over India. The British Parliament approved the Independence Act on 14th July, 1947 by which Pakistan came into existence as the biggest Islamic State of the world.

CHAPTER IV

DIFFICULTIES AND PROBLEMS ON THE ESTABLISHMENT OF PAKISTAN

Pakistan came into existence as the fifth most populous and biggest Muslim State on 14th August, 1947. Lord Mountbatten, the last Viceroy of United India came to Karachi to hand over power to the First Constituent Assembly of Pakistan and said, ` *the birth of Pakistan is* an event in *history. We who are part of history* and helping to make it *are not* well placed *even if wished to moralize on the event, to look back to survey the sequence of past that led to it. There* is no time to *look* back. There is *only* time to *look forward.'*

On 15th August, 1947, the last Friday of the holy month of Ramadan, a day to which the Muslims attach great sanctity, the Quaid-e-Azam assumed the office of Governor General of Pakistan. The National Flag with the crescent and star was unfurled. Cabinet was sworn in and Pakistan was born.

The emergence of Pakistan, after a long and strenuous freedom movement, was in fact a great victory of the democratic idea of life. The staunch faith of people in the idea of Pakistan and their ready acceptance of the dynamic leadership of the Quaid-e-Azam, made it possible to achieve Pakistan despite stubborn opposition from the British and the Hindus. The Muslims of India, happily and valiantly, laid down their lives and properties to achieve a destination in which they saw the fulfillment of their dreams of living an independent life. The Quaid-e-Azam won Pakistan for his people with his own unflinching spirit and people's trust in his sincere and dauntless leadership. The people were profoundly grateful to the father of the nation. The Quaid-e-Azam in his message to nation on 15th August, 1947 said, *'My thoughts are with those valiant fighters in our cause who readily* sacrificed all they *had,* including *their li*ves, *to make Pakistan possible.'*

The British and the Hindus, at last, had to surrender before the exemplary struggle of the Muslims of India and accept the demands of the partition of India. The Hindus and Congress, however, did not accept the partition from the core of their heart and always looked for the opportunities to harm Pakistan. The Indian leaders accepted partition with the hope of undoing it and establishing their hegemony over the whole of the sub-continent. According to Bracer, *most of Congress leaders and Nehru* among *them, subscribed to the view that Pakistan was not a viable state politically, economically, geographically or militarily -- and that sooner or later the areas which had ceded would be compelled by force of circumstances to return to the fold.'* With these sentiments the Congress leaders accepted Pakistan as for them Pakistan was a transient phase, a tactical retreat that did not affect their strategic aims. But the Quaid-e-Azam declared *'Pakistan had come to exist for ever and it will by the grace of God exist for ever.'*

The Congress leaders did their utmost to damage Pakistan. They took measures with the connivance of the British, to create problems for Pakistan so that it should not survive as an independent and sovereign State. The Indian Government adopted every possible means to strangle Pakistan's economy. Due to these steps Pakistan had to face great difficulties which are given below:-

FORMATION OF A GOVERNMENT
The immediate task before the nation, after independence, was to set up workable administrative and governmental machinery to run the affairs of the newly born State. The biggest administrative problem facing Pakistan was the acute shortage of competent and experienced personnel in the Central and Provincial governments. There were serious deficiencies in cadres of general administration as well as in the technical services.

The Quaid-e-Azam became the first Governor General of Pakistan. He had full authority on civil as well as on the armed assets. On June 3, 1947, Field Marshal Auchinleck was entrusted with the job of dividing the armed forces and army assets.

Congress and Indian Cabinet Ministers created many hurdles in the division of military assets. The assets were to be divided with a ratio of 36% and 64% between Pakistan and India respectively. All the Ordnance Factories, sixteen in number, were located in the Indian union. The Indian leaders were stubbornly opposed to the transfer of any Ordnance Factory to Pakistan. They were not even prepared to part with any piece of machinery, which may have been given to Pakistan.

A program for the transfer and division of army assets was chalked out. It was decided that the army soldiers and men, who opted either for Pakistan or India, should report in their countries of choice by the 15th of August, 1947. It was also decided that until the completion of division of armed forces and military assets, the armed forces would remain under the control of one Commander.

The armed forces personnel were given full liberty to opt for any country. It was decided that the Muslim regiments would go to Pakistan while the Hindu and other non-Muslim regiments would go to India. No problem was faced with regard to the division of army men and soldiers. But the Indian leaders created many hurdles in the division of military assets and equipments. The equipment, which was given to Pakistan, was mostly in shabby condition. The machinery was obsolete and out of order. A financial settlement was arranged and Rs. 60 million in lieu of Pakistan's share of ordnance factories was given to Pakistan. With this amount the Ordnance Factory at Wah was established.

The British Commanders, supervising the division of assets, could not get rightful share for Pakistan in the military assets. Field Marshal Auchinleck, who supervised and conducted the division of assets, was bitterly criticized and compelled to resign. Due to this determined opposition, there were no means by which Pakistan could get its due share and had to be content with what was given to her.

THE MASSACRE OF MUSLIM REFUGEES IN INDIA
During the movement of Pakistan the Hindus and Sikhs, with the blessings of the British rulers, had on many occasions, slaughtered the Muslim masses in India for their harassment and intimidation. These communal riots before the partition of India had been local affairs, which erupted for few days and then died down leaving no significant impact on the people. The 1946 massacre of Muslims of Bihar was the first organized attempt of extermination of the Muslims.

At the time of creation of Pakistan, the problem of refugees became a serious and difficult issue for the Government. The

Hindus and Sikhs had chalked out a systematic program for the massacre of Muslim refugees migrating to Pakistan. The Punjab massacre of Muslim refugees was not spontaneous but planned by the Sikhs with a certain motive and differed in kind from all previous disorders. They had defined political objective, and to gain it, controlled violence and terror were used. The Sikhs organized military offensive on the refugees that would end only when the objective was accomplished. They had at their disposal the trained and armed forces of Hindu and Sikh States and had planned the massacres at a time when the Governments of East and West Punjab were busy in the re-organization and, therefore, least capable of paying an effective attention to any other matter.

The Hindu and Sikh rulers of States played the most inhuman and ignoble role in this horrible tragedy in the history of mankind. They fully co-operated with the Hindus and Sikhs in the ruthless slaughter of the Muslim refugees. In the Punjab States of Patiala, Kapaurthala, Alwar and Bharatpur, the State troops joined with Hindus and Sikhs bands in the systematic extermination of the Muslim population. The State troops were employed in the massacre of Muslims with Hindus and Sikhs who were allowed to kill and mutilate Muslim men, women and children. The States of Kapurthala and Patiala provided secret *bases* to raiding Sikhs and Hindus to operate from. The State Governments also provided arms and ammunition to Sikhs and Hindus for killing the Muslims.

The Muslim massacres were not only confined to *the* countryside, worse things were happening in the *cities*. On August 15, 1947, the day of Indian liberation was celebrated very strangely in the Punjab. Sikh mob paraded a number of Muslim women naked on the streets of Amritsar, raped them on the roads and then cut some of them to pieces with Kirpans and burnt the others alive. In this way the revenge for the partition of India was taken from the Muslims.

The Sikhs were clearing East Punjab of Muslims, butchering hundreds daily, forcing thousands to flee and burning Muslim villages. The Sikh *'Jathas'* always attacked the Muslim migrants on their way to Pakistan. These raiding Jathas were given full protection by the authorities. The Sikhs slaughtered the poor men, women, young and old in the cold blood. The minor children were killed in a ruthless manner in the presence of their helpless parents. Women were raped and young girls were abducted.

Some migrants undertook their journey to Pakistan in trains under the protection of police and army. They also met the same fate. The trains were stopped at certain places and Hindus and Sikhs, armed with deadly weapons, would suddenly appear and killed the helpless refugees. They looted everything and left the trains in most miserable and horrible conditions. The trains reached Pakistan with large number of dead bodies and wounded persons to tell the tales of terrible atrocities committed by Hindus and Sikhs.

These were very hard days for the Muslims and the Government of Pakistan. The Pakistan Government was in great difficulty to provide shelter and food to the refugees who were pouring in large number. The Quaid-e-Azam was greatly perturbed over the miserable condition of the refugees. He strongly protested to the Indian authorities over the atrocities committed on the Muslims. The Indian leaders did not pay any heed to these protests and quietly sat with the most atrocious mass killings of the Muslims of India.

However, the Government with the help of social organizations ably and bravely dealt with the problem of refugees. The people of Pakistan also extended full assistance to their brethren in this hour of appalling distress. With the assistance of the people the Government was able to overcome the problem of refugees very soon.

DIVISION OF FINANCIAL ASSETS

The Indian leaders adopted every possible means to strangle Pakistan's economy so that the newly born state should not survive as an independent State. At the time of creation of Pakistan there was a cash balance of Rs. 4 billion which was lying in the Reserve Bank. This amount was to be divided proportionately amongst the two States by a Committee. When the division was decided Pakistan was to get 750 million rupees. The Indian authorities refused to transfer the amount on one pretext or the other.

The first installment of Rs. 200 million was paid. The rest of the amount was stopped on the advice of Sardar Patel who threatened that the amount shall not be paid until Pakistan acknowledged India's right over Kashmir. Mr. Gandhi intervened by a threat of going to hunger strike if the amount was not paid to Pakistan. On Mr. Gandhi's *insistence* Indian Government gave another installment of 500 million to Pakistan. The remaining amount of 50 million has not been paid till now.

CANAL WATER DISPUTE

The water dispute had its origin in the partition of Punjab. It came to light on April 1, 1948, when India cut off the flow of canal waters to West Punjab in Pakistan, causing dire threat of famine and loss of crops in West Punjab. The stoppage of canal waters, therefore, was a dire move on the part of the Indian leaders to satisfy their ignoble designs of damaging Pakistan's economy.

West Pakistan *has a* fertile soil but hot and dry climate. *The* rainfall is scanty and undependable. Agriculture, the mainstay of Pakistan's economy is, therefore, dependent almost entirely upon irrigation by canals drawn from the Indus and its five tributaries. The three western rivers, the Indus, the Jhelum and the Chenab, flow into Pakistan from the State of Jammu and Kashmir and the eastern rivers, the Ravi, The Bias and the Satluj, enter Pakistan from India.

In fact Pakistan's agriculture entirely depends upon the Indus water system, which is really a source of life for West Pakistan. On the other hand India has many river systems, which smoothly flow and fall into the sea unhindered. Much of Indian Territory also gets enough rains to support agriculture without irrigation.

It was decided at the time of partition that the canal Headwork would be given to India, which enabled India to cause a serious shortage of water. It also built dams over those rivers, which flow into Pakistan from India. Before partition India planned to build Bakhara dam on the river Satluj with a storage capacity of 4 million-acre feet. But before it could be completed, the downstream province of Sindh complained that the operation of Bakhara dam would adversely affect the functioning of its link canals.

The partition of Punjab cut across the rivers and canals, making India and Pakistan upper and lower beneficiaries of waters. India promised not to interfere with the waters of those rivers, which were very vital for the irrigation of West Pakistan. But only after six months of partition, India stopped the waters of the rivers Ravi and Satluj, which was a grave blow to the agriculture of West Pakistan.

Pakistan, however, managed to overcome its problem arising out of blockade of water with the assistance of the World Bank. Pakistan also purchased water from India on payment to avoid economic disaster. The canal water dispute remained the main source of trouble between the two countries and had adversely affected their mutual relations.

On September 19th, 1960, an agreement was concluded between the two countries at Lahore, which is known as 'Indus Basin *Water Treaty*'. President Ayub Khan represented Pakistan while her Prime Minister Pundit Jawhar Lal Nehru represented India. According to the treaty the waters of the rivers Bias, the river Ravi and the river Satluj would he used by India while the waters of the river Chenab, the river Jhelum and the river Indus would be given to Pakistan. It was also decided that to make best use of the waters of these rivers, two dams, 5 barrages and 7 link canals would be built. India would pay 200 million rupees of the total cost of this project while the remaining amount would he paid by the friendly countries of Pakistan. Pakistan to a greater extent was able to overcome its irrigation problems by this Treaty.

THE ACCESSION OF PRINCELY STATES

The Indian princely States, numbering 562, comprised of 1/3rd of Indian Territory and a quarter of population. These states were not the part of the administrative machinery of British India. The Indian princes who had agreed to come under the Paramountancy of the British Empire ruled them. These States were internally independent but came under the British control with regard to their defense and foreign affairs.

When the country was divided the division of the princely States was also considered. On May 12, 1946, The Cabinet Mission advised the princes to extend co-operation for framing of constitution so that their interests should also be safeguarded. The Cabinet Mission also urged the rulers of the princely States to conform to the wishes and desires of their people and their religious trends while deciding the accession of their States with one dominion or the other. The Cabinet Mission informed the States that the British control over States would come to an end with the partition of India and all treaties between the States and the British Government would cease to exist from that date.

The British Government announced on February 20th, 1947, that the British paramountcy would not be transferred to any Government of British India. The British Government reiterated that British paramountcy over India and princely States would come to an end in June 1948, the date set for the partition of India. The Government left it to the will of the States to decide whether they wanted to remain independent or join any Government after partition.

By 15th August, 1947, all princely States except Junagadh, Kashmir and Hyderabad had announced their accession with either India or Pakistan. These States were to fall victim to Indian aggression later on.

Junagadh

Junagadh was a small maritime State, 300 miles down the coast from Karachi. It had an area of 3,337 sq. miles and a population of about 700,000. It was ruled by a Muslim ruler while the majority of population comprised of Hindu and Non-Muslim residents. After independence the State announced its accession to Pakistan because it could maintain its links with Pakistan by sea. The Muslim ruler of Manavadar, a smaller State contiguous to Junagadh, also acceded to Pakistan. The Government of Pakistan accepted the accession of Junagadh and Manavadar and the Indian Government was accordingly informed. The Governor-General of India, Lord Mountbatten telegraphed to the Governor-General of Pakistan and said: *"Such acceptance of accession* by Pakistan *cannot* but be regarded by the Government *of* India as an *encroachment on Indian sovereignty and territory and* inconsistent with *friendly relations* that *should exist between* the two *dominions.* This *action* is in utter violation *of* principles on which *partition* was *agreed upon and affected.*

With these protests the Indian Government took steps to solve the problem by force. Junagadh was surrounded by the Indian troops. The Jam sahib of Nawanagar, a leading Hindu prince of the area, urged the Indian Government to take immediate steps to ensure protection of Kathiawar States which had acceded to India and which were regarded as threatened by Junagadh's accession to Pakistan. An economic blockade of Junagadh was imposed and rail communication with India was cut off. In consequence Junagadh's revenue from customs and railways dwindled and there was a serious shortage of food. The provisional Government of Junagadh, with Gandhi's nephew Shamaldas Gandhi, as President, was set up at Bombay. The provisional government moved its headquarters to Rajkot near Junagadh, recruited volunteers and continued raids were launched on Junagadh.

The Government of Pakistan offered to settle the dispute by negotiations. The Government of India was, however, bent upon to settling the matter by force. The blockade and raids had created such chaotic conditions in Junagadh by the end of October 1947 that the Muslim ruler had to leave hurriedly for Karachi with his family.

On November 7, 1947, the liberation army of 20,000 men with armored cars and other modern weapons entered Junagadh. Two days later India assumed control of the entire State. The Government of Pakistan strongly protested on illegal occupation of Junagadh by Indian army and urged the Indian Government to withdraw its forces. The Government of India paid no heed and held a referendum after two months under the supervision of its armed forces. Majority of voters cast their votes, as expected, in favor of accession to India. Pakistan took up the matter with the UNO which is still undecided.

Kashmir

The State of Jammu and Kashmir was the most important State in the sub-continent. It is situated in the northern part of Indo-Pak sub-continent. It was the biggest State in India and occupied 84,471 sq. miles of territory. It has its boundaries with Tibet, China, Russia and Afghanistan, which have placed it in a great strategic position. The total population of the State, according to 1941 census, was about 4,000,000 which comprised majority of Muslim residents. The Muslims were in clear majority in every province of the valley.

A Dogra ruler Ghulab Singh ruled the State of Jammu and Kashmir. The Dogra dynasty had purchased the State from the British

Government in 1846 for 7.5 million rupees. The Treaty of Amritsar sold the State to Ghulab Singh. Ghulab Singh and his successors had established a despotic regime and ruled the State in an autocratic manner. The Muslims, in particular, were ruthlessly subjected to the most inhuman treatment. They were heavily taxed and made to live a very poor life. The Hindus were given preference in Government jobs over the Muslims. Cruel punishments were awarded to the Muslim inhabitants for a simple and minor breach of law.

The first battle for the freedom of State was fought in 1930. It was in consequence to the repressive and arbitrary rule of Dogra dynasty. The movement was organized and led by Sheikh Abdullah and Ch. Ghulam Abbas from the platform of Kashmir Muslim Conference.

The movement was quelled with the assistance of the British Government. The Maharaja, as usual, adopted repressive and tyrannical measures to suppress the movement. There were large-scale arrests and firings. Muslims from the neighboring areas entered Kashmir to help their Muslim brethren. A Commission under Sir Glancy was appointed which recommended few constitutional reforms.

Geographically the State is a continuation of the plains of West Pakistan into mountains. The rivers Indus, Jhelum and Chenab, which are the source of life for Pakistan, flow into Pakistan from the State of Jammu and Kashmir making it a whole geographical unit. The State had its road and rail links with Pakistan. Its imports and exports moved through Pakistan. Timber which was State's most important and lucrative source of revenue was exported by being floated down the rivers into Pakistan. The cultural connections between the Muslims of the State and that of Pakistan are so close as to make them virtually identical. The destiny of Kashmir and West Pakistan is linked together by nature and by all possible interests such as economic, religious, cultural, and strategic.

When the sub-continent was divided, Maharaja Hari Singh who too was a tyrannical ruler ruled the State. The people of Kashmir, at the time of partition, felt that in view of Muslim majority population, the State ruler would accede to Pakistan and they would soon be out of the clutches of the oppressive Dogra rule. The Maharaja came under immense pressure from the public to announce the accession to Pakistan at an early date.

The Hindu ruler did not want to accede to Pakistan. In fact he wanted to accede to India in spite of all the factors favoring State's accession to Pakistan. When the public pressure increased, the Hindu ruler, to divert the attention of the people, concluded a treaty with Pakistan. The Government of Pakistan, through this treaty, was assured that efforts shall be made to keep the State situation normal and the cultural and religious connections with Pakistan would be maintained.

With the conclusion of this treaty, a large scale Muslim massacre was planned to turn the Muslim majority into minority. The people revolted against this mass killing of the innocent people and the despotic policies of the Hindu ruler. More than 237,000 innocent Muslim were executed and nearly 500,000 were made to leave their homes and seek shelter in Pakistan.

The Hindu Maharaja could not control the uprising and made an appeal to the Indian Government to extend assistance to control the situation. The Indian Government put a condition and first asked for the accession of the valley with India. The Hindu ruler immediately complied and announced the accession of Jammu and Kashmir with India. The Indian Government at once landed its armed forces in Kashmir. The Quaid-e-Azam, the Governor General of Pakistan, ordered General Gracie, the then C-in-C of Pakistan Army, to attack Kashmir which he (Gen Gracie) could not carry out the orders immediately for some technical difficulties, but later compiled.

The people of Kashmir fought in a valiant manner against Indian forces. The volunteers from tribal areas entered Kashmir to help and assist their Muslim brethren and bravely fought by their side. Most of the area was liberated from the Indian occupation. As the Indian forces had entered Kashmir, the Pakistani borders were in danger. Pakistan had to move its army for the protection of its frontiers. A war between India and Pakistan began. Indian forces suffered heavy casualties and the Indian position in the valley aggravated. Pakistan got hold of important posts and places.

India, in view of its bad military position in Jammu and Kashmir, made a frantic appeal to the UNO on 1st January, 1948. India complained that Pakistan had committed aggression by sending its forces to Jammu and Kashmir as the State had already acceded to India. Pakistan rejected India's plea and said that only the people of Kashmir had the right to decide the fate of the valley.

The Security Council passed two resolutions on 3rd August, 1948, and 5th January, 1949, and urged the belligerent states to stop fighting forthwith. It was decided by the UNO that there would be a boundary line drawn under the supervision of UNCIP. Both the countries should withdraw to their previous positions so that the verdict of the people of Kashmir, for accession either to India or Pakistan, could be ascertained. Pakistan, in spite of its better military position, accepted cease-fire because she wanted the settlement of issue in a peaceful manner.

The Indian Government, on the other hand, did not want to lose Kashmir. Sheikh Abdullah, who by now, had come under the influence of Gandhi and Nehru, also did not want to see Kashmir going to Pakistan. In a press statement in Delhi on October 21st, 1947, Sheikh Abdullah said, "Due *to the strategic position that Jammu and Kashmir holds, if this State joins Indian Dominion, Pakistan would be completely encircled.'* By getting hold of Kashmir, India would he in a commanding position against Pakistan. India, therefore, immediately accepted cease-fire.

After the cease-fire India did not hold plebiscite in the valley of Kashmir as was decided by the resolutions of the UNO. The problem is still unsolved and has created a perilous situation in the region. There have been several efforts to solve the Kashmir problem which all proved futile because of the stubborn attitude of India. Many UN Commissions have visited Pakistan and India to sort out solution of the problem, but so far there have been no success.

The Kashmir problem could not be settled in spite of the best efforts of UNO. India rejected UNO proposals about Kashmir in *1949.* In 1950 a delegation under Sir Dickson came but Indian Government did not accept its recommendations. In 1951 and 1952 Dr. Graham came with a Commission whose proposals were rejected by the Indian Government.

In *1954* India held a so-called plebiscite in the valley under the supervision of its armed forces. A bogus assembly was set up which confirmed the Kashmir's accession with India. Pakistan refused to accept these elections. The Kashmir problem is the main hurdle in the way of good relations between Pakistan and India. This problem caused armed conflict between India and Pakistan in September 1965.

Although Pakistan could not resolve Kashmir problem in 1965 but at least it was established that Pakistan was in a position to face comparatively much bigger power. On the other hand India felt humiliated and in order to vindicate herself made preparations at all levels before taking on Pakistan and thus successfully avenged her defeat of 1965 by dismembering Pakistan in 1971. In 1973 Pakistan signed Simla agreement whereby both the countries are committed to resolve their differences including Kashmir issue through peaceful negotiations only. Since then Pakistan has taken initiatives and invited world attention at different forums to persuade India to fulfill its commitment to give right of self determination to the people *of* Kashmir. During Zia's regime Kashmir was almost neglected and the cause of Kashmir suffered a setback but since 1988 the Kashmir issue has been a priority in *the foreign* policy *of* Pakistan. In 1993 the matter was put up on the agenda of O.I.C. but then it was withdrawn by Pakistan on the advice of some friendly countries. Since diplomatic efforts did not bear fruits, Kashmiris have launched liberation movement and it has been going on for the last many years. Thousands of Kashmiri youths have laid down their lives so far.

Pakistan is morally supporting the Kashmiri Mujahideen and has also stepped up its efforts to make the world feel the gravity of the problem. Delegations have been sent to foreign countries to apprize the world of the atrocities and violation of human rights committed by Indian army in the valley. However, development in global politics after 9/11 has brought a change in the approach of both India and Pakistan towards solution of their outstanding disputes that was observed in the 12th meet of SARAC held January last in Islamabad. India has agreed to resume talk on all pending disputes including Kashmir and Pakistan also seems to be flexible. A number of sessions of talks at Secretary and foreign ministers levels have taken place and the summit talks are likely to be held in a couple months Sept-October, In the light of past experiences high hopes cannot be attached – but an unexpected surprise decision cannot be ruled out which may be forthcoming not in a very distant future accepted to the parties including people of Kashmir.

The regime under the leadership of Gen. Parvez Musharraf had taken practical steps to resolve the issues by holding talks at Agra in 2000, and then again to bring the Indian leadership on the negotiating table in 2004 to resolve all outstanding problems including the core issue of Kashmir. A number of sessions on secretary levels have been held and during U.N. session at New York in October 2004 where both Indian prime ministers Jag Mohan Sing and president of Pakistan Gen. Parvez Musharraf met, have reiterated their resolution to discuss the Issue of Kashmir in the forthcoming meetings as per schedule. World powers, The United State and British Prime Minister Tony Blair are actively involved to bring about a settlement of the issue in the interest of a lasting peace in the region.

But after the terror attack of November 26, 2008 on Mumbai, like all other outstanding problems, Kashmir issue has suffered a great setback, as every other link other than the investigation on terror attack stand suspended between India and Pakistan.

Hyderabad
Like, Kashmir, Hyderabad was also a very important State of the sub-continent. It had an area of 82,000 sq. Miles and a population of 160,000,000. It was a rich State and its annual revenue were 260 million rupees. It had its own system of currency *and postage* stamps. *The* population comprised of both Hindus and Muslims. The Hindus and non-Muslims were in majority, while its ruler, the Nizam, was a Muslim. The Nizam had the title of *His* exalted Highness" and was very popular amongst his people, both Hindus and Muslims. He was a generous and kind ruler and looked *after his* people like his own children. He was considered as a faithful ally of the British government.

Hyderabad, being a prosperous and a populous *state and* because of its prestige and importance, felt justified in maintaining an independent status of a sovereign State. However, the Viceroy Lord Mount batten made it clear to the Nizam that it was not possible for the British Government to agree to the dominion status for the State. Mount batten also referred to the geographical location of the State and was of the opinion that the State could not remain independent for long as it was surrounded by the Indian territory from all sides. He impressed upon the Nizam to accede to India.

Being a Muslim, the Nizam of Hyderabad, would have desired to accede to Pakistan if ever need arose. The Indian Government, knowing the intention of Nizam, began pressurizing him for acceding to India. Lord Mountbatten, the Governor General of India, did his best to bring Hyderabad in India's fold. The Nizam was not willing to sign the document for accession to India. He was willing to enter into a treaty with India in respect of defense, foreign affairs and communications. The Government of India, however, insisted on accession and would not agree to anything less.

A standstill agreement between India and Hyderabad was concluded, in November 1947. The Nizam also gave a secret promise to Mountbatten not to accede to Pakistan. K.M. Munshi was appointed India's agent in Hyderabad. He was a staunch believer of United India. After taking charge he began inciting the Hindu population. Allegations of violating the standstill agreement were leveled against Hyderabad. Nizam was asked to arrest Qasim Rizvi, a nationalist leader of Ittehadul Muslimin. On August 24, 1948, Hyderabad filed a complaint before the Security Council of the UNO. But before the Security Council could arrange the hearing of the complaint, Indian armed forces entered Hyderabad. After a brief resistance the Hyderabad army surrendered on Sept. 17, 1948. In due course the State was dismembered and incorporated into the different provinces of the Indian Union. The complaint before the Security Council is still pending.

CONSOLIDATION OF THE NEWLY BORN PAKISTAN

ROLE OF QUAID-e-AZAM

Pakistan had to face many problems after its emergence created by the Indian Government and Congress leaders. The Congress leaders did not want to see Pakistan coming into being as a free and independent country. When *they* failed to stop the emergence of Pakistan, they created problems for the newly born country to cripple its administration from the very beginning.

The Indian Government refused to give equitable share to Pakistan in assets. The defense forces with their armory were neither divided equitably nor given enough time to get posted in their respective countries. The cruel and inhuman mass killings of the refugees followed. The poor migrants, after being looted and mutilated, were pushed into Pakistan to paralyze the Government. But Pakistan came out of this calamity triumphantly under the dynamic leadership of the Quaid-e-Azam who surmounted these hurdles due to his deep-rooted strength of conviction, indomitable courage, political tact and sincerity of purpose.

Lord Mount Batten, the last viceroy of India, wanted to become the joint Governor General of Pakistan and India. Pundit Nehru had already accepted him as the Governor General of India. But Quaid-e-Azam, knowing Mount batten's intentions and his close relations with Nehru family and other Congress leaders, refused to accept him as the Governor General of Pakistan. On Quaid-e-Azam's refusal to accept him as Governor General of Pakistan, Mount batten always carried an ill will against Pakistan and damaged Pakistan's cause on all subsequent occasions.

The Congress leaders, with the connivance of Lord Mount batten, created many problems for the newly born country. The Government of Pakistan had to face these difficulties with resolute courage and determination under the leadership of the Quaid-e-Azam who came forward with the unflinching faith to rescue the nation. The Quaid-e-Azam led the nation successfully out of despair and put them on the path of prosperity and progress. His dynamic leadership created great confidence amongst the people, who supported him to face every difficulty with courage and determination.

Quaid-e-Azam became the first Governor General of Pakistan on 15th August, 1947. He took oath as the first Governor General of Pakistan in the first Constituent Assembly of Pakistan on 14th August, 1947. The first cabinet of Pakistan was sworn in on 15th August, 1947 with Nawabzada Liaqat Ali Khan as the first Prime Minister of Pakistan. The cabinet included l .I. Chundrigar, Ghulam Muhammad, Raja Ghazanfar Ali Khan, Jogindar Nath Mandal (minority representative) and Fazal-ur-Rehman. Ch. Zafar Ullah Khan was made the first Foreign Minister of Pakistan in

December, 1947. The Quaid-e-Azam, after assuming the office of Governor General of Pakistan, paid his immediate attention to the following matters:-

REHABILITATION OF REFUGEES

The first and the immediate problem, which invited attention by the Government, was the rehabilitation of the refugees who had to leave their homes to begin a new life in Pakistan. The refugees, in miserable conditions, were pushed into Pakistan to create difficulties for the Government, which was busy in consolidating itself. Millions of mutilated persons were made to leave their hearth and homes for Pakistan simply to create economic problems for the newly born country and for its Government. The sinister objective was to overwhelm Pakistan with a torrent of uprooted and tormented refugees before the Government of Pakistan had time to set up workable administrative machinery.

Quaid-e-Azam met this challenge with courage and determination. He moved his headquarter to Lahore to give his personal attention to the grave problem of refugees. Quaid-e-Azam Relief Fund was created in which the rich and wealthy people were asked to donate generously for the rehabilitation of poor refugees.

The Quaid-e-Azam handled the situation arising out of the influx of refugees with vision, courage and wisdom. He made stirring speeches to revive faith and confidence in the distressed refugees. He said, "Do not be *overwhelmed* by *the enormity of the* task. *There are many examples* in *the history of young* nations building themselves up *by sheer determination and force of character. You have* to *develop the spirit* of Jihad, *you are a* nation whose history is full *with tales of heroism and bravery. Live up to your* tradition and *add to* another *chapter of glory."* The Quaid-e-Azam also appealed to the people for providing every possible assistance to their brethren. The people quickly responded to his call and came forward with every possible help and assistance for the refugees.

ADVICE TO THE GOVERNMENT OFFICIALS FOR CHANGE OF ATTITUDE

The Quaid-e-Azam warned the Government officials to change their attitude with the people after creation of Pakistan. He made it clear to the Government officials that they were no more the rulers and now should behave as servants of the people. The Quaid-e-Azam asked the Government officials to serve the people with national spirit. Quaid-e-

Azam addressed the Government officials on 11th October, 1947 and said, *"This is a challenge for us. If we were* to survive as a *nation we* will *have to face* these difficulties with a stern hand. *Our people are disorganized and* worried because *of the* problems they are *facing. We have to encourage them to pull them out of despair. It* has put *great* responsibility on the administration and *the people look for your guidance."*

The Government officials quickly took up the Quaid's advice and served the nation with zeal and national spirit in the most difficult conditions.

QUAID-E-AZAM'S CALL TO AVOID PROVINCIALISM AND RACISM

After the creation of Pakistan attempts were made from certain quarters to misguide the people. These elements, after failing miserably to stop the emergence of Pakistan, were trying to cripple Pakistan's administration. They spread rumors about Pakistan's viability to *exist as an* independent country. Sentiments of provincialism and racialism were aired to create administrative problems for Pakistan.

The Quaid-e-Azam immediately attended to this danger of provincialism and racialism. He advised the people to beware of such ignoble elements who wanted to destroy national unity and solidarity by spreading unfounded rumors. He addressed the nation and said, "In unity *lies strength. So long as we are united,* we *emerge victorious* and strong. If *we are not united we shall become* weak and disgraced. *We are* all Pakistanis. *None* of us is a Punjabi, Sindhi, Balochi, Pathan or Bengali. *Every one* of us should think, *feel* and act as a Pakistani and we should *feel proud* of being Pakistani alone."

The Quaid-e-Azam made strenuous tours of various provinces to attend to the problems personally. He aroused hope in the people of all parts of the country and reminded them of their responsibilities as members of *a free and* independent nation. A separate ministry was established for the States and Tribal areas to look into the problems of these areas. He ordered to withdraw forces from areas of tribal territories. He advised the tribesmen to look into their *affairs* by themselves as citizens of a free and independent Pakistan.

STEPS FOR CONSOLIDATION OF THE ECONOMIC SYSTEM

The Indian Government, as already mentioned, did everything to deny Pakistan its equitable share in the economic and other assets. The objective behind this denial was to cripple the economy of Pakistan.

Quaid-e-Azam immediately set to the difficult task of re-building the economic system of the new country. He had correctly realized that Pakistan will not be able to overcome its economic problems by the assistance of Reserve Bank of India alone. He, therefore, ordered that a State Bank of Pakistan be set up immediately and entrusted the job of setting up of the Bank to Mr. Zahid Husain. The State Bank of Pakistan was established on 1st July, 1948. The Quaid-e-Azam in his inaugural address said, *The* Bank symbolized *the sovereignty of our people* in *the financial sphere. He said that the* western economic *system has created many* problems *for* humanity. *He expressed* that the western *economic* system *will not help us* in setting *up a workable economic order.* He said that we *should evolve* an economic system based on Islamic *concept of* justice and *equality."*

SETTING UP OF ADMINISTRATIVE MACHINERY

Pakistan came into existence under the most appalling conditions. The Government of Pakistan could not get enough time to set up workable administrative machinery because of the immense difficulties. The Indian Government adopted delaying tactics in transferring the government servants and official records, which aggravated the situation.

The Quaid-e-Azam paid his attention towards setting up of the administrative machinery. Karachi was made the Capital of Pakistan where Central Secretariat was set up. The government officials began working with zeal and sentiments of sacrifice. There was no office equipment, no furniture, no official record and no stationery to pull the official routine. The high Government officials, full with national sentiments, did not care for the inadequacies they were facing and set to face the challenge under the dynamic leadership of the Quaid-e-Azam. Special trains were engaged to bring the Government officials who had opted for Pakistan. An agreement with the TATA Air Company was concluded for the transportation of the Government officials and their families.

In order to put the administrative machinery on smooth sailing, the civil services were re-organized in the light of the formula given by Ch. Muhammad Ali. The Civil Services Rules were drafted and the Pakistan Secretariat was established. Accounts and Foreign Services were introduced and the first Pay Commission was set up in February 1948. Headquarters for Navy, Army and Air Force *were* set up at different places. The Quaid-e-Azam, once again led the nation successfully in this crisis. In fact he created a great new country despite the difficulties and problems.

PRINCIPLES OF FOREIGN POLICY

Quaid-e-Azam paid his utmost attention towards foreign policy of Pakistan. He stressed on a foreign policy based on mutual friendship and equality. He gave priority to the relations with the Muslim countries. Foreign offices were opened which, in accordance with the instructions of the Quaid-e-Azam, set to the task of establishing relations with the other countries of the world. Diplomatic missions were set up in many countries, which worked day and night to make a happy image of Pakistan.

Pakistan became the member of UNO in September 1947 at the instance of the Quaid-e-Azam. Since then Pakistan has been playing its constructive and positive role for the international peace and justice.

Pakistan had to face difficulties in its foreign relations in the very beginning because of the Indian aggression in the States of Kashmir, Hyderabad and Junagadh. Pakistan had to fight a war imposed by India in the valley of Kashmir to liberate the poor Kashmiri Muslims and to save the Muslim population from the cruel atrocities of the Indian and State armies.

Quaid-e-Azam began negotiations with the Indian Government to solve the problem of Kashmir, Hyderabad and Junagadh. He also got in touch with the UNO and Commonwealth and impressed upon them to sort out some solution of the problems in order to finish tension and hostilities between the two countries.

Quaid-e-Azam lived for a very short time of little more than a year after independence. During this short period he fully devoted himself to the momentous task of consolidating and strengthening the newly born Pakistan. He worked continuous day and night ignoring the advices of his doctors. His health was falling rapidly because of intensive work. He died on 11th September 1948, on his way from Ziarat to Karachi in mysterious circumstances.

Chapter V

History of Constitution Making

After the partition, the first step for the framing of an Islamic constitution was taken by the Constituent Assembly, which passed the "Objective Resolutions" in 1949. The "Objective Resolutions" contained those steps and principles, which were to be taken for the fulfillment of the basic aim of the freedom struggle for the establishment of an Islamic society in Pakistan. After the passage of "Objectives Resolutions" the Constitutions of 1956, and 1962 Federal system of Government will be introduced in Pakistan.

- Principles of democracy, equality, freedom and social justice as enunciated by Islam shall be fully observed.

- Maximum efforts shall be made to enable the Muslims to order their lives in accordance with the teachings and requirements of Islam.

- The rights and interests of the minorities to freely profess and practice their religion will be safeguarded. They will also be provided the opportunities to develop their culture and civilization.

- All efforts will be made for the development and progress of the under-developed areas.

- Fundamental Rights of the citizens shall be fully safeguarded.

- Judiciary shall be independent.

ISLAMIC PROVISIONS OF THE 1956 CONSTITUTION

The first Constitution of the country was enforced on 23rd March, 1956. The Islamic provisions under this Constitution were as follows:

The name of the country will be *"Islamic Republic of Pakistan."*

The preamble of the Constitution embodied the sovereignty of God.

The Head of the State shall be a Muslim.

Islamic Advisory Council shall be set up to guide the people to order their lives in accordance with the Islamic principles.

No law, detrimental to Islam, shall be enacted.
A Commission will be set up by the Head of the State which will examine the present laws and will suggest changes-improvements.

The 1956 constitutions was not abrogated because of its deficiencies but it fell victim to selfish and short sightedness of the then head of state Mr. Sikandar Mirza, who having been frightened by long march of Muslim league under the popular leadership of Hussain Shaheed Suharwardy and Abdul Qayyum Khan, instead of holding elections and transferring power to the elected representatives invited army to perpetuate his authoritative rule. Gen. Ayub Khan, however, did not allow him to hold the slot of president and deported him to England, resuming powers as head of the state, abrogating the first constitution of Pakistan within its infancy

It was a highly undemocratic and unconstitutional step that paved way for the intervention of army in civil administration for all times to come and the country has already had such interventions in 1958, 1977 and 1999 in spite of the fact it entails capital punishment under the constitution for those who indulge in such intervention. The regime of *Gen.* Parvez Musharraf had adopted some constitutional measures to forestall any future recurrence. However, it is yet to be seen how far those measures remain effective and fool proof. In India our counterpart and immediate neighbor there army has never intervened in spite of worst civil crisis and allowed the politicians to settle their affairs themselves. India has fully exploited this weakness of Pakistan in the world to gain sympathies and to be known as a living example of western democracies in spite of her ill treatment of the minorities and denying the right of self-determination to the people of Kashmir.

The Constitution was enforced on 23rd March, 1956. It invited criticism from certain quarters because the condition of being a Muslim was meant for the Head of the State only. The political circles demanded that the condition of being a Muslim should have been laid down for the other important offices as well.

Gen. Muhammad Ayub Khan appointed a Constitution Commission under the Chairmanship of Justice Shahab-ud-Din in 1960 to frame the new Constitution. The Commission presented its recommendations to Muhammad Ayub Khan on 6th May, 1961. These recommendations were handed over to a Committee headed by Justice Manzoor Qadir for further scrutiny. The Committee thoroughly examined the recommendations and presented its report to President Muhammad Ayub Khan who promulgated the new Constitution in 1962.

SALIENT FEATURES OF THE 1962 CONSTITUTION

The name of the country will be 'Islamic Republic *of Pakistan"*

Islamic Advisory Council consisting of 12 persons shall be set up.

Sovereignty of God Almighty was re-affirmed in the preamble of the Constitution. It was also mentioned that authority and powers given to the representative of the people should be a sacred trust of God Almighty.

The Islamic Advisory Council shall be set up for three years. Islamic Advisory Council shall give suggestions to mould the laws in accordance with the Islamic principles.

The President of Pakistan shall be a Muslim by faith and belief.

The Constitution of 1962 remained in force till 1969. It also could not accomplish the desired target of political stability. The Constitution failed to establish a real Islamic system in the country because the Islamic provisions, introduced in the Constitution, were inadequate.

The Constitution was abrogated and Martial Law was imposed in the country for the second time in 1969. The nation had to bear the most unfortunate event of its dismemberment in 1971 because of Indian aggression. East Pakistan was separated from the rest of

Pakistan and emerged as an Independent State of Bangladesh on December 17, 1971. There was a great public resentment against the Government of President Yahya Khan who had to resign to make way for Mr. Zulfiqar Ali Bhutto to take over as an elected representative of the people.

Mr. Z.A. Bhutto, immediately after taking over the office of the President of Pakistan set himself to the task of Constitution making. The National Assembly was convened on 14th August, 1972 to discuss steps to be taken for making the new Constitution of the country. A resolution was adopted by which a Constitution Committee was set up under the Chairmanship of Mr. Mahmud Ali Qasuri. Mr. Mahmud Ali Qasuri resigned because of his differences with Mr. Z.A. Bhutto. After his resignation Mr. Abdul Hafeez Pirzada was appointed the Chairman of the Committee. The Committee, after a thorough examination, presented a draft Constitution before the assembly for approval on 2nd February, 1973. The Constitution was enforced on 13th April, 1973.

SALIENT FEATURES OF THE 1973 CONTITUTION
In spite of the fact, a socialist party drafted the Constitution of 1973, it is more Islamic in character than the previous Constitutions. It was emphasized that all efforts would be made to establish a real Islamic system in all aspects of social life and Islam would be the State religion.

It was made compulsory for the President and Prime Minister to be a Muslim by faith and belief and to profess faith in the finality of Prophet hood.

Clear and concise definition of a Muslim was laid down in the Constitution.

All laws of the State shall be brought into conformity with the injunctions of Islam.

The Government will take all possible steps to impart education of Islamiat and the Holy Quran.

f

The President and Prime Minister will take oath of their offices in accordance with the Constitution and openly express their faith in the Holy Quran and the finality of Prophet hood.

Islamic Advisory Council will be set up to recommend ways and means in order to bring the existing laws of the country in conformity with the Islamic principles.

It was emphasized in the Constitution that all steps will be taken to introduce 'Interest Free Banking System' in the country in the light of Islam.

The most significant feature of 1973 constitutions is that it has the approval of all the provinces and their legal representatives are signatory to the document. That is why Gen. Zia-ul-Haq in July 1977 when he staged coup against the democratic regime of Zulfiqar Ali Bhutto and imposed martial law did not abrogate the constitution and only suspended it and continued following it with certain amendments/Ordinances, realizing that once he abrogated the constitution it would be an uphill task to have consensus on the issues between provinces which were diplomatically settled by the previous regimes. Even Gen. Parvez Musharraf did not abrogate the 1973 constitution and kept it intact, only bringing amendments, with the approval of the constituent assembly. Undoubtedly this constitution is a remarkable feat of its creators; method to bring conformity with the Islamic principles of life.

CHAPTER VI

GEOGRAPHY OF PAKISTAN

AREAS AND LOCATION

Pakistan consists of four provinces; Balochistan, Punjab, Sindh, North-West Frontier and Federally administered tribal Areas. Of these Balochistan is the largest with an area of 347,186 sq. K. Meters., followed by Punjab with an area of 206,251 sq. k.m, inclusive of Federal Capital Area. Sindh has an area of 140,913 sq. k.m, North West Frontier 74,522 sq. k.m, and Federally Administered Areas 27,221 sq. k.m. Total area of the country being 796,095 k.m.

Longitudinal extent; Pakistan lies between 61 degrees east to 75 degree 31 minute east, stretching 885 K.M east to west.

Latitudinal extent; It lies between 23 degrees 30 minutes north to 36 degrees 45 minutes north, stretching 1600 K.M. north to south.

NEIGHBOURING COUNTRIES AND BORDERS

In the Northeast, it has a common border of about 595 k.m. with People's Republic of China along with its Gilgit Agency and Baltistan.

In the Northwest a narrow limb of Afghan territory, called Wakhan, separates it from Tajikistan.

In the West, it has a common border of 2,252 k.m. known as the Durand Line, with Afghanistan.

In the south of the Durand Line, there is a common border of about 805 k.m. with Iran.

The Arabian Sea lies in the south. In the East is the Indian territory of East Punjab and Rajasthan with a common border of 1610 k.m.

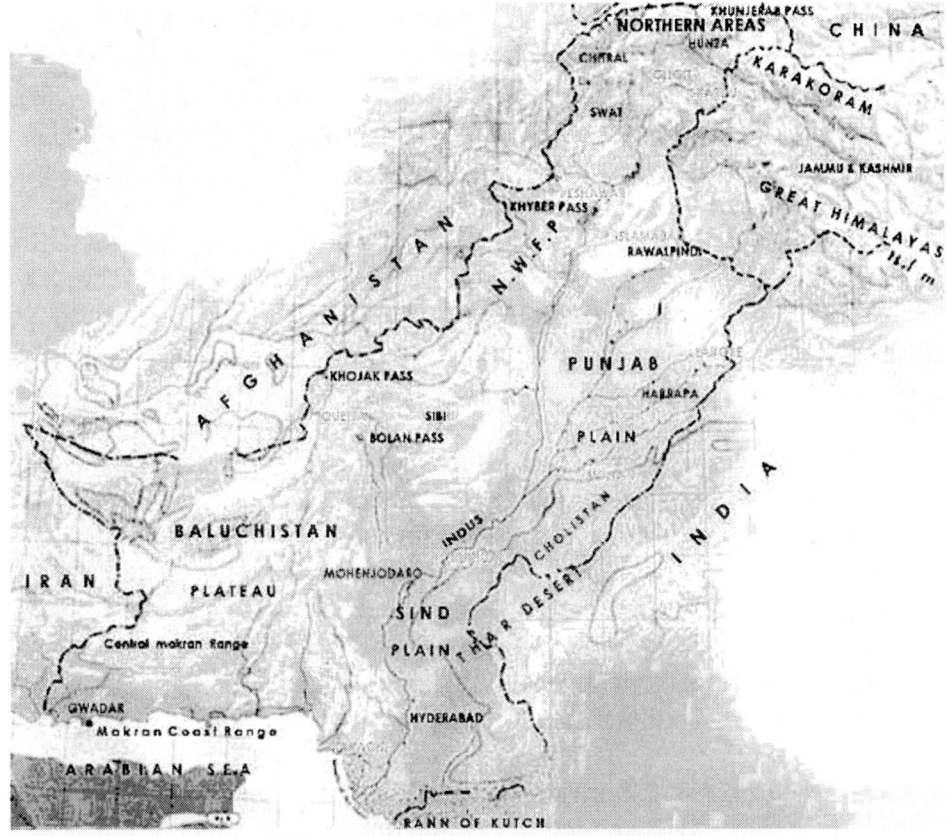

Figure 3: Pakistan Physical

STRUCTURE AND RELIEF

Structurally Pakistan consists of the highest mountain systems; the Himalayas, Karakoram, Hindukush and the Sulemans - a chain of young fold mountains uplifted in the quaternary era which surround it from north, and west. To its south and southeast there is a broad valley of river Indus and its tributaries; the Jhelum, Chenab, Ravi and the Satluj built by the eroded material which these rivers transport and deposited in the form of fine alluvium. Beyond this low lying region in the east and southeast lies the Deccan plateau- an ancient land mass made up of Basaltic lavas formed as a result of extensive volcanic activity. And to the west the Balochistan plateau.

It is believed that in the late Paleozoic times a great continent existed, known as Pangaea. Gondwanaland a part of the main continent got separated to be further splitting into Indian, Arabian, Burma and the Australian plates which having been detached from the main land drifted towards northeast. These plates normally move at the rate of few inches a year- Indian plate moves usually 2.4 inches a year. However, at times the plates slide abruptly as did happen in case of India Burma plates that slid about 50 ft. abruptly, resulting earth quakes of high intensity followed by severe tsunami, vertical sea waves, causing unprecedented colossal damage to life and property in the region. The Epicenter was located at Sumatra Indonesia-the worst hit, with 200,000 dead, followed by Sri Lanka 29,000 dead, India 9,000 dead, Thailand 5,000 dead, Maldives, 73, Malaysia, 66, dead and along the East African coast Somalia, 200 dead, Tanzania 10, Kenya 2, were reported.

This highest mountain wall of the world came into existence as a result of juxtaposition of north east moving Indian plate and the south west moving Eurasian plate to squeeze, fold and uplift a huge trough called Sea of Teethes located between the shields in which numerous rivers and glaciers deposited their eroded material. As a result of this convergence the deposited material in between got pressed and folded to form the world's highest and magnificent cordillera consisting of the chain of the great Himalayas, Hindukush the highest mountains of the world and the Sulemans a relatively lower range.

Similarly The Zagros, Elburz surrounding Iran and Ponitic and Taurus ranges of Turkey have been formed by the mutual movement of the Arabian and the Eurasian shields. The regions where the shields make the contact are known as the zones of convergence that bring about great structural changes and also result in great disasters. Rising of the great mountain wall and the recent Tsunami disaster in Indonesia, Thailand, Sri Lanka and India was the result of convergence of the northeast drifting Indian plate colliding against Burma plate The effect of such convergence is eminent by the fact that the Himalayan rim is still rising and gaining height and the instability in the region is manifest in the form of devastating earthquakes recently experienced in Turkey, Iran, and Pakistan. Pakistan is situated on the fault line at the collision of Indian plate with Eurasian plate, which is still in motion and hence the region has been geographically susceptible to earthquakes of mild and severe intensity:

Quetta experienced an earthquake of high intensity 8.1 on May 31, 1935, that left 33,000 dead and many injured, Bhisham Pattan earthquake of 1972 with intensity 7.5 also caused colossal loss of life and property in the area. The October 8, 2005 earthquake with an intensity of 7.6 occurred in the northern areas of Pakistan - Mansehra, Balakot, Kaghan and Muzaffarabad and adjoining areas both, falling in Pakistan and Indian held Kashmir. The catastrophe took a death toll of more than 70,000 and injured more than 100,000 and rendered millions shelter less. Countries of the entire world offered their sympathies and rushed to help to rescue the trapped victims. Volunteers from all over the world doctors, nurses, Civil and armed personnel participated in rescue work. Large sums of money were announced by many countries as Pakistan alone was not in a position to handle the catastrophe of that magnitude. Hundreds and thousands of people in view of the danger of repeated seismic activity had been forced to shift in the temporary huts tents and were provided with food, clothing, beds, blankets, medical facilities etc. as the life in the region practically came to stand still and no economic activity could be possible when the roads and almost all infra structures had been disrupted. Then again severe cold weather conditions, rain and snow fall further added to the miseries-hampered rehabilitation work.

STRATEGIC IMPORTANCE OF PAKISTAN

Pakistan is surrounded by India in the east, Iran in the west, Afghanistan in the North West, Russia separated by a narrow limb of Afghan territory in the north and China in the North East. Pakistan thus enjoys a bridge like position on one of the most important land routes connecting Europe and the Middle East Arabian Sea an important all season water body lies in the South. Because of its unique strategic location- gateway to the Sub-continent lying on both important land and water routes Pakistan enjoys an enviable strategic position in the world.

Highest continuous rim including Kara Kuram and the Himalayas in the north have served as natural barrier to the invaders - but comparatively lower and less contiguous ranges of Hindukush and the Sulemans in the west, crossed by rivers; provide easy access- passes; Khyber, Tochi, Gomal and Bolan to the sub-continent.- the region has thus a great historical past - its geopolitical significance has attracted one invader after another. Alexander the great swept in 329 B.C. who paved the way for subsequent adventurers. In 642 A.D, Arabs invaded the region and introduced Islam; followed by Persians, until conquered by Ghaznavids (Turks) in A.D. 998. Babar, the founder of Mughal dynasty stepped in 16th Century; large number of Sofia Kirams, Travelers, Scholars and Historians also used this route to have an access to a land of agricultural abundance (Indo-Ganges plains), a populous and prosperous area with advanced civilization and culture.

Arabian Sea a warm water body that washes the southern coast of Pakistan has all along been an earnest desire of USSR to gain its approach. Occupation of Afghanistan in 1979 by her was an attempt to fulfill that ambition. Her exodus from Afghanistan in 1989 by USA was primarily to frustrate that move, which could be possible largely with the help of Pakistan a key region. Again Pakistan has been instrumental in finishing Taliban regime and fighting the resultant terrorism. This significant geopolitical position and the role that Pakistan has played in the War against terrorism merited a frontline country in the global politics.

PHYSICAL FEATURES

Pakistan is a land of diversified relief. In the north, the Himalayan Ranges, the Kara koram Range and Hindukush lie beyond it. The Himalayas have an average elevation of 6,100 meters with some of the highest peaks in the world. K-2 (Mount Godwin Austin) 8,616 meters, is the highest peak of the Kara Koram Range, while Trich Mir, 7,736 meters is the highest peak of the Hindukush. Below the Kara korams is the parallel range of Himalayas extending far to the East and on the West ending up at the Nanga Parbat 8,215 meters.

Out of the total area of 796,095 sq. km. about 475,884 sq. km. in the North West and west form a highly differentiated mountainous terrain. The remaining 320,211 sq. km. presents a flat and gradational surface. The whole land, excluding most of Balochistan, falls into the Indus system of rivers. The unit includes the northwestern hills, northern and northwestern sub mountain, upper and lower Indus plains and parts of Balochistan, which is a region of small rivers. Large parts of it form areas of inland drainage.

PHYSICAL DIVISIONS

Pakistan comprises of six major physical divisions or regions:

1. Northern mountains

2. Western off shoots of the Himalayas.
3. Balochistan Plateau.

4. Potowar Plateau and Salt range.

5. Upper and Lower Indus Plains.

6. The Thar Desert.

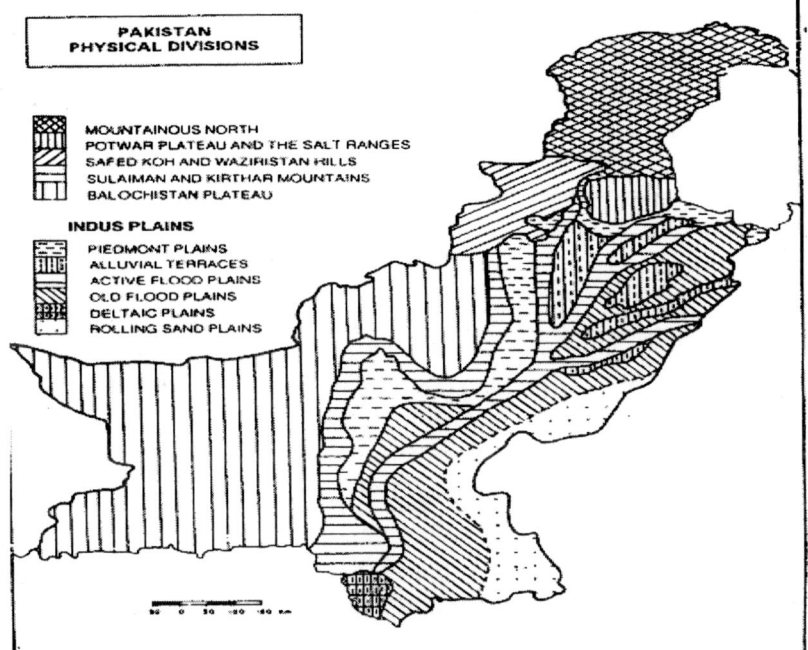

Figure 4: Pakistan Physical Divisions

NORTHERN MOUNTAINS

The north eastern mountains are the highest mountains of the world known as the "The Himalayas" comprising of a series of ranges situated in the north-east of our country. The Himalayas stretch like a how in the north of Indo-Pak sub-continent, having a length of about 2,700 km.

The part of this mountain which came into our share consist of four parallel ranges and between these ranges lie some beautiful valleys, like Gilgit, Hunza, Kaghan, Swat and the famous Kashmir valley; (a disputed preposition). According to their altitudes these ranges can be divided as under:

(a) The sub-Himalayas or Siwalik Range: These are lines of low altitude hills, situated adjacent to main areas of Hazara district in N.W.F.P. and Attock, Rawalpindi, Jhelum, Gujrat and Sialkot districts. Here these hills have a height of between 600 and 900 meters from the sea level. *They* extend over the Southern part of Hazara and Murree and include the Hills of Rawalpindi and the Pabbi Hills. Subjected to great strain and stress during the mountain building period, the Siwalik rocks are much faulted with many inverted and reverse folds and a high degree of dissection in the Pabbi Hills.

(b) The Pir Panjal Range: (The outer or lesser Himalayas) these ranges lie further to the north and mostly run parallel to the Siwalik Hills. Besides Murree and Hazara hills, Pir Panjal range is one of the famous ranges that lie in these areas. It has an average altitude of 4,200 to 4,500 meters; most of the peaks remain snow covered during winter. These are also covered with natural vegetation and forests are also seen at some places.

(c) The Central Himalayas: These Mountains lie in between the Pir Panjal and Kara koram Range. These ranges have an average height of 6,000 meters and most of the peaks-remain snow covered throughout the year. The highest peak of this range known as Nanga Parbat lies in Kashmir has a height of about 7,980 meters. The beautiful valley of Kashmir lies between the Pir Panjal range and the great Himalayas.

(d) The Kara koram Range: The famous Kara koram range lies to the north of central Himalayas in northern Kashmir and Gilgit area. This range has an average height of about 6,000 meters above sea level. The second highest peak of the world and highest peak of Pakistan Godwin Austin (K-2) having a height of 8,475 meters lies in this range near Gilgit. This peak was first conquered by an Italian expedition in 1954. The peaks having a high altitude remain snow covered throughout the Year.

The northeastern mountains of our country are quite high and it is difficult to cross them easily, but these mountains have a few passes which are used for communication purposes some of the important passes are:

The Babusar Pass: It is situated at a height of 4,317 meters from sea level. It serves traffic between Abbottabad and Gilgit.

The Lawari Pass: Its height is 3,069 meters and it connects Peshawar valley with areas of Chitral valley.

The Shandur Pass: It lies at a height of 3,161 meters and connects the areas of Chitral valley with the areas of Gilgit valley in Kashmir.

IMPORTANCE OF NORTHERN AREAS OF PAKISTAN

The region has great political and economic significance for Pakistan. Because of its great altitude and continuity it protects the country from being invaded by any power from this side. There are only few and difficult passes, which can be used by small caravans for trade purposes only: The completion of an all weather road, the Shahra-e-Resham with the collaboration of China has connected the country with our Northern neighbor i.e. China.

Besides, its political importance the region is very important from the economic point of view. Having been covered with snow for most of the year it forms a permanent reservoir of water. A number of rivers and glaciers start from this region and drain the country. They provide the most needed water supply for the country, river Swat, river Kunhar, Gilgit, and Hunza rivers are some of the more important tributaries of rivers Jhelum and Indus. All these valleys are littered with numerous small and insignificant glaciers but Hunza valley has world's famous glaciers like the Batura glacier.

Means of transport used vary with the changes in altitude, on the lower valleys and less steep slopes buses and cars are commonly used. On comparatively higher altitudes jeeps ply. Further up where roads and tracks are not well marked mules and yaks are the only means of transportation. Yaks are not only used as beasts of burden who can climb over steep altitudes carrying heavy loads on them, but they also serve as milk animals. Locally they are called as Khushgai and yield good quantity of milk.

The region is full of beauty and thus attracts a large number of tourists from home and abroad. There is adequate arrangement of boarding and lodging for the visitors, rest houses, Dak Bungalows, hotels, youth hostels etc., are always ready to welcome the visitors.

The mountains also protect the plain areas of our country from the cold winds of Central Asia during winter and thus the temperature remain high enough to continue out-door farming all the year round.

VALLEYS

Lower valleys are fairly hot in summer and cold in winter. Valleys of Kashmir, Kaghan and Swat get plenty of rainfall in monsoon season but rainfall in Hunza, Gilgit and Chitral valleys is not much. Nights are very pleasant in summer and snowfall usually starts in December and ends in March.

Valleys produce wheat, barley, maize and some rice. Mulberry, apricot, peaches, cherries and walnut are the main fruits. Dried Mulberry and apricot are used to sweeten the bread through winter months when the population is more or less confined to their houses. People are mainly farmers. Land is very less and growing season is limited but still *they* grow enough food to see them through a whole year. Lately with the spread of education, people have started coming down to plains for jobs and thus the area has shown tremendous leap towards modernization. In recent years many unskilled workers have gone to the Middle East and brought back money and new ideas.

DRESS AND CULTURE

People are staunch Muslims, most of them belonging to Agha Khani sect popularly known as Ismailees. Ladies do not observe 'Pardha' but they are very shy and rush to cover if they find an outsider near them. Marriage and other ceremonies are performed with the traditional pomp and show; still they lead a quiet, peaceful and contended life.

To a Pakistani, a visit to swat is most refreshing after the oppressive heat of the plains in summer. What strikes the beholder with wonder is the magnificent scenery. The spirit of the mountains seems to enter the soul of the beholder, and awed and entranced, he/she realizes the wondrous majesty of the 'everlasting hills'.

It is difficult to analyze the subtle appeal of Swat's scenery, first there is the grandeur of the hills themselves, with their rugged crests and lofty cliffs, beautiful at all times with an ever charming fascination. Sometimes they are ruddy with the light of sunset, another time they are calm and cold when darkness envelops them. At one time they are bathed by beautiful showers; at another thunder and lightning visits them. But the scenery at the top of the hill is most enchanting. The gigantic trees covered with thick foliage, with the white snow covering them in winter, and the swift gray clouds, passing just above them is a sight worth seeing.

The river of Swat adds greatly to the majestic beauty of the valley. Flowing downhill at a terrific speed the sparkling white water of this river reflects the shadow of every passing cloud. This river has always been a famous tourist's attraction due to its reputation as an extremely good trout fishing ground.

The inhabitants of these valleys though extremely poor, are very hospitable.

NORTH WESTERN MOUNTAINS

The northwestern ranges of Pakistan are also known as western branches of the Himalayas mountain - consist of several parallel ranges and *are* lower *in* altitude than the northeastern mountains. As most of these ranges lie outside the course of summer monsoons coming from Arabian Sea, so there the rainfall is low and they are almost bare of natural vegetation. These mountains act as a boundary between Afghanistan, Iran and Pakistan. These mountain ranges lie north to south, having some passes in riverbeds in the valleys. So the north western mountains can be sub-divided into following divisions:-

(a) The Hindu Kush: Between the Indus and Kabul rivers lies the Hindu Kush range. The average height of this range is between 3,000 to 4,800 meters above sea level. The highest peak of this area is known as Tirich Mir having an altitude of 7,708 meters. Most of the mountain remains snow-covered during winter months. The Kabul, Swat, Panjkora and Kunar flow through the minor ranges of this mountain. All these rivers join the Indus from the western side. This pass is a historical trade route between Peshawar and Kabul, the capital of Afghanistan.

(b) Koh Safaid: South of the Kabul River up to Kurram Pass lies the Koh Safaid range which runs east and west. These mountains have an average height of 12,000 feet and are often covered with snow in winter. The river Kurram lies to the south of this range. The Kurram Pass, which provides an easy route into Afghanistan, is situated near this range. Kohat is an important military base situated at the end of this pass.

(c) Waziristan Hills: Between the Kurram and the Gomal rivers lye the Waziristan Hills area. These hills have low altitude. The Tochi River joins the Kurram River from the west in North Waziristan. These rivers after passing through Tochi Pass join the Indus. Similarly Gomal River coming from Afghanistan joins Indus near Dera Ismail Khan. Bannu at Tochi Pass and Dera Ismail Khan at Gomal Pass are the important towns and military centers.

(d) The Sulemans: In the south of the Gomal river lies the Sulemans. It runs southward for a distance of about 480 km. Its highest peak is known as Takht-i-Suleman, whose height is 3,330 meters above sea level.

(e) At the southern end of the Sulemans Mountain, the Bugti and Marri Hills run from the southeast to the North West. The Bolan is the main river of this region. The Bolan River passes through the Bolan Pass, which provides communication facilities between Iran and Pakistan. Quetta is an important military base at the northern end of Bolan Pass.

(f) The Kirthar Hills: In the west of lower Indus plain lies a hilly area known as 'The Kirthar Hills'. These hills are not very high, their average height being about 2,100 meters. The Kirthar Hills are drained by the Hab and Lyari streams, which join the waters of the Arabian Sea near Karachi.

PASSES OF THE WESTERN MOUNTAINS

Passes through the western bordering mountains are of special geographical and historical interest. Comparatively broad passes, which are not difficult to traverse, occur south of the Kabul River. From north to south these are: Khyber, Kurram, Tochi, Gomal and Bolan. The Khyber is sufficiently wide for the passage of troops, only 1,067 meters high and Landi Kotal, its highest point, leads to the fertile valley of Peshawar at the head of the Indo-Gangetic Plain. The total length of the pass is 56 kilometers of which 40 k.m. lie (jamrud-Torkham) in Pakistan, and the remainder in Afghanistan. The Tochi Pass connects Ghazni in Afghanistan with Bannu in Pakistan via northern Waziristan. The Gomal Valley provides a route from Afghanistan to Dera Ismail Khan.

THE INDUS PLAIN

River Indus is the largest river of our country. This river after originating from Lake Mansarowar in Tibet (China) passing through the Himalayas enters in Pakistan territory near Gilgit. In the upper region a number of streams join it, but at the later stage, some of its western tributaries make it more huge and vast in volume and speed. Its western tributaries include rivers Swat, Kunar, Panjkora, Kabul, Kurram, Tochi, Gomal, Bolan and some minor streams.

All the plain areas of our country have existed by the sediment brought by River Indus and its tributaries. The whole of the Indus plain can be sub-divided into three parts for detailed study:

1. The Upper Indus Plain (from Attock to Mithankot).
2. The Lower Indus Plain (from Mithankot to Thatta).
3. The Deltaic Plain (from Thatta to coastal strip of Arabian Sea.

1. THE UPPER INDUS PLAIN

From the point of junction of eastern tributaries of river Indus is known as the upper Indus plain. It includes most of the areas of Punjab province. The Upper Indus Plain has a height from 180 meters to 300 meters. The northeastern part is comparatively higher. Although most of the plain area has existed by the alluvial soil brought by the rivers but near Sargodha, Chiniot and Sangla, some old dry hills appear above the plain. These are known as "Kirana Hills". The five big rivers of Punjab drain this plain. The land which lies between the two rivers is known as "Doab". Thus the area of Punjab plain can be divided into following Doabs:

(i)   Bari Doab: The area lying between rivers Beas and Ravi.
(ii) Rachna Doab: The Area lying between river Ravi and river Chenab.
(iii) Chaj Doab: The land lying between rivers Chenab and Jhelum.
(iv) Sindh Sagar Doab: The Land between Indus and Jhelum.

2. THE LOWER INDUS PLAIN

Mithankot is known as junction of Indus River and its eastern tributaries. Beyond Mithankot, river Indus flows alone and carries not only its own water, but also that of its eastern and western tributaries. While flowing from the province of Sindh, it becomes several kilometers wide especially during the flood season.

The *river* Indus flows *very* slowly and the silt carried by it is largely deposited on its bed, thereby raising it above the level of the sandy plain. The land on either side is, therefore, protected by the construction of embankments or bunds. Sometimes a number of difficulties have to be faced during flood seasons.

The Lower Indus Plain differs from the Upper Indus Plain because of its structure. The Lower Indus Plain has been formed by the changing course of a single great river and the deposits are of a comparatively recent origin. The Lower Indus Plain situated between the left bank of the Indus and Thar Desert is a level alluvial plain. It is more productive, but rainfall is scanty and agricultural activities cannot be performed without irrigational facilities. The areas situated on western side of Indus are comparatively less fertile and most of the areas lying northwest of the Indus have been suffering from the menace of water logging and salinity.

3. THE INDUS DELTA

The Indus delta begins near Thatta (Sindh) and river Indus by distributing itself into a number of branches joins the water of the Arabian Sea. The tidal deltaic area covers an area *of 36 to 45* km. It is submerged during high tides, and has mangrove swamps. The old deltaic lands in the south, are being reclaimed and irrigated by the canals of Ghulam Muhammad Barrage, still most of the areas of Lower Indus Plain are barren wastelands.

4. THE KACHHI-SIBBI PLAIN

The Kachhi-Sibbi Plain is bounded on the north by the Marri-Bugti ranges and on the west by the Qalat ranges. This plain is arid waste; most of it is barren, and cultivation is not possible without irrigation.

PLATEAUS
The Salt Range

The areas of Salt range begins in the east near the Jhelum in the Jogı Tilla and Bakralla ridges and runs south-west to the north of the river Jhelum for some distance before turning north west to cross the Indus near Kalabagh. West of the Indus the Salt range continues southwards into the districts of Bannu and Dera Ismail Khan. The average height of the range is about 671 meters, but near Sakesar it rises to about 1,525 meters above sea level. Large quantities of rock, salt and other minerals like gypsum and coal are found in this range.

Potowar Plateau

North of the Salt range the area of Rawalpindi, Jhelum and Mianwali districts are known as Potwar Plateau. These areas have also an uneven surface. The height of this plateau area varies from 300 to 600 meters above sea level. A large part of plateau has been dissected and eroded by the action of running water and it represents a varied landscape. The valleys of Haro and Soan rivers pass across the Potwar plateau. These are the important rivers of these areas and mostly flow during rainy season. Thus due to scanty rainfall and uneven surface these areas are not suitable for agricultural activities, but most of the minerals of our country, such as mineral oil, coal, iron, lime-stone, etc., are found from the Potwar Plateau area.

The Balochistan Plateau

This plateau lies to the west of the Sulemans and Kirthar mountains like Potwar Plateau, the dry hills run across the plateau *from the north-east* to the south-west. These hills are about 1,000 meters high. The Toba Kakar and Chaghi ranges in the north separate it from Afghanistan. The Brahui and Makran ranges lie in the center and the coastal Makran range skirts the south of the plateau. There is a large salt lake Hamuni-Mashke into which several small rivers drain. The only rivers of importance are the Zhob, which flows into the Gomal in the north, the Porali, Hangol and Dasht, which flow into the Arabian Sea in the south and contain valuable deposits of coal, iron, chromite and other minerals. These areas receive a small amount of rainfall and there is scarcity of water. So due to shortage of water and uneven surface these are not suitable for cultivation. In a few areas of Quetta and Pishin cultivation of various crops is possible with the help of Karez Irrigation System, but sheep rearing is the major occupation of the people living in this region.

THE DESERT AREAS

Although some desert areas of our country are parts of plain, but due to some different characteristics, where annual precipitation is insufficient to support permanent vegetation, these are known as deserts. The following are the main desert areas found in our Punjab and Sindh provinces:

Thal Desert

The area between rivers Indus and Jhelum is known as Sindh Sagar Doab. This includes the areas of Mianwali, Sargodha, Muzaffargarh and Dera Ghazi Khan Districts in the province of Punjab. These areas are called Thal desert. Here rainfall is very low and a large number of sand dunes are found here. Dust storms are frequent. Although canals have irrigated a large area of this desert, still a vast area is barren.

Cholistan Desert

The south border area of our Bahawalpur division is known as Cholistan. In fact, it is a part of Rajputana desert situated adjacent to it in India. Due to shortage of rainfall these areas have become dry barren lands.

Scattered sand dunes can be seen here and there. Although the soil is fertile enough, but due to scarcity of water, cultivation is not possible.

Nara Thar parker Deserts

The southern border area of Khairpur district in Sindh is known as Nara desert and border area of Mirpur Khas and Sanghar districts is called Tharparkar desert. These are also part of Rajputana desert situated in India. These are the driest parts of our country. Here rainfall is lowest, and except for the barren land with huge sand dunes and some scattered, stunted, thorny bushes, nothing can be seen.

RIVERS OF PAKISTAN

Indus is the largest river of Pakistan. River Indus flows in the center of our country. Our country is also known as the basin of river Indus and its eastern and western tributaries. After originating from Mansrowar lake in Tibet (China), which is situated in Kaile Range (Tibet), it flows Northwest wards through Tibet and Ladakh. It flows a long and nearly straight course in Ladakh running between the Ladakh Range and the Zanskar Range. Here the gradient of the river is quite gentle (about 30 cm per km). The Syyok and the Gilgit are its important right bank tributaries and the Zanskar its left bank tributary. After crossing the Himalayas through a very deep gorge (5,181 meters at Bunji north of the Nanga Parbat) it turns to the southwest and enters Pakistan. Like the other rivers having their sources in the trans-Himalayan regions, it has developed antecedent drainage in Jammu and Kashmir State. It leaves the mountains at Attock and flows roughly southwards until it falls into the Arabian Sea near Karachi. It has a length of 2,897 kilometers from its source to the Arabian Sea.

EASTERN TRIBUTARIES OF INDUS

Satluj, Bias, Ravi, Chenab and Jhelum are the main eastern tributaries of river Indus. All these rivers after originating from Himalayas Mountain and after passing through the areas of Kashmir enter into the territory of Pakistan. The river Bias joins Satluj near Harike in East Punjab (India). Similarly Satluj, Ravi, Chenab, and Jhelum after passing the areas o f Punjab in Pakistan join at a place known as Panjnad. After merging at that place they join collectively in river Indus at Mithankot. These rivers are of immense value for Pakistan. Because these rivers rise from such high mountains that serve as permanent reservoir- water resource which receive heavy rainfall during the summer

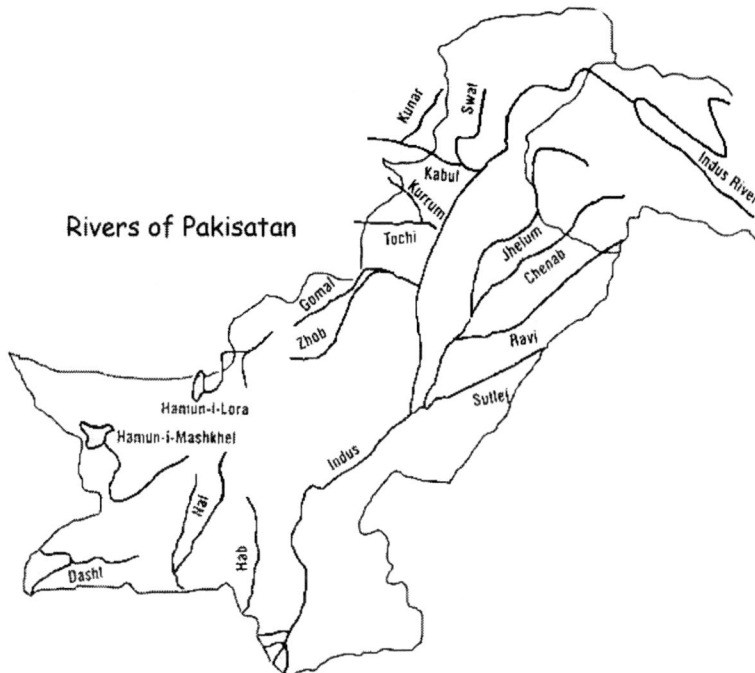

Figure 5: Rivers of Pakistan

and also heavy snowfall during the winter months. In summer due to heavy rainfall and thawing of snow, a huge quantity of water is available in these rivers, which serve as life line for the dry, fertile lands of both India and Pakistan and used for a number of purposes; irrigation, power generation, transportation etc.

INDUS WATER TREATY

To resolve dispute of water distribution between India and Pakistan Indus water Treaty was affected in 1962. According to Indus Basin Treaty the rights of Satluj, Bias and Ravi, the three eastern rivers of the basin have been given over to India, and Pakistan can use the water of Chenab, Jhelum and Indus only. India by virtue of occupying Kashmir valley where the upper courses of the rivers lie still keeps on creating problems for Pakistan and recently construction of Baggier Dam by India in violation of Indus water treaty. It has been brought to the notice of the World Bank by Pakistan.

CHAPTER VII
WEATHER AND CLIMATE

In order to have a clearer concept of the climatic conditions of a place it is essential to have understanding of the terms like weather, climate and season etc., involved in the study.

Weather is the actual condition of atmosphere; temperature, pressure, winds, humidity, cloudiness, precipitation i.e. rainfall, snow fall etc., of a place for a particular period - a day or a week. As for instance we say that weather today is or will remain during the week cool, calm, stormy, sunny, cloudy, dry or wet - but this condition is temporary and may change any time.

Climate, on the other hand is the average of weather observed at a place for a period at least 11 to 40 years - it may also be termed as the habit of weather at a particular place and time. For instance we can say that climate in the month of May at Lahore is hot and dry - meaning thereby that the averages of the elements of weather i.e. temperature, humidity, rainfall etc. exhibit hot and dry conditions of atmosphere there during that month. But it would be improper to say that weather of Lahore in the month of May is hot and dry; because weather gives the actual and spontaneous condition of atmosphere and not the averages.

CLIMATIC REGION, area that experiences almost similar averages of temperature and distribution of rainfall over the years is known as a climatic region.

SEASON, during the course of a year the weather and climatic condition keep on changing from warm, hot to cool and cold and dry to wet. On the basis of their record the months experiencing almost similar conditions of atmosphere can be grouped and be termed as season. The months having averages of temperature more than 70 degree F may be called hot season, the months having averages below 50 degree F as cool and the transitory periods when the temperatures are mild; spring or the autumn seasons, the months having excessively wet conditions as the rainy and the months receiving little or no rain as dry seasons.

Pakistan in the light of above stated definition has five seasons; namely cool, spring, hot, rainy season and the autumn, specific features of each season is separately described as under:

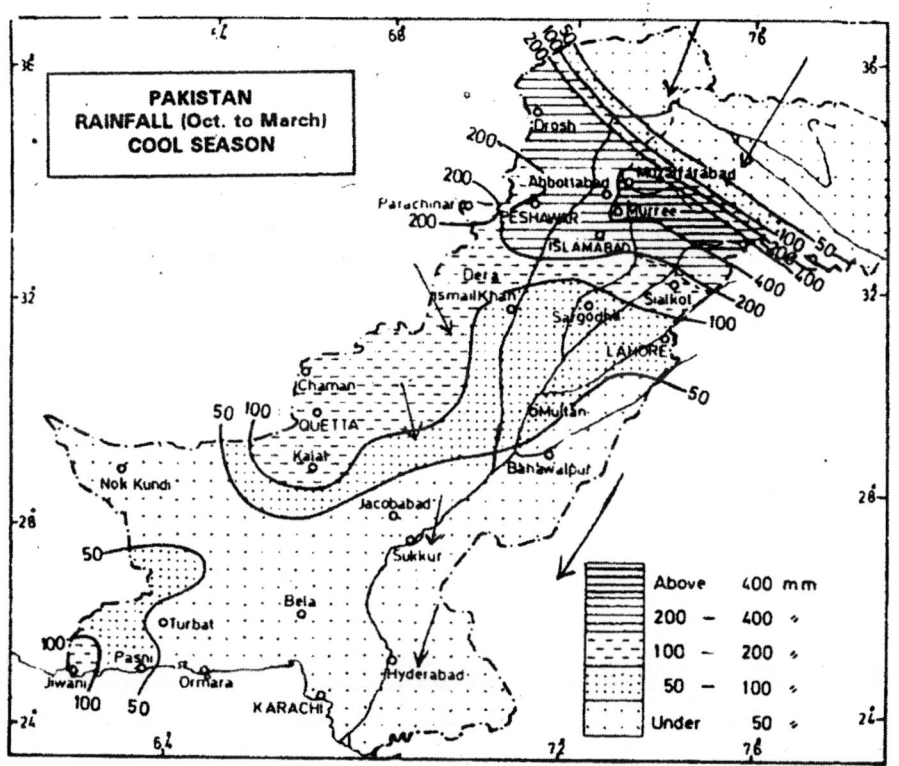

Figure 6: Distribution of Rainfall Cool Season

Cool Season (October to March)

Pakistan falling in the northern hemi-sphere experiences low temperatures during the months of October to February averages of nearly 55 degree F or 13 degree centigrade recorded because sun rays during this time fall oblique or slanting and the days are short and the nights long; the heat budget falls and cool conditions prevail. This season is a welcome season as it gives relief from the otherwise hot and sultry weather with averages soaring as high as 90 F/ 32 C and the maximal of 120 F/50 C. This is a season of maximum outdoor and crop activity on the plain areas; the major food/cash crops, wheat, barley, sugar cane and cotton are grown and harvested in this season. Business and trade also flourishes in this season.

The activity on the mountainous region, however, is reduced considerably because of freezing conditions due to high altitudes. Transhumance takes place at a large scale and thus the population abounds in the valleys and low-lying areas where there is enough activity and sufficient to feed the migrants and their animals.

Low pressure in this season is located on the Arabian Sea and a higher pressure on the lands. The winds, therefore, move from land to the sea-North East to South West as shown on the map.

These winds being cold and usually devoid of moisture do not give rain and hence cause dry weather conditions. However, occasionally warm Westerly Winds from the Atlantic Ocean moving eastward manage to penetrate pushing the high pressure located in the region, bring along with them a series of depressions or temperate lows that give winter rains on the plains and snow on the mountains and high altitudes.

The winter rains on the plains, which are clothed with wheat, the major food crop of Pakistan, oil seeds and other Rabi crops are very useful. The snow on the mountains replenishes the water reserves of the country. Like the summer monsoons the winter westerly winds are not very regular and occasionally fail causing great losses to the farmers and reduction of water reserves of the country.

SPRING SEASON (March - April)
Both spring and autumn in Pakistan are short lived and a transitory period of less than a month in each case.

SPRING in Pakistan follows cold weather when the high pressure, settled over the plains throughout the cool season, starts weakening or dissipating, temperatures start rising to allow the plants and trees to sprout, the flowers to blossom, cool breeze replace the chilly winds to give a sigh of relief to flora and fauna- natural world, and the poor folks who do not have sufficient clothing and shelter to protect themselves from the extremes of weather.

Inception of this season, however, varies from south to north; plains of Punjab and Sindh experience it early February whereas the northern hilly region a bit later in April or even May. The season entails spectacular celebrity throughout India Pakistan called Basant festival when men women clothe in yellow colors and particularly in Punjab, Lahore make it more hilarious by flying colorful kites and holding feasts on the roofs of their houses with loud music and dance parties that gives a grand festive color to the occasion. The festival is attended by people from all over the country and even Pakistanis abroad along with their foreign friends go to witness and participate in Basant Mela. Although the festival has been celebrated here since times immemorial, it has become more popular - almost an international celebration - since the last few decades.

AUTUMN SEASON (September-October)
This season conversely begins in October-early November in the northern hilly areas and late November or early December in the plains of Punjab and Sindh when the trees and plants shed their leaves and hide themselves under the cover of their bark, waiting for warmer conditions to sprout again. Before shedding leaves the trees cover them with eye bewitching yellow - crimson colors and from a distance, maple and walnut trees particularly appear to be in flames which present matchless- proverbial beauty, often described by poets and men of taste in their literary compositions.

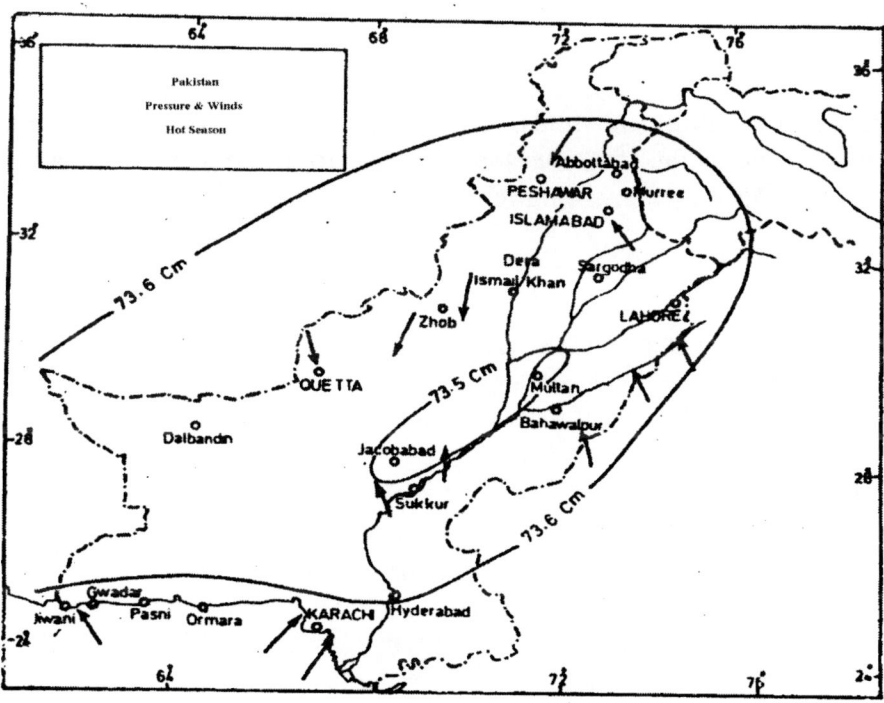

Figure 7: Direction of Pressure and Winds Hot Season

HOT SEASON (April to July)

In Pakistan the temperatures start rising after the spring equinox i.e. March 21st onward. It starts getting warmer day by day so that the averages of temperature April to May, are much higher than the preceding months - averaging more than 27 degree C (80 degree F). Due to dry sunny and soaring high temperatures activities on the plains and low lying areas are greatly hampered; Schools and Colleges are closed for summer vacation, business and trade is also affected, farmers also change their routine and carry out farming activities early morning or late in the afternoon to escape the scorching heat of the day time, those who can afford move to the hilly areas. June temperature on the plains, exceed 40 degree C (100 Degree F), with Jacobabad having recorded an absolute maximum 52 degree C (126 degree F). However, the humidity is low, hot dry dusty winds are the order of the day. Nights are comparatively cooler and windy that make the weather bearable and people spend nights in the open or on the rooftops of their houses. A low pressure gradually replaces the high pressure, settled on the land in the cool season, by June. The adjoining Arabian Sea, which comparatively is cooler than the land has a higher pressure.

Winds generally blow from southwest to northeast for the reason stated above. Tropical turbulent winds, and thunder storms are a common feature throughout the region in this season which are followed by brief rains lowering temperature and bring relief to the population from the soaring heat of the days.

As a rule this season is dry with the exception of the little rain caused by the thunderstorms stated above. But occasionally due to ensuing of early summer monsoons known as mango showers make the month of June wetter as compared to other months of the season.

RAINY SEASON (July to September)

Due to constantly rising mercury during the hot season the low pressure, which started building up in the hot season over lower Punjab and Sindh, is now fully developed - the low pressure incidentally is the deepest or the lowest in the sub-continent. In the month of July lowest (994.7 mille bars) pressure is found around Multan, 996.0 mille bars near Lahore and 997.7 mille bars around Karachi. A low pressure prevails over the land and a high over the neighboring cooler Arabian Sea to fill in the low pressure of the lands winds start moving from Sea to the land, South West to North East called summer monsoons.

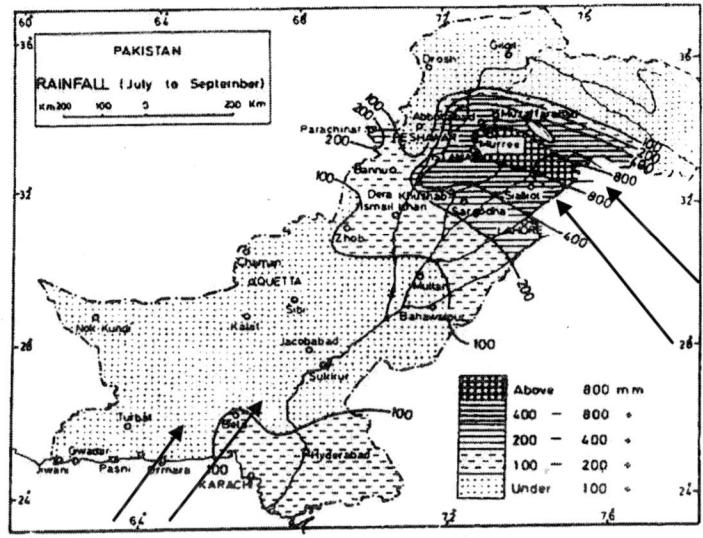

Rainy Season (July to September)

Figure 8: Distribution of Rain Rainy Season

Breaking of the Summer Monsoons

Rains in the sub-continent are associated with the summer monsoons that as a rule follow the hot sultry weather when humans, flora and fauna natural world are tired of heat and dry cloudless skies almost dying, anxiously wait for clouds and the much needed rain to quench and drench them and their fields. The rainy season begins in July and lasts up to September in Pakistan.

Lands of India Pakistan get very hot in summer, mercury going up to 45 degree centigrade. Low pressure is fully developed by the end of June. Cool moist winds from Arabian Sea and Bay of Bengal rush to fill in the low pressure. The sky is overcast with dark clouds; cool breezes as fore runner appear as a ray of hope, for all form of life, even the dry land. The phenomenon is called breaking of the Monsoons. The time of ensuing monsoon rains, however, varies from south to north and east to west; southern and eastern locations get an impact of monsoon rains earlier.

Heavy relief or Orographic rains occur when moist laden monsoon winds are checked and lifted by the Himalayas, Sometimes two streams of monsoons; one from the Bay of Bengal and the other from Arabian sea, converge over the foot hills of the Himalayas or even as far as lower Indus valley, Punjab and Sindh, producing unusually heavy rains and floods. The amount of rainfall varies from place to place depending on the vicinity of a water body or the place of condensation. In Pakistan the rainfall decreases from north to south; annual rainfall of Karachi is 200 mm, whereas Sialkot almost 900 miles, away from the sea – but due to its location on the foot hills of the Himalayas, gets 4 time more rain, 800 mm. This difference is due to the fact that Karachi although located near the sea, source of the warm moist winds, but being far from the place where these winds cool and condense, receives lesser rain.

Ravages of Monsoons

The variability of rain results in causing floods in the season of heavy rain ravaging life and property on a large scale and in case of failure of monsoon rains causing famine that result in loss of crops and death of animals on a large scale and in case of severe and persistent drought forces them to leave their home and hearth in search of food for them and their animals.

WINTER MONSOONS

Winter monsoons are dry winds as they blow from land to sea in this season when the lands being cold are occupied by high pressure and the sea being warmer has low pressure. As a rule this season is dry but occasionally westerly winds that manage to break in carrying depressions bring rain on the plains and snow on the mountains, Wheat the major winter crop of Pakistan depends on these rains.

CLIMATIC REGIONS OF PAKISTAN

Pakistan is a big country consisting of low-lying plains of the Indus, highlands of Himalayas, Hindukush and the Sulemans. Areas located on the tropic of cancer and close to the Arabian Sea and areas located far away from its moderating influences. As such a variety of climates are found in Pakistan.

An area that experiences almost similar conditions of average weather/climate over a long period of time is termed as a climatic region. On the basis of this criterion as per Kopen's classification we can divide Pakistan into the following climatic regions:

1. Sub-Tropical Coastal (Bwh)

This region includes the southern coastal strip of the Indus delta, almost 100 miles belt, from Karachi up to Hyderabad and the whole of Mekran coast. The sea- breezes, which dominate the region, keep

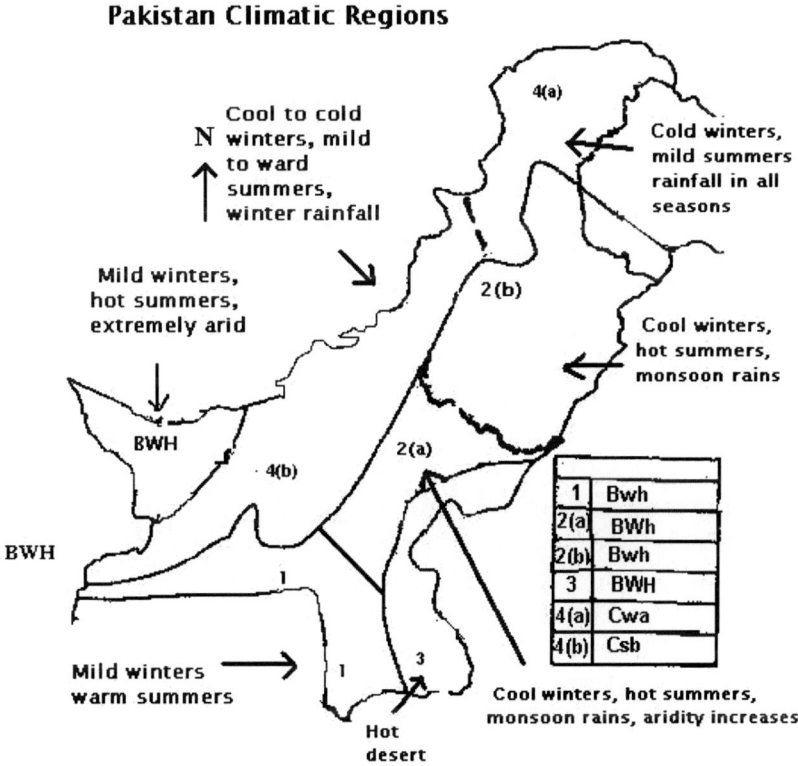

Figure 9: Climatic Regions

the climate mild; diurnal and annual ranges of temperature are lower than areas falling beyond the influence of the sea breezes. Annual rain fall is less than 10 inches with a summer maxima from the summer monsoons, which is not evenly distributed; there are years with no or scanty rain but on other times heavy down pours flood the region causing huge loss of life and property. Westerly winds that have already exhausted their moisture bring some winter rains. As a rule it is a dry coastal climate with warm winters and hot summers moderated due to cool sea breezes. Inland up to Hyderabad, tall wind trappers facing seaside are seen raised to trap the sea breezes to keep the houses cool in summer. The cover of thorny bushes and coconut palms that thrive on saline coastal strip to a great extent depict the climatic character of the region.

2(a) Sub-Tropical Continental Arid low land (BWh)

Lower Indus basin up to Bahawalpur and Multan falls in this region. It has extreme climate; summers are very hot with mercury rising to 52.5 C°, so that Jacobabad a representative town of the region is the hottest place of the world. In summer outdoor activities almost come to stand still; shops and businesses remain closed during the mid day, farmers plough the lands at night. The houses are plastered with a thick layer of mud on the walls and roofs to minimize heat absorption. Hot winds blow throughout the day and dust storms are a common feature of the region. Humidity is high cooling through evaporation is minimum making the conditions enervating and suffocating. Rainfall is low less than 10 inches a year with an average annual rain of 4 inches in Jacobabad. Multan receives about 10 inches because of its northern location. Winters are cool and pleasant night temperature fall nearly to freezing point in January. Annual range of temperature is high whereas the daily range of temperature particularly in the rainy season when the humidity is high, even the night temperature is above 27 C° to make it highly suffocating and enervating.

2(b) Sub-Tropical Continental Semi Arid Low land (Bwh)

The region includes the upper Indus plain from Sahiwal to the sub-mountain region including the vale of Peshawar. It has hot summer and relatively cool winters. Rainfall higher than the lower Indus region about 15 to 20 inches, comes from mainly the summer monsoons but winters are not totally dry and some rain which is helpful to raise the winter, Rabi crop is caused by the western disturbances brought by the westerly winds that blow here in this season. Lahore a representative town of the region receives 20 inches of rain annually, about 15 inches from the summer monsoons and the rest from the westerly winds in winter. Peshawar lying further northwest gets an annual rain of 15 inches half of which falls in summer and the rest half in winter from the westerly winds, which are more regular there, with February March being the wettest months.

3. Hot Desert (BWH)
Extreme hot and dry climatic conditions prevail in Thar and Cholistan desert that lie in the southeast of the country and also include Nokandi district of Balochistan lying in the extreme west. Days are very hot and nights cool, hot and dusty winds being a common feature that blow continuously from May to September. Rainfall takes place in summer partly due to convection followed by a dust storm, and mainly from the summer monsoons with an average annual rainfall of less than 5 inches.

4(a) Sub Tropical Highland (Cwa)
This type of climate is found in the northern mountainous region of the country that includes Murree-Hazara hills and the adjoining valleys. Due to high altitude more than 5,000 feet above sea level, summer is short and cool but the winters are cold with average temperature below freezing. This region because of its pleasant and cool summer attract large number of people from all around the country who want to have a break from the hot and sultry weather that prevails on the plains of Punjab and Sindh in that season. Rainfall that mainly comes in summer from the monsoons is fairly heavy more than 40 inches. Winters are dry with occasional rain and snowfall caused by the western disturbances originating from the Mediterranean Sea.

4(b) Sub Tropical Plateau (Csb)
This type of climate is experienced in the western mountainous region of the country mostly, included are the Balochistan plateau and the surrounding highland region. Quetta more than 5,000 feet above sea level has fairly cool summer. Being away from the influence of summer monsoons, get no or little rain in summer, and the entire annual rain of about 11 inches falls in winters, brought by the westerly winds. Thus the region has warm dry summer and cold wet winters.

Key to the Kopen's classification:
Kopen has divided climates of the world on the basis of temperature, distribution and effectiveness of rainfall: Tropical wet Climates are coded by letters A, and B denote tropical and sub tropical dry climates. Cool climates have been awarded letter C and

the cold climates as D. Tropical areas lie in between the tropics on either side of the Equator and the sub-tropical areas lie above the tropics.

Small letters
(a) Indicates hot summer warmest month 22 C° or above.
(b) Warm long summer with temperature between 10 C° and 22 C°.
(c) The region having short summer temperature above 10 C° but not more than 22 C°.
(s) Dry summers.
(w) Dry winters, capitol letter H denotes extreme drought and high temperatures.

CHAPTER VIII
NATURAL VEGETATION - FORESTS

Plants, shrubs and trees found covering the surface of planet Earth is called natural vegetation. Humans and animals are capable of shifting and migrating from one place to another to avoid extremes of weather- but the plants face the hazards of weather and climate located in the same environment. Hence natural vegetation is a more reliable indicator of the climatic features of a region as compared to human or animal kind. However, the thickness, quality and quantity of vegetation depend upon the prevailing temperature, rainfall distribution and their regimes from one season to the other. Existing climate and the vegetation cover of a region have, therefore, a positive correlation.

Looking at the natural vegetation distribution map and that of the annual distribution of rainfall at a glance one finds that the areas that have better distribution of rain are covered with productive forests whereas the areas suffering from drought have poor vegetation: thorny bushes, course grass or scattered dwarf trees of Acacia and Babul. It is, therefore, obvious that climate and vegetation are highly interdependent.

Pakistan being a sub-tropical country where temperature with the exception of highlands in the north and northwest remain sufficiently warm to hot throughout, the rainfall distribution is not only low but usually comes in the hot season when most of the moisture is lost through evaporation and as such the net moisture absorbed by the soil is insufficient to support good vegetation growth. As such Pakistan has a very small percentage of its area under productive forests, hardly 5% comparable to a minimal figure of 20% of a balanced cover of forests in a country. Government of Pakistan since independence is trying hard to achieve the target by encouraging tree plantation and adopting measures for the conservation of forests in the country.

This low percentage of forest cover is not only due to the climatic factor but also to a ruthless indiscriminate cutting and indifferent attitude of the people and the rulers towards this innocent useful - vital creation of nature - adversely affecting climate; reducing rainfall distribution and amounting to rise of temperature.

In Tuzk-e-Babari, an account of India, during Mughal period, it is mentioned that most of the area of northern Punjab was covered with thick forests, full of wild life: tigers leopards and grazing animals with cooler and wetter climate--but subsequently during Sikh regime and British occupation the trees were mercilessly cut for petty economic gains rendering the region almost devoid of its beautiful and useful covering and change of climate for the worst, which exposed the area to weathering and resultant leaching of once fertile homogenous lands - turning them into a badland topography as is found these days in Hazara and the Potwar area of Jhelum and Rawalpindi divisions in particular.

The government produces about 200 thousand cubic foot of timber and about 500 thousand cubic meters of firewood annually from its forest reserves whereas annual demand of timber at home is 1.7 million of timber and 16.7 cubic meters of firewood. The deficit is made up from farmlands and through imports. Current import of wood and wood products costs about Rs.13 billion. In order to reduce the burden on the exchequer and to narrow the gap between the supply and demand of forest products a number of measures have been undertaken:

Management of forests on scientific basis
Introduction of community forestry
Planting on waste and denuded lands in high rainfall areas
Raising industrial wood species on suitable soils
Raising nurseries to provide adequate plants for planting agencies and the farmers.

Classification of Forests
Distribution of forests closely corresponds with the climatic conditions, as both distributions are interdependent; mountain climates in Pakistan being wetter and cooler are covered with species of coniferous type, which thrive there. On the other hand the hot low-lying plain areas of Punjab and Sindh with low rainfall are covered with deciduous broad-leafed scattered growth. On the

basis of the climatic differences the natural vegetation also varies and classified as under:

Forests of Northern Mountains

The main natural forests of Pakistan lie in the northern areas including Murree, Swat, Dir, and Chitral, Malakand division of N.W.F.P. As these areas are higher enough above sea level, receive sufficient rainfall in summer from the southwest monsoons and in winter from the westerly winds so a large number of coniferous trees such as pines, fir, cedar, larks, spruce, and birches are seen there. The wood of these trees is soft and valuable, which is used for mainly construction purpose. Cedar (deodar) wood is particularly a valuable source of timber that is found on altitudes above 3,000 meters. Swat, Dir, Kaghan, Azad and Occupied Kashmir, are the main areas of its concentration.

The Balochistan Hill Forests

In the areas of Quetta and Kalat divisions, where rainfall is low but it mostly comes in winter from the western disturbances originating from the Mediterranean Sea, the region has open forests; mainly chilghoza pines, pencil pines, chestnuts, junipers and besides grow lot of fruits; apple, pears, apricots, vine and melons typical produce of Mediterranean lands.

Shrub Forest of the Hills and Plains

The region that lies on the foot hills / the piedmont area, which lie below the height of 900 meters the main trees found are deciduous broad-leaved like the oak, chestnut, walnut, maple, mulberry, wild olive, kao and phulai abundantly grow and their wood is used for furniture making and fuel.

The River Rain or Bela Forests

Such forests are found along the banks of rivers especially in the lower Indus plain, where due to hot conditions and low rain scattered dwarf acacias and Babul exist but along the rivers shisham, eucalyptus and date palms thrive.

Tidal Forests

These forests extend from Karachi to Kutch covering an area of about 750,000 acres. The coastal wastelands are covered with grasses and mangrove type of vegetation that is flooded with high tides twice a day. Besides coconuts and palms of different varieties, that like saline waters, also grow. Some valuable species are being experimented upon these days. A large amount of firewood is obtained.

Artificial Forests

In some areas of Punjab and Sindh a few irrigated plantation units have been established where hardwood species, such as shisham, mulberry and acacia trees are grown for commercial purposes. Changa Manga forest located 60 km. south of Lahore is the largest plantation of this type. Besides that artificial forests are being maintained at Chichwatni, (Sahiwal), Pirwala (Multan), Wan Bachran (Thal) and in some part of Ghulam Mohammad and Guddu Barrages.

Deserts and Semi Desert Vegetation

Deserts of Pakistan that include Thal and Cholistan in Punjab, Nara and Tharparker in Sindh and most of the areas in Makran and Kalat divisions of Balochistan have arid and semi arid climatic conditions and here due to shortage of rainfall only poor grass, shrubs and stunted bushes can be seen. In most of the area no vegetation is found except the sand dunes.

Importance and uses of Forests

According to an agriculture expert "A country can live without gold and silver- but not without forests." That greatly signifies the importance of forests in our day-to-day life.

As there is a shortage of power resource, coal and oil found in the country is insufficient to meet the requirements, a large rural population uses wood as fuel.

Pakistan has a hot climate, particularly mid days of summer are very hot. Rural population cannot afford cooling their houses; therefore, in order to escape the heat people spend the hottest part of the day under the shade of trees. A fully-grown tree produces cooling equaling to a three-ton air conditioner.

Timber obtained from the trees is used for furniture and house building industry. Forests supply raw material for various industries such as matches, paper, sports goods, resins, rayon and silk etc.

Forests help reducing temperature and increase the amount of rainfall of adjacent areas. The forested areas of our country serve as a pasture, for the livestock of the farmers. Forests particularly in the hilly areas help to control erosion. They grow and provide fruits that we use as food and different herbs that are used in making medicines. Forests reduce pollution and provide oxygen by consuming carbon dioxide. A large number of animals take refuge in forests, so forests provide hunting facilities for the hunters who get meat and skins from them. Forests help to save crops and orchards from dust storms.

CHAPTER IX
MEANS OF TRANSPORT AND COMMUNICATION

An efficient and adequate system of communication and transport is vital for economic development of the country. Men and material have to be carried from one place to another to meet the requirements of economic viability. The transport and communication facilities provide the most essential infrastructure needed for the socio-economic development of the country. These facilities are known as means of communication and transport, which are railway, roads, water ways, air ways, post, telegraph, telephone and television.

Modern advancement of technology has greatly enhanced the utility of means of transport and communication in the national progress. These means should be speedy, efficient and cheap to fulfill the requirements of social, economic and political uplift. The efficiency and swift mobility of these means stabilizes the economic, political and social set up of the country. The means of communication and transport create harmony and co-ordination between the different aspects of social and economic activity by effectively mobilizing their activity. They play an important and highly sensitive role in strengthening country's defense, for maintaining peace and security and for the development of knowledge and skill.

Means of transport carry the raw material to the industrial units and transport the finished goods to make them available in market in time. In this way the means of transport play a pivotal role in the economic and industrial growth of the country. They also help the workers, laborers and officials to reach their destination of duty so that they can contribute in the national progress and prosperity. The means of transport establish contact between the people living at distant areas by bringing them together. They help in maintaining links and increase mutual understanding and co-operation among the people. An efficient network of the means of transportation is necessary for running the administration and quick movement of the armed forces in any time of emergency.

PAKISTAN RAILWAYS

At the time of partition the railway was in a very bad shape. The engines, carriages and other machinery given to Pakistan were obsolete and mostly out of order. Pakistan received a paltry share of the trains and other railway equipment. Pakistan had to face numerous problems in technical and administrative sphere of the railway. The rails were put to intensive use during the World War II and repairs were not carried out to put them to work again. During the partition the trains were operated heavily to bring the helpless and homeless refugees to Pakistan. There was no time left for the repairs of the dilapidated trains and carriages. The government took effective measures to meet the challenge and for the time was able to overcome the difficulties.

The railway employees were given proper training in the country and abroad which helped the government to put the railway organization on stable footings. The conventional coal engines replaced by oil and diesel engines and the damaged railway tracks were repaired. At a number of places double railway tracks were laid. The narrow-gauge tracks were changed with broad gauge tracks.

Steps have been taken for the establishment of dry port at Peshawar railway station with the cost of Rs. 88.20 million. Between Khanewal and Multan double railway track will be laid with the cost of Rs. 190.76 million and telecommunication and signaling work will be improved with the cost of Rs. 821.46 million. Maintenance of tracks is the worst hit sector, which needs immediate attention. Only Rs. 11.5 million had been provided for the work during 1988-89, which was not sufficient amount to meet the total cost of the project.

The railway system in Pakistan comprises of 8,775 km of rail track, 880 stations, 109 train halts, 879 locomotives, 3,228 passenger and other coaching vehicles and 35,237 wagons. The government has started the work of replacement of out-dated assets. The track renewal program has been given top priority. Out of the total 1,681 km from Karachi to Peshawar, 914 km of the track has been doubled. The laying of double track between Shahdara and Raiwind and Chaklala-Golhra has also been laid while the work on Multan-Khanewal section is in progress.

The Risalpur locomotive factory has been completed with the cost of Rs. 1,800.69 million including Rs. 924.57 million of foreign exchange. It would produce 25 locomotives annually. With the exception of the diesel engines, which will be imported from General Motors, the entire locomotives will be manufactured within the factory. Mughalpura workshop at Lahore is rapidly undergoing improvement and modernization. A railway workshop has been set up in Islamabad for repairing diesel engines and to make new wagons. Karachi circular railway has started work to solve the problem of traffic of Karachi and its suburbs. However not a single locomotive has been produced since 1994. The Railway is constantly running in loss being over staffed due to political interference. Privatization of Railways is under active consideration of the present government. The three-pronged unprecedented accident in Sindh sector July 2005 has turned the attention of the government, to allocate adequate funds for the improvement of signaling and other equipment for the safety of the passengers.

ROADS

The roads are an important means of transport. They play a vital role in the development of national economy as they link the production centers with the market. In Pakistan the roads are maintaining links between Karachi, the country's major port, and the production centers. They transport trade goods to every corner of the country and also to the foreign countries. In view of the industrial and agricultural progress the utility of the roads, as an efficient means of transportation, has increased tremendously.

The existing road network in Pakistan has total length of 236,041 km including 129,865 km high quality and 106,176 km of low quality roads whereas the length of motorways is 770 km. The road network provides transportation facilities to 87,915 million passengers per km on which 3,500 vehicles ply.

Road transport is comparatively easier to carry the goods to their destinations. It is also cheaper than rail transport. Roads are used to carry industrial and agricultural products to the railway stations. The road transport is comfortable for the passengers. The buses and other means of transportation can pick the passengers from their doors.

The Grand Trunk Road linking Karachi and Peshawar is the main highway of Pakistan. Total length of G.T. Road is 1,750 km, of which 1,400 km. is single lane and 160 km. has already been doubled. Contract for another 450 km. has been granted. The volume-of traffic on this road is very high which averaged 5,282 vehicles per day at Attock Bridge and 9,716 vehicles per day on Jhelum Bridge in 1988. The traffic volume on G.T. Road has greatly increased by 1990.

Most of the roads in Pakistan are un-metalled and unable to meet the requirements of the developing economy. These roads are rendered unfit for use during heavy rains and floods. The roads have not been constructed according to the requirements of transport. A vast network of roads should be laid throughout the country. The old and damaged roads should be repaired. The roads should be constructed in such a way as to link the rural areas with the urban areas.

The roads transport is mainly in the private sector and adequate facilities are being provided to strengthen the existing transport fleet. In 1978 National Logistic Cell was established. It has 1,617 vehicles with a carrying capacity of 35,000 to 40,000 tones. Indus Super Highway has been completed which has reduced the distance between Karachi and Peshawar by 322 km. Two Urban Transport Corporations have been set up, one for Lahore and Rawalpindi-Islamabad and the other for Karachi, by the Federal government. These Corporations will provide transport facilities in the urban areas on cheaper rates.

MOTORWAY PROJECT

Total length of operational Motorways in Pakistan is 770 km whereas work is in progress on two other projects and many more are in the planning stage. The work on the Islamabad - Peshawar motorway M-1 was completed in 2007 by a Turkish firm, whereas Lahore – Islamabad M-2 section was completed and opened for traffic in 1997. Daewoo Ltd. has constructed the Lahore – Islamabad Motorway; 334 km in length. Similarly Pindi Bhattian – Faisalabad M-3, Karachi to Hyderabad M-9, and Karachi Northern Bypass M-10 sections of the motorways stand completed and operational. Different sections of motorway and their dimensions are as under:

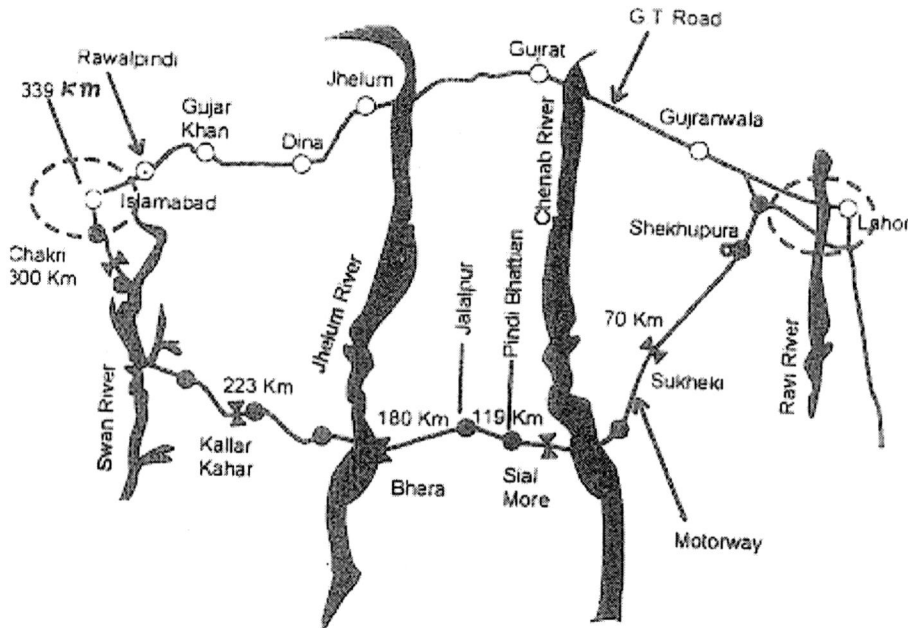

Figure 10: Motor Ways

Islamabad-Peshawar Motorway (M-1), 154 km completed
Islamabad-Lahore Motorway (M-2), 339 km, revised cost Rs. 35,486 million, completed since November 1997.
Pindi Bhattian-Faisalabad Motorway (M-3), 53 km, completed
Faisalabad Multan Motorway (M-4), 243 km
Multan-D.G. Khan Motorway (M-5), 85 km
D.G Khan-Radero Motorway (M-6), 895 km
Radero – Karachi (M-7), 341 km
Radero – Gwadar (M -8) Under construction, 2 lane road, completed
Karachi –Hyderabad (M-9) 138 km, completed
Karachi Northern Bypass (M-10), 57 km, completed
Lahore – Sailkot (M-11)

Motorways will not only help reducing traffic load on other highways but also save time and fuel consumption. It would bring a healthy effect on the industrial and commercial fields of the country.

WATER WAYS

Waterways are most suited to carry heavy goods and material from one place to another. They are the cheapest and oldest means of transport. The river transport is not in frequent use in Pakistan due to the uncertain nature of rivers. The water level of rivers keep falling and rising in different seasons, which make it difficult to resort to the river transport. The Federal government is adopting measures to improve the river transport in the country. The river transport, in view of the economic conditions of Pakistan, can be highly useful for promoting trade inside the country. Foreign trade is carried on by sea. Karachi and Muhammad Bin Qasim are the two ports in Pakistan, and Gawadar deep sea port has being operational in 2008 located 460 km west of Karachi in Balochistan will serve as a trading hub for western and northern Pakistan, China, Afghanistan and other central Asian countries.

At the time of independence Pakistan had only two ships, which were very small in size. The foreign trade was carried on through foreign ships, which involved a great amount of foreign exchange spent to charter the foreign ships. The Government of Pakistan took steps to reduce dependence on the foreign ships. A number of ships were purchased and the Pakistani fleet was considerably enlarged. The government announced the shipping policy under which the National Shipping Corporation was established in September 1963. The P.N.S.C. has fleet of 26 vessels with a deadweight tonnage of 410234. The ships are deployed on all the important routes and serve almost all the major ports of the world. A training center to produce efficient and trained sailors is working at Karachi.

Figure 11: Pakistan Air Routes

AIRWAYS/CIVIL AVIATION

In the modern age the air transport has received great boost. Regular air service is necessary to establish contact between the people living in foreign countries. Air travel is comfortable and quick. It saves lot of time. The air service is also highly useful in maintaining links between the areas, which are inaccessible by roads or other means of transport. There are some areas in Pakistan like Chitral and Gilgit, which can be approached by air service only. Moreover Pakistan is a country of vast plains, which is best suited for the aero planes to land and take off. It is, therefore, imperative to develop air service Pakistan to meet the needs of quick transport facilities.

At the time of establishment of Pakistan, there was only one Air line known as Orient Airways, which was established in Calcutta in 1946 and started its operations in June 1947, subsequently moved its headquarters to Karachi. The birth of Pakistan generated one of the largest transfers of population in the history of the mankind. Government of Pakistan started the relief operations and transportation of people between Delhi and Karachi by chartered aircrafts and with the help of Orient Airways. Afterwards, Pakistan International Airlines Corporation was set up in 1950, which, however, was merged with Orient Airways and named Pakistan International Airlines PIA which has full control over air transport in Pakistan. The P.I.A. has its own modern workshop and aircrafts. At present PIA fleet consists of Boeing 777, 747 and 737, Airbus 310, and ATR42 aircrafts.

At present there are 36 operational Airports in Pakistan. These airports are equipped with modern facilities such as Radio Navigation, fire-fighting equipment, night landing system, flight information system, instrument landing system, distant measuring equipment and sophisticated radars. Karachi. Lahore and Islamabad are major International airports. Peshawar and Gawadar too operate limited international traffic. The remaining airports are used for domestic operations.

The P.I.A. offers inland services and sends its flights to the foreign countries as well. It has spread a network of flights in the country and has linked the important trade centers with other parts of the country and the world. P.I.A. is the first non-communist organization, which has been granted permission to fly over Chinese territory. It is one of the best and most efficient airlines of the world.

Means of Communication

Means of communication (Mass Media) are equally important for the national progress, as are the means of transport. Their importance and utility for the economic growth of the country is over emphasized. In the last decade mass media has become a major sector of the economy. The electronic media has been transformed by the liberalization granted to the private sector by the government. It is estimated that an investment of about RS 5 billion will be made from 2005 to 2010. It has played a dominant role in the political and social life of the country. It is the Radio, Television especially news channels, newspapers, and internet which provides a link between the government and the people. The means of communication extend great help and assistance in expanding the internal and foreign trade. Radio and Television broadcast various programs for the recreation and amusement of the people. Means of communication in use in Pakistan are post, telegraph, telephone, radio, television, newspapers, magazines and the internet. Using the information technology the television and radio transmissions, and also newspapers and magazines are available on the internet.

POSTAL SERVICE

In 1947 it was established as the department of Post and Telegraph. In 1962 it was separated from the Telephone and Telegraph department. Postal department, besides providing postal service, is performing multifarious functions. It sells saving certificates, revenue stamps, issues radio licenses, provides facilities of savings and life insurance, collection of taxes and utility bills. During 1986-89 110 new post offices were opened in the country of which 100 were in the rural and 109 in the urban areas. At present the number of post offices in the country is 13,000 of which 9517 are in the rural areas. Working hours of more than 100 post offices have been extended. They remain open till late at night and are known as the 'Night Post Offices'. Air mail service is available within and outside the country.

Pakistan Post Office has introduced an Urgent Mail Service linking 31 metropolitan towns of the country. The articles are accepted at the counter and delivered to the addressee with proper receipts. A new inland remittance service through postal draft for an amount up to Rs. 10,000/- has been introduced. The postal department has floated Airex Service while Data post (International Express Mail Service) is already linked with U.K., Turkey, Netherlands, Japan, Belgium and Qatar.

TELEGRAPH

About 500 telegraph offices have been set up in the country. Tele-printer exchanges have been established at Karachi, Lahore and Rawalpindi-Islamabad. Pakistan has developed telegraph links with a number of foreign countries. FAX service has also been initiated in the important towns.

TELEPHONE

From the very beginning telephone facilities have been on the increase. In 1949 a telephone repair center was established at Lahore, which was later on shifted to Kotri. Another factory was established at Haripur for manufacturing telephones. By June 30, 1989 there were 1100 telephone exchanges and 664,499 working telephones in the country. Facilities and direct dialing are now available between important places in the country. Pakistan is presently linked with 151 countries of the world and about 29.96 million calls per year are being handled on the international routes. The department planned to provide 250,000 new telephones during 1989-90.

In 1991 the government decided to privatize Pakistan Telecom Corporation and issued 6 million vouchers which were converted into shares later on in 1996 when the Pakistan Telecommunication Company Limited was formed. PTCL launched its mobile and data services subsidiaries in 2001 by the name of Ufone and PakNet. 26 % of the shares of PTCL were sold to Etisalat, a Dubai based company by the government. At present PTCL has around 2000 telephone exchanges across the country whereas GSM, CDMA and Internet are other services provided by PTCL. After the liberalization of telecommunication industry in 2003 about a dozen of other telecommunication companies including giants like Telenor and China Mobile have entered the competition providing services ranging from cellular phones to DSL and broadband at very competitive rates and making the industry customer oriented.

RADIO

Pakistan has greatly progressed in the field of Broadcasting. At present Pakistan Broadcasting Corporation has 31 radio stations that broadcast programs in seventeen languages daily and 10 FM stations. Whereas PEMRA (Pakistan Electronic Regulating Authority) has issued licenses for establishment of more than 100 FM Radio stations in the private sector including some for universities for educational purposes and about 75 of these are operational.

TELEVISION

Pakistan Television Corporation was set up in February 1965. It has set up five T.V. stations at Lahore, Karachi, Peshawar, Islamabad and Quetta. These stations are being run on commercial basis. At present there are about 500,000 T.V. sets being used in the country. More areas are being brought within the operational reach of the P.T.V. by installing boosters at different places. Multan T.V. station has been recently inaugurated.

Parvez Musharraf government gave permission to set up private satellite channels and issued 20 licenses. Prominent private channels operate at home and overseas besides making profits have been helpful in maintaining contacts with Pakistanis serving abroad but also introducing Pakistani culture through popular plays, and dramas keenly watched all over in the Middle East, Europe and USA. News channels like Geo and ARY provide live coverage of national, local and international events around the clock. At present there are about 25 TV channels that are operational whereas Geo TV, Indus TV, and ARY are the prominent private channels.

After the deregulation and liberalization of the media, in addition to private channels, PEMRA has issued licenses to cable operators. At present there are more than 1600 cable operators throughout the country and about 3.5 million cable subscribers.

CHAPTER X
POPULATION OF PAKISTAN

Pakistan is an important country of South Asia and the Islamic world and ranks third in both cases by virtue of its inhabitants. According to the last census present population of Pakistan is about 172.8 million with an annual increase of nearly 1.6%. As of 2010 estimated population is 175 million with an annual increase of 2.2 %

The present increase in the population in Pakistan is high no doubt but not alarming in view of available resources in the country. A growing population is considered to be healthy one. Look at USA, Canada, Australia and most of the European countries where the growth rate is very low and the structure of population is imbalanced; the number of old people is far more than the young population and as such they have to rely on immigrants to square their population deficit. Pakistan has immense natural resources but unfortunately due to political instability proper planning could not be done and the country largely depended on the foreign aid. Pakistan's foreign benefactors have, therefore, rightly been objecting to the high rate of growth, as they had to feed ever-increasing numbers. On the other hand if Pakistan can utilize this population resource of her own it would prove to be an asset rather than a liability for the country.

POPULATION GROWTH
Low literacy and poor economic conditions are the major factors, which have contributed a great deal towards the enormous rise in population. With the efforts of population planning department and also due to rise in literacy figures growth rate has come down to some extent as is evident from the result of the last census.

The majority of Pakistan's population, about 72 per cent consists of rural population, while the remaining 28 per cent is urban. The province of Balochistan is the most thinly populated province of Pakistan in spite of its vast area. The percentage of urban population is the highest in Sindh, 43.37 percent, followed by Punjab 27.53 per cent, Balochistan 15.16 percent and N.W.F.P. 15.13 percent.

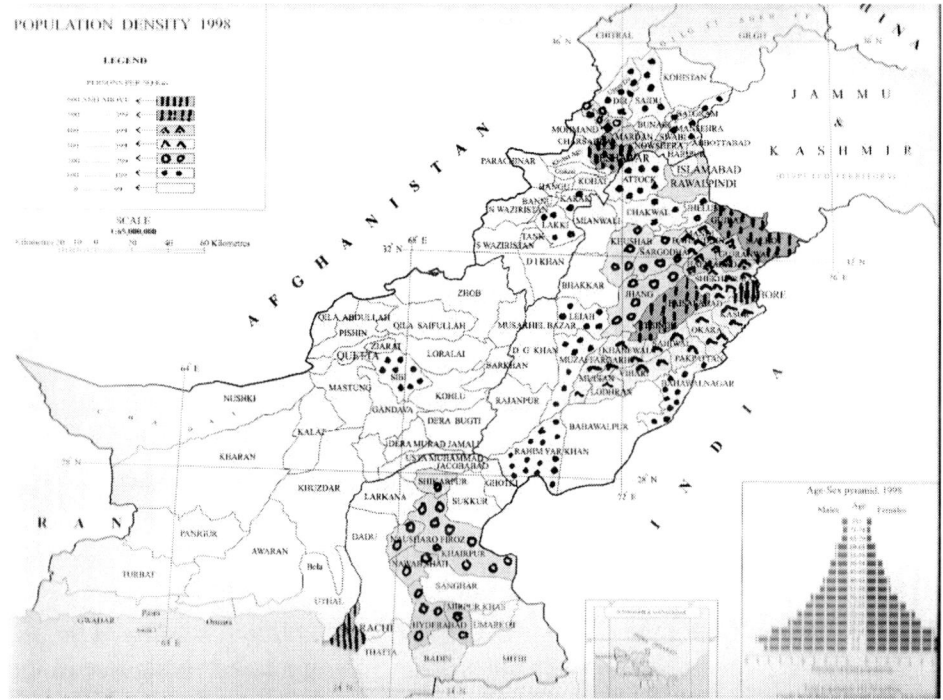

Figure 12: Population distribution

Following table shows province-wise population and land area:

No.	Province	Land *Area*	Population
1	Balochistan	43.6 per cent	5.1 per cent
2.	Punjab	25.8 per cent	56.1 per cent
3.	Sindh	*17.7* per cent	22.6 per cent
4.	N.W.F.P.	12.8 per cent	15.7 per cent

REASONS FOR THE HIGHER GROWTH RATE OF POPULATION

WARM CLIMATE

Warm climate accelerates puberty process. The females particularly in villages get married soon after attaining puberty in early teens with an extended fertility period, which is a major factor in the rapid increase of population in Pakistan.

LACK OF RECREATIONAL ACTIVITIES

There is an acute dearth of recreational facilities in Pakistan, especially for the people living in rural areas who do not have enough recreational facilities to pass their leisure.

LOW LITERACY

Pakistan has a low literacy rate 53% where majority of people cannot even read or write and are not aware of the economic liabilities involved in an unplanned population growth. The ignorance of the masses is also a big impediment in the way of family planning. The people due to lack of education are not able to understand the benefits and measures of family planning. They consider it highly un-ethical and against Islamic principles to restrict and control the birth rate by artificial or medical methods.

DEATH RATE

For the last few years the death rate in Pakistan has fallen sharply. The death rate has decreased all over the world causing an enormous rise in the world population. The reasons for the falling death rate in the world are the advancement in the field of medicine and technology. The technological and scientific advancement have effectively played their role in curbing and arresting the genesis of various diseases.

Pakistan is saving the lives of over 100,000 children every year since 1982 by launching a program of immunization. Due to this program there has been a dramatic change in child survival in Pakistan. The programs of mother childcare have also been instrumental for controlling infant mortality rate. The life expectancy has increased from 54 years in 1982 to 60 years by 1998. The amazing progress of surgery in the field of medicine is another factor in the sharp decline of the death rate. In Pakistan advanced medical facilities are now within the access of majority of the population, which has enhanced the life expectancy of the people and thus is instrumental to low birth rate.

BIRTH RATE

High birth rate is another important reason for the rapid growth in population in Pakistan. At present the birth rate is 3.1 per cent (55 per thousand), which is likely to shoot up to 6 per cent at the end *of* the century. This trend is highly precarious in view of the scarcity of the resources in Pakistan. The birth rate has got to be checked and kept within the ratio of the availability of the resources.

LARGE FAMILIES CONSIDERED A BLESSING

In Pakistan, generally in villages, large families are considered an asset and a symbol of prestige in the rural society being helping hand in pursuit of agricultural activities on their lands. The people, therefore, consider the large families as blessing and thus are unmindful of the size of the family.

JOINT FAMILY SYSTEM

Joint family system is still prevalent in Pakistan on a large scale. All the earning members thus dilute the economic stress to share the economic burden of a family and as such can support and maintain a larger family without much hassle.

GROWTH OF POPULATION IN PAKISTAN

Census	Population of growth in Thousand	Annual rate
1941	28,282	1.8%
1951	33,740	1.7%
1961	42,880	2.4%
1972	66,309	2.6%
1981	88.725	2.98%
1983	88,223	3.0%
1988	89,767	3.1%
1989	98,090	3.1%
1992	1,14,782	3.1%
1995	1,25,425	3.1%
1997	1,33,064	3.1%
2004	150,000	2.85%
2007	169,000	2.4%
2010	175,800	2.2%

DENSITY OF POPULATION

The density of population differs from country to country. Even within a country it *varies from one* region to another. The best examples of the variation of population density within a country are the provinces of Punjab and Balochistan. Punjab is the most densely populated area while Balochistan is the most thinly inhabited province in spite of its vast territory.

There are a number of factors, which contribute to the density of population in a particular area. These factors are climate, fertility of land, rain and irrigation system, soil, peace, and security of the area, availability of means of communication and transport, development of trade and industry and mineral resources. All these factors, more or less, are available in the province of the Punjab, which is the most densely populated province of Pakistan. Following factors are responsible for higher density of population in the Punjab province:

FERTILE AGRICULTURAL LANDS

Punjab has better agricultural facilities in the whole of Pakistan. Punjab being the land of five rivers has fertile soil to support agriculture that is why Punjab supports higher rural population. Most of the people from the rural areas are farmers and earn their livelihood by working on land. Cotton, wheat, rice and sugarcane are the main crops of Pakistan, which after meeting home requirements are available for export as well.

IRRIGATION FACILITIES

Punjab has the best irrigation system in comparison with other provinces of Pakistan. Punjab, the land of rivers, has naturally better water availability of both surface and ground water resources. Besides, has 'Mangla Dam' the second largest dam of the world built on the river Jhelum and also Tarbela dam. There are a number of small dams and heads, which help supplying water to the lands all the year round and thus, keep the lands and the farmers busy throughout the year.

INDUSTRIES

Industries have played an important role in increasing the population of Punjab. Industries attract labor from other provinces that come and settle there to get employment in the factories scattered all over the province.

TRANSPORT

Being mostly a plain area Punjab has a better network of roads and railways as compared to other provinces. Besides the above stated facilities, the routes are comparatively secure and without hazards.

DAILY NECESSITIES OF LIFE

The Punjab has also better comforts of daily life. For example electricity, gas supplies, availability of fresh water, supply of fresh milk, vegetables and fruits are available at reasonable rates as compared to other provinces.

CAUSES OF LOW DENSITY IN BALOCHISTAN

The conditions in Balochistan on the other hand are completely the opposite as compared to Punjab where land is thin and infertile, rainfall is low and irrigation is almost negligible. Population is mostly rural; life is full of hazards and lacks security. Proper communication and transport facilities are not available. Mineral resources are available but due to lack of funds exploration is limited. Industry is inadequate and as such job opportunities are scarce. Because of these factors population density in Balochistan is very low: 46 persons/sq km.

MIGRATIONOFPOPULATION FROM RURAL TO URBAN AREAS

The study of distribution of population between the urban and rural areas in a country is very essential for any planning. As a country develops, there is a shift of population from rural to urban areas because the cities provide better job opportunities in expanding industrial and commercial sectors. A country like Pakistan whose economy is agrarian, cannot afford the large scale shifting of people from rural to urban areas as it involves heavy expenditures.

There is no doubt that mobility is an important characteristic of the development process but we can devise other measures lessening the impulse of rural population to urban areas. The villages should be connected with roads. The small-scale industry should be encouraged and properly organized in the rural areas technical education and health facilities should also be made available to them. The villagers should also share in building up the infrastructure. According to the 1972 census, out of the total population of 65.3 millions, 25.4% were living in urban areas and 74.6% in rural areas. The ratio has changed a little and at present it is 28 to 72%.

Sex	Total
Pakistan	
Both Sexes	46,737,010
Males	24,840,503
Females	21,896,507
Urban	
Both Sexes	13,591,289
Males	7,462,132
Females	6,129,157
Rural	
Both Sexes	33,145,721
Males	17,378,371
Females	15,767,350

POPULATION AND NATURAL RESOURCES

Natural resources are a boon from the heavens for a nation. The presence of natural resources in great quantity plays a pivotal role in the economic development of a country. Natural resources, therefore, are very vital for social uplift and economic stability.

Although nature has endowed each region with ample resources but much depends on the people how best they make use of these resources. It is the human endeavor only, which can fully exploit the resources for the happiness and welfare of the people of a certain area. There are numerous examples of the nations progressing through sheer hard work to put an end to their economic impoverishment. The amazing success and economic betterment of China, South Korea and Japan is a living example of dedication, devotion and burning desire of the people of these countries to accomplish the desired goals of life. Till 1949 these nations were not in reckoning in any walk of life. But their astonishing economic progress at present has bewildered the entire world. The major factor in these countries development is the dedication and devotion of the people. The availability of natural resources is not the only factor required for the economic development. It is also imperative that every individual should sincerely participate in the process of nation-building in order to achieve the lofty ends of life.

Pakistan is short of technical experts, which is a major factor in its economic lethargy. There is an acute dearth of skilled personnel in the country such as surveyors, geologists, engineers, scientists, and other experts. The population of Pakistan is rapidly increasing which leaves its adverse impact on the process of economic development. Manpower can be helpful in the economic prosperity only if the people are hard working and love to see their country prospering.

The presence of natural resources can be of great utility in raising the standard of life only if the people are trained and capable of utilizing the available resources to the best of their capacities. It will then bring prosperity in spite of the huge population. If, however, the people are not well trained and lack skill and expertise, the economy will stagnate even if the population is very small. The economic prosperity is always due to the quantity of natural resources and the way they are being exploited.

AGE COMPOSITION

According to the 1997 census; 45 percent of the population is under 15 years of age; 51 percent is between the age group of 15 and 64 years of age and above. The highest percentage of age group 15 to *64* years indicates that the population growth potential of Pakistan is high (nearly 3 percent). This high rate of growth is due mainly to the factors mentioned earlier.

The literacy rate in Pakistan has considerably increased and is nearly 53%. Sindh has the highest rate followed by Punjab, N.W.F.P. and Balochistan. By achieving higher literacy rate and with the improvement of living standards the population growth rate, which has declined to *2.85* percent at present, is likely to fall further in the years to come. Present regime is making hectic efforts to achieve the targets.

CHARACTERISTICS OF POPULATION OF PAKISTAN

1. The age group population statistics reveal the ratio of population of young people is high followed by children under 15 years and the percentage of older population is the least only 4% that goes to prove that Pakistan has high growth potential - a valuable man power resource.

2. As it is evident from the sex distribution table the male population is higher than the female about 51 to 49%. It is partly to natural

higher birth rate of males and partly due to lack of care to females in infancy and improper maternity facilities for adults.

3.   Most of the population lives in villages, ratio of rural urban population being 72 to 28%. It is due to the fact that Pakistan has primarily an agricultural economy and there is greater opportunity for the people to get work on lands. Growth of cities and of industries has to some extent diverted their attention and there is a trend of migration from rural to urban centers.

4.   People of Pakistan are healthy, energetic and hard working endowed with clean habits. HIV occurrence in Pakistan is, therefore, negligible as compared to her immediate neighbor India largely because of cultural differences - Adherence to Islamic way of life is the main factor.

CHAPTER XI

POLITICAL DIVISIONS OF PAKISTAN PROVINCES

Pakistan consisted of two Provinces, East Pakistan and West Pakistan before 1971. The Eastern part was separated from the rest of the country as a result of Indian aggression in 1971. The present Pakistan is divided into four provinces known as Punjab, N.W.F.P. Sindh and Balochistan. The four provinces of Pakistan are further divided into divisions and districts for administrative purposes.

Before partition the province of Punjab consisted of 28 districts. Eleven districts fell in East Punjab (India) and 17 districts were included in Western Punjab (Pakistan). This distribution of districts remained unchanged till 1956 when a scheme of One Unit was introduced in Pakistan. The province of Punjab was dismembered and merged into the province of West Pakistan, created under the One Unit Scheme.

The One Unit was dissolved in President Yahya's regime in 1969 and Punjab once again attained the status of a province. Three more districts were created namely Bahawalpur, Rahimyar Khan and Bahawalnagar bringing the number of districts to 20 in the Punjab.

There were only three divisions in the Punjab before President Ayub came to power. Two more divisions were created known as Sargodha and Bahawalpur Divisions, which raised the number of divisions to five in the province of the Punjab.

When Mr. Z.A. Bhutto came to power, Qasur and Vehari were given the status of districts thus bringing the total to 22 districts in the province. Later under Martial Law regime of Gen. Muhammad Zia-ul-Haq, Khushab, Leiah, Bhakkar, Toba Tek Singh, Rajanpur and Okara were raised to district Level while two more divisions Gujranwala and Faisalabad were constituted. Dera Ghazi Khan and Larkana were declared as Divisions. The new districts started functioning with effect from July 1, 1982. Lodhran, Pakpattan, Chakwal and Narowal in Punjab and Haripur in N.W.F.P. have also been given the status of districts and these districts have started functioning with effect from 1st July, 1991 and Nankana Sahib District from July 2005.

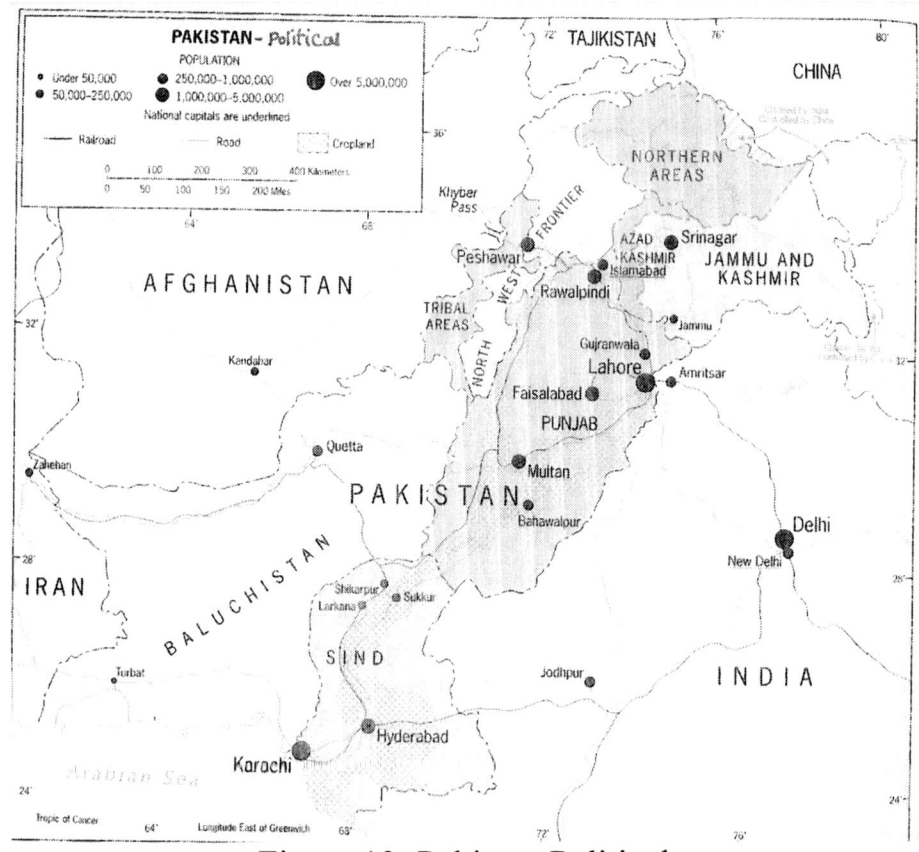

Figure 13: Pakistan Political

NEW DISTRICTS
Seven new districts were created and recently the eighth one Nankana Sahib in Punjab has been announced officially in July 2005.
Mandi Bahauadin, Hafizabad, (Gujranwala, Div, Punjab, July 1993)
Ghotki (Sukkur Div, Sindh) April 1993.
Omar Kot (Mirpur Khas Div. Sindh) April 1993

KEY REGION CITIES
Population of Pakistan is mainly concentrated along the rivers and the population pattern also follows the trend of the Indus valley. River basins being made up of the fine alluvium deposited by the flowing

rivers and streams that provide fertile lands for cultivation - but being low lying are also vulnerable to devastative floods. Cities or settlements are located on river bluffs; a higher ground, much above flood level, that a river constructs during its journey to its mouth in its middle and lower stages when the speed of the river is reduced and no longer can carry and transport the eroded material start depositing - the same. Over a period of millions of years, such a feature is formed; Multan and Lahore are good examples of this habit or characteristic of the rivers that has helped formation of sufficiently higher ground to make it possible to growing of these settlements in the basins of Chenab and Ravi respectively. Pakistan consists of four provinces and each province has a key region, which is represented by a prominent city like Lahore for Punjab, which has been a natural center of activity and hence administrative pivot of the region.

Divisions – SINDH
Sind division consists of: Hyderabad, Sukkur, Karachi, Larkana and MirpurKhas Divisions.
Districts of Karachi Division: Karachi West, Karachi East, Karachi South and Karachi Central, Malir.
Hyderabad Division: Hyderabad, Dadu, Thatta, and Badeen.
Sukkur Division: Sukkur, Khairpur, Nawabshah, Naushero Feroze and Ghotki.
Larkana Division: Larkana, Jacobabad and Shikarpur.
Mirpur Khas: Mirpurkhas, Thar, Sanghar, Umerkot.

Divisions and Districts – N.W.F.P.
Peshawar Division, Mardan Division, Kohat Division, Malakand Division, Dera Ismail Khan Division, Hazara Division, Bannu Mansehra Division.
Districts of N.W.F.P. Division wise are:-
Peshawar Division: Peshawar, Nowshera.
Mardan Division: Mardan, Swabi and Charsadda.
Kohat Division: Kohat, Karak and Hangu.
Malakand Division: Swat, Upper Dir, Lower Dir, Chitral, Bunner, Shangla Pur and Malakand.
Dera Ismail Khan Division: Dera Ismail Khan, Tonk and Kulachi.
Hazara Division: Abbottabad, Hazara and Haripur.
Bannu: Bannu, Lucky Marwar.
Mansehra: Manshera, Ghazar, Ghanchi, Dia Mir.

Divisions and Districts - BALOCHISTAN

Divisions and Districts of the province of Balochistan are as follows:
Quetta Division, Kalat Division, Mekran Division, Sibbi Division,
Nasirabad Division Zohb Loralai Division.
Districts of Balochistan Division wise are:-
Quetta Division: Quetta, Pasheen and Chaghi, Killa Abdullah.
Kalat Division: Kalat, Khuzdar, Lasbella, Kharan, Oraan and Mastung.
Mekran Division: Turbat, Panjgur and Gawadur.
Sibbi Division: Sibbi, Kohlu, Dera Bugti and Ziarat.
Nasirabad Division: Nasirabad, Kachhi, Hat Pat and Jaffarbad.
Zohb Loralai Division: Loralai, Zohb Agency, Barkhan, Musakhil and
Killa Saifullah.

CITIES OF INDUS BASIN PAKISTAN

Cities in river basins, are located on river bluffs a feature which a river
makes in its mature stage when it deposits the eroded material in the shape
of mound, a much higher firm land, than the surrounding low lying area,
much above flood level, become site of cities in river basins.

Figure 14: Hazuri Bagh and Bad Shahi Mosque, Lahore

LAHORE

Lahore is an important historical city named after a son of Hindu Raja Lahoo, which in course of time became Lahore. It is located on the left bank of the river Ravi on a much higher firm ground built by the river and the entire old city of Lahore, built as a fort with high walls and huge gates around almost 12 in number. Over looking dry bed of the river to the north stands the magnificent Lahore fort originally built by Hindu Rajas and rebuilt in present shape by Shah Jahan. Opposite Lahore fort is the big beautiful mosque of red stones called Shahi mosque built by Emperor Aurangzeb that has a capacity of fifty thousand worshippers. On its eastern corner is the grave of Dr. Allama Iqbal the poet philosopher of Pakistan. Lahore has been an administrative center of Punjab during British period and continues to enjoy that position. It is also the city of colleges and gardens; Shalimar garden built by the Mughal emperor Shah Jahan, has been well-maintained but other old gardens like Chauburji garden and Hazuri Bagh have been turned into residential areas. However, a number of new ones; Lawrence garden, Iqbal park, Race course park and several other such parks add to the beauty of the city. Iqbal parks formerly known as Minto Park attained historical position as the Pakistan Resolution in the year 1940 was passed here in a meeting of All India Muslim League.

Lahore has been a center of politics and almost all Political parties have their head offices located here. A center of education; one of the oldest University of India, the Punjab University is situated here was created in 1862 that has a number of colleges, schools and institutes; affiliated to it. Independent Engineering University at Lahore and Agriculture University at Faisalabad have also been created. Engineering University has a number of technical institutes attached to it. King Edward the oldest Medical College has attained the status of a Medical University and there are a number of Medical colleges, including Allama Iqbal and Jinnah Medical Colleges with attached hospitals have also been added where free medical facilities are provided. Almost all the colleges and universities have boarding facilities and students from all over the country come to pursue their studies here. Lahore is also a market that serves the entire Punjab for its agricultural produce, industrial products; textiles, handicrafts, sports goods cutlery, automobile and a huge market for old spare parts, called Bilal Ganj is located here.

Above all Lahore is a cultural center of not only Punjab but represents Pakistani culture; Basant Mela of the spring season at Lahore, is joined by people from all over the country and even by Pakistanis living abroad come all the way to attend it. But at present due to the use of chemical and metallic strings used for flying kites which are responsible for the loss of many innocent lives and damages to electric transformers, resulting in frequent failure of electric supplies, the chief minister Punjab Mian Shahbaz Sharif has banned the sport- an historic seasonal colorful event. Mazars of Data Ganj Bakhsh, Hazrat Mian Mir, and Imam Bargahs are largely attended. Moharram gatherings and processions rank it No.1 amongst the religious cities of Pakistan not because of its geographical central location, but for its above stated activities, that Lahore is rightly known as the heart of Pakistan.

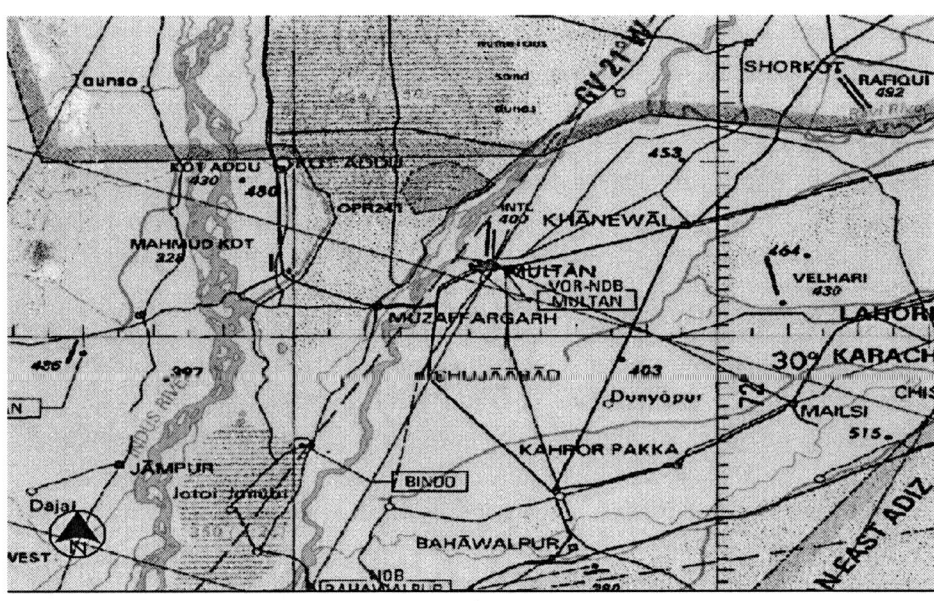

Figure 15: Location of Multan

MULTAN

Multan's population is about 2 million, and is located on the bank of river Chenab, a tributary of river Indus. It is the center of cotton growing and textile industry. It is an old historical town - a city of graves and graveyards. Alexander the great came here in 326 B.C and was wounded during combat when he jumped in a fort during his mission to conquer the world. Mohammad been Qasim from Arabia came up to Multan and stayed here, a garden of date palms is said to have been planted by him and is known as Qasim Bagh.

KARACHI

Karachi with a population of 20 million is located on the Arabian sea coast, and so far the only harbor, whose hinter land spread thousands of miles including Afghanistan and Russian states. It is center of engineering and manufacturing industry. It accommodated a large number of immigrants from India in 1947 and these immigrants have gained a political status in the city, Named "Mohajir Qaumi Party"

Figure 16: Shah Faisal Mosque, Islamabad

RAWALPINDI- ISLAMABAD

Rawalpindi was a village in the beginning. It grew into a town and then into a city during the pre-historic (stone age) up to the present time. The capital was shifted from Karachi to Rawalpindi in 1959. Rawalpindi is situated on G.T Road. Government offices were shifted to Islamabad, the new capital of Pakistan. Rawalpindi and Islamabad are known as "Twin Cities".

Rawalpindi acquired greater importance when capital was shifted from Karachi. It is the General headquarters of the Pakistan Army. The Air Headquarters and Naval Headquarters have been shifted to Islamabad. The Rawalpindi Cant. is the largest military establishment in the country. It is a divisional and district headquarters.

Rawalpindi has tremendously expanded within the last few years. It is a big commercial and industrial center. It has a number of industrial factories, which include cotton and textile mills, steel mills and oil refineries.

Rawalpindi is also a seat of learning. It has quite a few educational institutions. It has an Army medical college besides other reputed institutions, which are affiliated with the University of the Punjab. The only hill resort in Punjab, Murree, is situated nearly 40 miles away from Rawalpindi. Estimated population of Rawalpindi at present is about 3 million.

Islamabad is the new Capital of Pakistan and one of the few modern capitals in the world. It was constructed during President Ayub Khan's regime in 1959. It is situated 9 miles (14.4 km.) away from Rawalpindi and lies at the base of Margalla Hills. The world's famous and renowned town planners, Co Buster, John Stone and Geo Panti have designed the plan of Islamabad, which is the blend of traditional Islamic architectural characteristics with modern requirements.

The total area of Islamabad is approximately 350 sq. miles with a population of about 1 million. Islamabad is a beautiful place with pleasant climate and excellent environs. Shakarparian Hills, Rawal Lake and Dam are the fascinating resorts in Islamabad. A beautiful and picturesque garden known as Daman-e-Koh has been built on the Margalla Hills from where the whole of Islamabad lies before one's eyes to give a captivating view. Faisal Masjid has recently been constructed to add grandeur to the beauty of Islamabad. Islamabad is expanding rapidly. At present there are Government offices. It is an important seat of learning with a number of educational institutions. The Quaid-i-Azam University, Allama Iqbal Open University, Pakistan Institute of Engineering and applied Sciences, National University of Science and Technology, and Islamic University are the most prestigious seats of higher learning.

PESHAWAR

Peshawar is the capital of N.W.F.P. It is an ancient city with a population of about one million. It is situated nearly 1,100 miles away from Karachi and at a highly strategic position being few miles away from the Khyber Pass. It has a common border with Afghanistan and commands routes through Khyber Pass to Kabul and Central Asia.

Peshawar is a city with great historical background. It is famous for its handicrafts, museums, Gandhara sculptures and other antiquities. There is the Warsak Dam, built on the Kabul River 29 km., from Peshawar, with-Canadian assistance. Peshawar is also famous for producing excellent guns and pistols produced by the skilled craftsmen in a small village of Barra in the Tribal area situated near Peshawar.

Peshawar has many places of interest. The famous Qissa Khawani Bazar occupies great historical significance. Chowk Yadgar is another important place of Peshawar. The Qissa Khawani Bazar has been the center of professional storytellers who used to tell stories and sing songs for peoples' amusement. In this way it was given the name of Qissa Khawani Bazar.

The famous educational institution, Islamia College Peshawar, has been the center of freedom struggle in the N.W.F.P. This great institution has produced a number of celebrated men who worked for the freedom movement. Peshawar has one Engineering University and one Medical College. The University has a beautiful residential campus. Besides these institutions, there is one Agricultural University of Peshawar and one Forest College. Peshawar is the biggest city of NWFP with the population of 0.988 million (1998 census).

QUETTA

Quetta is the Provincial Capital of Balochistan. It is situated 536 miles away from Karachi. It is situated at the Bolan Pass and occupies a highly strategic position. It is 5,500 feet above the sea level, which has made it a hill resort. It gets its first snowfall with the arrival of the New Year.

Quetta has a dry and chilly climate. It is very cold in winter and extremely pleasant in the summer. Hanna Lake and Ural Valley are picnic resorts near Quetta. A plan is underway to develop a new hill station 30 km., from Quetta at an altitude of 8,000 feet. It will have all modern facilities to attract tourists both the domestic and foreign. Quetta is a fruit-producing city where different types of fruits are planted in large quantity.

Quetta is a famous Military Cantonment. The Staff College, Quetta is an excellent army institution. It is an important trade center of Balochistan. Quetta has many higher education institutions; University of Balochistan, Balochistan University of Information Technology Engineering and Management Sciences, and Bolan Medical College being the outstanding ones. Quetta is the biggest city of Balochistan with a small population of 0.56 million (1998 census), and at present estimated at 0.75 million.

CHAPTER XII
SOILS OF PAKISTAN

The soils of Pakistan belong to dry groups having high calcium carbonate content and are deficient in organic matter. These vary in color from reddish brown in the north to red or gray in the south. These soils are generally fertile due to their process of formation.

The newly deposited alluvium near the river is called Khaddar and mostly consists of sand. The old alluvium of the bar uplands, called Bangar, consists of finer particles - loams. At the foot of the mountains the soil is sandy and generally becomes finer towards the plains where

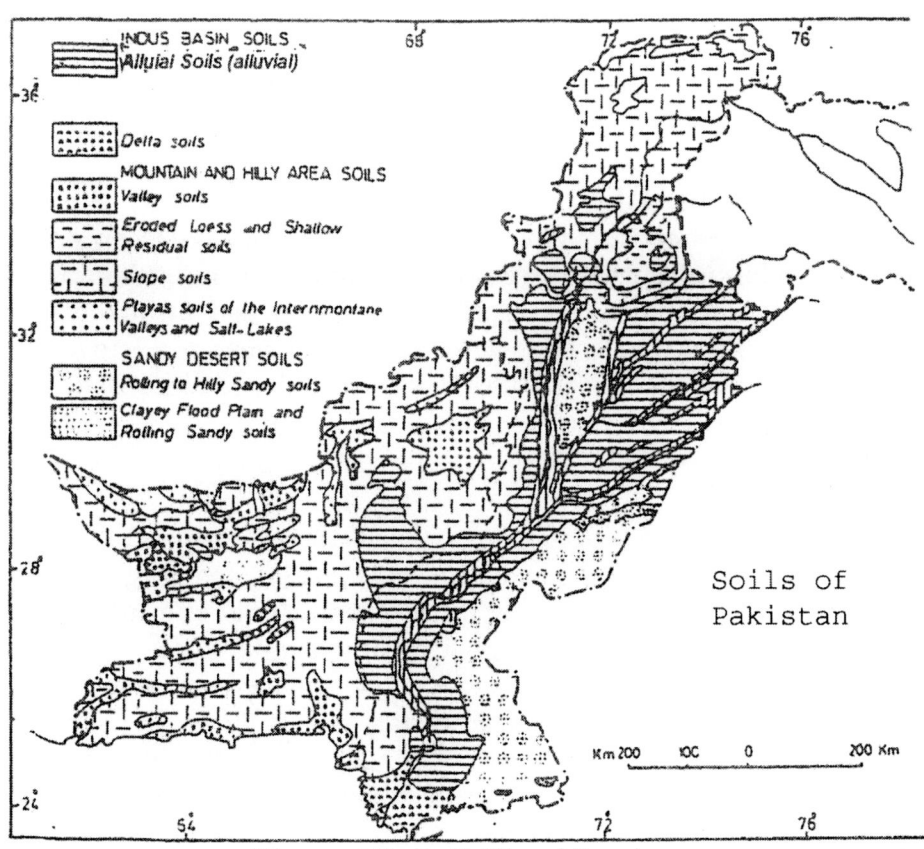

Figure 17: Soil Classification

Khankah, limestone concentration, is occasionally found. The soils of the Thal and the Thar deserts, and of Balochistan are wind-blown. In southern Potwar a thin layer of residual soil covering is found. In parts of the canal irrigated lands, salt efflorescence is found, generally in the areas of high water table. These saline areas are known as Thur or Kallar.

FACTORS IN SOIL FORMATION

Soil is defined as that part of the unconsolidated material covering the surface of the earth, which supports plant growth. It has three major constituents. (i) Solid particles: Salts, mineral and organic matter, (ii) air and (iii) water. The type of soil formed is a function of topography, climate vegetation and the parent rocks from which the soil material is derived. Soil material transported and deposited by running water is known as alluvium, which that is transported and deposited by winds forms Aeolian soil. Soils formed in silt are termed residual. Soil forming processes are complex and continuous. As a result, soils vary in their chemical composition color, texture and organic content from place to place.

INDUS BASIN SOILS

The Indus basin comprises of a vast area of alluvial plains deposited by the Indus and its tributaries, and a small area of loess plains. Most of the material is sub-recent or recent in origin, calcareous, and low in organic content. The soils can be divided *into three* major *categories:* Banger Soils (old alluvium); Khaddar Soils (new alluvium); and Indus Delta Soils.

Banger Soils

Banger Soils cover a vast *area in the* Indus Plain, including most of the Punjab, Peshawar, Mardan, Bannu and Kachhi plains, and the greater part of the Sindh Plain. These soils are deep, calcareous, of medium to fine texture, low in organic matter, but very productive when irrigated and fertilized. In some ill-drained areas, these soils have become waterlogged, and capillary action has carried salts to the surface. Some areas show a puffy salt layer at the surface, but simple leaching can reclaim these, if supplied with plenty of irrigation water. Over very small areas, strongly alkaline soil patches have developed, and these, being nonporous, are difficult to reclaim.

In the upper Chaj and Rechna doabs, the sub-montane area bordering the Peshawar-Mardan Plain, and in the eastern Potwar, the Banger soils have developed under sub-humid conditions. Because of the higher rainfall, they have been leached of lime and are non-calcareous, medium *to fine* textured, and have a slightly higher organic content. These soils are also fertile when supplied with plenty of water and manure.

Khaddar Soils
Khaddar soils are formed from recent and present-day deposits along the rivers. Parts of these soils are flooded each year, adding depositional layers of silt and clayey loams.
The organic content of these soils is low, but they are usually free of salts.

Indus Delta Soils
Indus Delta Soils are formed of sub-recent alluvium and estuarine deposits. They cover the entire area of the Indus Delta from south of Hyderabad to the coast. Clayey soils, developed under floodwater conditions, cover about one-third of the area.

MOUNTAIN SOILS
Mountain soils occur in the highland areas of the north and west, and are residual as well as transported. Along the steep crests and slopes, and in the broken hill country, shallow residual soils have developed. Under arid and semi-arid conditions, these soils are usually strongly calcareous, with low organic content. Further north, under sub-humid conditions, there is more leaching, and a higher organic content. In the mountain valleys, soils are formed from the alluvial in fills of the streams. These soils are calcareous silt loams and sandy loams of low organic content. They are cultivated in patches only.

In the sub-montane area of the Potwar Plateau, shallow residual soils and silty eroded loess have been formed. In places these soils are massive, susceptible to erosion, and strongly gullied, producing a dissected landscape. Lime content is high and organic content low, but with plenty of water, these soils are relatively productive.

In the lowest parts of the inter-montane valleys and interior basins of the arid and semi-arid regions, strongly saline soils develop. Excess of evaporation over precipitation leaves a thick crust of salts at the surface of the intermittent lakes. For the most part, these soils are barren. The margins carry low shrubs and saltbush, used for poor grazing.

ALLUVIAL SOILS OF THE FLOOD PLAINS

Within the flood plains of Pakistan, flood conditions differ from one region to another. Areas close to rivers are flooded every year. Areas at some distance from the rivers are inundated in years of severe floods, while the coastal areas are subject to tidal flooding. This has affected the soil texture, the soil water, the soil pH and other soil characteristics. Accordingly, different areas have developed different types of soil.

Loamy and some sandy soils
Loamy and clayey soils
Mainly loamy saline estuarine soils
Saline soils of the tidal flats

Loamy and some Sandy Soils

The active flood plains are covered with loamy and some sandy soils. They occupy the narrow strips along the Indus River *and its tributaries, the* Jhelum, *the Chenab, the Ravi and* Satluj. They are most extensive along the Indus River where they are 25 to 40 km wide. The two heads between the braided channels of the stream are also covered with these soils. *They* are flooded almost every year during the rainy season (July-August). They are thoroughly flooded and are free from salinity. They are renewed with fresh deposits of alluvium whenever the flood comes. Loams dominate the area. Sandy soils occur on the towheads and in other areas in small patches.

Loamy and Clayey Soils

The old flood plains are covered with loamy and clayey soils. The old flood plains lie between the active flood plains (bet) and the Bar Uplands in the northern Indus Plains and between the active flood plains and the desert region in the southern Indus Plains. The old flood plains were subjected to flood in the recent past. At present they remain free from flood in most years. Only in years of heavy rainfall are they locally flooded. Therefore, the soils have experienced considerable stability and are appreciably homogenized. Saline and alkaline patches are observed here and there, particularly close to the desert areas. In such patches the pH ranges from 8.0 to 8.4 and in exceptional cases up to 9.0. Loam is the predominant soil with patches of clayey soils on the back slopes and in the meander scars and the channel in fills. The levees and meander bars are covered with sandy loams. The color ranges from brown in humid and well-drained areas to grayish brown in dry areas.

Mainly Loamy Saline Estuarine Soils

A major part of the Indus Delta excluding the tidal plains is covered with loamy saline soils. The soils are graded from levees to the back slopes of the Indus and its distributaries. The meander bars are covered with sandy loams and the channel in fills with clayey soils. In general the soils are porous. They are low in organic content. Homogenization has not progressed much. In most parts, the soils are saline. The pH values range from 8.0 to 8.5. Over large areas Solonchak soils have been recognized.

Soils of the Tidal Flats

The tidal flats occupy the coastal areas along the Indus Delta. The soils are mainly clays derived from the sediments deposited by the Indus and reworked by the tides. In low-lying areas the tides visit twice a day whereas in slightly higher areas they come twice a month. The soils are stratified. The sea water has turned the soils highly saline. Sodium chloride is the main salt. There are some tidal lakes, which are occasionally filled with seawater. The seawater evaporates after some time and a crust of salt is left behind.

ALLUVIAL SOILS OF THE BAR UPLANDS

The Bar Uplands (the Kirans Bar, the Sandal Bar and the Nili Bar) are Pleistocene alluvial terraces. They are well above the flood plains and have developed mature soils. *They* are classed as Noncalcic Brown in the sub humid areas where the soils have been leached almost free of lime. In the arid areas they are classed as Brown Soils or Sierozems. Considerable leaching of lime has taken place from Sierozems also but not as thorough as that from the Noncalcic Brown. In both the soils, a layer rich in lime occurs at about three feet from the surface. Texturally the soils are silt loams and clay loams. The soils are quite fertile and are extensively cultivated with the help of irrigation.

SOILS OF THE PIEDMONT PLAINS

The Piedmont Plains cover an extensive area between the Sulemans-Kirthar Mountains and the Indus River. Two relatively smaller areas occur in the northern part of the Punjab along the Pir Panjal Mountains. The foothills of these mountains are occupied by stony fans and aprons, which are formed of loose material washed down from the mountains by occasional heavy rainfall. The stream beds are filled with gravels and coarse sands. Some fine material is arrested between the gravels and stones. These predominantly stony soils are strongly calcareous and are of little agricultural importance. Gently sloping plains lie beyond the foothills. They are formed by alluvium laid down by sheet floods and shallow intermittent streams with shifting channels. They are covered mainly with sandy loams and silts, and are strongly calcareous. In some areas dunes have developed by wind action. The soils are quite fertile and produce good crops after rains and on application of irrigation.

DESERT SOILS

There are three large areas of desert soils in Pakistan: Thar-Cholistan, Thal, and Kharan. These soils are generally classed as regosils. The Thar-Cholistan is the most extensive. It is about 720 km long and 80 km wide. It is located in the eastern part of Pakistan. In the South it is covered primarily by latitudinal dunes and in the north by transverse dunes. The sands involved are yellowish to pale brown in color. They are calcareous and rich in minerals. Dunes occupy loamy sands and the interdunal valleys by soils of inner texture (sandy loams). They are very weakly developed soils. The Thal area lying between the Indus and the Jhelum rivers is a river terrace covered with a comparatively thin layer of *gray* sands. Dunes oriented in various directions cover the region. Calcareous loamy sands form the ridges and sandy loams cover the interdunal areas. When the calcium carbonate is leached from them, they are classed as Sierozem. Old river channels are filled with silt and clays. The Kharan Desert occupies a large area of western Balochistan and is covered with sands. With the virtual absence of vegetation, solid formation is minimal.

SOILS OF THE POTWAR PLATEAU

The Potwar Plateau is covered with three types of soils: (1) Loess, (2) Alluvial, (3) Residual. All the soils are extensively eroded, deeply dissected and badly gullied. The wind-deposited loess is brown in color and moderately alkaline in reaction. They are very fertile. Unfortunately they do not occupy large areas and are badly eroded. The alluvial soils cover the narrow river valleys and the alluvial terraces. The soils of the river valleys are fine sands and loams whereas those of terraces are clay loams. They are fertile soils and are suitable for farming.

The residual soils of the Potwar Plateau have been derived primarily from the decomposition of shale and sandstone. They have formed into brown clayey soils. Part of calcium carbonate has been elevated from the surface to a foot below. They are poor soils and are suitable for pasture.

SOILS OF THE WESTERN HIGHLANDS

Steep rock outcrops bare of soils dominate the Western Highlands. Some parts of the extreme north are covered with glaciers; therefore, over large areas soils are absent. Wherever soils are found lithosols and regosols cover the hills and mountains and alluvial soils fill the river valleys and basins.

Lithosols and Regosols: Limestone, shale and sandstone are the main rocks involved in the formation of the Western Highlands. Volcanic rocks cover the area in patches. Limestone yields very little soil. Shales, sandstone and volcanic rocks have produced a thin veneer of soils. Most of the soils formed on the slopes are removed by wind, water and gravity. Thin stony sods lie over the bedrock and are classified as lithosols. Over the flatter areas, regosols dominate. They are also thin soils but unlike lithosols, they are usually not stony. In the northern sub humid region podzolization on a limited scale has started. Agriculturally lithosols and regosols are of very little importance.

Alluvial Soil

The wide basins bounded by hills and mountains are covered with alluvial soils. So are the narrow river valleys which wind through and run between hills and mountains. The foothills are covered with talus cones and alluvial fans generally composed of gravels, pebbles, and coarse sands. Beyond the foothills, the valley floods are covered with silt and loam. They are fertile soils of great agricultural value in the rocky waste of the Western Highlands. The most extensive and important areas of alluvial soils in Balochistan are the Lasbela Plains drained by the Porali River, the valleys of Dasht, Mastung, Quetta, Pishin and Zhob. In N.W.F.P. the Valleys of Kabul River, Kurrum and Swat are important.

Chapter XIII

IRRIGATION IN PAKISTAN

Most of the cultivable areas in Pakistan with fertile lands have low and unreliable, rainfall less than 10 inches annually, which is insufficient to raise crops and carry on agricultural activities profitably. However, with the construction of Barrages, Dams, and perennial canals rather a network of such facilities has helped bringing large areas in Punjab and Sindh under plough that once were dry and barren lands.

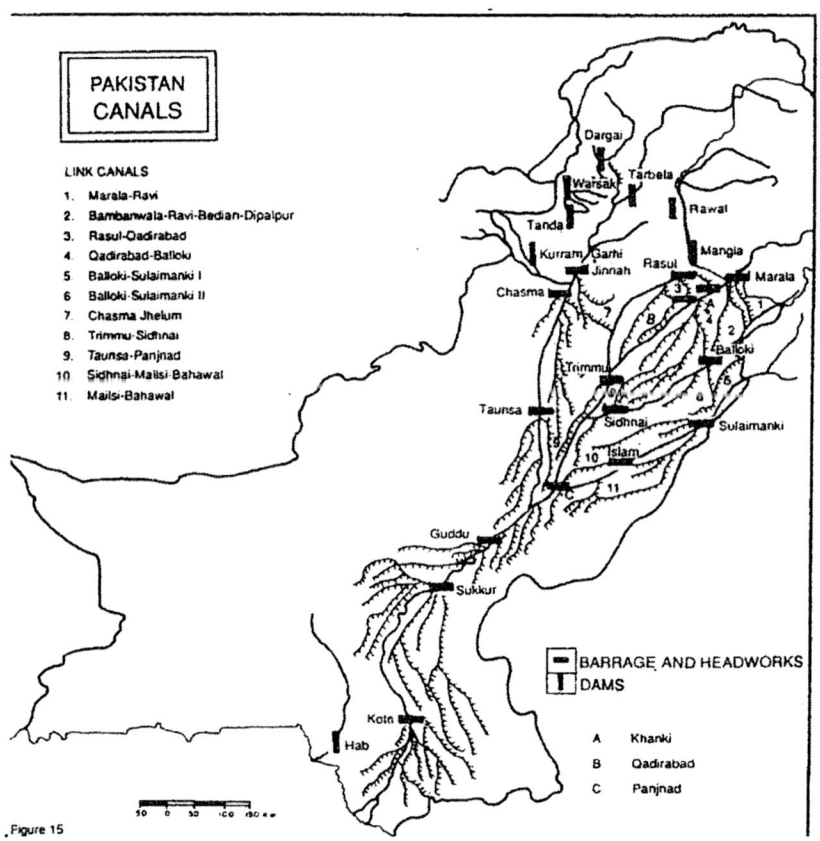

Figure 18: Canal Irrigation of Pakistan

Although irrigation on a limited scale was being done before British occupation of India, particularly in the Mughal period when inundation and flood canals were dug and used for irrigation, yet it was during

British period that irrigation on a large scale was undertaken and besides flood and inundation, perennial canals were introduced and new canal colonies were established where the farmers were allotted lands to be settled and brought under cultivation.

Pakistan, thus has one of the largest and cleverest systems of irrigation in the world. The Irrigation Department, after taking over from the British, continued development of its projects and added considerable irrigated areas in Punjab and Sindh. In the late 1950s WAPDA (Water and Power Development Authority) was organized that had the support of the World Bank. The Authority having huge funds at its disposal under took construction of multipurpose works like Warsak on River Kabul, Mangla at Jhelum, Tarbela at Indus, and a number of small dams at different sites to boost irrigation and Power generation throughout the country, that helped running tube wells as well, which in turn has helped bringing green revolution in the country. Today Pakistan has a number of big and small dams, and barrages that supply water throughout the year to the thirsty lands, thus reducing dependency of the farmer on rainfall alone.

Besides canal water a large number of tube wells have been dug, which have not only helped supplementing canal irrigation but also have been useful in treating water logging and salinity that has resulted from extensive canal irrigation system in the country. It is with the planning and efforts of the Irrigation Department and WAPDA that Pakistan is not only self-sufficient in food and cash crops but also in a position to export and earn foreign exchange for the country.

INDUS WATER TREATY

All the rivers of Pakistan rise from Indian occupied Kashmir region. Thus India is in a position to divert the waters of these rivers at her will. After partition India used this weapon of persecution and more often than not Pakistan had to pay for the water for irrigating fields. In 1960 with the efforts of UNO India and Pakistan signed a treaty of division of Indus waters, which deprived Pakistan of the use of waters of Satluj, Beas and Ravi. Thus Pakistan was restricted to the use of Chenab, Jhelum and Indus. In order to compensate the loss of waters of the three eastern rivers the World Bank helped Pakistan in the construction of two dams Mangla and Tarbela and five barrages for meeting the needs of irrigation in Pakistan. This treaty is known as Indus Water Treaty.

Although Pakistani Engineers opposed such an unprecedented agreement but the military dictatorship prevailed and signed the treaty ignoring technical and professional objections raised by the Engineers. India and Indian Engineers rejoiced it. The bad effects of losing flow of the three eastern rivers in their original beds have since started appearing in the form of going down of water table of sweet water; the water which was available at a depth of about 300 feet in Lahore has now gone below 500 feet or more and this depth is continuously falling and not only that large area of productive lands, according to one expert will be rendered barren and uncultivable. The expert, an American scholar, commenting on the Treaty had pointed out its draw backs and paid rich tributes to Pakistani Engineers acknowledging their depth of knowledge for having opposed the deal tooth and nail. He expressed these views in his research volume on the subject available in the library of the Punjab Irrigation Department's office at Lahore. The other menace a result of digging extra link canals alternate to the existing arrangements has appeared in the form of water logging and salinity on a large scale due to which rich agricultural lands to the tune of hundreds of thousands of acres are being affected annually.

The Treaty has given an upper hand to India who still keeps on violating the treaty whenever she likes; construction of Bagyar dam at River Chenab and another at Jhelum in occupied Kashmir are the glaring examples of Indian violations of the treaty. The dispute has now been referred to the World Bank who has already appointed a committee from three independent member countries to decide the issue on merits. Both the countries are committed to honor the decision of the committee.

Mangla Dam

Mangla Dam is constructed over River Jhelum. It is 3,352.8 meters long and 116 meters high. Mangla Lake is 64 kilometers long and it can hold 55 acres feet water. It was completed in 1967. The design of the dam has a provision of future extension; the height of the dam about 100 feet and the storage capacity to 9,900,000 acre-feet. The present government has granted approval and funds for increasing its height and the holding capacity of water, to make up for the silting that has taken place since 1967. Extension work on the project has already started. It is a multipurpose project and besides irrigation it is providing electricity as well. At present it is providing 400,000 kilo-watts of electricity but after completion of extension work the capacity would be substantially increased.

Tarbela Dam

This is also a multipurpose project and is built on river Indus at Tarbela, which is 34 kilometer from Haripur and 48 kilometer from Attock. The dam is 2,743.2 meters or about 2.7 kilometer long and 146.3 meters high. An 80 kilometers long reservoir has been built behind it. Construction work of the dam was started in 1968 under Indus Water Treaty and completed in 1974. It has a potential of generating 2.1 million kilo watts of electricity and supplying 9,300,000 acre- feet of water. This dam also has the provision of future extension of generation power and capacity of storing water.

KALABAGH DAM

KalaBagh dam was proposed decades before at a site 147 km downstream of the Kabul-Indus rivers confluence at Attock. It was designed to have a generation capacity of 3,600 MW and storage of 6.1 MAF water. The dam would have cost Rs 272 billion in 80s. It will have the world's largest catchment area of over 275,000 sq. km. with a height of 260 feet above the river and two spillways; the one on the right bank to be used for the disposal of flood water and the left bank shall have a power house connected to 12 tunnel conduits having a diameter of 36 feet each with an ultimate generation capacity of 3,600 MW.

KalaBagh dam was the first proposal of dams of its nature. Its feasibility and survey was conducted in early 50s. The dam geographically and geologically ideally located as per survey report submitted by local and foreign experts and the country has already spent a billion Rupees on the same. It is a pity that in spite of availability of funds from the World Bank the project could not be started. Even a strong dictatorial regime of Zia-ul-Haq that could hang an elected popular Prime Minister did not use its discretion to initiate a project, which, according to independent experts could have changed the fate of the nation by improving its economy by many folds. But due to conflicting statements of some individuals, vested with political antagonism the otherwise a feasible project of national interest has been given to un-ending provincial controversy and the politicians have taken it as an issue to give vent to their differences with the government in power, that is sincere and wants to solve water and power deficiency faced by the people of all the provinces, to usher an era of prosperity in the country.

Every proposal has its pros and cons, advantages and disadvantages, which should be judged in the light of national interests irrespective of provincial priorities. The father of the nation had warned against such tendencies that have already cost us bifurcation. We must learn a lesson from that. If the project is not in the best interest of the country it should be set aside otherwise one should go ahead with it forgetting about provincial rivalries. Instead of politicizing the issue and to finish the controversy, a high powered committee consisting of Engineers and Economists from the four provinces under some judicial authority be constituted to look into the apprehensions and objections being raised by the parties to decide either to carry out the proposed project as such or to modify the existing design to accommodate the criticizers but to abandon it altogether on which millions of dollars have been spent, conducting surveys and preparation of feasibility etc., would be a sheer waste and a big national loss. The decision and verdict of the committee should be final.

NEED FOR CONSTRUCTION OF NEW DAMS

Pakistan has many good sites identified for building new dams besides Kalabagh dam. Construction of new dams will not only provide cheap energy but it would also bring arid area of 27 million acres under cultivation by supplying sufficient water for irrigation purpose. Further dams will help manage floods which year after year cause colossal loss of life and property. Thus unless these dams are built Pakistan will be unable to produce adequate food and fiber, and to generate enough power to alleviate poverty and hunger. Industrialized countries have already harnessed their rivers to the maximum. Accordingly developing countries should be given opportunities for building more dams. In case dams are not built atomic power would be next choice with its own peculiar hazards and disadvantages.

SMALL DAMS

Small dams are vital for the economy of Pakistan. They no doubt command small area but can easily constructed with indigenous resources. A number of such dams have been constructed in the hilly regions of Punjab and Balochistan. Some of these dams have been built by WAPDA and others by Small Dams Organization.

RAWAL DAM

It is one of the small dams built in Punjab on a small stream called Rawal. It is a multipurpose dam and besides irrigating about 5,000 hectares of land supplies drinking water to Rawalpindi Islamabad.

KHANPUR DAM

It is located on Haro River in NWFP. It irrigates 14, 760 hectares in Haripur Abbottabad area.

NARI-BOLAN DAM

It is located on River Bolan in Balochistan. It irrigates 9,700 hectares of Sibbi.

NARACHIP PROJECT

It irrigates 1300 hectares of Loralai district. Hab dam in Lasbela district irrigates 34,000 hectares of Lasbela and Karachi.

MIRANI DAM BALOCHISTAN

A multipurpose project, located on Dasht River, about 30 miles west of Turbat in Makran Division of Balochistan. Inaugurated in 2002 is nearing completion by 2007 costing more than Rs. 5.8 billion. It will irrigate 35,000 hectors of rugged and dry lands of the southern Balochistan besides other benefits.

BARRAGES

Five barrages, a gated siphon and a number of link canals have been constructed under the Indus water treaty.

Chashma Barrage

It is located on the river Indus 64 km downstream from Jinnah Barrage. It was completed in 1970. It can divert one million cusecs into Chashma–Jhelum link by which it irrigates areas served by Sidhnai-Mailsi-Bahawal link system, Haveli and Rangpur canals.

Rasul Barrage

It is located on the Jhelum, 4 km downstream from Rasul weir. It was completed in1968. It supplies water to Rasul-Qadirabad link canal and upper Chenab canal.

Marala Barrage

It is located on the Chenab and completed in1969. Its flood discharge capacity is 1.1 million cusecs. It supplies water to Ravi link Canal and Upper Chenab Canal.

Qadirabad Barrage

It is located on River Chenab 32 km from Khanki weir. It was completed in 1970. Its discharge capacity is a million cusecs. It feeds Qadirabad-Balloki Link.

Mailsi Siphon

It is a gated siphon located on River Satluj near Mailsi. It carries water on the Sidhnai-Mailsi Link across river Satluj into the Bahawal canal.

Link Canals

Link Canals are the main water careers from the western rivers to the eastern and from rivers into the canals. The link Canals constructed under the Indus treaty are:

1. Rasul-Qadirabad Link Canal. It carries water from Rasul Barrage on River Jhelum to the Chenab.

2. Qadirabad –Balloki Link. It is an extension of Rasul-Qadirabad Link by which the water of river Chenab is transferred to the river Ravi.

3. Balloki-Sulemanki Link connects the Ravi and the Satluj.

4. Trimmu-Sidhnai Link. It transfers water from Trimmu Barrage into the River Ravi.

5. Sidhnai-Mailsi Link. It takes the water carried by the above Link Canal to Satluj.

6. Mailsi-Bahawal Link. It carries water to the Bahawal canal.

7. Chashma-Jhelum Link transfers water from Taunsa on the Indus to the Jhelum.

8. Taunsa- Panjnad Link canal is 38 miles long. It carries water from Taunsa on the Indus to the Chenab River to feed the Panjnad canals.

Water Logging and Salinity

Whereas extensive canal irrigation has ensured water supply for crop activity all the year round, it has its disadvantages as well. Water from the unlined canals keeps on seeping and thus raises the water table and after choking the soil, the seeped water reaches the surface rendering the lands water logged. This water brings salts in solution on the top, which on evaporation leaves a white layer of salts on the surface, which is called salinity.

Remedies for Water logging and salinity

The above stated facts show that vast areas of fertile agricultural lands are becoming waterlogged and falling victim to salinity. The danger of these menaces is so great that if not checked the country would face acute shortage of food grains. Government has taken a number of steps to reclaim the affected lands to make them fit for cultivation again, such as stated below:

Tube wells in large number have been dug and the farmers are encouraged to install them in canal irrigated areas to supplement irrigation and to lower the water table to reclaim the waterlogged lands. The program is known as SCARP (Salinity Control and Reclamation Project). WAPDA has been assigned work for the implementation of the program.

Gravity canals or Sem nallas have been dug to drain away the seeped water. Canals are being lined cemented to stop seepage of water from the canals. Special varieties of grasses and paddy cultivation are suggested for treating the affected lands.

These measures taken by the government have been helpful in arresting the menaces of water logging and salinity to a great extent. Not only large affected areas have been reclaimed by now but also further spread of the menace has been reduced appreciably.

CHAPTER XIV

Pakistan-Agriculture

The agricultural sector is the backbone of the national economy. It provides food to the ever-growing population and is a source of supplying raw material for the industrial sector. Agricultural development not only brings prosperity to the nation, but is a major source of foreign exchange earnings and capital formation as well. The foreign exchange earned through agriculture can be used to import machinery, technology and other inputs which are not locally produced. It can also be used for the development of industrial and other non-agricultural sectors.

Primarily because of a long growing season, almost the whole year round and fine alluvial soils of the river plains, Pakistan has inherited an agricultural economy where about 80 percent of its population earns its livelihood, directly or indirectly, from the agricultural sector. The agricultural sector in Pakistan, however, remained under-developed because of conventional methods of cultivation and irrigation. Many other factors such as under-utilization of cultivable land, scarcity and loss of irrigation water through seepage, inadequate supply of inputs quality seeds and manure, water logging and salinity, and lack of sufficient funds available to the cultivator were also responsible for the backwardness of our agricultural sector. These shortcomings are being looked after and a number of measures have been adopted by the government to remove the snags to enhance capacity of this vital sector.

AGRICULTURAL PROBLEMS OF PAKISTAN

Agricultural sector is the mainstay of Pakistan's economy. As already mentioned, 80 percent of our population is dependent for their livelihood on the agricultural sector. It contributes one fourth of GDP. In spite of the fact that our economy is predominantly agricultural, this sector has remained underdeveloped for various reasons. It is often exposed to natural calamities such as shortage of rains, floods and locust swarms. Apart from these, backward and conventional methods of cultivation and irrigation also add to the difficulties faced by our agricultural sector. The agricultural problems of Pakistan are discussed below:

Floods

The agricultural sector has to face a natural calamity in the shape of floods every year. Floods play havoc with the crops and undermine the productive capacity of the land. The Government is trying hard to control the problem of floods by erecting bunds and constructing dams on various rivers.

Water-Logging and Salinity

The twin menace of water logging and salinity is a great threat to the agricultural sector of Pakistan. It is a dangerous disease of the land and is considered as the 'Land cancer,' which quickly destroys the fertility of the cultivable land. It is caused when the water table rises to 1.5 meter or less under the surface of the ground. Stagnant water then adversely affects the growth of plants. Water evaporates leaving salts on the surface, which renders the agricultural land unproductive. It is one of the major reasons of the low productivity of land, as the salinity-affected land is rendered unproductive. It has damaged millions of acres of our agricultural land, thus, seriously lowering our national income. The Government, in spite of its best efforts, has not been able to control this evil completely so far.

Irrigation:

Water gives life to the crops and, therefore, is a vital requirement for the agricultural development. Artificial means of supplying water to the lands is called irrigation. Water for irrigation purposes is acquired from two major sources, which include canals and the sub-soil water pumped by installing tube wells. Pakistan has world's largest system of canal irrigation. The conditions favorable for it include: availability of water in the rivers, dam sites, rich lands, soft cover of soil to allow digging of canals, natural slope of land and qualified and competent engineers.

Ignorance of the Farmer

Our farmers are generally illiterate and ignorant about the modern farming techniques. They depend on the conventional methods of cultivation and are reluctant to adopt the modern *methods*- the technical knowhow, which is necessary to get higher yields. Being ignorant, Pakistani farmer is unable to put his land to the best use.

Lack of Funds

The farmer in Pakistan is poor and lacks funds to manage his cultivation. Most of our farmers possess small units of land, which are insufficient to provide them with adequate means of income. They are not in a position to develop their holdings in order to get greater yield to overcome their financial worries. They cannot acquire modern technology to enhance the fertility and productivity of their land. The credit system in our country is cumbersome and small farmers are unable to obtain loans. The Government is taking steps to improve the credit system in order to streamline it with the requirement of our poor farming classes.

Land Erosion

Soil or land erosion is another serious problem, which our agricultural sector is facing. It is adversely affecting the large areas by dividing the cultivable land into small units thus curtailing their yield and productivity. In Punjab a sizeable portion of cultivable land about one million acres has been destroyed by land erosion.

Under Utilization of Cultivable Land

The total cultivable area in Pakistan is about 79.61 million hectares. Out of this, only 20.43 million hectares is actually cultivated. This means that a major portion of cultivable land is not being cultivated. The Government is taking steps to increase the cultivated area in the country.

Inadequate System of Transportation

The Pakistani farmer has to face difficulties in taking his production to the market in time for lack of transport facilities. Our transportation system is inadequate, under-developed and unable to meet the requirements of quick and speedy transportation of goods. There are few metalled roads linking *our* farming areas with the market. As a result of this difficulty the farmer is unable to bring his yield in the market on time.

STEPS TAKEN BY THE GOVERNMENT TO SOLVE THE AGRICULTURAL PROBLEMS OF PAKISTAN

Control of Water logging and Salinity

Water logging and salinity has become an evil in Pakistan and has to be brought under effective control to increase the productivity of our agricultural land. The Government had launched an effective program of salinity control and reclamation project (SCARP) to arrest the evil of water logging and salinity. Forty-one different projects under the scheme of SCARP were launched out of which two third have already been completed. Under SCARP I project 2,069 tube wells were installed to pump out the access water out of the water-ridden soil. The drainage system is being improved by constructing 748 kilometers of drainage channel to suck out the extra water lying under the soil.

SCARP II was launched for an area of 0.79 million hectares. 3,026 tube wells were installed for pulling the extra water out of the soil to increase its fertility. SCARP III was launched to an area *of 0.79* million hectares and is meant for the districts of Jhang and Muzaffargarh. It included the installation of 1,969 tube wells and a drainage system of about 240 km.

Flood Control

Floods play havoc with the standing crops and destroy the productivity of the cultivable land. Besides floods, heavy rains and thunder-Strom, too, badly damage the crops. The Government being alive to this problem has taken effective measures to protect the land from these hazards. Flood control centers have been set up which give information about floods well in time to cope with them effectively. At least 4.0 million acres has been protected from floods, rains and thunderstorm.

Steps for the Increase in the Agricultural Growth

After 1960 there has been a steep fall in the agricultural growth and production. The green revolution of 60's has come to a standstill, which has decreased the rate of production. Another factor, which was responsible for the low productivity was fragmentation of land amongst its owners in shape of small units, which curtailed the fertility of land holdings affecting its yield and production. Soil erosion on a large scale was also responsible for the low yields.

The Government has taken several steps to increase the growing capacity of the agricultural land. The steps include: provision of fertilizer, availability of improved seeds and a simple and easy way of giving loans to the farmers for acquiring the modern agricultural technology, growing of forests in the catchment areas to protect the lands from erosion. The Government has also taken steps to give education on agricultural development and has encouraged research work on agriculture. The agricultural sector has been developed on the modern lines by mechanization of the agriculture. Storage facilities have been provided for storing the agricultural yield to save it from being wasted. Better means of transportation have been provided to shift the production to market well in time. To put an end to the difficulties of the farmers in marketing their produce, the Government set up PASSCO (Pakistan

Agricultural Storage Services Corporation) in 1973, which purchases the agricultural products directly from the farmer on reasonable prices.

Training of the Farmer

The Pakistani cultivator still follows the conventional methods of ploughing. He is unaware of the scientific and modern developments in the field of agriculture. As a result of this ignorance our farmer is unable to improve his agricultural yield. The Pakistani farmer lacks technical knowhow and is unable to acquire it to make the best use for improving his productivity.

The Government has taken concrete steps in this direction. Arrangements have been made to educate the cultivator in the use of modern farming technology. The cultivators were persuaded to adopt modern means of cultivation by leaving the conventional and obsolete methods. The Government has also given lavish loans to the farmer for acquiring the modern agricultural technology. Agricultural Development Bank and other commercial banks have been directed to provide maximum financial assistance to the farmers for obtaining the modern agricultural equipment.

Consolidation of Holdings

Fragmented land holdings were a great hindrance towards increasing production by using new techniques. Revenue department was asked to consolidate the holdings to help the farmer to concentrate at one place and also to convert otherwise fragmented uneconomical units to economical ones.

Establishment of Agriculture University

A full-fledged Agriculture University was established at Faisalabad in 1962, with strong research, and extension system that developed close interactive relationship with the state agriculturists. High yielding variety of Mexican wheat, assured canal and tube well irrigation, use of fertilizers and pesticides, spread of rural approach roads network, tractors and price support procurement system - intensity of cropping started increasing, the foundations of the GREEN REVOLUTION were thus laid and enabling infrastructural technological, economic environment was rendered conducive, which resulted into the green revolution of 1970s. Dwarf varieties for paddy crop increased production manifold. Gross sown area also increased from 4.73 to 5.68 million hectares with G D P increase of 3.4%. Production of food grains increased more than double from 3.15 million tonnes to 7.1 million tonnes.

Present Scenario

84% of the total geographical area of the state stands cultivated and only 28 thousand hectares classified cultivable waste. 16 % of the area is under cities town, villages, rivers, canals, roads, and buildings, waste forest etc. Intensity of cropping is over 181 %.

CROPS OF PAKISTAN
Kharif and Rabi crops:

Pakistan enjoys a long growing season because of high enough prevailing temperatures, to allow the cultivation of crops all the year round. A variety of crops, therefore, are cultivated in Pakistan. Those crops, which are cultivated before the beginning of winter season and harvested in early summer, are known as 'Rabi Crops', they include wheat, barley, grams oil seeds, pulses etc. But those crops which are grown in the beginning of summer and their picking or harvesting takes place in early winter are called 'Kharif Crops'. These include rice, sugarcane, millets, maize, cotton etc. The following are the main crops cultivated in Pakistan.

KHARIF CROPS

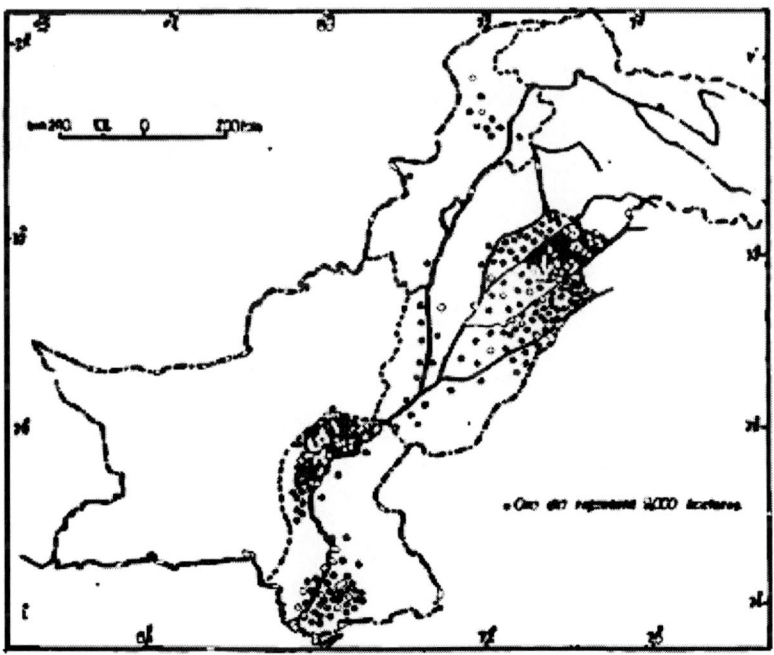

Figure 19: Rice Cultivation

RICE

Rice holds an important position among the food crops of Pakistan. Pakistan produces enough high quality rice to meet both domestic demand and allow for export of 1 million tons. It occupies about 10.2 per cent of the total cropped area. According to the preliminary estimates for 1997-98, its production was estimated at 4,325 thousands tones which showed an increase of 0.5% as compared to the produce of 4,305 thousand tones during 1996-97. While produce of the crop in 2001-02 was 5,156 thousand tones. Rice needs hot and moist climate. In our country the crop is cultivated almost entirely on the irrigated areas of Punjab and Sindh in summer. Districts of Sheikhupura, Gujranwala and Sialkot in Punjab and Larkana in Sindh in particular are famous for the finest quality of Basmati rice that besides having special flavor, on cooking spreads like vermicelli or pasta. Being expensive is served as a delicacy in marriage parties or on special occasions. Because of its high quality the variety has a demand all over the world, and a source of earning foreign exchange for the country. In the hilly areas it is cultivated on terraced lands but the quality is different mostly Irri rice. High quality rice has buyers mostly in Japan, US, Europe, UAE, and Saudi Arabia whereas Irri rice is exported to Bangladesh and African countries.

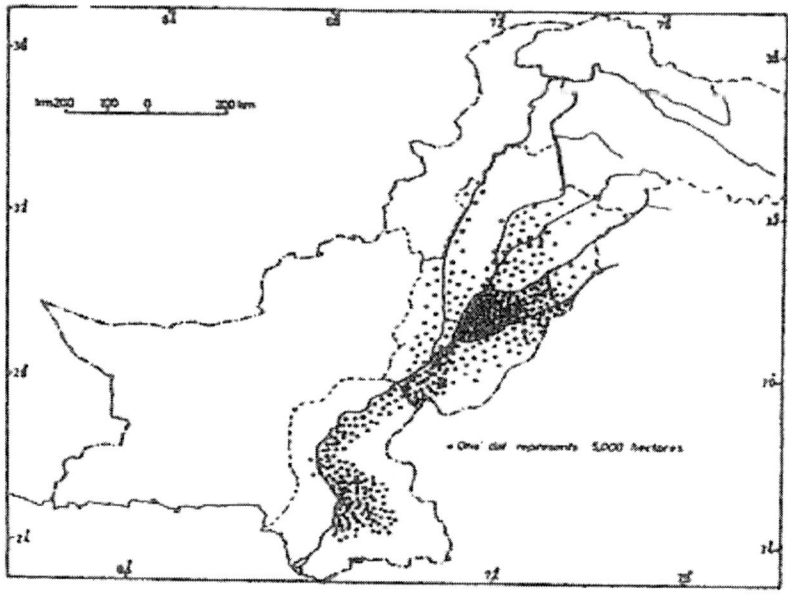

Cotton

Figure 20: Area under cotton cultivation

COTTON

Cotton is a precious cash crop of our Country. It is not only used for the manufacture of yarn and cloth but also for a number of other products. Pakistan earns a lot of foreign exchange from its export to other countries. It is known as silver fiber. It contributes about 5 per cent to the GDP and 55 per cent to the foreign exchange earnings. Major exports come from cotton, and its by products, cotton yarn and cloth. According to the preliminary estimates for 1997-98, cotton was planted on an area of 2959.5 thousand hectors as compared to 3,149 thousand hector1996-97.

The production of cotton crop was estimated at 9.2 million bales in 1997-98 as compared to 9.4 million bales in 1996-97. The area under cotton however fluctuates due to weather, pests, viruses and market conditions. Decline in production in 1997-98 was due to severe attack of leaf curl virus, spread of white fly, attack of Aphid, Jessed, and dry weather. In the year 2005 due to better weather conditions and supply of unadulterated pesticides, a bumper crop had been harvested that not only benefited the farmer but also helped earning more foreign exchange with enhanced exports of the commodity. Estimated area under production is 9.7 million Hectares with a produce of 51.6 million tons.

Cotton being a Kharif crop needs temperature between 24 - 28 C° (75-80 F) in the growing season, but at the time of harvest or in the picking season it requires cooler condition - temperature between "10 C° to 15 C°" (50-60 F). Cotton, therefore, is a crop of both sub-tropical and warm temperate regions. The irrigated areas of Southern Punjab and Sindh are most suitable for its cultivation where temperature and soil are suitable and the deficiency of rainfall is met through irrigation.

SUGAR CANE

Sugar cane is another cash crop of Pakistan. Sugar cane needs high temperature and well-drained soils rich in lime. In Pakistan Sugar cane is cultivated on the irrigated areas of Punjab 57%, Sindh 40% and N.W.F.P. 3 %. Total area in 1999 was 1,010 thousand hectares that however fluctuates due to weather and local supply and demand factors. Cane sugar is largely the chief source of sugar in our country supplemented by beet sugar particularly in N.W.F.P. Pakistan is now self-sufficient in her sugar needs. The estimated crop produce in the year 1997-98 was 52.00 million tones, which stood at 53.1 m tones in 2000-2001.

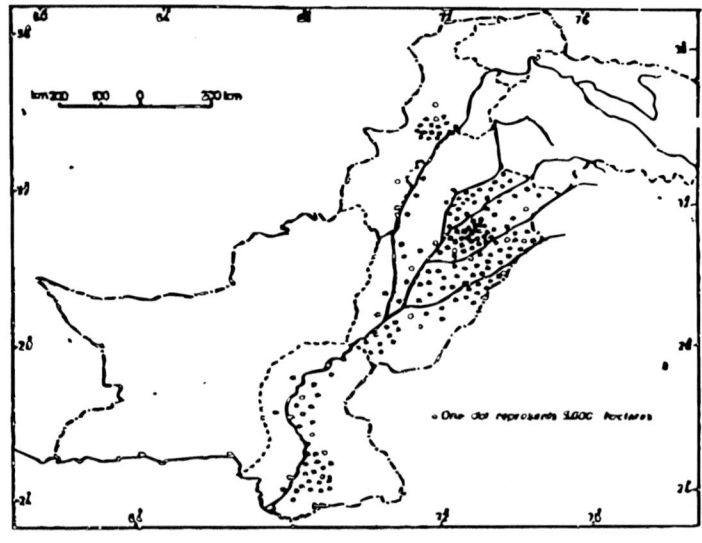

Sugar Cane (Kharif Crop) ·

Figure 21: Area under sugar cane cultivation

MAIZE

Maize is an important food and fodder crop of our country. In the hilly areas of Pakistan it is the staple food of the people. Corn oil is edible oil extracted from the ripened crop. Two crops of maize are obtained in our country. One is grown in spring and the other in July and August. Severe cold and frost is harmful for the corp. It is, therefore, harvested before winters.

Main areas of production are: irrigated areas of Punjab, Sindh and N.W.F.P. But good quality sweet corn is cultivated in the hilly areas of Haripur, Hazara, and Azad Kashmir. Total annual production is about 1 million ton.

MILLETS (JAWAR AND BAJRA)

Barani areas of Rawalpindi division and districts of Bahawalpur and Dera Ghazi Khan Division in Punjab, Tharparker, Sanghar districts of Hyderabad in Sindh are famous for the production of these crops. Annual produce of both Jawar and Bajra is 250,000 tons each.

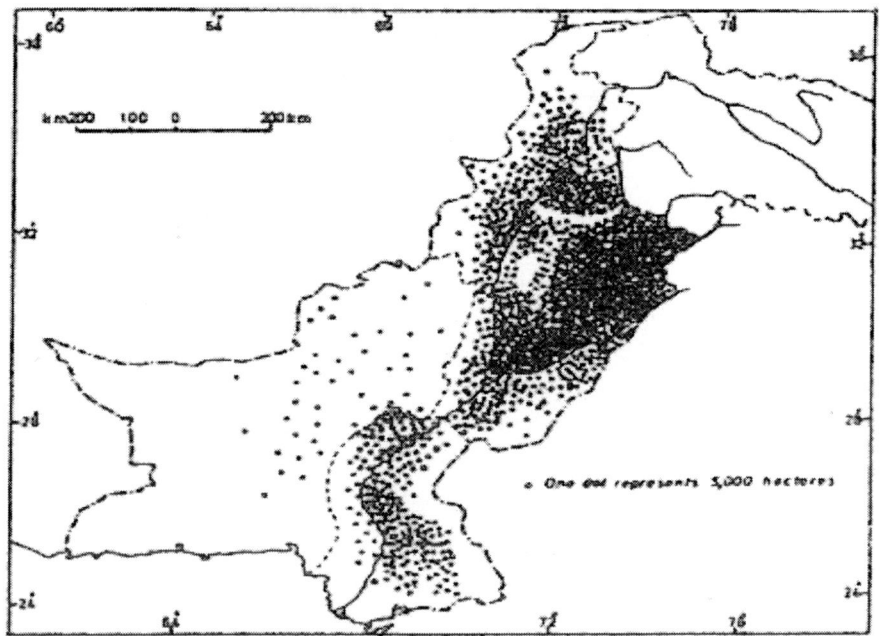

Figure 22: Area under wheat cultivation

RABI CROPS
WHEAT

Wheat is the staple food of the majority of our population and existed in the region from ancient times. It is cultivated in all the four provinces of Pakistan, and covers 3 times more hectares than other three food crops; rice, millet and maize put together.

Wheat needs temperature "between" 4.5 C° to 15 C° (40-60 F). It is, therefore, a cool season 'Rabi' crop. It is planted in early winter and harvested at the end of the spring season. Late and quick growing varieties, however, can be cultivated even by the end of December and 1st week of January. Harvesting season almost remains the same.

As the rainfall in our country is low, wheat is mostly grown under irrigation on the plain areas of Punjab, Sindh, and N.W.F.P. Besides, some wheat is also cultivated in the hilly and plateau areas of Potwar, Balochistan, and Azad Kashmir on barani lands that mostly depend on rain. According to preliminary estimates, production of wheat for 1999-2000 stood at 18.7 m tones as against 16.6 m tones of the previous year's showing an increase of 12 per cent. A bumper wheat crop in the year (2005) like cotton had been possible due to the enhancement of support prices of wheat Rs. 400 per kg., sufficient soil moisture at sowing time in barani areas because of well distributed monsoon rains, availability of quality seeds, and increased use of manure the produce figures touched 22 million tones.

In 2007-2008 in the world market, the price of food commodities including wheat have gone up sharply as corn and wheat are being used for bio-fuel since the price of oil has more than doubled in the world market. In Pakistan also the price of wheat, and wheat flour has gone up sharply, there is shortage of wheat, in spite of importing wheat. The total production of wheat was 21.7 million tones whereas the estimated consumption was 22 million tone. There is stagnation in production of wheat because widespread rust disease, not enough irrigation water and rainfall, shortage of electricity to run tube-wells, and tremendous increase in price of fertilizers.

BARLEY
It is a Rabi crop and almost needs similar condition of climate as wheat. Being a hardy crop it can bear greater fluctuation of temperature and rainfall and can thrive on less fertile soils as compared with wheat. Besides food of the poor people it is used as a fodder crop. Total annual production is 150,000 tons.

OIL SEEDS
These may include seas mum, rapeseed, mustard, Soya beans, sunflowers, canola, etc. and cottonseeds. Although a large quantity of oil seeds are grown in various areas of our country, but the amount of oil which is being extracted from these seeds is insufficient to meet our requirements because we use that oil in our vegetable oil industry. So to meet our requirements we have to import a large quantity of edible oils from foreign countries. Total requirement of edible oil for 1996-97 was 1.6 million tones of which 0.538 m tones (32 per cent) came from local production while remaining 1.062 m tones (60 percent) were imported at a cost of US $ 612m.

The edible oil requirement for 1997-98 was estimated at 1.7 m tones. Of this local production contributed 0.588 million tones and rest 114 m tones (66%) had to be imported. In Punjab, Multan, Bahawalpur, Sargodha, Faisalabad districts, Peshawar in N.W.F.P and Khairpur district of Hyderabad division are famous for the production of oil Seeds.

LIVE STOCK & FISHERIES

Cattle goat and sheep assume special importance in the agrarian set up of Pakistan. In the past an average farmer for tilling the land owned a pair of bullocks, whereas cows and buffaloes were kept for the production of milk and butter. These days with the extensive use of tractors, cattle are mostly reared as milk animals. Cattle, goats, and sheep provide meat, hides and skins. Poultry development is important to supplement the food and improve protein contents. Fish also form an important source of meat.

CATTLE

Generally the stock of cattle in Pakistan is of low quality. However, some good breeds are also found. In order to improve the quality of cattle, government, has not only established organized cattle farms at various places at their own but have also encouraged the private sector to follow suit. Large government dairy farms are at Sahiwal, and Mirpur Khas. Important military dairy farms are in Peshawar, Rawalpindi, Lahore, Okara and Karachi. Besides, large dairy farms for the general public have been set up in Lahore, and Faisalabad. Dairy supply schemes are in operation in Karachi, Lahore, Hyderabad, and Islamabad.

There are no organized farms for beef cattle and the chief producer of meat remains dry cows, buffaloes or their calves. Cattle supply *23%* of the total production of meat. Buffaloes have a slight edge over cattle. Recently goats have made great headway and they account for about *25%* of meat supply.

SHEEP & GOAT

Sheep and goat abound the areas that are inhospitable for cattle and buffaloes. Therefore, they are found in large number in the tribal area, Balochistan Plateau, Thar Parkar, Cholistan and Thal deserts, and also in the well-watered canal irrigated areas of the Punjab and Sindh. Sheep are kept both for meat and wool. Production of wool and meat are on the increase and their output has more than doubled in the past one decade. Sheep besides supply of meat are good suppliers of hides and skins but a poor source of milk.

POULTRY

Poultry production has emerged as a good substitute of beef and mutton. Its importance can be judged from the fact that almost every family in rural areas and every fifth family in urban areas are associated with poultry production activities in one way or the other. Government is providing every possible incentive to develop it at an accelerated pace. Poultry farming has gained great importance due to pressing needs to supplement protein contents in our food there are thousands of commercial poultry farms supplying *4,28,000* tones of meat annually. Supply of eggs has considerably increased keeping into consideration a constant increased demand of eggs.

Annual growth rate of poultry has been 10-15% due to veterinary care treatment and vaccine action facilities available. There is huge concentration of poultry farms around urban centers like Karachi, Lahore, and Islamabad.

FISHERIES
Development of fisheries is being given great importance to meet the deficiency of meat in Pakistani diet. Fish is the best animal protein and source of white meat. The production of fish has grown at an average rate of 6 percent. There are two sources of fish in Pakistan, marine and inland fisheries.

Marine Fisheries
Pakistan has about 1,000 km. of coastline the coast is divided into two parts; the Sindh coast and the Balochistan coast. Although Sindh coast is shorter in length as compared to Balochistan but accounts for 68% of the total marine catch. Fisheries of Sindh are known for prawns, and these and other fish are distributed from Karachi.

Inland Fisheries
Fishing from inland waters is carried on all over the country lakes; large dams and abandoned river channels are the principal producers. Manchhar Lake in Dadu, Kalri and Haleji Lakes near Karachi and Mangla and Tarbela dams, Sukkur, Kotri and Thatta are also important fishing centers.

FISH PRODUCTION
During 1997-98, inland and marine fish catch production was 590,000 tones, with total exports of 83,138 tons of fish and fishery products, yielding export earnings of Rs. 7.27 billion.The inland and marine fish catch production totals 519,000 tones with exports earnings amounting to Rs. 2,865 million that makes 2 per cent of the total export earnings. In order to boost up fishing a number of projects like Pasni fish harbor,

Korangi fish harbor and expansion of existing Karachi fish harbor have been under taken by the government. About 80% of the total catch of the Makran coast is dried for export to Middle Eastern Countries. During calendar year 1999, about 90 million tons of fishery products were exported to Japan, UK, USA, Germany, Middle East, and other countries.

CHAPTER XV

MINERAL RESOURCES OF PAKISTAN

Pakistan is rich in mineral resources, but these immense potentials remained unexploited over the years due to absence of venture capital, inadequate planning, geological mapping and exploration coupled with remoteness of the area not easily accessible that greatly add to the cost of production, limited demand for many minerals from domestic industries. Moreover much of the wealth is found in Balochistan that also entailed law and order - security problems. Now the Government is adopting new Policy measures to give a boost to this sector by the establishment and expansion of mineral based industries; widening exploration activities, creating safer heaven in the troubled area, scientific research, and raising the financial allocation for its speeded development. Foreign collaboration in specialized fields is also being utilized.

In order to encourage mineral exploration and exploitation in the country, a Mineral Co-operation Board (MCB) was established in 1979 to co-ordinate public sector agencies and the private sector.

The Ministry of Petroleum and Natural Resources is responsible for mineral development in the country. It has five main agencies namely:-

1.   Geological Survey of Pakistan (GSP)

2.   Gemstone Corporation of Pakistan (GEMCP)

3.   Oil and Gas Development Corporation (OGDC)

4.   Pakistan Mineral Development Corporation (PMDC)

5.   Resource Development Corporation (RDC)

These institutions are responsible for various activities connected with the exploration, development and industrial exploration of natural resources. Besides these institutions the following public sector agencies are also engaged in mineral exploration, research and development.

PROVINCIAL AGENCIES
Punjab Mineral Development Corporation.
Sarhad Development Authority
Balochistan Development Authority
Federally Administered Tribal Areas Development Corporation
Azad Kashmir Mineral and Industrial Development Corporation
Pakistan Industrial Development Corporation.

The Geological Survey of Pakistan has completed regional geological mapping of an area of 5,500 sq. Kilometers on 1:50,000 scale, in parts of Loralai, Chaghi and Lasbela districts of Balochistan, Attock and Dera Ghazi Khan districts of Punjab, Thatta and Dadu districts of Sindh and Kotli, Poonch and Muzaffarabad districts of Azad Kashmir.

The minerals which have already been found and have potential for commercial and economic exploitation in the short and medium term, initially for domestic use are classified as under:

Metals (Basic Minerals)
Iron ore, copper, lead, zinc, nickel, tungsten, antimony, bauxite, and chromite.

Energy (Power Resources)
Coal Petroleum, Gas, and Nuclear minerals besides; Gypsum, Limestone, Marble, Rock Salt, precious stones, Silica, baryte are also important minerals.

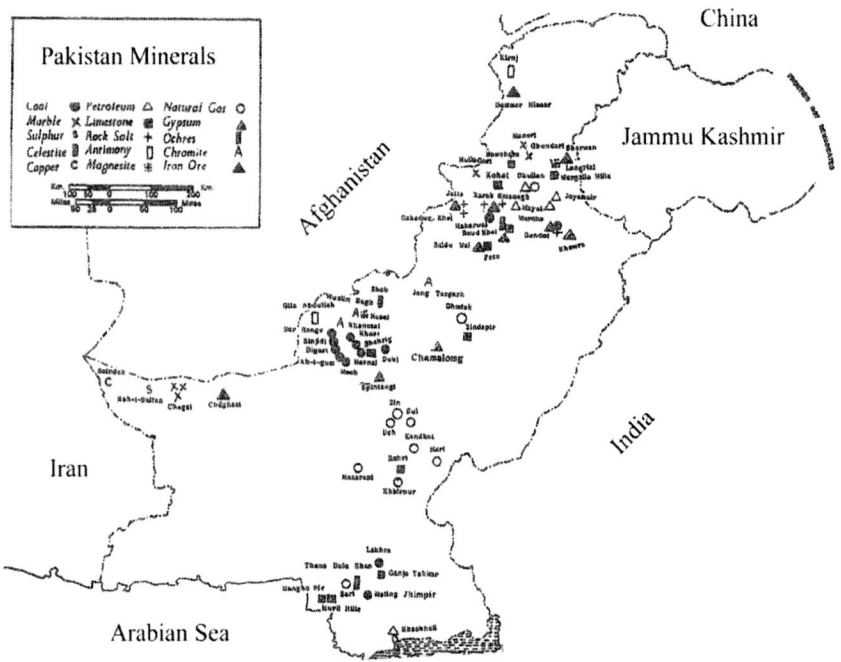

Figure 23: Basic Minerals

BASIC MINERALS
IRON ORE

Iron ore has been found in various areas of our country. The total reserves of iron ore deposits are estimated up to March 1995 to be over 6.065 million tons. The following are the main centers of iron ore deposits in our country.

Deposits of Kalabagh

Iron ore deposits have been found in areas of Salt Range near Sakesar and Kalabagh districts, Mianwali (Punjab) in the Surghar Range. These are considered as the largest deposits of iron ore in Pakistan, but here the ore is of low grade having 30% to 35% ore iron contents. The iron ore deposits here are estimated about 300 million tons.

Deposits of Sargodha

High-grade magnetite deposits of iron have been found near Sargodha, Punjab. The ore has iron contents of 62.2 % certified by PCSIR labs at Lahore. Production, however, is low being 100 million tons per month to be increased in the near future. The mine site has an easy access of transport from where the mineral can easily be loaded. The ore is being supplied to Pakistan steel mill at Karachi, and in the year 1992, only 937,000 tons of the ore was sent to the plant for smelting.

Deposits of Dommel Nisar

At about 20 miles from Drosh in Southern Chitral, (N.W.F.P.) high quality (Magnetite) iron ore deposits have been found at Dommel Nisar. These deposits have 55% to 65% of iron contents. Here the reserves are estimated to be about 3 million tons.

Deposits of Langrial, Galdanian & Abbottabad:

At Langrial in Tehsil Haripur district Hazara (NWFP) iron ore deposits have been found. Langrial deposits are situated at about 20 miles south of Abbottabad. The iron ore deposits found here contain about 50% of iron contents.

Galdanian Deposits

Galdanian deposits are situated about 10 miles north east of' Abbottabad. The ore found here is of low quality, having about 20% of iron contents. Some iron ore deposits have also been found on the eastern side of Abbottabad city. The ore contains about 14% to 46% of iron contents. The total reserves deposits of iron ore at all the three places of Hazara district are estimated to be 100 million tons.

Deposits of Chil ghazi

Some high-grade iron ore deposits have been found at Chil ghazi in district Chaghi of Balochistan province. The ore deposits contain about 55% of iron contents. These reserves are estimated to be over 3 million tons. Few iron ore deposits have also been found at Khuzdar, Ziarat, and Naukundi in the province of Balochistan.

At present iron ore in our country is not being exploited commercially, due to quality being poor, the sites being inaccessible and insecure, production being low and inadequate as such not suitable for a big or medium size steel mill. Pakistan Steel Mill near Karachi, therefore, until increased production of good quality supply at home is and will keep using imported iron ore. Pakistan Industrial Development Corporation is considering a proposal to establish a small steel mill at Naukundi Balochistan.

SAINDAK MINERAL PROJECT

It was developed in early 1990s but by 1993 had not made any notable success. Located in Balochistan the project area contains 3 separate large deposits of copper and iron ore, molybdenum, baryte, silver, gold and sulfur. Government of Balochistan (GOB) has granted BME a joint venture 50:50 bet GOB and PPL for the development of barite and other minerals. Baryte has proven reserves of 1.50 million tones, mainly used in oil drilling process. During 2004-05 total quantity of 36,695 tons baryte has been sold to oil and gas companies. BME has already supplied 98,400 tons of iron ore to Pakistan steel mill in the year 2003-04 and contract for future supplies is being made for the supply of its high-grade iron ore.

CHROMITE

Chromite is also an important mineral of our country. It is used for making stainless steel, high-speed tools, precision instruments, dyes, and in photography. A few years back, we exported all the production of our chromite to foreign countries, but nowadays we are using our chromite in Pakistan Steel Mills near Karachi.

Huge deposits of chromite are found at Muslim Bagh in Zohb valley of Balochistan. The mines of Jang Torgarh and Khanozai rank at the top. Besides these, some chromite deposits have also been found in areas of Chaghi and Kharan districts. A few deposits of chromite have also appeared in Malakand and Mahmand Agencies of N.W.F.P. Average annual production of Chromite is 350,000 million tones.

ROCK SALT

Salt is being used in our country from ancient times. Pakistan has vast deposit of salt. The salt range had been discovered before the Mughal period. There is reference of salt mines in "Aaeen-e-Akbari". The salt deposits of our country are considered as one of the largest salt deposits in the world. These deposits begin from the western bank of Jhelum and go up to the northwestern mountains. These salt deposits have a width of 600 to 1,000 miles and their depth reaches up to 275 feet. The following are the main salt mines of our country.

Khewra Salt Mines

These are the oldest mines of our country. Here the depth of these mines reaches up to 60 feet. Khewra has a railway link with Makarwal, a branch line of the Pakistan Railways. These are the important salt mines of district Jhelum in Punjab. Here the present production is about 0.4 million tons.

Warcha District Sargodha Mines
These mines are situated at Warcha; district Sargodha in the province of Punjab. It lies about 10 miles north west of Gunjital Railway station. Here the depth of the mines goes up to 50 feet. These mines have an average annual salt production of about 50 thousand tons.

Kalabagh District Mianwali Mines
A small quantity of salt is found near Kalabagh. The production being low, are less in importance.

Bahadurkhel District Kohat Mines
Vast deposits of salt have been found at Bahadurkhel district Kohat in NWFP. Here the depth of salt mines is up to 350 feet. Besides this, some salt has also been found in Jatta and Karak. The reserves deposits of these areas are estimated to be 50 thousand tons. The reserve salt deposits in all the above-mentioned places are estimated to be over 100 million tons. The total salt production during July-March 1994-95 was 685,000 tones. Besides, some salt is obtained from seawater and salt lakes. Large deposits of salt have also been discovered in Tharparker area of Sindh. At Mauripur near Karachi and on coastal area of Makran, salt is obtained from seawater.

Salt does not only provide the basic requirement of our foods, it is also used in various industries particularly chemical industries such as caustic soda, washing soda, manufacturing of sulphuric or hydrochloric acids, tanning of leather etc. ICI soda ash plant at Khewra and sulphuric acid plant at Kalashah Kaku use rock salt as raw material supplied by Khewra mines.

GYPSUM
Gypsum is an important mineral mined in the country. It is used as raw material for cement, Plaster of Paris, fertilizer and various other industries. It is also used for reclamation of soil in waterlogged and salinity ridden areas. Gypsum in Pakistan is found in a large quantity at Mianwali, Jhelum, and Dera Ghazi Khan in Punjab, Quetta and Sibbi in Balochistan, Kohat in NWFP, are the main producers but some quantity of Gypsum is also found in Bahawalpur (Punjab), Dadu and Sanghar districts (Sindh),

and Dera Ismail Khan (NWFP). The total reserves of Gypsum found in our country are estimated at about 350 million tons.

SULPHUR
Sulphur is used as a raw material in various industries such as chemicals and matches etc. Its deposits have been found at extinct volcano Koh-e-Sultan in Chaghi district of Balochistan province. Besides, some sulphur deposits have also been found at Sanni, District Kachi of Balochistan Province. The sulphur reserves are estimated to be about 0.8 million tons.

Annual average production of sulphur is about 1,100 tons. We are not self-sufficient in our requirements of sulphur, and we have to import a large quantity of sulphur from foreign countries.

BARYTE
This ore is used for the preparation of digging material of oil wells. The deposits of baryte have been found in district Khuzdar of Balochistan province, some other deposits of baryte have also been found at Kachhi district, Lasbella of Balochistan, and some deposits near Haripur (NWFP). The total reserves of baryte are estimated to be about 5 million tons. The production of baryte is 750 tons.

COPPER
Copper is considered as an important mineral of modern age. It is being used in electric goods, especially in the manufacturing of copper wires. It was used for making coins and domestic utensils in the past. Its importance is significant due to its increasing demand. The deposits of copper have been found at Saindak and Amuri in Chaghi districts of Balochistan province. Sandak deposits are estimated to be 412 million tons. At present copper is not being extracted on commercial basis in our country. It is hoped that within a few years time we shall be able to produce copper in sufficient quantity with foreign collaboration.

Recently, one of the largest deposits in the world were discovered in south west Balochistan Chaghai province at Reko-dik. According to development experts12.3 million tons of copper and 20.9 million ounces of gold lie in the Reko-Dik area that are believed to be larger than Sarcheshma of Iran and

Escondida in Chile. Three Australian mining companies, BHP Billiton, Tethyan TCC and Mincor are engaged for the exploration of copper gold and other base minerals in district Chaghai with an investment of $ 152 million. Under the agreement 75% of the share were given to Australian companies and 25% to the Balochistan devepment authority (BDA). An annual production of 200-500 lbs copper is estimated. Work on the feasibility has commenced and expected to be completed by 2012. Balochistan government particularly the chief minister Mr. Raieesani is opposed to the agreement and instead of only 25% demands much higher share about 80% and has challenged the same in the supreme court of Pakistan. According to him gold and copper prices have since been doubled and as such the terms of the contract are not acceptable to Balochistan government the owner of the deposits. The court is hearing the case and the matter is sub-judice.

CHINA CLAY

The deposits of China Clay have been found at Shah Dheri district Swat and Tamar Garth near Dir in NWFP. The reserves of china clay are estimated to be about 4.5 million tons. A ceramic industry has been established at Swat, which is using about 4,800 tons of china clay every year. We are not self-sufficient in our requirements of china clay, and we have to import a large amount of china clay from other countries.

LIMESTONE

A large number of limestone deposits are found in various areas of our country. It is used for various industries, especially in cement manufacturing. The deposits of limestone are at Daudkhel, Wah (Punjab), Rohri, Hyderabad, and Karachi (Sindh). Cement industries have been established at these places. The average annual production of limestone is 8.5 million tones.

PRECIOUS STONES

A large number of Gemstones are found at Swat, Mardan, Malakand, Chitral (NWFP), Gilgit and Hunza (Northern Areas). Gemstone Corporation of Pakistan, established in 1979 is working for the exploration and development of Gem-stone Industry. The Corporation's annual earnings from the sale of Gemstones is about Rs. 4.5 million.

MARBLE

In various parts of our country, good quality marble is found in a wide range of colors. The best deposits are located at Mullaghori near Peshawar in the Khyber Agency. Besides, Maneri, and Gundai hills in Mardan, and Nowshera, and Swat in NWFP, are famous centers. Some important deposits are also found at Kala-Chitta range in Attock district. A few deposits also appear in Chaghi district of Balochistan, and Muzaffarabad areas of Azad Kashmir.

The reserves of green marble deposits are about 8.6 million cubic feet and reserves of other qualities are estimated at about 700 million tons.

SILICA SAND

This particular type of sand is used as a raw material in glass industry. The main deposits are located at Jangshahi (Sindh), Makarwal in district Mianwali, Dandot in district Jhelum (Punjab), and district Hazara in NWFP. The reserves of Silica Sand are estimated to be about 325,000 thousand tons. The annual production of Silica sand is 90,000 tones.

BAUXITE

Aluminum is extracted from this ore. Its deposits have been found in Hazara district of NWFP and at Chashma, Khaqan-e-Cheen in district Loralai of Balochistan. Its reserve deposits are estimated to be about 74 million tons.

GOLD AND SILVER

Gold and silver are found in very small quantity in our country. Some gold is also extracted from the sand of river Indus. Now it is hoped that the Saindak Deposits besides copper will also provide gold and silver in enough quantity.

POWER RESOURCES OF PAKISTAN

Energy is the essential need of the present age. It plays an important role not only in the economic development of the country, but it also helps in providing the basic needs of the people. Today, economic development is not possible without the availability of energy. Progress in power resources such as coal, mineral oil, gas, hydro-electricity etc., improves the economic condition of a country. So now-a-days all the countries of the world are in search of more and more power resources so that the living standard of their people can be raised. Pakistan is self-sufficient to the extent of about 67% of its energy requirement. The deficit is being met through imports, mainly of crude petroleum and refined petroleum products. The following are the main power resources of our country.

COAL

Coal was being extracted in the present areas before the existence of Pakistan. Mining of coal began in 1887 in areas now constituting Pakistan. In the beginning a very small quantity of coal was taken out, but after the establishment of Pakistan some more mines have also been discovered. The coal areas mainly occurred in Sedimentary rocks of Tertiary age ranging 50 to 60 million years ago its seams are generally thin. The coal is of bituminous and lignite quality. It has both a high ash and sulphur content and is of low heat value. About 80% of the coal found in our country is used in bricks and lime-burning kilns; besides, some quantity is used for railway locomotives and domestic purposes.

Coal mining in Pakistan is mainly in the hands of private sector, which accounts for 85% of the total production. Pakistan Mineral Development Corporation (PMDC), a public sector organization, which is operating four coal mines; three in Balochistan and one in Punjab are producing the rest of the 15%.

The total production of coal in March 1994-95 was 2,297 thousand tons as against 3,214 thousand tons in 1993-94. During the year 1990-91, 2,888 thousand tons were produced as against 2,751 thousand tons during the corresponding year of 1989-90. The total production of coal by PMDC during July-March 1993-94 was 3,214 tons showing a rise of 17.4 percent over the previous years. The following are the main coal mines of Pakistan:

COAL MINES OF THE PUNJAB

SALT RANGE MINES

The coal region of the salt range extends from 20 miles north of Khushab to 15 miles northeast of Khewra, an area of about 100 square miles. The coal found in these areas is of low quality, which contains a large quantity of ash, sulphur contents. Its seams are not very thick and have maximum depth of about 5 feet. The main centers of coal mining in this area are Dandot and Pind. Besides, some coal is also mined at Ara Khatha, Chilal Pir, Jahania, etc.

MAKARWAL COAL MINES
The coal deposits at Makarwal district Mianwali are the largest coalmines of our country. It begins a mile west of Kalabagh and extends unto Makarwal. The seam of coal in these mines is 2 to 10 feet deep; its quality is better than that of the salt range mines. The expansion scheme of Makarwal collieries costing 44.46 million is aimed at increasing the production capacity of the mines from 1,20,000 tons at present to 3,00,000 tons by the end of the fiscal year 1994-95. This project is being implemented on self-finance basis.

BALOCHISTAN COAL FIELDS
The coalfields of Balochistan are mostly located in the northeastern part of the province and can be considered in three groups: (i) Khost-Shahrig, Harnai; (ii) Mach; and (iii) Sor Range-Degari.

KHOST-SHARIG, HARNAI
Khost-Shahrig, Harnai: This is the largest coalfield in Balochistan. The coal bearing strata extend in northwest southeast direction for a distance of about 60 kilometers. At present three seams up to 1.5 meters thick, are being mined. The coal is high volatile bituminous, and has the highest heat value among Pakistan coals. Reserves are estimated to be about 40 million tons Production capacity of the mines is being raised from 50,000 tons to 100,000 tons per annum.

MACH COAL FIELD
Mach coalfield covers an area of 40 sq. kilometers on both sides of the Sibbi-Quetta railway line. The coal is of inferior quality and occurs in shallow and discontinuous seams, only four of which are economically workable. Further, since most seams extend into low-lying areas, there is a problem of excess water in the mines. Reserves to a depth of 300 meters are small.

SOR RANGE-DEGARI
Coalfield covers about 45 sq. kilometers, 15 kilometers east of Quetta. Several coal seams, ranging in thickness up to 3 meters are present but only two are working. The mines are shallow, following the dip of the seams. P.I.D.C. has constructed a 1.6 km long haulage tunnel in the

central block of the field. The coal is sub bituminous in quality, of low ash and sulphur content and is suitable for brick kilns and briquette Reserves are estimated at 54 million tons.

SINDH COAL FIELDS
Two coalfields occur in the lower part of the Indus Plain one at Lakhra and the other at Meting-Jhimpir.

LAKHRA COAL FIELD
Lakhra coalfield lies about 16 kilometers west of Khankot railway station on the Kotri Dadu branch line of Pakistan Railways. It extends over an area of 200 sq. kilometer. The coal beds are associated with a gently folded anticline, have a thickness of 0.5 — 2.5 meters and occur at depths of less than 45 meters. The coal is of inferior quality lignite, has a high moisture contents, and tends to crumble on drying. Reserves are about 22 million tons and the total annual production capacity being 200,000 tones.

METING-JHIMPIR
This coalfield lies about 130 kilometers north of Karachi near Jhimpir and Meting railway station. It extends over an area of 900 sq. kilometers. The coal beds occur at the base of low lime-stone hills, but there is only one workable seam, this is thin and of poor quality. Reserves are about 28 million tons. Annual production at present being 30,000 tons, underground development works are being carried out as per schedule. Coal is also found in other localities of Pakistan but because of the smallness and inferior quality of the deposits, mining is uneconomical.

NATURAL GAS AND OIL

OIL
The search for oil in the area now in Pakistan started in 1968 when the first test hole was drilled at Kundal near Mianwali and continues to the present day. In Pakistan, large areas are covered by sedimentary rocks, which have petroliferous members. The search is for stratigraphic and structural traps where oil could accumulate. Such favorable structures are usually not found in areas of intense folding, such as the northern mountains. The possibility of major discoveries, either in on-shores or

off-shores areas, is considered quite bright. Parts of Pakistan adjacent to the oil and gas producing fields of Iran have a similar geological history.

At the time of Independence, Pakistan inherited four producing fields, Khaur, Dhullian, Joya Mir, and Balkassar. Later, four more fields were discovered, Karsal, Tut, Sarang and Me'al. All of these lie in the Potwar Plateau.

DHULLIAN OIL FIELD
Dhullian oil field is located about 16 kilometers northwest of Khaur. Discovered in 1937, this is one of the big fields in the country, which produces substantial quantities of gas. The structure is a gentle dome, about 90 sq. kilometers in area, and the oil is obtained from the Lani and Ranikot horizons of the basal Murree beds.

JOYA MAIR OIL FIELD
The Attock Oil Company discovered Joya Mair oil field in 1944. The structure is a narrow anticline, and the oil-producing horizon, Sakesar limestone. The oil is heavy asphaltic oil, and is transported to the Morgah refinery by railway.

BALKASSAR OIL FIELD
Balkassar oil field is located west of Joya Mir in Jhelum district. Attock Oil Company drilled the first well in 1945/46. The structure of the field is a gentle anticline, with two producing horizons, both of Eocene limestone. The oil is asphaltic suitable for furnace fuel.

KARSAL OIL FIELD
Karsal oil field was the first field discovered after Independence. It lies a few miles north west of Balkassar; to which a pipeline joins it. The Karsal anticline is exposed on the surface and the oil occurs in limestone. Quality is similar to that of Balkassar oil.

TUT OIL FIELD
Tut oil field was discovered in 1968, the Kot Sarong, and Meyal fields still later. All are located in Attock district. Meyal is presently the most productive field with an annual yield of over 2,500,000 barrels. While the production of most of the oil fields is declining whereas that of Meyal is increasing. It also produces gas in substantial quantities. The oil field at Khaskheli has recently come into production, with an annual yield of

about 50,000 barrels. The production of crude oil was 69,000 barrels (25.19 million barrels annually) per day in 1990, which in recent years due to extrusion of old oil fields has declined to 14.58 barrels by 1994-95. But still most of Pakistan's crude oil requirements are met through imports, which account for 81 percent of total oil consumption. The decline in production has been very significant during the year 1989-90 when exploration and development efforts were intensified. During 1990-91 (July - March) 23.49 million barrels were produced as against 19.47 million barrels in the period (July-March) in 1989-90. The imported crude oil is refined at Karachi.

NATURAL GAS

Gas was discovered at Sui in 1952, while drilling for oil. As a result of an extensive program of test drilling, additional fields were found at Zin, Lich, Khairpur, Kandkot,, Meyal, Mari, Mazarani, Sari, Jacobabad and Dhullian. The natural gas of Pakistan has high methane content, usually 70-90 percent. Of the total estimated productions of nearly 10 million meters of natural gas in the country Balochistan produces 7 million cubic meters.

SUI GAS FIELD

Sui is the major producing field. It lies in the Sibbi district of Balochistan at the foothills of the Marri-Bugti range and is one of the biggest fields in the world. The reservoir rock is known as Sui main limestone. One reservoir covers an area of 190 sq. kilometers. Sui accounts for over 80 percent of production. Mari gas is next in importance followed by Meyal, Dhullian and Sari.

Natural gas is used for power generation and by the different industries. Power stations using natural gas have been built at Karachi, Hyderabad, Jamshoro, Multan, and Faislabad, and about 30 percent of total production is consumed in power generation. Fertilizer factories use 20 percent, cement factories 11 percent, and other industries including textiles 25 percent. Natural gas is playing a vital role in the economic development of Pakistan by providing a cheap fuel for industry. Commercial (3 percent) and domestic (6 percent) consumption is still quite limited.

ELECTRICITY

There are three main sources of electrical energy in Pakistan. Hydel (53 per cent) and Thermal (45 per cent) are major producers, while nuclear is a small producer (2 per cent).

HYDROELECTRICITY

Hydroelectricity is a major source of energy in Pakistan. Most of the hydel plants of Pakistan are located on the rivers of the northern hilly and mountainous areas where the rugged topography provides a good head for the generation of electricity. A good head makes the waterfall from a sufficient height on to the turbine wheel to move it. A regular flow of water is also essential to ensure year-round generation of electricity. But the rivers of Pakistan experience low discharge in the winter season, which reduces their power-generating capacity; therefore, in the winter season power shortage is generally experienced. A few low artificial falls along the canals have been utilized to develop small hydel plants. According to an estimate made by WAPDA, the hydel power potential of Pakistan is 30,000 MW of which 20,000 MW can be utilized economically. The installed capacity of hydel power plants was 2,898 MW.

At the time of independence there were 2 hydel plants in Pakistan namely Renala and Malakand. Since seven more important hydel plants have been added. Of them Tarbela, Mangla and Warsak are large projects. Tarbela is a magnificent earth-fill dam about 445 feet high on the Indus River (Fig. 27). It is a multipurpose project primarily constructed to supply water for irrigation. But it also produces electricity. Its installed capacity is 3,500 MW. Mangla is another gigantic multipurpose project. It is located on the Jhelum River at a point where the river leaves the mountains. Besides provide water for irrigation, it generates 1,000 MW of electricity. There is a proposal to increase the capacity of the reservoir to compensate for the storage capacity lost to silting by increasing the height of the reservoir by 30 feet which would increase the storage capacity by 2.9 million acre feet and electricity output by 772 MW.

Warsak is yet another multipurpose project designed to provide water for irrigation and generation of electricity. It is Located on the Kabul River about 32 km (20 miles) from Peshawar. Its installed capacity is 240 MW. In 1989-90, 493 million KWh of electricity was produced with plant utilization factor at 62 per cent.

There are a number of small hydel plants in Pakistan. One of them is Renala, located on the Upper Bari Doab Canal. Commissioned in 1925, it is the oldest hydel plant of Pakistan. Its installed capacity is one MW. Rasul hydel plant utilizes a head of 27 meters between the Upper and

Lower Jhelum Canals. Its installed capacity is 22 MW. It was commissioned in 1952, after which the import of electricity from India was stopped. Cichokimallian hydel plant makes use of a seven-meter fall on the Upper Chenab Canal. It is about 45 km from Lahore. It was completed in 1959 with a capacity of 13.2 MW. Nandipur hydel plant is located about 17km (11 miles) northeast of Gujranwala on the Upper Chenab Canal. It was commissioned in 1963. Its installed capacity is 13.8 MW. Shadiwal hydel plant, with an installed capacity of 13.5 MW utilizes an artificial fall seven meters high on the Upper Jhelum Canal. Malakand hydel plant was constructed in 1938, utilizing the water of Upper Swat Canal with an installed capacity of 16.7 MW, which was raised to 20 MW in 1952. The water of Malakand plant is reutilized to turn the turbines of the Dargai Project. This was completed in 1954 with a capacity of 20 MW. Kurramgarhi hydel plant takes advantage of the canal taken off from the Kurram River and produces 4 MW of electricity. Chitral is a new hydel plant (1983-84). Its capacity is one MW. With a total installed capacity of 0.7 MW as many as 50 units of micro-hydel plants have been developed in remote areas.

The demand for electrical energy in Pakistan is increasing rapidly. A quick solution to this problem is required. Giant hydel projects like Tarbela and Mangla are no answer to this problem. Such projects take about 15 years from the preparation of a feasibility report to the commissioning of the plant. They involve heavy investment, and return takes a long time. Small plants can be completed in a much shorter time, investment is considerably less and the return starts much more quickly. Pakistan should go for small plants for which many sites are available. China and Japan have gainfully utilized many small hydel plants.

THERMAL POWER

The contribution made to the electrical energy by the Thermal Power plants in Pakistan is slightly less than that by Hydel plants in 1984-85; thermal electricity generated was 10,416 million KWh as against 12,241 million KWh by hydroelectricity. The increase in the generation of electricity by thermal plants has been appreciable during recent years, about three times from 1971-72 to 1984-85. Guddu Unit-IV of 210 MW and the Guddu gas turbines of 400 MW have recently been commissioned. Water and Power Development Authority (WAPDA) and Karachi Electrical Supply Company (KESC) are the two commercial producers of electricity. Besides, there are a number of private producers. They have installed small generators for their personal use. The total amount of electricity generated by them is not known but it is very small. The Government is encouraging Private investors to enter into commercial production of electricity.

The thermal plants are well distributed over the country unlike the hydel plants, which are concentrated in northern Punjab and NWFP. Karachi is the single largest center of thermal electrical plants in the country. Its six plants produce more than 43 per cent of the total thermal electrical energy of Pakistan. Pipri Thermal Power Station produces 21 per cent and Korangi Thermal Plant 15 per cent to the total thermal energy. Another plant has been setup by Hubco Pakistan which produces 1,292 MW. Besides Karachi, other stations in Sindh, which have large thermal plants, are Kotri, Hyderabad, Sukkur and Guddu (21 per cent). In the Punjab large thermal plants are located at Faisalabad (12 per cent), Multan (12.5 per cent), Lahore and Rawalpindi. Outside Sindh and Punjab, Quetta has a large thermal plant producing about 2 per cent of the total thermal electricity of Pakistan. In the eighth five-year plan making use of local coal, estimated deposits 100 billion tones, an additional 5,000 MW could be produced.

NUCLEAR POWER

A nuclear power plant was installed at Karachi with Canadian aid. Its installed capacity is 137 MW. It contributes about 1.5 per cent of the total electricity produced in Pakistan. The supply has sharply fluctuated. From 104 million KWh in 1971-72, it reached its peak in 1975-76 when it produced 610 million kWh. Thereafter the production declined and reached a low level of 2.0 million KWh in 1989-90. Since then the production has steadily increased and was 346 million Kwh in 1994-95. Technical difficulties have been the main cause of fluctuation. Another large nuclear plant has been set up at Chashma. Its installed capacity is 300 MW, and a second one also with 300 MW has been installed.

SOLAR ENERGY

Pakistan has abundance of sunshine all over the country. The length of the shortest day of the year in Pakistan is about 9 hours. Cloudy days even in the rainiest areas are not many. Continuous occurrence of cloudy conditions interfering with the solar electric generation is rare; therefore, conditions in Pakistan are ideal for the development of solar energy. However its economic implications and organizational problems are not easy to solve. The generation of electricity by solar energy is still in its experimental stage in Pakistan.

Starting from 1981 eight plants have been installed and eleven are in various stages of completion, while the feasibility studies for some are under way. It was in December 1981 that the first solar photo static system was commissioned. It is located in Mumniala, a village 60km from Islamabad. Its capacity originally was 6.8 kWp, which was later increased to 8 KWp. The plant supplies electricity to 30 houses and streetlights and maintains storage of 10,000 gallons of drinking water. The storage capacity is to meet three days requirement of the village: Electricity is supplied only for limited hours. The second photovoltaic system is located at Kankoi village in Swat. It was commissioned in 1983.

CHAPTER XVI
INDUSTRIAL SECTOR

INDUSTRIAL DEVELOPMENT OF PAKISTAN

Industry is the second commodity-producing sector of Pakistan's economy. It provides consumer, intermediate and capital goods. The industrial sector of Pakistan was very weak after partition. There were very few industries in the country and the industrial production was very low. The industrial sector in 1949-50 contributed only 7.7 percent towards national income. It slightly improved during next ten years. By 1983-84 the industrial sector's contribution in the national production reached 20 percent level, thus becoming the second largest sector, after agriculture, in the national economy.

Since Independence, the Government has been desperately trying to utilize all available resources at its disposal, for the rapid development of the industrial sector. Great stress was laid on the quick development of industry by setting up industrial units and factories in the public sector as well as in the private sector. A clear-cut policy was devised for the industrial development by the manufacturing of arms and ammunitions and steel industry. Electricity and means of communications were kept under Government control. The private sector was allowed to invest in the remaining industrial enterprises.

In 1959 the Government devised a new policy by which emphasis was laid on the establishment of those industries for which the raw material was available within the country. Apart from these steps and measures several corporations were set up with an objective of rendering assistance for the rapid industrial development of the country. The most important of these were Industrial Development Bank of Pakistan, Pakistan Industrial Credit and Investment Corporation. Besides these, the major industrial units were exempted from tax and the foreign investors were given incentives to invest in the industrial sector of Pakistan.

With these steps and measures Pakistan was able to achieve a fairly broad base in manufacturing. Apart from essential consumer goods, Pakistan is now producing chemicals, steel, and heavy engineering machine and tools, car and motorcycles assembly and manufacturing units. Pakistan has also been able to produce items of domestic use like cement, sugar, fertilizer and steel items. Pakistan has earned a substantial amount of foreign exchange by the export of these items. A Steel Mill, with Russian assistance was completed at Pipri near Karachi, which provided a great boost to industrial development in Pakistan. Not only its capacity has been recently increased but also privatized to further enhance its efficiency.

INDUSTRIAL PROBLEMS OF PAKISTAN

Since Independence, Pakistan has faced many problems in the development of its industrial sector. These difficulties were mainly due to the wrong and biased policy of the British Government in the United India. The British Government deliberately over-looked the industrial development of Muslim majority areas, which fell in Pakistan after partition. Thus on partition, Pakistan received only 34 industrial units out of 921 operating in the United India. The areas which fell in Pakistan were mainly the producer of raw material which could not be locally used because industries were located elsewhere in regions which were included in the Hindu India. Former East Pakistan was a major producer of jute, but there was not a single jute factory in East Pakistan, which could use jute for domestic use. Similarly cotton was a major crop of West Pakistan but the province had no significant indigenous cotton textile industry to make use of the raw cotton, which had to be shipped abroad. Pakistan also had no steel mill, which is considered a pre-requisite for the rapid industrialization of a country.

As a result of this policy Pakistan had to take a fresh start to build up its industrial sector on stable foundations. The Government of Pakistan faced many problems for its industrial development which are discussed below:

Biased British Policy

As already mentioned, the British Government adopted a wrong and biased policy with regard to the industrial development of Muslim majority areas. This bias was particularly manifest in the Muslim majority areas of Northern India, inhabited by martial races, which provided good soldiers to the British. Industrialization of these areas would have deprived them of excellent fighters and soldiers for their Armies. Thus when Pakistan came into existence it had to take a start from a scratch.

Lack of Capital

Capital occupies a key position in any country's economic development. It particularly carries great importance in building up a modern industrial sector on stable footings. Capital is like blood which runs into the veins of economy to give it life and vitality. It provides fill up to the industrial growth by building up the infrastructure of the economy and installation of producer as well as consumer goods industries. The major industries like steel; iron, chemicals, automobiles, sugar, carpets and textile need huge amount of money for their effective running.

Unfortunately, Pakistan is extremely deficient in capital resulting in the low level of capital formulation in the economy. Political chaos and instability also weakened resolve of the capitalists to come forward in a big way to risk their investment. It compelled Pakistan to seek foreign assistance, but it too, proved inadequate for the huge task involved in the industrial progress. Moreover, the donor countries paid with one hand and took away with the other in form of fat salaries of technical advisers, which accompanied the aid agreement.

Non- availability of Basic Minerals

Pakistan also lacked badly in the supply of coal and iron ore the basic minerals and other mineral resources needed for the production of iron and steel and certain industrial items. The Government, therefore, had to spend a substantial amount of foreign exchange on the import of minerals and chemicals required to produce industrial goods. The only steel mill established with the collaboration of Russia depends on imported coal and iron ore.

Problems of Industrial Labor

Pakistan's industrial sector has suffered greatly because of the attitude of the employers towards the labor force; low wages, indiscriminate terminations, lack of health and education facilities, and above all no security of bread and butter, were among the factors, which resulted in frequent unrest strikes and lockups that affected their attitude towards their work and good performance.

The political conditions remained unstable for a very long time after Independence. Political chaos and unrest were rampant in the society, which left their unhealthy impact on every aspect of our social life. The Government could not formulate and implement labor policies. The original owners in the first place did not like nationalization of Major

Industries during Mr. Z.A. Bhutto's regime and also the laborers stopped working with that zeal without fear of losing their jobs or to be reprimanded for inefficiency.

Lack of Technical Know- how
Pakistan lacks in technical know-how, which is very essential for industrial progress. There is an acute shortage of skilled personnel in the country such as surveyors, geologists, supervisors, administrators and managers for efficient running of the economy. There is a tendency of flight of skilled 'manpower to other countries in pursuit of more lucrative jobs causing a brain drain in the country.

Pakistan also lack in facilities of the technical education, which is necessary to produce trained and skilled workers for the industrialization of the country. The country, therefore, has to rely on the foreign technicians, which is costly and against national interest. However, taking due cognizance of this deficiency a number of technical institutes in public and private sectors have been added to overcome the problem.

Frequent Power Breakdown
Power resources such as electricity and gas are very vital for running factories to utilize maximum industrial capacity in a country. Most of our industrial units run on these power resources. But there has been too frequent power breakdowns/load shedding, adversely affecting the industrial production.

GOVERNMENT'S ROLE FOR THE SOLUTION OF INDUSTRIAL PROBLEMS

ESTABLISHMENT OF GOVERNMENT ENTERPRISES
The Government took immediate steps for the solution of industrial problems by setting up a few Government enterprises controlled and run by the Ministry of Production. The major objective of these enterprises was to provide maximum assistance to industrial sector for its growth. Besides this objective, these enterprises took over the management of those industrial units, which the private sector had abandoned. These enterprises are as follows:

Pakistan Industrial Development Corporation: Pakistan Industrial Development Corporation was set up in January *1952.* The main objective of the P.I.D.C. was to encourage and guide the industrialist to solve his problems. It also encouraged the private sector to invest in various industrial projects. It took over the control of those industries where the private sector was reluctant to invest.

Industrial Development Bank of Pakistan:
The I.D.B.P. was set up in 1961 with an objective of providing financial assistance for the industrial development. The bank extends financial assistance to industrial sector.

Scientific and Industrial Research Council:
The Council was established in *1952* to do research on the industrial development. It has set up its own laboratories where extensive research on the industrial development is being conducted under the supervision of industrial experts.

National Fertilizer Corporation of Pakistan:
The N.F.C. was established in 1973 at Multan at the cost of Rs. 2243 millions. It is operating with maximum capacity.

State Cement Corporation of Pakistan:
This Corporation was established in 1973. It has completed several projects such as Kalat Cement Factory, Thatta Cement Project and White Cement Expansion Project.

Small Scale Industries Corporation:
This Corporation was set up in 1955 with an objective of encouraging the establishment of industries on a smaller scale. It gives financial assistance for the establishment of industry on a small scale to those investors who are unable to invest from their own resources.

DENATIONALIZATION OF INDUSTRIES
The Bhutto regime nationalized a few industries in 1973, which however, could not produce desired results. The Government, in order to accelerate the process of industrialization, decided to denationalize some of the units. In pursuance of this policy the cotton ginning factories, rice husking, and flourmills were returned to their previous owners. The denationalization of heavy industry has also been approved and the Nowshehra Engineering Co. and LEFO (Lahore Engineering and Foundry

Ltd, former Ittefaq Foundry) have been returned to their former owners. The only Government owned steel mill at Pipri Karachi was sold to Saudi Arabian, Russian, and Pakistani investors but the Chief Justice of Supreme Court of Pakistan took Suo Moto notice, and declared the transaction null and void.

INCENTIVE TO THE INDUSTRIALISTS
To provide incentive to the industrialists the Government announced a Five Year Tax Holiday and allowed remission in the import duty on machinery to be installed in those industries, which are to be established in the under-developed   areas. Lavish reduction in various taxes has been allowed to encourage investment in the industrial sector.

LENIENT POLICY OF CREDITS
The government adopted a lenient policy in giving loans and credits to the industrial sector. The commercial banks have been authorized to extend credit facilities to industrialists. Price control has been lifted from most of the industrial products to set an incentive to the investors.

PRIVATIZATION PROGRAMME
As mentioned above the basic objective of the state enterprises was to assist the private sector and accelerate economic growth. However, the state enterprises failed to achieve this target and they soon began to choke the private sector. These enterprises became a play thing in the hands of politicians and bureaucrats. The Government frequently interfered in their working due to which these institutions suffered heavily. Some of them were extinguished while a few still exist doing nothing positive. Due to failure of Government enterprises the private sector suffered a setback.

In order to re-activate the private sector, the Government of Pakistan decided to launch privatization program. A privatization commission was set up with the task of privatizing Government owned enterprises and to lure the private sector to come forward in a bigger way. The basic objective of privatization is to create a market based economy and promotes the expansion and efficiency of private sector.

So far 91 State owned enterprises have been privatized and 46 other are available for privatization including non-industrial units. Privatization of HBL, Pakistan Telecommunication Company LTD (PTCL), Faisalabad

Area Electric Board (FAEB), and Jamshoro Thermal Unit of WAPDA, and UBL has been completed.

Eighty-five industrial units have so far been privatized during 1996-97. The privatization of National Press Trust Newspapers: daily Mashriq, Pakistan Times and Progressive Papers Ltd. has been accomplished. Following table gives the industry wise breakup of the privatization activities during 1991-92 to 1996-97.

PRIVATIZATION OF INDUSTRIAL UNITS

	1991-92 1993-94	1994-95	1995-96	1996-97	Total
Automobiles	7	x	x	x	7
Cement	9	x	2	x	11
Chemicals	7	2	3	x	12
Fertilizer	1	x	x	x	1
Engineering	5	x	2	x	7
Ghee	16	x	x	x	16
Rice	7	x	1	x	8
Roti Plants	12	x	x	x	12
Miscellaneous	3	3	4	1	11

With these measures adopted by the Government the industrial sector has shown a significant progress during the last two decades. The Government is still giving preference to the uplift of the industrial sector and huge amounts are allocated in the Five Year Plans for the industrial development.

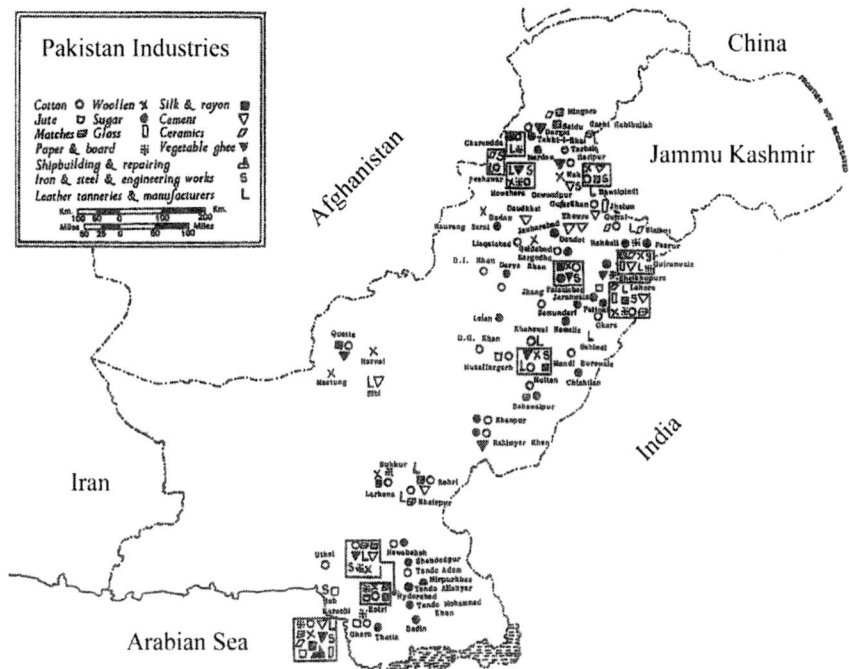

Figure 24: Major Industries

MAJOR INDUSTRIES OF PAKISTAN

TEXTILE INDUSTRY

Textile Industry in Pakistan is mainly based on agricultural or mineral raw materials. At the time of partition this area was not given much attention for manufacturing. Initially there were only 17 textile mills in the country. Pakistan is an important producer of cotton, which was mainly exported to U.K. and Japan, but now Pakistan is consuming most of the cotton produced in the country. Textile is most important sector of Pakistan's economy. Excluding synthetics its weight in the country's industrial production is 18.0 percent. Its total share in exports is 62.2 percent. The government has introduced a broad based package to give a boost to the textile industry. This package includes the reduced interest rate on loans extended to textile mills, re-financing of borrowings were exempted from payment of excise duty, lavish reduction in income tax, freight concession @ 25 per cent on the export of woolen and silk products.

The scattered nature of the industry is in the first instant affected by the market which is there all over the country and secondly by the labor. However, there are some centers of cotton textile manufacturing in the country, which include Faisalabad, Karachi, Hyderabad, Multan, and Lahore. There has been 5.7 per cent increase in the production of cotton yarn while the production of cloth declined by 2.07 percent during 1995-96. At present the number of textile mills in the country is 503.

SUGAR INDUSTRY
Sugar industry has made a tremendous progress and the number of sugar factories has increased to 76 as against 9 at the time of partition. Sugar industry is also scattered over N.W.F.P. 6, Punjab 39, and Sindh 31. It is, however, concentrated in the sugar cane growing areas because sugar cane cannot be stored and transported over longer distances as compared to other raw materials. Although most of the sugar industry in Pakistan uses sugar cane as raw material, yet some mills in the N.W.F.P. use Sugar-beet as well for one or two months when sugar cane is exhausted. Total production in 1997-98 was 3,232.8 thousand tones.

CEMENT INDUSTRY
Cement industry has also made remarkable progress and at the moment Pakistan has 23 Cement factories (4 in public sector and 19 in private sector) with a capacity of 13,029 thousand tons per year. The cement factories are located in Punjab 8, Sindh 9, NWFP 5, and Balochistan 1. The total production, however, still falls short of our requirements, which are increasing because of development going on in various fields. Total production was 6,676 thousand tones in the year 1997-98 as compared to 6,945 thousand tones during 1996-97 showing decrease of 3.87 per cent in production. The shortfall is attributed to closure of prestigious Zeal Pak Cement factory and some other units and owing to low demand in the market due to escalating prices.

PAPER INDUSTRY
Pakistan had established its 1st paper mill at Karnaphuli and the 2nd one was established at Khulna in 1959. These were the only paper mills Pakistan had. After the separation of Eastern wing, Pakistan was totally deprived of paper production. At the moment, Pakistan has paper mills at Sheikhupura and Lahore, which are producing 62 thousand tons of paper, and 109 thousand tones of board as per 1996-97 report of ministry of industries.

CIGARETTES INDUSTRY
A large amount of tobacco is planted in various parts of our country and we produce enough amount of tobacco every year. In the beginning there

was no factory for the manufacturing of tobacco products and we had to export it in raw shape and import tobacco products from other countries. Today we have not only become self sufficient in our tobacco products but are also able to export a large number of tobacco goods to other countries. There are at present 30 cigarettes manufacturing units situated at Jhelum, Multan, Lahore (Punjab), Karachi (Landhi Mauri), Sukkur (Sindh), and Nowshera (NWFP). Total production during 1996-97 was 34.3 m cigarettes.

IRON AND STEEL INDUSTRY

Iron and Steel industry plays a pivotal role in the development of the country. At the time of partition, Pakistan did not have even a single Iron and Steel mill. The first Iron and Steel Mill was located at Chittagong, which was completed in 1959 and soon after it went into production. Pakistan was deprived of it as a result of separation of East Pakistan. However, we now have established first big steel mill at Pipri near Karachi with the assistance of former U.S.S.R. with a capacity of 1 million tons of steel production. The production capacity of Pak. Steel is 1.1 million tons of raw steel per annum with built in potential to expand to over 3 million tones.

Iron ore was mainly imported from Australia, Mauritania, India and Iran but now about 250,000 ton/ year is obtained from local high grade deposits of Saindak, Balochistan and Sargodha Punjab. The steel mill is producing coke, pig iron, billets, hot rolled coils/sheets, and cold rolled coils/sheets, formed sections like channels, angles and galvanized sheets, Iron grills, coils and plates for pipe industry.

Another Heavy Complex has been located at Taxila, which was completed with the assistance of China. Besides that there are a number of big and small units like Ittefaq Foundry producing iron and steel goods. The demand for iron and steel is, however, more than its present production, which is partly being met through scrapes and dismantling of ships at Karachi. Total production of pig iron in the year 1996-97 was 839 thousand and that of Billets was 302 thousand tones.

VEGETABLE GHEE INDUSTRY

There are 150 units producing vegetable ghee and cooking oil with an installed capacity of around 2.5m tones and 1.6/1.7m tones of vegetable ghee/cooking oil is being produced to meet annual national requirement of about 1.4m tones. Out of 150 units only 109 are operative. GCP now produces fraction of total production while major production activity is concentrated in private sector. After the privatization of 16 ghee units, 7 ghee mills are left with the GCP.

SMALL-SCALE INDUSTRIES

Small-scale industry accounts for 5.9 percent of gross Domestic Product, and is widely recognized as a powerful instrument in the economic growth of Pakistan. It provides employment to large number of people; it employs about 80 percent of the industrial labor force. Its share in manufacturing sector is 32.8 per cent. The government has been providing financial support. The World Bank credit equivalent to US $ 30 million was obtained for the development of small-scale industries. The Government has also provided institutional set up for the promotion of small scale industries. It includes technical services, training centers, marketing facilities, and the establishment of industrial estates.

Small and household industries can play a vital part in increasing rural income and reducing the pressure of migration to the cities. Small-scale rural industries have their origin in the historical self-sufficiency of the village. Every village had its own weavers, carpenters, tailors, shoemakers, black-smiths, gold and silver smiths, and other craftsmen. These rural crafts were based on skills passed on from generation to generation. As urban centers developed, craftsmen migrated to the cities where they are able to play their skills for a large market and in some instances expand their operations to small-scale industries. Some of the typical Pakistani fancy goods have developed a market abroad. It is convenient, therefore, to distinguish between those industries, which have remained in the rural areas, and those that are widely developed in the cities.

RURAL AREAS

Most rural settlements are not well connected with outside areas and tend to fulfill most of their requirements within the village itself. These cottage industries and rural crafts are largely governed by local raw materials and local demand. Such industries include atta chakies (flour milling), rice husking, oil-seed milling, rope making, bakery and basketry and these are found in almost all villages. A survey of these agro-based industries by the Pakistan Small Industries Corporation showed them to be second to agriculture itself in providing employment in rural areas.

The village craftsmen produce a wide range of articles and consumer goods. Carpentry, shoemaking, leather tanning, weaving, dyeing, printing, pottery and tailoring, together with the working of iron and gold and the making of bricks, are the most common and widespread rural crafts, Carpenters produce cartwheels, agricultural instruments, cots doors and other small items of furniture. Tanners and shoemakers produce sandals, horse-bridles and saddles, whips, and other leather goods. The blacksmiths produce iron and other instruments. Certain of these artifacts are made in distinctive local styles; locally made khaddar cloth and darrees (coarse rugs) have their traditional designs. Earthen wares are made from local clay, and in some instances, such as the *glazed* tiles of Hala, have achieved national repute.

The total value of these crafts is not easy to estimate. In most areas, it is three to four times that of the agro-based industries, and some rural districts employ 16 percent or more of the population.

URBAN AREAS
The small and craft industries of urban areas fall into two categories, household units and small manufacturing units. Household units are located in residential premises and have assets not exceeding Rs. 50,000. Small manufacturing units have fixed assets up to Rs. 500,000 excluding land. There are some 60,000 household and small manufacturing units, employing more than 400,000 people, and having a total value of fixed assets of over Rs. 5 million. About half of them employ 2-4 workers and about one-quarter employ only one person, in addition to family members, larger units employing more than 50 persons are very low. Most are in the major cities, and the larger the city, the greater the number. According to a survey, 87 percent of all the small and household units were in Karachi, Lahore, Sargodha, Multan, Peshawar, Rawalpindi, and Hyderabad.

TEXTILES
Among these small industries, textiles are the most important group. Cotton spinning and weaving of rough khaddar cloth is widespread, and some centers have gained greater importance because of their production of a special type. Lungis and Khases are made in Peshawar, Kohat, Multan, D.I. Khan, Thatta and Gumbat. Durrees are made in Karachi, Lahore, Sahiwal, Gujranwala, and Gakhar. The cotton carpets are made in Lahore, Multan, and Jacobabad. Blankets, Lois and pattu are prepared from homespun wool. Blankets, are a specialty of Multan, Jhang, and

D.G. Khan. Lois comes from Mingora (Swat), and thick rough woolen cloth is woven in Swat, Chitral, Gilgit, and Kalat. Woolen carpets are made in Lahore, Multan, Hyderabad, Peshawar, D.I.Khan, Kalat, Bannu, Leila, Bahawalpur, and Landhi. Silk cloth and turbans are made in Peshawar and Kohat.

EMBROIDERY AND NEEDLEWORK

This industry is centered in urban areas such as Karachi, Lahore, Hyderabad, Multan, Bahawalpur, and Quetta. Phul kari work, silk embroidery over rough cotton cloth, is done in many centers in the Punjab, Swat, and N.W.F.P. Sindhi and Makrani embroidery and golden thread embroidery is done in Quetta, Karachi, Lahore, Hyderabad, Multan, Bahawalpur, and Peshawar. These goods are exported in substantial quantities.

LEATHER, POTTERY AND FURNITURE

Embroidered leather sandals and shoes are a specialty of Peshawar, Multan, Bahawalpur, Lahore, Karachi, and Rawalpindi. These fancy sandals and embroidered handbags have found a market in America and Europe. Fine pottery is prepared from good quality clay in Sialkot, Gujrat, Gujranwala, Peshawar, Bahawalpur, and Multan. Articles like ashtrays, flower-vases, fruit bowls, and plates are exported to the Middle East. Carved wooden articles and art furniture, inlaid with copper, brass, and ivory, are made in Lahore, Chiniot, D.G. Khan, Gujrat, Karachi, and Peshawar.

MISCELLANEOUS

Utensils made from brass, copper, silver, iron and aluminum are hand-made at many places. Peshawar, Guiranwala, Sialkot, Larkana, and Shikarpur are the main centers. Sialkot produces sports goods from mulberry wood. Other Pakistani crafts include glass bangles (Hyderabad), marble lamps, bowls and ashtrays (Karachi), camel skin lamps (Balochistan and Multan). These latter items are exported and also appeal to tourists.

FACTORS INVOLVED IN LOCATION OF INDUSTRIES

There are considerations for locating any unit - may it be a residential, commercial or an industrial proposition. For a residential accommodation the basic facilities like availability of water, electricity, connection of road, vicinity to school, college, office, security etc., are kept in view. Similarly there are preferences in mind while locating a commercial organization. Since industry is a bigger venture and involves huge expenditure and investment, a careful deliberation and planning is, therefore, required before taking any decision regarding its location.

The function of an industry is to reshape or mould raw material into some finished product. A small scale or a cottage industry mostly serves the local market, in which manual labor and limited use of power is involved, hence it can be carried on anywhere without giving much thought. On the other, a factory/industry cannot be initiated without proper planning. Those agencies which issue licenses for installing industrial units take into account all the factors that are essential for a smooth functioning of a unit.

Factors that influence the location of a factory/industry include labor, power, raw materials, capital, transport, market etc.

LABOR
A large number of skilled and unskilled workers are needed in a factory. One of the reasons for encouraging industrialization is to help providing employment to the people. A site close to some inhabited area from where labor can easily be available is advantageous and economical; because it would help avoiding huge expenditure on providing housing facilities to the labor.

POWER
In order to run the machinery availability of power in the form of coal, oil, gas, hydro-electricity, depending on the nature of industry is very important. For an Iron and Steel industry a site close to a coal producing area is useful whereas for an aluminum or metal smelter availability of cheap hydro-electric power is more advantageous. In Pakistan industrial development was only possible after the development of hydro-electricity and the discovery and exploitation of the extensive resources of natural gas. Natural gas besides its use as power is also used as raw material in fertilizers and petro-chemical industries.

RAW MATERIAL
Where bulk or use of fresh raw materials like iron ore or cane sugar is to be made, site closer to the sources of raw materials is more suitable. Tata

iron and Steel Industry at Jamshedpur, Ruhr Steel Industry West Germany, Pittsburg Iron and Steel Works, U.S.A. are all raw materials oriented in the same way cotton textile industry in Punjab and Sindh is also based on local cotton produce. Sugar cane factories necessarily have to be located in the sugar cane growing areas as sugar cane besides being in bulk has to be crushed within 48 hours of its harvest; otherwise sugar contents are reduced to the extent of about 30 to 40% because of chemical decomposition.

CAPITAL

The pre-requisite of a factory industry is the availability of capital. Adequate arrangement of funds is essential for undertaking any such venture. In order to encourage investors Government has offered Industrial loans at reasonable terms. Industrial Development Banks have been established all over the country for the purpose.

TRANSPORT

For the transportation of goods from and to the factory and movement of labor, availability of efficient means of transportation is very important. Development of means of communications is, therefore, closely linked with, industrialization in a country. With the development of rail and roads industries also come up with the same speed.

MARKET

Market is a very important factor in determining location of industries. Areas close to the markets are most suited for the industry e.g. Iron and Steel industry of Pakistan is entirely market oriented. Because Pakistan lacks basic minerals like coal and iron ore and yet the industry has been established at Karachi. It is purely because of demand i.e. market.

PRICE OF LAND

Price of land near urban centers is very high. Factories, therefore, are located at a reasonable distance from the urban centers to avoid huge expenditure on land.

POLITICAL CONDITIONS

Stable government and areas at a safe distance from politically explosive regions and enemy territories are preferred for industrial location.

SOCIO-ECONOMIC FACTORS

Before setting up an industry Socio-Economic survey of the surrounding area from where the labor has to be recruited is desirable. Social and moral conditions of the population greatly influence the working atmosphere of the factory. An area having high rate of crime is not suited for industrial location.

Geographical factors

Geographical factors play an important role in determining location of industry. Coastal climate besides an attraction for import and export facilities is an added attraction for the textile and heavy industry. Heavy machinery can be installed in coastal locations without incurring extra freight. Moreover, for textile industry high humidity is suitable and a requirement of the industry, but this can be compensated if other factors are favorable. Idealism in industry is not much supported as in other aspects of practical life. Compromises in industrial location have, therefore, to be made. Ideal location in industrial planning is very rare yet possible.

TOURISM

Pakistan is endowed with immense natural scenic beauty; lofty mountain peaks, colorful valleys, and historical buildings attract tourists from all over the world. Tourism, therefore, is an important industry of Pakistan. Besides foreign tourists people from all over the country in large number to escape heat of the plains and to relax visit north mountainous country in summer and to enjoy snowfall in winter. Pakistan has some of the world's highest peaks which are over 6,000 meters high. Mountaineers to scale the lofty peaks flock in summer when the snow line recedes, and also to enjoy the beauty of the region. Availability of drugs has also been an attraction to the youngsters in the past.

Tourism not only provides jobs to the people but also the government earns foreign exchange; annual foreign exchange earnings range from four to five million dollars. Government is paying great attention to promote and expand the industry and a full-fledged Ministry has been created for the purpose that has chalked an elaborate program to further popularize and attract people to visit Pakistan in greater numbers. Following measures have been adopted to enhance attraction and scope of the Industry:

Extension of communications

New roads and approaches to the sites of attraction are being planned and implemented. Rest houses, youth hostels, and prestigious hotels are being made and encouraged in the private sector. Safety measures for the tourists, particularly the foreigners, are being adopted to ensure security to the visitors. New sites of attraction and sports have been planned to widen scope of the industry. But since 2001, due to the increase in terrorist attacks tourism has been hit hard.

CHAPTER XVII
TRADE

EXPORTS AND IMPORTS

No country or region is self-sufficient. In order to meet our requirements we have to depend on one another. Some areas are rich in minerals and industrial products but they depend for the food and raw materials on other areas. Pakistan is basically a producer of food and raw materials and therefore, the composition of imports and exports is reflected in its foreign trade. Balance of trade in Pakistan, however, is negative which means that our exports fall short of our imports. In order to improve this ratio a number of steps have been taken. Newly sworn Government of PPP hopes that in the near future the balance in foreign trade will be achieved.

EXPORTS

During the five-year period, 2000-06, exports have been doubled. However, the growth has been unsteady for various reasons, principally owing to the variable demand from year to year of our export items in the world market. The export of raw cotton, cotton yarn and sometimes rice is more affected by the changing trends in the international market.

VALUE (US. $ in MILLIONS)

Year	Imports	Exports	Balance of Trade
2000	10,309	8,568	
			- 1,741
2001	10,728	9,201	
			- 1,527
2002	10,339	9,134	
			- 1,205
2003	12,220	11,160	
			- 1,060
2004	*15,591*	12,313	
			- 3,278
2005	20,623	14,410	
			- 6,213
2006	24,990	16,468	
			- 8,522

COMPOSITION OF EXPORTS

Under the Second, Third and fourth Plans, efforts were made not merely to increase exports but diversify them and reduce dependence on a limited number of primary products. This policy is presently gaining momentum. By replacing the export of unprocessed primary products with that of manufactured products, foreign exchange earnings have increased.

In order to reduce, and if possible eliminate, the negative ratio of exports to imports, several measures have been adopted. The Export Promotion Council and Export Promotion Bureau have been set up to provide assistance and information to potential foreign buyers. Pakistan has participated in international trade conferences and fairs, and sent trade delegations abroad.

PAKISTAN'S MAJOR EXPORTS in US$ in millions

Year	2000	2001	2002	2003	2004	2005
Primary Commodities	896	949	808	1,006	1,010	1,330
Textile Manufactures	9.1	8.6	9.3	9.2	8.0	7.2
Rice	5.6	6.0	4.7	3.6	5.6	5.8
Synthetic Textile	5.7	6.1	7.4	9.5	7.1	6.2
Sports Goods	2.2	2.0	1.9	2.9	3.2	2.8
Others	16.4	16.0	16.9	16.9	17.4	14.9

Pakistan's exports are highly concentrated on few items namely cotton and textile, rice, synthetic textiles, and sports goods. These categories of exports, accounted for 83.6 per cent of the total export in 1990-91.

Although Pakistan is trading with a large number of countries, its exports are highly concentrated in few countries. Almost 50% of Pakistan's exports are directed towards seven countries (USA, Germany, Japan, UK, Hong Kong, Dubai, and Saudi Arabia), among these countries the shares of USA and Hong Kong have been raising while those of Germany, UK and Dubai remained almost same with minor fluctuations.

IMPORTS

The import policy of Pakistan has been varying. Availability of foreign exchange has been the main constraint. Edible oil, POL, fertilizers, tea, chemicals, drugs, and medicines, machinery, iron and steels, and transports equipment constitute bulk of the imports, generally accounting for about 70 percent of all imports. It has been attempted, with some success, to curtail imports, by increasing domestic production of oil energy, fertilizers, engineering goods, food grain etc. However, a liberal import policy is being pursued to improve the value of industrial production, by making available the required machinery and raw material.

Although Pakistan is importing from a number of countries, the major portion of its imports, however, come from a few countries. Almost 50 per cent of imports originate from seven countries namely USA, Japan, Kuwait, Saudi Arabia, Germany, UK, and Malaysia.

Food grains are imported mainly from U.S.A. and Canada, metals and ores from the European Common Market, Japan, U.S.A. and Canada, electrical goods from U.K, U.S.A, Japan, and West Germany, petroleum from the Middle East, principally Iran and Saudi Arabia, transport equipment from U.K, U.S.A, Japan, and West Germany, tea from Sri Lanka, and vegetable oils from U.K and U.S.A.

Imports are broadly categorized into:

1. Consumer goods
2. Raw material for consumer goods
3. Raw material for Capital goods.

The general trend has been for consumer goods to form a decreasing percentage of total imports, both because of the emphasis on capital goods for the developing economy and the substitution of domestically manufactured products for imports.

CHAPTER XVIII
ECONOMIC PLANNING

MEANINGS OF ECONOMIC PLANNING
Economic planning, broadly speaking, is an activity aimed at utilizing the human and material resources available with a nation in a way as to bring maximum economic prosperity and happiness to the people. Planning is done with a prime objective of erecting the national economy on stable foundations keeping in view the national resources and requirements. The sole objective of planning is to utilize, more effectively, the resources available to a country with a view to achieving the well-defined target of economic progress within a given time limit. It is a central authority usually called the Planning Commission, which carries out the task of planning by harnessing the potential human and material resources of a country for economic well being of its people.

ECONOMIC PLANNING IN PAKISTAN
The overwhelming importance and utility of planning in Pakistan cannot be ignored because Pakistan has always been facing problems in its economic development. All Governments, from time to time, have been well aware of this problem and had always given their utmost attention towards its solution. For this purpose economic planning was always done in shape of development plans and other developmental projects. The Government of Pakistan, immediately after Independence, set up the institution of planning in the country. A Development Board was set, up in 1948 with a view to carrying out economic planning in the newly born nation in order to promote economic growth. A Planning Advisory Board was also established which was to extend assistance to the Development Board in its work of planning for economic development.

The Development Board began its work with a Six Year Development Plan on the recommendation of the Colombo Plan. The plan, however, could not succeed because of the internal political unrest. In 1953 the Development Board was dissolved and a Planning Board was assigned the job of preparing the First Five Year Plan, which was designed and released in 1955. With the First Five Year Plan, the systematic economic planning in Pakistan set in.

The planning machinery in Pakistan was once again reshaped in 1958 when the Planning Board was raised to the status of the planning Commission. The Head of the state was to be its Chairman and a Deputy Chairman with the status of a Cabinet Minister was to be appointed as its operational Head who was either a senior member of the Civil Service or a professional economist. The commission had several other staff members such as Secretary Planning, Chief Economist and joint Chief Economist. Also a separate Ministry of Planning and Development was created in early eighties. Dr. Mahbub-ul-Haq, a renowned Economist, was appointed as the first Minister of Planning and Development.

The Planning Commission, since coming into existence, has given eight Five Year Plans to the country. These plans, to a great extent, have given sufficient boost to the national economy. The Five Year Plans are discussed below:

THE FIRST FIVE-YEAR PLAN 1955-60

The Planning Board prepared the First Five Year Plan in 1955. It was released to the public in 1956 for acquiring the public opinion. The National Economic Council finally approved the plan on 15th April, 1957 to be launched to achieve its objectives.

The total expenditure of the plan was estimated to be Rs. 1,080 crore out of which Rs. 750 crore were to be spent in public sector and the remaining amount of Rs. 350 crore in the private sector. As it was the first developmental plan of the country, a great deal of emphasis was laid on the accomplishment of several projects.

The plan, however, could not achieve its target for many reasons. Due to unstable economy, balance between imports and exports could not be maintained. Exports could not be enhanced while greater expenditures had to be incurred on imports. The delay in obtaining the approval of the plan from the National Economic Council greatly damaged the plan by hampering the developmental work for two years. The non-developmental expenditures rose to unexpected and unseen limits, which adversely affected the implementation of the plan. Many projects took longer time to complete than was expected because of lack of co-ordination between the Government agencies. Acute shortage of equipment, personnel and material became a key impediment in the implementation of the plan.

In spite of its short falls and failure in achieving its target, the First Five Year Plan provided a strong base for the Second Five year Plan. The Second Five Year Plan was prepared keeping in view the short falls of the First Plan. Maximum efforts were made to prepare the Second Plan in the light of the experience gained during the implementation of the First Plan.

THE SECOND FIVE-YEAR PLAN 1960-65

The second five year plan was prepared in 1959 and approved by the N.E.C. in 1960. The total expenditures of the plan were estimated at Rs. 2,300 crore. A more vigorous role was assigned to private sector whereas public sector was to act as a gap-filler. Out of the total size, Rs. 1,240 crore were to be spent in public sector, Rs. 680 crore in the private sector and the remaining Rs. 380 crore in the semi-public sector.

The Second Five Year Plan, in comparison to the First Plan, was a great success. It succeeded in achieving most of its expected targets. In some sectors the achievements even surpassed the targets and Pakistan's performances became the envy of other developing countries.

THE THIRD FIVE-YEAR PLAN 1965-70

The Third Five Year Plan was formulated in the year 1964. After the approval by the N.E.C. the plan was launched in 1965 as a part of 20-year Long Term Perspective Plan to be completed in 1985. The 20-year Long Term Plan was devised in the light of the experience gained during the previous plans.

Some ambitious objectives were laid down in the Third Five Year Plan. The implementation of the plan unfortunately, fell in jeopardy at the *very* outset because of the Indian aggression in 1965. The Government had to divert its energies towards the defense of the country in wake of Indian attack. However, in spite of the dire situation, created by the war, the objectives and the targets of the plan were not altered.

The total expenditures of the plan were estimated at Rs. 5,200 crore. Out of this amount Rs. 2,200 crore were to be spent in the public sector and the remaining amount of Rs. 3,000 crore was to go to the private sector. Development expenditures were distributed amongst the two provinces of Pakistan. The former East Pakistan got a share of Rs. 1,600 crore and the West Pakistan received Rs. 1,400 crore out of Rs. 3,000 crore allocated in the private sector. The two wings got the equal share from the proposed investment of Rs. 2,200 crore of the public sector.

The plan could not accomplish its targets in total because of multifarious reasons such as 1965 war with India, stoppage of US Aid, floods and cyclones in East Pakistan. The country had to face these crises during the early years of the launching of the plan. There was political turmoil too, which adversely affected the implementation of the plan. Despite enormous odds, the plan achieved most of its targets.

THE FOURTH FIVE-YEAR PLAN 1970-75

Fourth five year plan was prepared as a part of the 20 Year Long Term Perspective Plan of 1965-85 like the Third Plan. The estimated expenditures of this plan were Rs. 7,500 crore. Out of this amount Rs. 4,900 crore were allocated for development work in the public sector and Rs. 2,600 crore in the private sector.

The Fourth Plan met a different fate, as it could not be implemented because of the 1971 war with India and the secession of East Pakistan. Although it aimed at achieving some ideal objectives of establishing a just society and reducing disparities in the per capita income, it had to be scrapped because of the separation of country's Eastern part as a result of Indian aggression just after a year of its launching. The Fourth five-year Plan later was, replaced by Annual Development Programs.

THE FIFTH FIVE-YEAR PLAN 1978-83

The Fifth Five Year Plan was launched on July 1, 1978. The estimated expenditures of the plan were Rs. 210.22 billion out of which Rs. 128.22 billion were given to the public sector and Rs. 62.00 billion were allocated for the private sector. A sum of Rs. 20.00 billion was spent outside of the ADP.

THE SIXTH FIVE-YEAR PLAN 1983-88

The sixth five year plan was launched on July 1, 1983 with a total expenditure of Rs. 490 billion. The private sector was allocated Rs. 200 billion while the public sector received Rs. 290 billion. At the time of launching of the Sixth Plan it was felt that Pakistan needed rapid economic growth to eradicate the increasing volume of poverty. The economic experts were of the opinion that the economic growth was of no use if it did not reach the poor classes. They pointed out, rightly, that it was essential for the masses to participate fully in economic life.

THE SEVENTH FIVE- YEAR PLAN 1988-93

The Seventh Five Year Plan was launched on July 1st, 1988. It envisaged a total fixed investment of Rs. 660.2 billion at 1987-88 prices. The public sector was allocated the fixed investment of Rs. 368 billion, which was higher than the public sector development outlay of Rs. 350 billion the private sector's fixed investment in the Seventh Five Year Plan works out to be Rs. 292.4 billion.

Out of Rs. 350 billion earmarked for the public sector, the Federal Government ministries and departments were to receive Rs. 91.4 billion while Rs. 101.7 billion were fixed for the provinces and the rest for the Federal public sector Corporations.

The Seventh Five- year Plan had been formulated within the context of the perspective plan, which covered the period from 1988 to 2003.

The seventh five year plan envisaged balancing the Government expenditures by the current revenues. The Government borrowing would be restricted to the size of the five- year total of A.D. of Rs. 315 billions. The plan also aimed at taking institutional steps to impose a discipline on the federal budget by legislative means. It also intended to raise taxation from the present level of about 13 percent to 16 percent by the end of the plan period.

CHAPTER XIX

CHILD LABOR

In the recent years the producers of certain commodities like carpets and sports goods have showed an increasing global interest on the plight of the children. All sorts of child labor are not exploitation. In developing societies it is almost a necessity mainly due to the absence of social security cover and low wages of unskilled workers.

PLIGHT OF' CHILDREN IN PAKISTAN

In Pakistan more than half of its population approximately 64 per cent falls under 18 years of age. The highest concentration is in age group of 5 to 9 years and under 4 years. This major portion of our society upon which the future of the nation depends, is unsafe in every respect. Nearly *600,000* children under 5 years of age die of preventable diseases in Pakistan every year.

According to UNICEF's estimates, the world average of child mortality per thousand is 97, 128 in India, and 138 in Pakistan.

Nature of Child Exploitation

Child labor is differentiated from child work. Child labor is the negation of childhood and child education and development. Child work is an occasional form of work requiring at the most a few hours in a day working with other members of family. This form of work is considered healthy for the child as it enables him in acquiring traditional skills and expertise. Opposed to this are the conditions of work where children are found working on adult's jobs. The work is regular and has longer duration and contains an element of exploitation. The children are overworked and deprived of education.

The conditions of child labor are defined as working too young, working for long hours, working under strain, working on the streets in unhealthy and dangerous conditions and working for very little pay.

Health Hazards

In addition to be deprived of education, and getting low wages, the working children are very much prone to health problem while on work.

Children working in carpet weaving industry, embroidery and heavy weight lifting fall victim to postural deformity. Anemic, fatigued, and inadequately slept children are more susceptible to infectious diseases, and tuberculosis. Half of 50,000 child laborers in carpet industry in Pakistan never reach the age of 12.

Quite a few other child workers, who are working in restaurants on roadsides and cleaners in trucks, are highly vulnerable to accidents and infectious diseases.

STEPS FOR THE ELIMINATION OF CHILD LABOR

Poverty conditions alone are not responsible for the prevalence of child labor. What is needed is more vigorous enforcement of the laws prohibiting child labor. About 40 countries of the world have ratified the ILO convention on "Child Labor minimum age".

The problem of child labor needs concerted efforts with focus on contributing factors. In this regard the ILO is of the view that the issue of Child Labor can be tackled by a focus on:

(i)   Improving and enforcing legislation
*(ii)   P*romoting school education
*(iii) R*aising public awareness
*(iv) S*upporting community action
(v)   Targeting hazardous occupations

But these steps alone would not be able to eliminate the basic causes of Child Labor such as existence of widespread poverty, unemployment and under-employment. It is, therefore, imperative to re-organize the educational and training system, there is also need to develop comprehensive labor market information system, preparing an employment policy, eliminating poverty, evolving a social security system and raising public awareness. It is also needed to enforce legislation strictly.

Pakistan has taken some initiative in the right direction for the elimination of Child Labor. Steps have been taken to promote self-supporting village communities with emphasis to sending children to schools and preventing them from joining the ranks of child Labor. Efforts have been launched to further strengthen the process by evolving safety net mechanism for vulnerable groups of society, streaming anti-poverty Islamic institution of

Zakat and Ushr, enforcing the existing labor legislation and developing a comprehensive labor market information system.

Giving and receiving of all 'advances' and 'peshgis' be stopped and made an offence punishable under law. Prohibition against Child Labor should be strictly enforced in Brick Kiln industry. A commission at the National level to be set up to suggest further remedial measures not only for the Brick Kiln industry but in all the areas where the Bonded Labor in vogue.

However, despite the presence of numerous legislations on the prevention of Child Labor/Bonded Labor, Child labor continues to be employed in Pakistan and its violations are unabated. At present there are more than 15 acts and ordinances, federal as well as provincial dealing with the children in one form or another. They are children (pledging Labor) Act 1933, Workers children Education Ordinance 1972, Sindh children Act 1955, Punjab Children Ordinance 1983, Sindh Borstal Schools Act 1955, Child Elders Act, and Child Marriage Restrained Act.

It is because of non-enforcement of the provisions of law the children are being exploited criminally. The irony of the fate is that Pakistan is a signatory of UN convention on the rights of the children. Since children cannot organize themselves into pressure groups or lobbies and express their grievances, their cause appears to be going by default.

CHAPTER XX

CULTURE

Culture may be defined as the sum total of a people's way of living - a behavior peculiar to human beings, together with the material objects used. Constituents of culture are language, beliefs, customs, rituals, ceremonies, techniques, works of arts, and so on.

The concept of culture emanated fairly recently. The first definition of culture as a sociological term was put forward in 1871 by E.B. Taylor, a British anthropologist who describes "culture is the complex whole which includes knowledge, belief, art, morals, custom and any and all other capabilities and habits acquired by man as a member of the society." In 1919, Clark Wissler, an American anthropologist, stated that culture has to be learned. In 1920's A.R. Radcliff and his contemporaries emphasized the fact each culture is an integral whole, like a living being. According to Margret Mead "culture is an abstraction from the body of learned behavior which a group of people who share the same tradition, transmit entirely to their children. It depends not only on art and services, religion, and philosophies, but also the system of technology, the political practices, the small intimate habits of daily life such as the way of preparing or eating food, as well as the method of electing their chief or the prime minister or changing the constitution.

Some cultures belong to large groups and others to small tribes. No two cultures are exactly alike. Culture is the history of a society. It reflects and preserves its social past and leads to the future. Culture depends and is affected by a number of factors of which history, geography, faith, and religion are more important.

Whereas civilization is a wider term and denotes average behavior of man spread over a long span of time like Indus valley civilization, culture is the behavior of a specific group or a society at a particular period of time. Cultural values differ from place to place. In the same geographical region there may be different practices of preparing and eating food, housing, dress, worship from society to society e.g. in the sub-continent of India Pakistan which is more or less the same geographical region, but they speak different languages, dress differently, Muslims eat and slaughter cow whereas Hindus worship it and consider a sin to kill it. Muslims bury the dead bodies whereas Hindus cremate them. Muslims believe in one God and Hindus practice polytheism and so on. Here history and geography of the people is the same but religion and faith is the main factor that matters and brings radical change in the way of life as soon as one changes one's faith.

Language, food, dress, and seasonal festivals are the products of local geographical conditions and keep changing with the changing times. It may, therefore, safely be concluded that culture and cultural values pertain to a particular time and place. Every socio-cultural system exists in a natural habitat and of course environment exerts influence upon the cultural system. We can break down each culture in to a number of traits. In western culture a man can be married to only one wife at a time, but in the Arab culture, polygamy is a normal feature and one may have four wives at a time.

When the people of one culture meet another culture as the groups grow, they usually exchange ideas and products. The impact of one culture on another is called acculturation. For example when the ancient Romans conquered the Greeks who had a more advanced culture in arts and sciences became teachers of Romans. When Alexander the great, along with his army attacked the sub-continent, the Greeks learned sculpture and Astronomy from Indians and taught them Mathematics and philosophy.

THE IMPACT OF ISLAM ON THE INDIAN CIVILIZATION AND CULTURE

Muhammad Bin Qasim, a great Muslim hero and commander, came to India in 712 A.D. as a conqueror and lived there for about three years. He introduced Islamic system; respect for humanity regardless of cast, creed or position in the society and thus made an indelible impact of Islam as a faith and system of life, and won *many* followers in India because of his high moral character.

Before the coming of Islam to India, the people were divided in several religious factions and a deep struggle was going on between Hinduism and other religions. Conditions, which extremely perturbed the people, prevailed in the society. The prevailing conditions were ripe for the introduction of a new religious faith and system, which would negate the existing religious philosophies based on inhuman trends and customs. When Islam was introduced to the people of the sub-continent, it attracted many followers because of its simple and easily understandable principles. The introduction of Islam completely transformed the Indian society into a well-knit social fraternity.

Islam and Hinduism basically differ in their attitude towards life. Islam strongly believes in the concept of 'Tauheed' and insists on the equality of mankind before law. It does not entertain any distinction among the people on the basis of such inhuman principles as caste, creed, and social status. Hinduism on the other hand believes in the multiplicity of Gods, and is based on the unethical caste system, which has divided society into privileged and underprivileged classes.

Islam came as a blessing for the oppressed sections of India whose life had become miserable because of the deep-rooted caste system. Islam brought a new way of life for them, which they had never seen before in the Hindu society. The respectable way of life, shown to them by Islam, gave them a feeling of being human beings. Islam infused a different thinking and sentiments among the people of the sub-continent.

The spread of Islam in the sub-continent, owes much to the selfless and dedicated services of eminent Sufis, mystics, and religious leaders such as Hazrat Data Ganj Bakhsh, Khawja Mueen-ud-Din Chishty, Sheikh Baha-ud-Din Zakria, Khawja Bakhtiar Kaki, Baba Farid-ud-Din Shakar Ganj, Nizam-ud-Din Aulia, Mujadid Alf Sani, Shah Wali Ullah and many others of those times.

Islam also made its impact on the Hindu temples and their architecture began reflecting the Islamic way of construction. The religious leaders of Hindus, also influenced by the Islamic principles, reshaped their religious philosophies in the light of Islamic values and principles. They started advocating the Islamic principles of equality, love, brotherhood and oneness of God in their teachings and impressed upon the people to abandon idol worship. The main leaders of Hinduism, influenced by the teachings of Islam, were chafing who introduced the Bhagti movement and Baba Guru Nanak, the founder of Sikh religion.

IMPACT ON ART AND LITERATURE
The Indian art and literature also showed influence of Islam. The people rejected the out-dated and absurd customs of Hindu society and showed tendency towards the new trends of life. Muslim thought and trend influenced native art and paintings. The old languages Sanskrit and Parakrit had a tinge of Arabic, Persian and later on Turkish languages. By the interaction of these languages new languages like Urdu and Hindi emerged. Urdu, later on became the language of the Muslims and left its impact on many other languages of India.

IMPACT ON ARCHITECTURE
The Muslim conquest of India left a considerable impact on the Indian architecture and there was a unique development in art during the Muslim rule. Muslim architecture frequently mingled with the Hindu style of buildings. The Hindu temples, their pillars and domes reflected some glimpses of Muslim architecture. In the new buildings red stone and marble was used which was a significant characteristic of the Muslim way of construction.

IMPACT ON HISTORY
The arrival of Muslims in the sub-continent marks a new development in the art of recording historical events. Historical literature, which existed before the arrival of the Muslims, was mostly legendary and not authentic. In a series of geographical works the Arabs explained topography and political and cultural geography of the sub-continent entitled *'The Tarikh-al-Hind Wa al* Sindh", which is regarded as the first reliable historical record *of* the sub-continent. It was translated from Arabic to Persian and is known as *"Chach Nama"*. Various branches of historiography developed during the sultanate period, which included World History and Dynastic History. The *"Tabqat-c-Nasiri'* and the *Tarikh-Feroz Shahi"* are excellent examples of the art of historiography developed during this period.

Besides the above mentioned areas Islam made its impact on every other aspect of Indian society. A sense of homogeneity and oneness developed in the social set-up after the arrival of the Muslims in India. Indian society was now a well knit whole and a sense of centralism had evolved amongst the various sections of society. With the arrival of the Muslims, India established relations with the other countries of the world. Diplomatic and trade links were established. This had a happy effect on the economy of India.

During the reign of Sher Shah Suri the public welfare sector was given special attention. Roads and means of communication were improved. New roads, hospitals, inns, and post offices were constructed for the convenience of the people. First census was held in the time of Muhammad Tughlak. Ala-ud-Din Khilji introduced trade and agricultural reforms.

Salient Features of Pakistani Culture

Every nation has its cultural past, which reflects the identity of that nation. Many nations lived in India. They had their own cultures and civilization, which left an indelible impact on the local social conditions. Consequent upon the invasions of Arabs, in 712 A.D. and then by Ghaznvi, Ghauri, and Mughal dynasties who established their rule here that lasted for about 600 years and as such left a lasting impact of Muslim culture on the local Buddhist and Hindu society. The social life in the sub-continent saw a great change with the advent of Islam in India. Significant changes occurred in the way of life of the people who entered the fold of Islam in great numbers. Islam has, therefore, played a dominant role in molding social pattern in the sub-continent particularly in the areas that now constitute Pakistan with the Muslim majority.

Islam unlike other religions is not only a faith and a way of worship but it is culture, a code of conduct − by practicing which in every sphere of one's life a purposeful lasting experience is achieved. Going to the mosque, wearing a special dress keeping beard is not Islam − Islam means complete submission to the will of Almighty and to observe discipline in all walks of life − at home, in business, dealing with others, young or old, friends and foes. He, who is very regular in praying and giving to the poor, and has performed pilgrimage, but is not fair in his dealings with others; does not care for the comfort and welfare of his relatives, neighbors is not a follower of Islam in its true sense. God loves those who avoid evil and love His creation. Pakistan was achieved in the name of Islam but there are people who are Muslims only by name; dishonesty, corruption, amassing wealth by unfair means, theft, murder, ill treatment of women and children, sectarian killings is a common feature and the frequency of such crimes in Pakistan that claims to be a land of the pure free of vices, is no less than other countries of the world.

To find true followers of Islam is a rare thing these days – fault lies somewhere – with parents, teachers or the community that have failed to create the real Islamic values in the individuals and the society. That is why in spite of gaining freedom more than half a century ago, Islamic law could not be enforced in the country – the law has been framed but it is not implemented because it neither suits the people at the helm of affairs and nor the society. Allama Iqbal in this respect had rightly said, " Jahan Mein Ho Saki Na Qaim Kabhi Hakumat-e-Ishq Sitam Ye Hai Keh Mohabbat Zamana Saz Nahin." In a nut shell the philosopher and poet of the east admittedly said, "No rule in this world could ever be established that followed justice-cause, justice does not believe in compromises." Perhaps, it was because of this rarity that he had advised his son to adopt a line of judiciary who, (Justice Javaid Iqbal) retired as a chief Justice of Pakistan. Anyhow by the grace of God Almighty most of Pakistanis declare themselves as Muslims primarily to reap the benefits of being so in a Muslim State where Muslims are considered first class citizens.

Language is another important feature of culture. Although many languages are spoken in Pakistan yet Urdu is accepted as the National language. People of all the provinces besides their local language speak and understand Urdu. The language, therefore, is another binding force between provinces besides religion in Pakistan. English still is the official language and medium of instruction in most of the colleges and universities of Pakistan.

Mixed Culture

Influence of Hindu and British culture is manifest in customs and traditions of Pakistani society. Festival of Basant, primarily a tradition of Hindu culture is observed and celebrated with great enthusiasm in Pakistan in the spring season particularly at Lahore. In the same way Christmas and New Year, primarily Christian festivals, largely legacy of British influence find a great fascination with youths of the country; dance and music parties are held in hotels and clubs and Jamaat-e-Islami workers (Lath Bardars) keep chasing them considering it an un-Islamic act.

Moreover, life style, dress, food etiquettes, and manners in high society conform to the western culture rather than the eastern. In rural societies of Punjab and Sindh, the populous provinces, where on occasions of marriage and death almost the same rituals are followed as prevalent in Hindu society. For example in Hindu culture a female does not inherit movable or immovable property of her parents, instead they spend lavishly on the marriage ceremonies of their daughters in the form of dowry and feasting bridegroom his friends and relations along with other guests. Bridegroom practically does not spend any thing. Almost same is the practice of marriage ceremonies in Pakistani society; "Walima" feast on behalf of the bridegroom a tradition of Muslim culture is mostly ignored and not religiously followed. In rural Punjab and Sindh women are forced to forego share of their landed property in favor of their brothers against Muslim inheritance law. Women in case of death of their husband are not encouraged to marry again and rather considered a bad omen and are downgraded. All these practices are contrary to Islamic version but are in practice in Pakistan as well.

In case of death of a senior the funeral is carried with the beat of drums and the whole village is served with a sumptuous food. On the other hand, if it happens to be the death of a youth it is mourned for several days; the women folk assemble in the courtyard of the deceased at night, sit in a circle with their arms and heads close to one another and recite mournful notes with a loud voice for many days. Neither the traditions of marriage nor of death find any conformity with the customs and traditions of the Muslims, which clearly shows an influence of Hindu culture in Pakistani society.

Women's Position in Pakistani Society

Pakistani Society is male oriented. It revolves around the male members. Male member heads the family. He is mostly the sole earner and his word is considered final in matters concerning family affairs. Particularly, in the rural areas women seldom have any say even in the selection of their life partner and have to submit before the will of their elders. Those who try to break the tradition are severely dealt with and often killed in the name of honor killing called 'Karo Kari' and no action is taken against the defaulters. These traditions have been a legacy of ancient Hindu culture and are against Islamic laws and traditions. Islam does not create any distinction between the two sexes; marriage contract cannot be executed without her approval and she is represented by a counsel to settle the terms of the contract. Then again a woman is fully competent to dissolve the marriage contract if she feels that she cannot pull on like the husband who can divorce at his will. Unfortunately, our society largely follows ancient cultural practices rather than Islamic laws and traditions.

The present government has taken practical steps to implement the laws pertaining rights of women. A bill has been passed in the National Assembly to stop discriminatory practices against the females; to end heinous crimes like 'Karo Kari'. Death penalty has been recommended for those who are found involved in such crimes.

More than 70% of the overall population of the country lives in villages that not only earns its own livelihood from the lands but also produces food and cash crops to meet the needs of the country. Women in the rural areas besides looking after the house hold help the farmers particularly at the time of sowing and harvesting crops when labor is greatly needed; rice planting, cotton picking, feeding and milking cattle, and many auxiliary jobs on lands are performed by the women folk. Then again most of the handicrafts and small industry; spinning, weaving, sewing, and carpet making, etc. is carried out by them except the hard jobs like ploughing the fields, by bullocks or by tractor, carrying the produce to the markets, etc. is done by the male members.

In the towns, where the cost of living is high and the women have got the basic education, to subsidize income of the family they work in offices, hospitals, business, advertising, teaching, etc. But the percentage of working women in the towns is still very small and they do not come out to work unless forced by the circumstances. Primarily, they like to shoulder the household responsibility only because some conservative families do not allow women to go out and work along with other men.

Figure 25: Women in rural Punjab

Purdah system
Segregation of sexes again is an influence of Hindu culture and an act of oppression against the weaker sex. In Islam Purdah is emphasized for

both men and women, as mentioned in Sura al Noor, Holy Quran. "Whereas women have been directed to cover their heads and shoulders men have also been forbidden at staring and to keep their eyes low". But this directive is only imposed on the female members to suppress and dominate them.

Role model for women are the pious ladies of Islam as also mentioned in the holy books; Sara wife of Abraham peace be upon her, Aacia the wife of the Pharaoh, "Firaun", Mary the mother of holy Christ peace be upon her, Khadija and Aisha wives of the holy prophet and his daughter Fatima Zehra. Allama Iqbal has emphasized to follow tradition of the daughter of the prophet Fatima also called 'Batool' and has advised the women folk to adopt her as a role model to shape their lives following her tradition. Paying homage to the great lady he said, "Aien-e-Haq Zanjer-e-Pa ast, Pas Farman-e- Janab-e- Mustafa ast. Warna gird-e- turbatash gardid mein. Sajdaha dar khak-e-ou pashidme." He is much overwhelmed by her character that he declares, "Had it not been forbidden by Almighty to prostrate before anyone else except Him as also endorsed by the holy prophet (PBUH), he would have continued taking rounds of her grave and performed prostration on the dust of her sacred grave." In these words, Allama has depicted how much he cared and respected ladies; the better halves, mothers, sisters, and above all daughters.

Dress and Food

Dress is an important manifestation of culture. Dress in a Muslim society are designed and intended to cover human body as nudity is prohibited in Islam and particularly women are supposed to cover their hair all the time and not to expose their makeup when they go out of their houses for work or to attend a mixed function. But over the years due to globalization, a radical change in the dress of both men and women has occurred. Jean culture has replaced 'kurta pajama'; shirt and pants without 'Dupatta' (a covering on head and shoulders) has become popular particularly among the younger generation in the cities.

People eat simple food; wheat is the staple food of the people, however, rice, maize, and millet also form part of the grain intake. Special rice dishes are served on the occasions of marriage ceremonies and other social functions. Halal / (Kosher) meat, poultry, eggs, and fish are commonly used and Pulses, vegetables, and fruits form an essential part of the diet of a common man.

However, like dress eating habits have also undergone a change with the passage of time; Halva Poori and Lassi Kulcha, Kulfi Falooda culture of Punjab for instance has been changed to 'Pai Nihari', fish Nan Kabab, Tikka and recently to hot dogs, burgers, fries, pizza, and coke culture.

'Thara Culture', a special feature of Punjabi culture that meant after day's job men folk dressed in neat embroided silk Kurta and Dhoti with a shawl on their shoulder discussed various topics from family affairs to local politics addressing each other 'Pahlwan', thereafter, helping themselves with a draft of cold or hot milk, kulfi falooda, sweets and carry some of it for their family who remained confined to their homes – but now the old 'Thara Culture' has been replaced by Food Street or Macdonald culture. That 'Pahlwan' is no more dressed in embroided shirt, lungi or shawl but in Bushirt, pants or jeans sits in a restaurant – food street, Kentucky Fried Chicken or McDonald's along with the entire family and instead of kulfi, falooda or lassi enjoy burgers, fried chicken, french fries, ice cream, and coke.

Burger – coke culture in the west has led to obesity on a large scale and an alarming percentage of men and women are found overweight mainly due to excessive use of fats and carbohydrates. These days, a tendency towards use of low carb and fat free foods, diet beverages or spring water is being preferred and according to some experts in a matter of few decades they would revert to low fat and plain water society altogether. It would follow suit in the East and would affect Pakistani-Indian culture as well.

Literature and Poetry

The poets and writers express human feelings in a captivating manner. As they are attached with every individual of the society, they present their desires and feelings in a beautiful way. Most of our poets reflect Islamic trend in their poetry. The Radio and Television also present the cultural aspect of our society. They broadcast cultural programs and dramas, which portray local, social, and cultural values in an effective style. Similarity of thought amongst our poets and writers of all regions is an important fact of our cultural life. Heer Warris Shah a legend in Punjabi poetry is full of mystical and philosophical views and his verses are used as quotations that match with the realities of life. Warris Shah is buried near Sheikhupura in Punjab and his poetry besides other occasions is particularly recited on his death anniversary by famous folk singers. Baba Bulleh Shah of Qasur, and Sultan Bahu, highly respected saints of Punjab are also famous for their philosophical and classical poetry. They are very popular with the people of Punjab. Hazrat Lal Shahbaz Qalandar was a famous Sufi poet of Sindh who is buried in Sehwan Sharif. He wrote many books in Persian and Arabic. Satchel Sarmast, and Shah Abdul Latif Bhithai are other great Sufi poets of Sindh who spread the light of Islam through their mystical compositions and attractive verses revealing the truth of life.

Handicrafts

Pakistani craftsmen are considered best in their craftsmanship. Their handicrafts are very popular all over the world. Province of Sindh is famous for high standard items of glasswork embroidery and silver industry. Multan and Bahawalpur in Punjab are famous for making beautiful things from camel's skin; whereas Chiniot also in Punjab is famous for making furniture from Shisham wood with beautiful engraved designs. Lahore and Karachi are famous for embroidery particularly of golden bridal dresses. Metal work and carving is done at Lahore. Gujranwala specializes in engineering works, and Sialkot in cutlery, surgical instruments, sports goods and leather wear.

Games-Sports

Sports and games form an important part of the national culture. Many games and sports are played in Pakistan that reflects its cultural identity. These games include: wrestling, Kabaddi, Cricket, Hockey, Soccer, Squash, Badminton, Tennis and athletics. Pakistan's Hockey team has been world champion for more than once, in cricket also Pakistan has a good ranking and has won the world cup (1992-93). Cricket is a very popular game particularly in Punjab and Sindh, so is hockey, national teams of both sports constitute players mainly from these provinces. Imran Khan, former captain of the winning team of world cup, now turned a social worker and a politician has been popular with the youngsters because of their love for the sport. Inzmam-ul-Haq, present skipper of the national cricket team has also attained fame after a successful tour of India (2005). The whole team was given a tasteful reception on their return by the government and the public at Islamabad. Other old and young players of repute include, Nazar Mohammad, Fazal Mahmood, Hafiz Kardar, Imtiaz Ahmad Waqar Hasan, Mahmood Hussain, Javed Mian Dad, Mohammad brothers (Hanif, Wazir, Mushtaq and Sadiq), Muhammad Yousuf, Shahid Afridi, Younas Khan and many more that have helped projecting the name of the country in the world. Similarly Jahangir Khan and Jan Sher Khan who won world champion ship several times in squash have earned fame because of that.

In the field of hockey the players that earned fame are: Naseer Bunda, Samiullah, Akhtar Rasool, Hasan Sardar, Sohail Abbas and many more. Tennis though not very much played in Pakistan but only this year Pakistan has qualified in this sport as well and achieved a world ranking. Ex-President Gen. Parvez Musharraf particularly took keen interest in the promotion of games and raising the standard of performance of the players by giving recognition and cash awards as an incentive to the players. This policy has started showing results.

Sports not only bring fame to the country but also help a great deal in inculcating discipline, tolerance, a healthy spirit of competition, to take defeat and victory gracefully. These rare qualities can best be developed by making sports an essential part of our curriculum at all levels. A sound mind in a sound body is a famous maxim, which is very true. Promotion and giving due place to sports in our daily programs will go a long way to reform and bring a healthy change in our society physically, mentally, and morally. For this purpose government and the private sector should provide playgrounds, sports facilities including sports gears at reasonable rates and hold tournaments to maintain interest and love for the sports. In return the country would get a healthy, disciplined and a responsible nation.

Monsoon Culture

Pakistan falls in the dry belt of sub-tropical lands and is very much influenced by the monsoon regimes the seasonal winds, which prevail there, both in summer and winter seasons, which exercise great influence on the life and culture of Pakistan.

Monsoon is not only a weather phenomenon but it is a culture – a way of living- predominant in the social, moral, economic, recreation, sports, and political activities. Seasonal festivals; Deevali, Dusehra, Basant, social and political functions; marriages election schedule are mostly regulated with monsoon timings rather than the calendar. Prevalence of warm weather, above freezing point, even in winters lengthens the growing season – to almost the whole year in the plain areas that keeps the lands and the farmers busy all the year round, agriculture, therefore, is the main occupation of the people and is manifest in their culture and way of living; houses, dresses, manners, habits, means of transportation, poetry, literature, religion, custom and traditions.

A good year of monsoon rains brings happiness and prosperity to the people and on the other hand when the monsoons fail entails misery, hunger and destitution. This uncertainty and unreliability of monsoon regime has made the people highly superstitious and happen to be very religious, they have blind faith in religious lords; Pundits and Pirs, who they consider godly – molders of their fate and turn to them for any problem. Instead of going to a doctor for the treatment of an ailment, or to a marriage bureau for finding a match for their daughter or to a lawyer for a legal problem they invariably go to these religion tycoons who fully exploit that weakness and thus have prosperous business. They are found everywhere as their cliental is also spread all over the country.

LANGUAGES

Language plays an important role in the development and progress of a nation in every field of its activity. Language is the media by which we express our ideas, emotions and feelings. It is a symbol and interpreter of human consciousness and intellect. Language is the only media of communication, which makes it convenient for us to accomplish our objectives of human needs and prosperity. Collective ideology and interests can best be under-stood and safe guarded by the help of common language. Besides the national language each region has a local dialect mostly corresponding to its geographical environs for instance in Pakistan languages spoken other than Urdu the national language include; Sindhi, Balochi, Pashto, Punjabi and Hindko. Primarily, they are the product of the times when there was little inter regional contact between people. But gradually as the means of communication developed and contacts increased common language like Urdu intelligible to the people of all the contiguous regions came into use.

Figure 26: Pakistan major ethnic groups

URDU Language

Urdu is the national language of Pakistan and thus carries immense importance for every Pakistani. It is nearly 300 years old, and was considered as the language of the Muslims from the very beginning. The Muslims of the sub-continent had played an active role in the development of Urdu as their culture left an indelible impact on every aspect of local cultures. The local languages in the sub-continent, therefore, could not escape a marked influence of the Muslim Culture.

The blending of Arabic, Persian and Turkish gave birth to a new language which was called Hindi, Hindustani, Shahjahani and finally as Urdu. Gradually the new language became the media of expression of the Muslims of the sub-continent. They adopted this language for the expression of their social, cultural and regional feelings and emotions. Urdu soon became a popular language after passing through different stages of development. It was spoken and understood in the different regions of the sub-continent. It did not stick to one particular region but moved with the Muslims who took it with them wherever they went.

The poets and writers have played a significant role in the development and progress of Urdu. Amir Khusro was one of the early poets who adopted Urdu for his poetry. Sir Syed Ahmad Khan rendered meritorious services to safeguard Urdu from Hindu and British domination. He wrote several articles and essays in Urdu in order to make it a popular language amongst the people. Maulana Shibli, Allama

Iqbal, Deputy Nazir Ahmed, Munshi Zaka Ullah, Maulana Hali, Ghalib and many others adopted this language, in their poetry and writings. Maulvi Abdul Haq, the Baba-e-Urdu dedicated his entire life for the development of Urdu.

Due to the efforts of poets and writers, during different periods of history, Urdu progressed well and reached almost all parts of the sub-continent in the 16th century. The Muslims, from time to time, brought about changes and amendments in it to make it more simple and easy to understand according to their needs and requirements.

After Independence, Urdu became the national language of the people and a symbol of unity between the different regions of Pakistan. It became the media of expression in all parts of the country. It has helped the Muslims of Pakistan in understanding their religion, culture and civilization to a great deal. Lectures on Islamic education and religion are delivered in Urdu throughout Pakistan. The religious leaders, mystics and Sufi poets spread the light of Islam in the sub-continent with the help of Urdu. The translations of 'Holy Quran' and 'Hadith' have been printed in the Urdu language in great numbers to enable the Muslims to understand them properly. In this way the Urdu language has played a pivotal role in keeping the Muslim nationhood intact.

Urdu language is the medium of instructions in most of the institution in Pakistan. Urdu literature, Political Science, History, Islamic Studies and other subjects are taught up to even Masters level in the Urdu language. Concrete steps have been taken to shift to Urdu language from English in the office routine on the national level. The offices have adopted Urdu language in their official work and the Government has published a dictionary containing Urdu terminology for the office work. The Government is making hectic efforts to impart advanced education in science and technology in Urdu language.

After the emergence of Pakistan, a great deal of work has been done for the progress of Urdu language. The Urdu language has crossed its evolutionary stages after Independence, and is now on its way to the road of progress and development. Each Pakistani feels proud of speaking, reading and writing Urdu. Most of our national leaders, while visiting other countries, deliver their speeches in Urdu language, which enhances its prestige on the international level. Several Committees have been formed for the development and enforcement of Urdu language as a media on the national level. Being the national language of the country, it is the binding force between different parts of Pakistan. Those who try to divide Pakistan on language or regional basis do not do any service to Pakistani nationalism.

PUNJABI

Punjabi is the local language of the province of the Punjab, which is the biggest province of Pakistan with regard to population and development. The Punjabi language, before partition, was spoken in Delhi, Dhirpur, Peshawar and Jammu. It was a popular language amongst the Sufi poets who used it for their traditional romantic folk poetry. The famous poetic tales of Punjab like Heer Ranjha, Mirza Sahiban, Sohni Manhiwal and Sasi Punnu were written in Punjabi. These immortal classics of literature contributed greatly towards the popularity of Punjabi language. The great Sufi poets like Waris Shah, Hazrat Sultan Bahu, Baba Bulleh Shah and Hazrat Ghulam Farid are the famous poets of Punjabi language. Their writings and poetry is the precious asset of Punjabi literature.

Punjabi is a very simple language and easy to understand. It was given various names during different periods of history. Famous historian Masoodi called it Multani, while Al-Beruni used the name of Al-Hindi for it. The famous Sikh religious leader Baba Guru Nanak gave it the name of Zaban-e-Jattan. In the NWFP it was known as Hindko.

Hafiz Barkhurdar was the first person to have used the name of Punjabi for this language in 1080. Maulvi Kamal-ud-Din also used this name for this language in his selected works. It is understood that Amir Khusro was the first poet to adopt Punjabi in his poetry. After him the Sufi poet Sheikh Farid-ud-Din also wrote his poetry in Punjabi language. During the reign of Mughal Emperor Akbar, the Sufi poet Shah Husain wrote his Sufi verses in Punjabi. Hazrat Sultan Bahu produced his excellent poetry in Punjabi language. Warris Shah's poetic version 'Heer' is another famous classic widely appreciated and recited.

Before partition Punjabi was spoken and understood mostly in eastern Punjab. After Independence, however, concrete steps were taken for the promotion and development of this language, which made it a popular language in other parts of the province as well.

Dr. Iqtidar Hussain Zaidi professor of Geography of Syracuse University USA contributed a research article on Punjabi culture, published in Annals a reputed magazine of the University. He based his study using the variable per capita daily consumption of milk and curd and on the basis of his study statistically determined Gujranwala-Lahore region as the heart of Punjabi culture. As per his study eating habits and the type of food mostly used forms an important determination factor of a culture. Various other studies also affirm and acknowledge Lahore as the heart of not only Punjabi but also that of the Pakistan culture. Punjab Government is making efforts for the progress of Punjabi language and extending support to those institutions, which are striving for its development. At present the Punjabi literature is taught up to M.A. level in Pakistan.

SINDHI

Sindhi is the language of the province of Sindh and is the second major regional language spoken in Pakistan. Sindhi is an ancient language. History reveals the stages of its evolution and development and tells how it has reached its present status. Chach Nama, being an authentic document proves that the dialect of Sindhi language was the same in the 12th century as it is today.

In the beginning Sindhi was written in 'Marwari' and 'Arz Nagari' way of writing. This way of writing was subsequently changed into Arabic with the advent of Arabs in the sub-continent whose culture and literature greatly influenced the Sindhi literature. It is because of this reason that we find many Arabic and Persian words in the Sindhi language.

The poets and writers have played commendable role in the progress and development of Sindhi language. They are Makhdoom Ahmed Bhatti, Makhdoom Noah Shah Karim, and Makhdoom Pir Muhammad who are regarded as the early poets of Sindhi language. The Sindhi writers made efforts to simplify the language by introducing beautiful phrases and idioms in this language. Most of the writers belonged to the Somroo period, "1050 to 1300", when the Sindhi literature reflected literary trends in its folk songs and conventional folk tales. The authentic period of Sindhi literature is said to fall between "1685 to 1783".

Shah Abdul Latif Bithai was a great Sufi poet of Sindhi language. His poetry gives an excellent description of the natural beauty of Sindh and fascinates the reader. The poetry of 'Sachal Sarmast' and 'Ramazan Qandhar' is deeply influenced by the environmental atmosphere and is considered a valuable contribution to the Sindhi literature.

By the year 712 the Arabs had a complete hold on the province of Sindh. During this period the Sindhi language enjoyed a reputation of a popular language and was widely spoken and understood in the whole of province. Poetry and prose could easily be produced in Sindhi language, which rapidly increased its utility. The advent of the Arabs in Sindh greatly influenced every aspect of social life in the province. They inter-married the local people, which influenced the local traditions and customs. Far-reaching changes occurred in the Sindhi society with the advent of Islam as a social order. These factors also left an impact on the Sindhi literature. Sindhi and Arabic languages crossed stages of development side by side and deeply influenced each other. However, the impact of Arabic on Sindhi was greater and indelible.

After Independence effective steps were taken for the progress and promotion of Sindhi language. Sindhi Literary Board was set up in 1948, which printed many books and magazines in Sindhi. Besides, several books have been published on Sindhi folk literature. Shah Abdul Latif Bithai, Shah Qadir Bux and Faqir Nabi Bux are the eminent personalities of Sindhi literature. Numerous compilations of these great writers have been published which have greatly enhanced the prestige of Sindhi literature. In 1954 'Bazm-e-Talib-ul-Muala' was set up which is rendering meritorious services to Sindhi literature. Similarly, Dr. Ali Akbar Drazi established 'Sarmast' academy, which has published several books in the memory of Sachal Sarmast.

PASHTO

Pushto is the language of the people of NWFP. It is an ancient language and is widely spoken and understood in the province of NWFP. Pushto is greatly influenced by other languages. Many of its words have been taken from Pali, Prakarat, Pehlvi, Persian, Arabic, Greek, German and French.

The history of Pushto literature is divided into three different periods. The first period begins with the second century and ends with the 10th century. The second period of Pushto literature begins with the Mughal annexation of India and goes up to the advent of the British while the third period lies from 1100 to 1300.

Bayazid Ansari was the most famous personality of the 1st period of Pushto literature who wrote on 'Sufism'. His famous and prominent work is known as 'Khair-ul-Bian' which was published in Pushto, Arabic and other Indian languages at one time. The first poet of this period is known as Amir Khan Pehlvan who used simple words in Pushto for his poetry. The other important poets of this period are Khawja Khan, Sheikh Suleman, Sheikh Razi, Bait Baba, Sheikh Saleh and Raghoon Khan.

The second period of Pushto literature begins with the year 1200 when the Mughals had started the invasion of India. This period extends to the British rule and is considered as the golden period of Pushto literature. Akhund Dardeeza is the famous writer of this period who wrote many books in Pushto. Khushal Khan Khattak is another great writer of this period who rendered great services for the development of Pushto literature. He produced some excellent books and one compilation. Rahman Baba is a popular figure of the second period of the Pushto literature. He was a Sufi poet whose poetry was widely admired by the masses.

The third period of Pushto literature falls between "1200 to 1300". The Pushto prose was at the pinnacle of glory during this period. Hazrat Mian Omar was a great scholar of this period who was a contemporary of Ahmed Shah Abdali, a great spiritual leader. Mullah Abdul Rashid, Saadat Ali Khan, Qasim Ali Afridi, Nawab Rehmat Ali Khan and Amir Muhammad Ansari are regarded as other famous literary personalities of this period. The poetry of this period reflects emotional sentiments and is full of nationalism. The poets and writers played significant role in the freedom struggle. Some of them are Muhammad Akram Khan, Fazal Muhammad Mufti, Abdul Kabar Khan Kabar, Fazal Rahim Saqi, Muhammad Aslam Khan Shirare, Abdul Hakim, Ahmed Shah Barister, Abdul Ghani Khan Ghani and Amir Nawaz Jaila.

Pushto literature received great boost after Independence. The services rendered by the Pushto poets and writers in the freedom struggle, in fact contributed a great deal towards the promotion of Pushto literature. Sahibzada Abdul Qayyum worked very hard to create political awareness in the people of NWFP, The Islamia College, Peshawar which became the citadel of freedom movement, in NWFP, was established because of his dedicated services. Peshawar University was established after three years of Independence. An academy for the promotion of Pushto literature was set up under the supervision of the Government. The Pushto academy was set up in 1954 and Maulana Abdul Qadir (Alig) was appointed as its Director. This academy prepared Pushto dictionary.

BALOCHI

Area-wise, Balochistan is the biggest province of Pakistan. The language spoken in this vast area is known as Balochi. This language contains many words of Persian. Other languages like Pushto and Brohi are also spoken in the province. The Balochi language, spoken in Balochistan at present, is of two kinds i.e., 'Sulemanki' and 'Mekrani'. The second language of Balochistan is known as 'Brohi', which is said to be the language of Drawars. Another language spoken in Balochistan is known as 'Khait Rani'.

The Balochi literature could not progress very much because the Balochi people were basically the nomads who wandered from one place to another. Moreover, Balochistan is a mountainous region, which greatly lacks in facilities essential for the promotion and progress of social life. These difficulties of life and the unsettled character of the Balochi people have in fact hindered the development of Balochi literature. Balochi prose, like Balochi poetry is very rare. However, in spite of these inadequacies, the Balochi poetry has rendered invaluable services for the progress of Balochi literature.

The history of Balochi literature can be divided into four periods. The early medieval period begins with the year 1430, and ending with the year 1600. The later medieval period of the Balochi literature began after the year 1600 and ended with the year 1850. Modern and contemporary periods of the Balochi literature can be divided into two different periods extending from 1850 to 1930. The first time the Balochi literature came to light was in 1830 when a British traveler W. Leech, after conducting his research in Balochistan, wrote his report in the 'Journal of Asiatic society' and revealed the presence of Balochi literature.

Since the Balochi literature could not progress very much there are no names worth mentioning belonging to the Balochi literature. The Balochi prose, mostly contains the tales of bravery and romantic stories of the tribal chiefs. The literary work in Balochi is very rare. The Balochi poetry, too, could not attain a high level of literary worth. Jam Darag is known to be the only famous poet of Balochi who wrote a few romantic verses.

The Balochi literature was on the verge of decline before partition. After partition, however, it received little boost when Radio Pakistan, Karachi began its broadcast in Balochi language. Balochi programs were relayed from Radio Pakistan Karachi, which enhanced the developmental process of Balochi language. The Balochi literary

Association was set up which published many magazines and articles in Balochi language: A weekly magazine known as 'Nan Kessan' was published and a monthly known as 'Classics' was also published.

With the establishment of Quetta Television Station the Balochi language has received great fillip. Atta Shah is a famous Balochi poet of Pakistan. Ishaq Shamim is another famous poet of Balochi language whose poem 'Dulhan' is very popular. The renowned politician Gul Khan Naseer is also considered a good poet of Balochi language. Balochi prose has also developed a great deal after partition. Translation of the Bible has also been published in Balochi language.

CHAPTER XXI
EDUCATION IN PAKISTAN

Education is of immense importance for everyone, man or woman. Without education one is like a horse without reigns. Knowledge is light and ignorance is darkness. A knowledgeable person enlightens its surroundings. Ali (K.W.) while comparing knowledge and wealth has said; knowledge is the wealth that increases by spending, knowledge protects its owner whereas the owner of wealth has to look after it, knowledge generates friends and wealth harbors enemies, wealth leaves its owner after death but knowledge accompanies its owner.

When a child is born he/she has no knowledge of things and objects around and slowly starts recognizing the mother, father and other members of the family. First of all the child learns the words mama and papa and gradually his/her vocabulary increases, start recognizing and naming other objects. In this way knowledge of his/her surroundings keeps on advancing day by day. Mother's lap is the first school of learning and a child learns and forms basic values from home; a child is a true reflection of one's parents. Education of women is, therefore, very important. It is well said: "if you teach a man you teach an individual but if you teach a woman you teach a family". German rulers had stressed a lot on women education and said, "Give us good mothers and we will give you good nation."

The holy prophet Muhammad (peace is upon him) has also stressed and made compulsory the education of both male and females and said, "learn and seek knowledge from cradle to grave; go to China – a far fledged country – in pursuit of knowledge." The ability of a person is judged by ones knowledge and not on the basis of riches and inheritance. God Almighty when created Adam (peace be upon him) first taught him and the angels, names of certain objects and then tested both; angels failed to associate the names with the objects when they were presented before them but Adam (peace be upon him) could do that. So it was by dint of Adam's superiority of knowledge that the angels were ordered to bow before him and he was appointed as His viceroy (caliph) on earth.

The holy prophet (peace is upon him) declared that he is a teacher and the Almighty in Sura Jumma introduced him with the words, "He has sent the apostle from amongst you who purifies you and teaches you wisdom and things of which you had no knowledge before." It was custom of the holy prophet that after prayers he addressed the people and Sahaba kiram in the mosque and whenever a new revelation from God would come call them to assemble and would explain the significance and text of the message to educate the people. The highest exalted position of our prophet Muhammad (PUBH)) is because of his knowledge and quality of extreme patience that he exercised throughout. The holy prophet talking about himself said. " I am the city of knowledge and Ali is the entrance." That is why the Caliphs of the prophet always referred problems concerning interpretation of the holy Quran to Ali (K.W.). Caliph Omar (R.A) was particularly a great admirer of Ali (K.W.) and there existed understanding between the two reverend companions of the holy prophet. Omar (R.A.) always consulted Ali (K.W) in administrative and other matters.

Once a case for decision came before Caliph Omar (R.A) that perplexed him; two women had a dispute over the ownership of a male child; each claimed to have given birth to the male child. Ali (K.W) was called to decide the matter. Ali (K.W) asked the contestant mothers to pour their milk in two separate pots of equal volume and then ordered to weigh the pots containing the milk. The balance showed difference in weights of the pots containing the milk of the women. He interpreted that the pot that weighed less belonged to the woman who had given birth to the girl and the heavier one to the boy. Then the women were asked to come out with the truth the one who had a false claim admitted that she had lied because her husband had threatened to divorce her in case she gave birth to a girl that time. Caliph Omar (R.A) for his satisfaction enquired Ali (K.W.) about its source from the holy Quran. At this Ali (K.W) referred the verse of the holy Quran regarding law of inheritance (Sura Nisa), where it is stated that male receives double the share out of inheritance as against female and in the light of this divine distribution the density of milk of the mother of a male child should also be greater as compared to the mother of the female child; that was why the weights differed.

 Once Ali was going to lead evening prayers someone put him a question to test his knowledge, which he thought would be so lengthy that would delay his evening prayers but Ali (K.W.) promptly replied without taking a pause and proceeded towards the mosque. The question put to him was to tell the names of all species of animals that lay eggs and the one who give birth to their off springs. Ali (K.W.) concisely replied that the one who have their ears in side lay eggs and those having ears outside give birth to the young ones, which is a biological truth that could not be refuted till date. Ali (K.W.) is also the founder of algebra, which forms an essential basic course in Mathematics.

From the foregoing discussion importance of education and its need for the promotion of a healthy society cannot be overemphasized. Those who strive and work hard to seek knowledge, teach, manage, subscribe and help in the extension of knowledge do so in obedience to His command and the tradition of the Prophets and would be rewarded for their efforts in this world and the world hereafter.

Literary meaning of education is to bring a healthy change in one's behavior, to overcoming wild, outrageous instinctive tendencies a second nature of man. It was because of these characteristics of man related to them that angels had opposed the creation of such a species who in their opinion would create trouble and cause bloodshed and as for them, they were always there who bowed before Him day and night. Almighty disagreed with them saying He knows better. He was confident that such a creation if educated and harnessed would prove to be a better one than all other creations; angels, Jins, plants, animals etc. Therefore, to prove His point of view, He accepted the challenge; created man and undertook to educate this dangerous yet wonderful of His creations. It was on the creation of humans that Allah felt proud and called Himself as the best of the creators (Ahsan-ul- Khalqins).

In the light of the emphasis laid on education it is not only the duty of the state but everyone to participate in this noble cause. The progress of nations and their strength primarily rests on the level of achievement and superior technology. Muslims entered and established their rule in the sub-continent on the basis of their superior technology. They lost control of territories and their superiority when they stopped paying attention to research and advancement of education. The system of education adopted and contributed by Muslim scholars of repute like Ibn-e-Khaldun was based on three axes: Compulsory, Free and Technical Education. During Muslim rule in India education was compulsory; everyone was obliged to send one's child to school, the education was not only free but the students were given food and provided money to buy other necessities. Besides learning languages, religion, maths, etc. were also required to attain proficiency in at least one trade, like carpentry, masonry, black smith, gold smith, painting etc. to be able to earn their living after completion of their studies. Teachers were given great respect and even the king would rise as a mark of respect before them. The whole expenditure on education, stipends etc. was dispersed through teachers. The system worked very well and proved fool proof; it not only helped producing highly knowledgeable persons but great technicians in the field of industry, masonry, paintings, wood and metal carving and also made progress in the production of warring techniques and equipment. A fine cotton cloth called "malmal" in local dialect used to be so fine that the whole length of 40 yards could pass through a ring. The quality of masonry is eminent from the buildings erected by the Muslims without any support and the quality of adhesives used to join big blocks of stones is a mystery. Quality of paintings and engravings that exist almost in the same magnanimity today speak themselves of the proficiency of their creators. Development of gunpowder and use of heavy guns was also the result of research in the field of warfare.

British who took over from Muslims tried to damage the existing Muslim set up in all the fields to establish their hegemony; first of all they spoiled the system of education, reduced the authority and respect of the teachers, highly qualified teachers of Persian, Arabic and other faculties who did not learn English language were degraded, considered inferior to the teachers of English language. Education no more remained compulsory and neither technical education imparted on those lines. In the field of industry to popularize their own cloth and textiles, discouraged those technicians, who wowed fine fabrics. Instead of aiming education on the lines prescribed by Muslim educationist for the development of a balanced personality to be able to earn his living independently, introduced a system to produce 'Baboos' clerks to help them in administration. For Hindus it was a change of masters, readily adapted to the system but it were mostly Muslims who suffered and as such literacy rate amongst Muslims sharply declined.

After independence, like other areas, Pakistan followed the same set up designed by the British in the field of education, at the most introducing the teaching of Islamic studies or Pakistan Studies. A number of times Curriculum development conferences were held, recommendations after great deliberations of scholars submitted but the same could not be implemented due to political instability, frequent change of, or due to lack of funds. There is a need of bringing radical changes in the scheme of studies. Present government is not only trying to raise rate of literacy in the country but also stressing on technical education to solve the problem of unemployment in the country on the one hand and raising exchequer by increasing manufacturing and their export. These measures would also solve the problems created because of large number of unemployed youth in the country would bring healthy change in our political system – attitude of the electoral and the electorate.

WOMEN EDUCATION

Before British occupation of sub-continent, women studied at home learnt religion, holy Quran and concentrated on household to manage the home. They also learnt embroidery, tailoring, making baskets, pottery, paintings and such pursuits that could be done at home that were why their contribution in cottage industries of the country is not less than men.

There was no concept of co-education or girl schools or universities, which started during British occupation, who established separate schools and colleges for girls and co-education at higher levels. After independence, Pakistan has maintained the British policy and encouraged women education. Girl schools in urban and rural areas have been established and the number of educated women has greatly increased. Besides medicine, women have taken up engineering, computers, accounting, business administration, aeronautics, and are pilots in civil aviation and air force. Women have also been taking active part in politics and the contribution of women in the freedom movement has also been praiseworthy. The present government has allocated special seats besides general seats in the National and Provincial assemblies to encourage women participation in politics.

AIMS AND OBJECTS OF EDUCATION IN PAKISTAN

Pakistan is an under-developed country of the Third World. It is an Islamic and democratic state. Pakistan is fully aware of the importance of education and due attention has been given to the educational sector in the 7th Five Year Plan. It is imperative that the students in Pakistan should be imparted education in view of the Islamic ideals in order to enable them to fully understand their social and political commitments. It is also essential to train the young generation of Pakistan in a way as to inculcate national spirit in them so that they should always keep national interests above personal motives.

Moreover, the technical and professional education should be emphasized in order to prepare the youth to take on the national responsibilities. The educational system in Pakistan should, therefore, be built up on the foundations so as to reflect national aspirations and goals. Following are some of the objects of our educational system.

Safeguard of Ideology of Pakistan

The main object of the educational system of Pakistan is the preservation and protection of Pakistan Ideology, which was the basis of Pakistan Movement. The educational system of Pakistan should he based on the Islamic ideals which was the primary purpose of the freedom struggle.

National Unity

Our educational system should strive to develop national unity by creating social and cultural harmony. It should be accomplished in view of the Islamic ideology.

Character Building

Character building of the individual should be the prime objective of educational structure in Pakistan. This very purpose should be achieved in a way to infuse courage in the youth to enable them to face truth.

Eradication of Ignorance

As education is meant for the elimination of illiteracy, Pakistan's educational set up should attain this target by launching a comprehensive program of primary, secondary and adult education as quickly as possible.

Promotion of Technical and Professional Education

In the modern age technical and professional education has acquired greater importance due to the advancement of modern technology. The educational structure in Pakistan should be devised on the pattern, which can ensure the promotion of scientific, technical and professional education. The students should be offered different disciplines to make a choice of their own.

Welfare of the Teaching Community

Teacher is the pillar of every educational set up. It is the teacher, who by his dedicated efforts, helps in building up a stable educational edifice. The teacher, by edifying the student community, gives to the nation the future leaders, administrators, soldiers, engineers, businessmen and many others who are in a position to take on the national responsibilities in a befitting fashion. The educational system should, therefore, be established in a way as to ensure maximum welfare, dignity and security of the teaching community.

STAGES OF EDUCATION IN PAKISTAN

FORMAL EDUCATION
Primary Education
Primary education is the bases of the educational structure and, therefore, carries immense importance. Due to the extreme utility of the primary education the Government has given priority to this form of education in Pakistan. Primary schools have been set-up in large number to meet the requirements of imparting education at this level. The government has taken over the control of all the primary institutions in the country.

The basic purpose of primary education is to give elementary knowledge to the students to enable them to read or write something. It is also meant to impart basic information about the daily household accounts; the government considers the primary education as the basic necessity and, therefore, intends to enforce compulsory primary education all over the country. Primary education is free in the country and the parents who do not send their children to schools could be punished.

The government plans to open new primary institutions in the country during 1993-98. It intends to open 20,687 primary schools while 2,780 primary schools will be upgraded to middle, and 1,881 from middle to high School level. With the assistance of World Bank, 6,000 additional classrooms have been constructed in 19 districts of Balochistan, N.W.F.P, and Sindh. In the next stage 15,000 classrooms will be provided in the Punjab. One primary school, each for boys and girls, with five teachers each, has been provided in each Union Council of the country to serve as a model institution. Ex-Prime Minister, Nawaz Sharif announced the National Education Policy on 21st February, 1998. He gave this policy for the next 12 years (1998-2010). The National Education policy laid greater stress on the Primary Education. In this direction 40,000 new formal primary schools and 20,000 mosque schools will be set up.

The National Education policy, as announced by Nawaz Sharif, was meant to enhance the existing participation rate of 31 per cent at secondary level to 48 per cent by the year 2010. The policy provided to establish 15,000 middle schools and 7,000 secondary schools during the next five years.

Secondary Education

The secondary education occupies supreme position in the national educational set up as the skilled manpower is trained and prepared at this level. The importance of the secondary education is due to the fact that it prepares the students to take on the higher and university education. In view of the overriding utility of the secondary education such syllabi have been included at this stage, which could develop the sentiments of patriotism and hard work amongst the students. Syllabi have been segregated into several departments, which was the essential requirement of the time. Emphasis has been laid on the scientific and technological education at this stage. A number of professional subjects have been included in the syllabi for ninth and tenth classes. Syllabi for all the subjects have been revised and efforts have been made to include material, which would promote national integration. Adequate arrangements have been made for religious and physical education. Science and mathematics have been made compulsory subjects. Students have been allowed to make a choice of elective subjects from technical, home economics, and agricultural and industrial subjects.

Intermediate education has been separated from the university education. The courses for intermediate education are covered during two years. The intermediate examinations are conducted by the Secondary Boards according to the syllabi prescribed by the Boards of Intermediate and Secondary Education.

Special Education

The government has special responsibility for giving education to the handicapped children. Separate institutions for the handicapped children have been set up in Pakistan. The Federal Government has allocated the sum of Rs. 1.33 billion for setting up educational centers for the disabled children in four categories-hearing impaired, mentally retarded, visually impaired, and physically handicapped at divisional and district level in the four provinces of the country. Special training to the teachers has been imparted to give education to handicapped children at these centers. A 'talking book center' is also being established at Islamabad to provide textbooks for blind children. The National Education Policy provides to set up 7,000 secondary schools during 1998-2003. One model secondary school would be set up at district level for qualitative improvement of Education.

Higher Education

After the secondary stage, it is the higher education Commission formerly University Grant Commission established in 2002 September is the primary regulator of higher education in Pakistan which includes Engineering, Medical, Law, Bachelor's and Master's Education – All the institutions imparting higher education were run by the government but the private sector has now excelled in this field and scores of private institutes have emerged in the recent years. Not only that a number of Government run colleges; Government college Lahore and Lahore college for women have been raised to universities, Foreman Christian college has been privatized, the two years degree courses has been enhanced to four years while further two years are required for a Master's degree. Different courses are offered for technical and medical education.

Higher education is given under the supervision of the university. There are 120 universities/degree awarding institutes at present in the country, which include agricultural and engineering universities. Medical universities have also been set up which are; Agha Khan Medical University, Karachi and Lahore University of Medical Sciences. Islamia University, Bahawalpur is giving Islamic education.

New universities have been opened to give education in different fields of higher education. University Grants Commission has been set up to co-ordinate the work of universities. University Grants Commission is also responsible for maintaining a link between the government and the universities.

The government has taken a number of steps to enhance the standard of education at the university level. The university teachers are given training in Pakistan and abroad under different Schemes. The courses and syllabus are regularly reviewed and revised in order to introduce the latest developments and advancement in different disciplines. Research programs have been launched in order to promote research and training between selected universities of Pakistan and foreign universities. The Vice-Chancellors Committee, comprising six Vice-Chancellors, has been set up to gauge the academic and administrative environments in the campuses. The libraries and laboratories have been equipped with the latest books and scientific equipment.

The foundation stone of the University of Islamic Studies was laid in Karachi on 16th April, 1987. This University has been completed in 1990. It is assisting in the promotion of Islamic teaching and research work in Islamic Studies. In the later stages similar universities will be established at Islamabad, Lahore and Quetta. The Al-Azhar University of Egypt has agreed to extend assistance and guidance in conducting the classes at this university.

PROFESSIONAL EDUCATION

Medical Education

Medical education is essential for keeping of good health. For this purpose the government of Pakistan has stressed the acquisition of Medical education. The Pakistan Medical and Dental Council, in its revised curriculum for M.B.B.S. courses, has emphasized on medical ethics and human behavior. The medical students will be offered intensive research work during the final years of under-graduate medical education. Emphasis has also been laid on the hospital administration in order to acquaint the students with the working and management of the hospitals.

Special courses in surgery and other fields are being conducted in the King Edward Medical College, Lahore. These courses and programs are meant to impart training in advanced fields to the doctors desirous of doing F. R. C. S., M. R. C. P. and other higher courses of Medical education in a wider scale.

There are a number of excellent Medical institutions in the country which are giving Medical education to thousands of students in Pakistan. These institutions are also providing educational facilities in the medical profession to many students from other countries. Some of the most important Medical institutions are Jinnah Post-Graduate Medical Center. Karachi, Sindh Medical College, Hyderabad, General Services Hospital, Islamabad, King Edward Medical College, Lahore, Mama Iqbal Medical

College, Lahore, Fatima Jinnah Medical College, Lahore, Nishtar Medical College, Multan, Army Medical College, Rawalpindi, Bolan Medical College, Quetta, Ayub Medical College, Abbottabad and Khyber Medical College, Peshawar. Besides these institutions, there are several other Medical institutions operating in the country.

Technical Education

In the beginning the technical education was merely a diploma education at the Polytechnic Institutions, but none of the polytechnic institutions have been raised to the status of technical colleges and degree courses have been introduced in these colleges. Technical subjects such as Electronics-Technology; Plastic and Rubber Technology have been included in the syllabi. The government is making efforts to give technical education to the maximum number of people in view of the scientific and technological advancement of the modern age. The National Education Policy envisages enhancing enrollment in poly-techniques from 42,000 at present to 62,000 by the year 2002. Besides, Technical Institutions in the private sector are also being encouraged, which impart training in various trades to share the burden of the government in this field.

The Punjab government has taken a lead by providing greater opportunities of the technical education to the students. Training centers and vocational institutes have been set up at the Tehsil headquarters in the Punjab from the academic year beginning from September, 1987. By 1988 nearly 24 vocational centers began functioning in the province. Each vocational center will give admission to 50 girls. Each commercial training institute has a capacity to accommodate 100 students. The new centers will provide job opportunities to 150 teachers.

There are a number of Engineering Universities functioning in the country. The most famous of these universities are University of Engineering and Technology, Lahore, University of Engineering, Peshawar and University of Engineering, Karachi. All subjects relating to the engineering and Technology are taught at these Universities.

Legal Education

The legal education has received tremendous impetus with the advancement in other fields of education. Today, the legal education is considered essential and vital for social uplift and peace as other branches of human activities. In view of the overwhelming importance of the legal education the government of Pakistan has given due attention towards the promotion of Legal education. There are several institutions in the country, which are giving legal education to the students. The government has encouraged the private sector for playing a positive role in the spread of legal education.

Legal education in Pakistan is conducted under the supervision of the universities, which prescribed the syllabi. The Bachelor's degree in Law is a two years program. LLM classes have also been started in some of the institutions in the country. All the Law colleges are affiliated with their respective universities. Some of the famous institutions imparting legal education are Law College, Lahore, Anjuman-e-Himayat-e-Islam Law College, Lahore and Urdu Law College, Karachi. A new Law College in the private sector is being established at Karachi. The college will give legal education in accordance with the principles of Islam. The college will he named after the name of great' ulema and a close ally of the Quaid-i-Azam, Allama Shabbir Ahmad Usmani. Since the curricula of this college will be framed in the light of Islamic Ideology, it would greatly help in accelerating the Islamization process in the judiciary. The College will be affiliated with the University of Karachi. A number of law colleges have been opened in the private sector in the major cities of Pakistan.

INFORMAL EDUCATION

Adult Education

The state owes its responsibility to educate every individual. It is, therefore, imperative that every person of society must receive education. The scheme of adult education is aimed at achieving the target of educating every citizen.

Pakistan is a country where literacy rate is very low. The percentage of illiterate persons is very high in Pakistan. However, the government is trying to extend the educational facilities to every member of society. To accomplish this objective a scheme of adult education has been launched in the country. Centers have been set up in the country where education is given to the adults who could not enter school at proper age due to some unavoidable reasons. The scheme of 'Nai Roshni Schools' launched by the government of ex-Prince Minister Muhammad Khan Junejo, was in fact aimed at educating the adults of society who missed the entry in schools due to their pressing reasons. Arrangements of an integrated program of adult education have been made at the Allama Iqbal Open University, Islamabad. This university caters for education through correspondence courses, radio and television program and tutorial service in the country.

Madrassah Education

In order to increase literacy rate in Pakistan Madrassah education scheme was encouraged. The scheme was initiated at primary level. According to that one mosque school was to be set up for 300 residents, which would be a part of general scheme of education and observe same curriculum as other schools. Under this program the government had to spend Rs 1,468 million on primary education during 1986-87. The target for the year was 5683 schools.

The scheme was meant to use the mosque as Maktab in the villages, which had no schools with the following objectives:

1. Impart religious and basic education to the young boys and girls of the villages.
2. Build character of the children according to the Islamic teachings.
3. Make use of the mosques as community centers for the social moral and economic uplift of the villages.
4. Attach Libraries and small dispensaries with the mosque schools.

The Maktab scheme helped achieving the goals to some extent. Madrassah Education existed in Pakistan, a legacy of ancient times, and there were 189 such institutions in 1947. The number increased rapidly and by 2002 according to National Education census, their number was between 10,000 to 13,000, registerd and un-registered, and in 2008 it had increased to over 40,000 serving about 1.9 million students boys and girls.

There exist at present five Boards belonging to different school of thought about 80% sunni and 20% shia respectively they are:

i) Tanzim-ul-Madaris (Brelvi)

ii) Wafaq-ul-Madaris Deobandi
iii) Wafaq-ul-Madaris (Ahl-e-Hadith)
v) Wafaq-ul-madaris (shia)
v) Rabita-ul-Madaris jamaat-e-Islami.

Unfortunately due to policies of General Zia-ul-Haq extremism erupted and these religious institutions were blamed for that. General Parvez Musharraf was, therefore, asked particularly to control these schools, which were teaching radicalism and to stream line their educational system. Huge funds were allocated for the purpose. The owners of the institutions refused to accept any grant to avoid interference from the government. They have, however, reconciled to follow prevalent curriculum in other schools; teaching of English, Maths, Science and Pakistan Studies. But not agreeing to their students appearing in Government Secondary Boards examinations. The Islamic Boards want to keep it an internal affair but the government argues that if they are going to accept the grades and degrees awarded by them, they have a right to check their performance, one can't be a judge of one's own doing.

Otherwise the government has recognized the above stated five Boards in spite of criticism from the opposition to establish sectarianism in the country for which the nation has already paid a heavy cost in the form of valuable lives lost and earning a reputation of an extremist society in the world. Islam teaches tolerance and unity, we are all Muslims and not Shias, Sunnis, Deobandis or Ahl-e-Hadith. Difference of opinion is a sign of a progressive society, interpretation of law by different scholars should be discussed in a civilized way, dialogue rather than resorting to violence and labeling others as Kafirs.

CHAPTER XXII
PAKISTAN IN THE COMITY OF NATIONS

SOUTH ASIAN ASSOCIATION for REGIONAL COOPERATION (SAARC)

Asian nations: Bangladesh, Nepal, India, Bhutan, Pakistan, Sri Lanka, Maldives agreed to the proposal of President Zia-ur-Rehman to organize South Asian Association for Regional Cooperation (SAARC) in the region.

ZIA-ur-Rehman defining its activities had said that the scope of the Organization would be limited to economic, technical and cultural co-operation with major objective being promotion of welfare of the people of South Asia and to improve the quality of their life. The Organization has been established on the lines of EU, which is also engaged in creating harmony and understanding between member states and helping out the needy and underdeveloped nations.

SAARC has been instrumental in resolving issues between member countries. It was though the good offices of SAARC that Pakistan India acceded to discuss outstanding disputes between the two countries including the core issue of Kashmir, which India has been avoiding on one pretext or the other. Like EU membership of SAARC may as well be extended to widen its scope and usefulness in Asia.

Pakistan is an active member of SAARC and generously contributes for its requirements. Pakistan has recently voluntarily doubled its share in South Asian food program and is the second largest contributor towards all SAARC related activities and budget of its secretariat. The highest decision making authority of the Organization are the heads of state. They meet once a year or more often as and when required. Next meeting of the organization was scheduled in January 2005, but it was postponed on the behest of India for reasons best known to her that has raised some concern amongst the members for this unprecedented step of India without taking the members in confidence. However, with the efforts of the members the meeting could be held at Islamabad in April 2005.

ORGANIZATION OF THE ISLAMIC CONFERENCE (OIC)

OIC in fact is the realization of the dreams of the Islamic world for unity and sharing problems faced by the Muslim Umma at the hands of Zionists.

The First Summit meeting of the Heads of the Islamic states was held at Rabat, the capitol of Morocco, on 22nd September, 1969. Shah Hassan presided over the meeting. The meeting was of great significance, as it made clear to the non-Muslims that the Islamic world had been united to face any challenge from them. The main purpose of the organization was to protect the rights and interests of the Muslims all over the world. The participants unanimously accepted the proposal, thus OIC was established with its secretariat at Jeddah.

Second Summit Conference; the second Summit Conference of the OIC was held at Lahore (Pakistan) from 22nd to 24th February, 1974. It was mainly due to the dynamic personality of the then Prime Minister of Pakistan Zulfiqar Ali Bhutto that it was a great success. Almost all heads of Islamic states attended. It was a great honor for Pakistan to play host to such a large number of heads of states of the Muslim world. It was first and the last occasion when the heads of the Islamic countries had assembled in Pakistan in such a large number. Pakistan had sent a special plane to fetch Sheikh Mujeeb-ur-Rehman and persuaded him to attend which he had graciously consented and thus rapprochement between Bangladesh and Pakistan could be possible.

The summit meeting at Lahore did not have the consent of US and that was why Shah of Iran did not attend. The success of the conference and the decisions taken directly clashed with the interests of the world powers. They never wanted the emergence of another rival in the shape of a Muslim bloc. Z.A. Bhutto, King Shah Faisel and Col Qaddafi who were found mostly active and enthusiastic were targeted; King Faisel and Z.A. Bhutto both got eliminated, former by his nephew and the latter by his confided Chief of Army Staff. Apparently neither of them had any grievance against their victim that goes to prove that they were hired for the job. Then a number of murderous attacks were made on the life of Col. Qaddafi, which he escaped but were sufficient to warn him to refrain from pursuing the agenda of OIC.

Although a number of OIC Conferences have been held but the spirit and enthusiasm shown in the Lahore summit has been lacking and the

Organization is no more effective. Israel has become stronger and kills Palestinians like ants at her will and the OIC and its members are helpless spectators. In the same way India is busy in the genocide of Muslims in Kashmir and Gujarat but Muslim world is not in a position even to protest against that. There was time when a few women and children in the Indian Ocean near Dabel were ill treated, and captured by sea pirates. One Muslim ruler Hajjaj on the denial of the Raja had sent his soldiers to set them free and gave a befitting thrashing to the defaulters. But out of scores of Muslim States there is not one Hajjaj to reply to the in human treatment of the tyrants. Present regime is making efforts to revive the old spirit and enthusiasm in the organization that remained inactive for quite some time. Gen. Parvez Musharraf has already held meetings with the heads of Islamic States to emphasize need of reviving the Organization in view of the challenges faced by the Muslim world.

ECONOMIC COOPERATION ORGANIZATION (ECO)

It is the new name of RCD formed in 1964 at Istanbul between Turkey, Iran and Pakistan. A number of projects for the regional development were initiated but could not be completed because of political changes and due to Iran Iraq war.

In the year 1990, the original members of RCD met in Islamabad to reactivate the treaty of Izmir, which became the charter of the economic cooperation. The RCD was reborn and converted formally into ECO. The political and economic pattern in the three former RCD countries has been completely changed. The ECO nations were in many ways different from the ones that had come together at Istanbul more than 30 years ago in 1964. The three member states have earnestly desired to make ECO a viable economic forum for the uplift and prosperity of the people of their respective countries.

Organizational Structure

The organizational structure consists of the Council of Ministers, Council of Deputies, Technical Committees, ECO Secretariat and specialized agencies. The Secretariat has started working to identify the potential areas for common endeavors to be launched. A number of studies to explore the potentialities of the ECO and the relevant areas for the economic cooperation have already been initiated. The ECO Secretariat is taking all possible steps to ensure that necessary data on economic cooperation and projects is available in the member states.

Membership was extended to Central Asian Republics who also joined after the fall of Soviet Union in 1991, and many of its Republics overnight emerged as independent states that included Baku, Ashkabad, Tashkent, Dushanbe, Azerbaijan, Turkmanistan, Uzbekistan, Kirghizstan and Kazakhstan.

These independent republics formed Commonwealth of Independent States, CIS to chalk out the course of their future destiny. The CIS wanted to join ECO being an Organization of Muslim states. An extraordinary session of the foreign Ministers was held in November 1992 at Islamabad to consider expansion of ECO and to develop a broader economic and trade region in Asia. Delegates from the independent Republics were also invited to attend. The new states were welcomed by the participants of the Conference and formally inducted in the ECO fold as full members. With the addition of the new members the membership of ECO has jumped to nine. With a population of 300 million located in the heart of Euro-Asian land mass with an area of over 600 million sq. miles equaling the area of USA is bound to play an important role in the global political order in the 21st century.

Besides efforts at government level business community in Pakistan is exploring opportunities available in the area. Delegations from Federation of the Pakistan Chambers of commerce and industry and from businessmen visited Central Asian states in October 1992. A team of Bankers led by governor State Bank of Pakistan also visited Uzbekistan and set up a branch of National Bank of Pakistan at Tashkent.

Quaid-e-Azam high lighting principles of foreign policy of Pakistan emphasized that our foreign policy is based on the principle of friendship and brotherhood on equality basis with all the countries of the world. Pakistan does not cherish hostile attitude towards any nation and strongly believes in honesty and peaceful co-existence in international relations. It is a clear indication of a non-aligned policy of Pakistan.

With the approval and finalizing of the Charter of the ECO, its organizational structure is now in place. The organizational structure consists of the Council of Ministers, Council of Deputies, Technical Committees, ECO Secretariat and specialized agencies. The Secretariat has started working to identify the potential areas for common endeavors to be launched. A number of studies to explore the potentialities of the ECO and the relevant areas for the economic Cooperation have already been initiated. The ECO Secretariat is taking all possible steps to ensure that the necessary data on economic cooperation and projects is available in the member states.

CENTRAL ASIAN REPUBLICS INDUCTED IN THE ECO FOLD

In 1991, the Soviet Union fell apart and many of its Republics emerged as independent states on the world map. Almost overnight Baku, Ashkabad, Tashkent, Dushanbe, Furenze (Bishkek) and Alma Ata became the seats of the sovereign states of Azerbaijan, Turkmanistan, Uzbekistan, Kirghizstan and Kazakhstan. Nearly 60 million Muslims had been set free.

The independent Republics of the Central Asia, after the collapse of the Communist structure and demolition of the Soviet Empire, formed CIS, the Commonwealth of Independent States, to chalk out the course of their future destiny. The new development and the establishment of the OS obviously provided the Muslim Republics of the CIS an opportunity to look southwards to the brotherly Muslim neighbors like Pakistan, Iran, Turkey and Afghanistan for joint ventures.

In order to expand the ECO and to develop a broader economic and trade region in Asia, an extraordinary two-day session of the Council of Foreign Ministers of the original ECO states, i.e., Pakistan, Iran and Turkey was held on November 28-29, 1992, at Islamabad. Besides the ECO founding members – Pakistan, Iran and Turkey – delegates from Afghanistan, Azerbaijan, Kirghizstan, Turkmenistan, Uzbekistan and Kazakhstan were also invited to attend.

The agenda of the conference included the following four main issues:
1. Admission of Afghanistan as a permanent member of the ECO.
2. Amendment to the Treaty of Izmir.
3. Formal induction of the new member states which include Azerbaijan, Kirghizstan, and Tajikistan.
4. Adoption of modalities for the participation of Turkish Muslim community of Northern Cyprus.

The new states were welcomed by the participants of the conference and formally inducted into the ECO fold as the full members. With the addition of the new members the membership of the ECO jumped to nine with a population of 300 million people. The ECO states are strategically located in the heart of Euro-Asian landmass with the territory of over 3 million sq miles, equal to the area of the USA. The Islamabad Conference indeed heralded a new global factor which is bound to play an important role on the global political order in the 21st century. ECO is a 21st century phenomenon, therefore, must be viewed and perceived in the same perspective.

PAKISTAN AND THE ECO

A long history of cultural and political affinity between Pakistan and the CAR (Central Asian Republics) had existed ever since the establishment of Pakistan as an independent sovereign state in 1947. A substantial part of the Soviet delegations who had visited Pakistan as well as of the Soviet diplomats stationed in the Soviet diplomatic missions in Pakistan hailed from Central Asia.

When Pakistan's Minister of State for Economic Affairs visited the CAR in 1991 (Central Asian Republics) for developing diplomatic relations, several avenues of cooperation were explored. Pakistan was of the firm view that it could offer assistance to the CARs with respect to industries like banking, insurance, management and English language training as well as market for raw material from these republics. It could supply many consumer goods, which were in dire need.

Pakistan signed an agreement with the CARs of understanding and joint ventures in culture, education and the economy. The CARs needed credit for food, engineering goods and medicines. To get trade rolling, Sardar Assef Ali offered long-term credits of 10m dollars and 30m dollars each.

The lack of transport and communications turned out to be the major obstacle to Pakistan's ambitions of developing closer ties with Central Asia. The problem was deepened with the internal turmoil in Afghanistan, which was sandwiched between the two regions. The railway lines of South and Central Asia ended at the Afghan border.

It was easier to start air traffic. From May 1992, PIA has started a weekly service between Islamabad and Tashkent. This was after a civil aviation agreement had been signed in February 1992. Also regular air service to Kazakhstan is in the offing. The talks were held repeatedly to establish a Central Asian Airlines which would feed all the Central Asian republics and connect them with Kabul, Istanbul, Tehran, Islamabad and Karachi.

However, it is the rail and road links, which is crucial for trade and potential military use. There are three railheads on the Pakistan side one each near Peshawar (Landi Kotal) and Quetta (Chaman) facing Afghanistan and one terminating inside Iranian Balochistan at Zahidan. On the Central Asian side Chaman would be linked with Kasha at the Turkman-Afghan border leading railroad through southern Afghanistan.

The independence of the CARs has opened a new era of opportunities for Pakistan in the economic field. Besides Afghanistan, the CARs and the western regions of China, which also have a predominant Muslim population, Iran, Pakistan and Turkey may form a regional economic bloc of sizeable proportions. The Karakoram highway (Silk Route), the Salang Pass route which carries cargo by road from Kabul to the CARs, and now – the new inland roads in northern Pakistan should provide the necessary road networks for intra-regional trade.

Pakistan can provide port facilities at Karachi and Bin Qasim. Pakistan can also export electric goods like air-conditioners, washing machines, plastic goods, ceramic products, some food items, textile goods and engineering goods. Besides, can provide them with cotton ginning machinery, machine tools, road building equipment, power looms and help them develop their textile industry. Due to the geographical proximity, we can carry their cargo in transit to other parts of the world.

Nevertheless, Pakistan government and businessmen will have to plan carefully and meticulously to improve relations with CARs as India and Russia besides the USA and European countries have also started maneuvering for exercising their economic influence there.

Besides efforts at government and ECO levels, business community in Pakistan is also exploring the tremendous opportunities waiting in the CARs (Central Asian Republics). Two delegations one from the businessmen's forum and other from the FPCCI (Federation of the Pakistan Chambers of Commerce and Industry) visited Central Asian States in October 1992. A team of Bankers led by governor State Bank of Pakistan also visited Uzbekistan and set up a branch of NBP at Tashkent.

The FPCCI delegation had visited Central Asia to exploit the trade and economic opportunities existing in the newly independent states. The delegation made on-the-sport studies at Tashkent, Samarkand, Bokhara,

Moscow, Ashkabad and Alma Ata to explore the possibilities for expansion of Pakistan's economic relations with those countries.

UNITED NATIONS ORGANIZATION (UN)

When the First World War ended in *1919* the civilized world seriously thought to establish a world organization, which could save the mankind from the scourge of war in future. The aftermath of the First World War was so dreadful that all nations were now unanimously in favor of eliminating the chances of any future armed conflict which could damage the world peace. For this noble aim the League of Nations was set up which, however, could not save the world from the war and thus dissolved after 20 years of its existence.

The Second World War broke out in 1939, which proved more dreadful and devastating for the peace-loving world. Atomic bomb was used for the first time in this war, which shook the shallow foundations of world peace by cruelly eradicating the mankind from earth.

The world leaders, horrified by the results of the war, painstakingly felt that an effective world body should he set up to promote peace, tranquility and friendship in the true sense among the whole world. The leaders of USA, France, Great Britain, Russia and China played a pivotal role for the establishment of a world organization different from the League of Nations. They assembled at San Francisco on 25th April 1945 to discuss the details. A conference of 50 states was convened which discussed in details all possibilities pertaining to the formation of a world body with the lofty objectives of avoiding all chances of war and promoting social and economic well-being of the world. On 26th June, 1945 the participants agreed to set up UNO. A Charter of UNO was drawn up which was agreed and signed by the participants. The initial membership of the UNO was restricted to fifty nations who took part in the San Francisco Conference. The Charter of UNO came into effect on 24th Oct. 1945. The head office of the UNO is located in New York.

AIMS AND OBJECTS OF THE UN

The basic objective of the UNO is the maintenance of world peace and to foster friendly and brotherly feelings among all countries *of* the world. It also aims at creating greater harmony and co-ordination among the member countries *of* the UNO in order to promote and enhance social and economic well-being of the people. The major objectives, as laid down in the Charter of the UNO are as follows:

To maintain international peace and tranquility, and to take appropriate steps for its fulfillment.

To foster friendly relations amongst the nations of the world on the basis of human rights, promote mutual co-operation between the nations of the world for economic, social, cultural and educational uplift irrespective of race, color, religion and creed.

ORGANIZATIONAL STRUCTURE OF THE UN

1. General Assembly

The General Assembly is comprised of the representatives of all the member countries of the UNO. By mid 1997, the present membership of the UNO had risen to *194* member nations. Each member has one vote to cast in the deliberations of the General Assembly. "However, every country can send five representatives to the meetings of the General Assembly. It is the most important organ of the UNO which conducts the working of the world body. The assembly holds its regular sessions. The Secretary General can convene emergency meeting of the Assembly on the request of the Security Council or of a majority of the members of the UNO. All issues are decided by voting in the Assembly and *2/3* majority is required to decide a highly sensitive issue. On other routine matters a simple majority is sufficient to decide the matter.

The General Assembly gives approval to the budget and distributes expenditures among member countries. It watches the overall working of the UN by keeping a surveillance on the activities of the UNO. It is the General Assembly, which confers membership on the new entrants.

2. Security Council

Security Council consists of 15 members. Five members are permanent while the remaining 10 are elected for 2 years term by the General Assembly. The temporary members are not eligible for immediate re-election. China, France, USA, Great Britain and Russia are the permanent members of the Security Council with a 'Veto' right.

The primary responsibility of the Security Council is to maintain world peace and security. The Council may take up any matter, at its own, which may threaten the world peace and security in any way. The Security Council holds its meetings at least once every two weeks. The Presidency of the Council changes every month by rotation on alphabetical order.

The Council reports to the General Assembly by submitting detailed reports annually on all matters, which it had decided.

Decisions on procedural questions are made by an affirmative vote of a member country. On all other matters the affirmative vote of nine members must include the positive vote of the permanent members. In case of a negative vote by any permanent member of the Council on any matter, the issue will be 'vetoed' and considered as undecided. The Council takes immediate steps to stop the war between the two countries. It tries to hold negotiations between the belligerent states and presents its own solution of the dispute. The Council can impose economic and social boycott with the help of other members on the country, which refuses to accept the solution offered by the Council.

3. Economic and Social Council
The economic and social council consists of 54 members elected by the General Assembly for a term of 3 years. The Council is responsible to the General Assembly for its work, which mainly pertains to the international economic, social, cultural, educational, health and related matters. For this purpose the Council co-ordinates the functions of UNESCO, ILO, and WHO. The council holds its meeting twice a year.

4. Trusteeship Council
The management of trust territories is under UN supervision. Trust territories are those territories, which have achieved freedom from foreign rule and are going through the initial stages of their independent life. These territories have yet to acquire complete sovereignty after throwing away the yoke of slavery. The UN takes over the charge of all such territories, which have been liberated and are considered as trust. Togo land, Cameroon and Tanganyika were put under England for their management before they acquired full sovereignty. At present pacific Island is the only trust territory administered by the USA.

5. Secretariat
Secretariat is the Headquarter and one of the most important organs of the UNO. Secretary General is the chief administrative officer who heads the secretariat. The Secretary General has a large number of officers, assistants and officials to run the work of the secretariat. The members of the secretariat are not allowed to get instructions from any Government and also are not supposed to be influenced by any country.

The Secretary General is elected by the General Assembly for a period of five years. The Secretary General can seek re-election for another term of five years. So far there have been eight Secretaries General of the UN that is as follows: Trygve Lie, Dag Hamergshold, U Thant, Kurt Waldhiem, Perez de Cuellar, Butros Ghali, Kofi Annan, and Ban Ki-Moon.

Secretary General enjoys vast powers. He convenes the meetings of General Assembly, Security Council and Trusteeship Council. He presents the annual report of the working of the UN before the General Assembly.

The Secretary General is usually taken from a nonaligned country having no war designs against any other Country. Since the Secretary General plays a pivotal role in the maintenance of peace in the world he is known as the 'World Peace Maker'.

6. International Court of Justice

The International Court of Justice is the supreme judicial organ of the UN. All member countries of the UN become parties to the statute of the Court. They are bound by the statute to comply with the decisions of the court. There are three non-member states to the statute as Switzerland, San Marino and Liechtenstein.

The Court consists of 15 permanent judges who are elected for a 9 years term by the General Assembly and the Security Council. Retiring judges can seek re-election. The Court is always in session except during vacations. All disputes and matters, brought before the Court, are decided by the majority vote. The Headquarter of the Court is located in The Hague (Netherlands). There can be no appeals against the decisions of the I.C.J.

7. SPECIALIZED AGENCIES OF THE UN

Apart from the organs of the UN, there are several specialized agencies, which are autonomous with their own membership and organs.
However, they have financial relationship or working agreement with the UN headquarters. The agencies are as follows:

I.L.O. (International Labor Organization)

The major aim of I.L.O. is to look after the interests of the laborers all over the world. It strives to promote employment, improve labor conditions and living standard.

F.A.O. (Food and Agriculture Organization)
It aims at increasing the agricultural production, improving farms, forests, fisheries and the condition of the rural population.

UNESCO (United Nations Educational, Scientific and Cultural Organization)
It aims to promote collaboration among nations through education, science and culture.

WHO (World Health Organization)
It works and provides assistance for obtaining highest possible health level.

IMF (International Monetary Fund)
It works to promote international monetary co-operation and currency stabilization.

UNICEF (United Nations Children Emergency Fund)
It provides aid and development assistance to children and mothers in the developing countries.

PAKISTAN'S ROLE IN THE UNITED NATIONS ORGANIZATION

The Quaid-i-Azam, while highlighting the governing principles of Pakistan's foreign policy, emphasized that our foreign policy is based on the principle of friendship and brotherhood with all the countries of the world. Pakistan does not cherish hostile attitude towards any nation and strongly believes in justice, honesty and peaceful co-existence in international relations. Pakistan will always be in the forefronts in siding with and extending moral and material assistance to the poor and oppressed nations of the world in the light of the UN Charter.

In pursuance of the policy, as enunciated by the founder of the nation, Pakistan became the member of UNO on 30th September, 1947. Since the day Pakistan entered the UNO, it has been striving hard to make UNO an active world body. Pakistan has played an effective role in the UNO and contributed a great deal towards its activities in ensuring international peace and tranquility which is the prime objective of the UNO. Pakistan's role in the UNO is discussed in the following lines:

1. Support for the International Peace

Pakistan has been a chief spokesman in the UNO for the maintenance of international peace. It has always supported the cause of peace and advocated the solution of all disputes by mutual negotiations. Pakistan has always tried to develop a sense of brotherhood amongst all nations of the world in the light of UN Charter. Pakistan has recognized the liberty and equality of other nations of the world. It has raised its voice on the forums of the UNO in favor of respecting others independence, sovereignty and liberty. Pakistan has endeavored for the promotion of bilateral relations based on equality and friendship and has always shown respect for human rights and liberties. Pakistan always extended maximum co-operation to the UNO and quickly acted upon the advice of the world body for the accomplishment of the noble aim of peace and prosperity of the world.

2. Favor and support for Nation's Independence and Freedom

Ever since Pakistan achieved independence after an intense freedom struggle, it has, therefore, sincerely advocated the independence of all nations of the world. Immediately after acquiring membership of the UNO, Pakistan objected to the unlawful occupation of Indonesia by Holland. Pakistan also acknowledged Indonesian right over the Western Irian Territory. Pakistan extended its support to the Libyan freedom struggle, which greatly accelerated the Libyan freedom movement and gained independence for Libya in 1952. Pakistan came forward with its support in favor of the freedom movements of Morocco, Tunis and Algiers on the forums of the UNO.

3. Opposition to the Nuclear Weapons

Being a peace loving country, Pakistan has openly opposed the proliferation of nuclear weapons. It has stood by the side of the UNO in its efforts to cheek the mad race for the nuclear weapons by the developed countries.

4. Condemnation of the Racial Discrimination

The UN Charter clearly lays down that the racial discrimination will be condemned and any country adopting the policy of racial discrimination shall be opposed and checked. Pakistan fully supports this policy and extends its maximum assistance for checking racial discrimination.

5. Palestine Problem

Palestine problem has been a source of unrest for the entire Islamic world. The people of Pakistan continue with their support for the Palestine problem and have always recognized the rights of the Palestinian people. Pakistan took up this issue with the UNO and persuaded the whole world to solve this sensitive issue for the maintenance of world peace.

NON-ALIGNED MOVEMENT (NAM)

MEANING OF NON-ALIGNMENT

Non-Aligned Movement (NAM) is an important world organization of the Third World countries that do not wish to be aligned with any of the big powers. They are rather more alive towards their economic, social and cultural development by keeping away from the expansionists designs of the super powers. The NAM, however; does not mean that the super powers should be left free and unchecked to do whatever they wish. It is a positive concept of condemning the policy of expansionism and supporting all efforts aimed at achieving mutual co-operation, international peace and tranquility. The NAM can be defined as the International forum of the people of the Third World who openly condemn and negate the lust for creating the spheres of influence by the super powers and thus is an important and effective organ against colonialism and imperialism.

BACKGROUND

The result of the Second World War had divided the whole world into power blocs quite distinct from each other. The western bloc was headed by the USA, while the socialist bloc openly toed the policy given and dictated by the former USSR. The two super powers, therefore, involved in the cold war created great problems for the smaller nations and the under-developed countries. The smaller nations had to face serious difficulties in the formulation of their foreign policies as none of them could afford to invite the annoyance of any of the super powers, which usually came in shape of economic blockade and military intervention. The smaller nations were greatly worried by this difficulty and seriously pondered over devising a line of action, which could save them from this touchy situation.

Pakistan, India, Burma, Egypt, Iraq, Syria, Jordan, Indonesia, Philippines, Sri Lanka and Lebanon had achieved their independence soon after the Second World War. Apart from these countries many other nations were engaged in their struggle for freedom. It was, therefore, not in their interest to have sided with any of the power bloc, headed by the super powers, in the initial stages of their independence as it could seriously jeopardize their development. The best policy for them would have been to keep away from the cold war of the super powers and fully concentrate on their economic, social and cultural uplift.

BANDUNG CONFERENCE

The Prime Ministers of Pakistan, India, Indonesia and Burma met at Kandy (Sri Lanka) from April 28 to May 2nd, 1954 to discuss problems facing their respective countries. The Indonesian Prime Minister proposed that another conference of Afro-Asian countries be convened. The Pakistani Prime Minister Mr. Muhammad Ali Bogra supported the proposal. The Prime Ministers of the five Asian countries once again met at Bogor (Indonesia) and decided that a conference of Afro-Asian countries would be held at Ban dung (Indonesia) on April 24th, 1954 to discuss the problems of these countries in details.

The Ban dung Conference, as decided at Bogor, was held on 24th April, 1954 to discuss the problems of the Afro-Asian countries in detail. The main objective of this conference was to provide a forum to those nations who wished to keep away from the 'Tug of War' of the super powers and was desirous of mutual co-operation for peaceful aims. The participating countries mutually concluded five governing principles in the conference as the aims and objects of the newly proposed platform. The principles were declared as 'Ban dung Principles' or 'Panjshilla'.

The principles were as follows:

Respect and safeguard for each other's sovereignty and territorial integrity/ independence Refrain from acts of aggression or use of force against any other nation
Non-interference in others internal affairs
Recognition of equality, importance and liberty of all nations
Peaceful co-existence

The conference outlined the major objectives as follows:

To promote goodwill and co-operation among the Afro-Asian countries
To consider social, economic and cultural problems of the participating countries
To consider the problems of special interests to Afro-Asian countries like racialism and colonialism

To assess the position of Afro-Asian countries and their people in the world

SUMMIT CONFERENCES

IST SUMMIT CONFERENCE
The first NAM summit conference was held at Belgrade (Yugoslavia) in *1961* in which 25 nations took part. Great personalities like Marshal Tito, (Yugoslavia), Jamal Abdel Nasar (Egypt), Jawahar Lal Nehru (India) took active part in this conference. The rules for obtaining membership of the NAM were drafted in this conference.

SECOND SUMMIT CONFERENCE
The second summit conference of the NAM was held at Cairo (Egypt) in 1964.

THIRD SUMMIT CONFERENCE
The Third Summit Conference of the NAM was held at Lusaka (Zambia) in 1970. By this time the membership of NAM had jumped to 51 countries. A Committee of 17 nations was set up in this conference with a purpose of getting in touch with other countries.

FOURTH SUMMIT CONFERENCE
The Fourth Summit Conference of the NAM was held at Algiers (Algeria) in Sept. 1973. President Boumedine of Algeria presided over this conference. A number of participants in the Fourth Conference advocated the inclusion of China and Pakistan in the NAM. Due to deep opposition from India Pakistan could not become the member of this organization.

FIFTH SUMMIT CONFERENCE
Great and significant changes had taken place in the international politics in between the Fourth and Fifth Summit conferences. Democracy had been acknowledged as a popular political system all over the world. The concept of national liberties and peaceful co-existence had gained immense *boost*. Race for the nuclear weapons had set in within the developed regions of the world. New ideas and political trends had emerged because of these developments. The countries that had enhanced their military power were interfering in others internal affairs.

The Fifth Summit meeting of the NAM was held in August 1976 in Colombo, (Sri Lanka). By this time the membership of NAM had risen to 86 member countries. It was stressed in this meeting that conditions for membership should be made stricter than before and membership should not be conferred on those countries that have joined defense pacts with super powers. Since Pakistan had concluded military pacts under SEATO and CENTO with USA and other western countries, it could not - become the member of NAM.

A number of highly important decisions were taken in this meeting. It was decided that the NAM should put up a firm resistance to racialism and expansionism *by* openly condemning those countries that have adopted the policy of racialism and expansionism. The meeting supported the Arab cause and -urged the UNO to use its influence over Israel to settle her disputes with the Arabs. The Fifth conference also stressed upon the USA to smother the war impact in Viet Nam and help restore normalcy. The participants also demanded the USA to lift its embargo on Cuba.

PAKISTAN SEEKS MEMBERSHIP OF NON-ALIGNED MOVEMENT

While formulating its foreign policy, Pakistan had always pursued the policy of Non-Alignment and had never attached itself with a particular power bloc. Pakistan always tried to keep away from the cold war of the super powers. She developed its relations with other countries on the basis of bilateral relationship and friendship.

In pursuance of this prime objective, Pakistan had been desirous of seeking the membership of the NAM. Pakistan failed in her endeavors because of the resolute opposition coming from India. The involvement of Pakistan in the defense pacts of SEATO and CENTO proved an impediment, which delayed Pakistan's entry in the NAM. Pakistan had to join the SEATO and CENTO agreements simply because of security threats from India and Afghanistan, which invited the annoyance of a powerful neighbor like former Soviet Union and a few Muslim countries as well.

In these circumstances, Pakistan gave serious thoughts to its involvement in the defense treaties and re-considered its policy of relying on the western countries in order to expand its foreign relationship. This change in Pakistan's policy and outlook was mainly because of the 1965 war in which Pakistan's western allies did not come to her help. Pakistan had to face numerous problems because of stoppage of arms supply and other assistance by her allies. The western countries adopted the same attitude during 1971 war against India, which deprived Pakistan of its eastern part. Pakistan, therefore decided to leave SEATO in 1972 and CENTO in 1979 to adopt a more independent foreign policy.

After quitting SEATO and CENTO Pakistan formally applied for NAM membership. The 25member NAM bureau considered Pakistan's application during summit conference at Colombo and finally accepted it. The Foreign Ministers meeting gave its approval to Pakistan's participation in the Sixth NAM Conference to be held at Havana (Cuba).

SIXTH SUMMIT CONFERENCE
The Sixth Summit meeting of the NAM was held at Havana (Cuba) on 3rd Sept. 1979 and continued till 9th Sept. 1979. Pakistan was attending this meeting for the first time as a member of NAM. President Fidel Castro of Cuba formally extended invitation to President Zia-ul-Haq to attend the summit conference. President Zia-ul-Haq led Pakistan's delegation to the Sixth Summit Conference. President Castro at the Havana airport warmly received the Pakistan delegation on 2nd Sept. 1979.

President Zia-ul-Haq addressing the participants emphasized on peace, equality, and international brotherhood while giving details of Pakistan's nuclear program President Zia-ul-Haq said that our atomic program was aimed at peaceful objectives and negated the false propaganda by other nations about Pakistan's nuclear program. President Zia declared Pakistan's unflinching support for the Arab cause and demanded that Israel should immediately vacate the occupied territories of the Arabs. He also extended support to the struggle of South - African people and condemned the South-African Government for adopting the policy of racial discrimination.

SEVENTH SUMMIT CONFERENCE
The Seventh Summit Conference of the NAM took place in New Delhi, capital of India in March *1983*. The NAM membership had considerably jumped by the 7th conference in which 101 countries took part. Pakistan by now had become an active member of the NAM and President Zia's speech in the 6th summit meeting had greatly enhanced Pakistan's importance in the NAM set up.

The international political situation was discussed at large in this meeting and a number of decisions of far reaching significance were made. The summit meeting emphasized checking proliferation of nuclear weapons by all states of the world. The participants of the conference expressed their grave concern over the continued 'Cold War' between the super powers, which posed serious threat to the world peace and, therefore, demanded that negotiations between USA and former USSR be initiated to end the cold war. Besides these decisions the conference took effective decisions pertaining to the evacuation of Arab_ territories, freedom struggle of the people of Palestine, South Africa and Namibia. USA was bitterly criticized for assisting Israel.

EIGHTH SUMMIT CONFERENCE

The Eighth Summit Conference of the NAM was held at Harare (Zimbabwe) on 1st Sept. 1986. The Prime Minister of Zimbabwe Robert Mugabe inaugurated the conference. Delegations from 101 countries took part in the eighth summit. Their Heads of States represented fifty countries while the remaining participants sent their high officials to represent them. President Zia-ul-Haq led the Pakistani delegation. The Indian Prime Minister Mr. Rajeev Gandhi had been elected as the Chairman of the NAM at the Delhi Summit, after the death of his mother Mrs. Indira Gandhi. Since Mr. Rajeev Gandhi had completed his tenure, Robert Mugabe was elected as the Chairman of the NAM for the next term of three years.

Robert Mugabe, the new Chairman, while inaugurating the conference, demanded the withdrawal of foreign troops from Afghanistan and Kampuchea. He invited the attention of the delegates towards the growing tendency of arms race, which was adversely affecting the world peace.

The 8th Summit Conference discussed sensitive issues like Iran-Iraq war, Afghanistan problem, M.E. problem and liberation movements of Palestine and Namibia. It also focused its attention on the racial policy of the South Africa to combat it effectively by imposing economic embargo against South Africa in order to get back the rights of the black majority of South Africa. A nine member Committee consisting of Zambia, Zimbabwe, Algiers, Nigeria, Congo, Peru, Angola and Yugoslavia was formed to draft the action plan against South Africa. It called upon all states to sever political, economic, cultural, military, and sports relations with South Africa. The conference also condemned the continued occupation of Namibia by the racist regime and assured full support to SWAPO in its liberation struggle.

The NAM summit meeting reiterated its earlier position taken by NAM on Afghanistan and demanded immediate withdrawal of foreign troops from Afghanistan. The NAM summit expressed its desire to see Afghanistan as an independent and Non-Aligned country.

The Harare conference called for immediate check on arms race and urged the two super powers to re-open their dialogue on nuclear disarmament. The summit meeting also discussed the adverse impact of economic and trade problems of the developing countries of the Third World on the economic systems of the developed nations. It focused its attention on the economic disparities between the rich and poor nations. The summit formed a committee on economic collaborations among the developing countries and called for the establishment of a new economic order.

PAKISTAN AND THE MUSLIM WORLD

The freedom movement of the Muslims of the subcontinent was based on the Islamic ideology, which meant, the safeguard of the Islamic culture and civilization. It also aimed at protecting the rights and interests of the Muslims who were being suppressed and dominated in every walk of life by the Hindu majority in United India. Pakistan, therefore, was demanded with the ultimate objective of making it a strong citadel of Islam and enabling the Muslims to live according to the principles and tenets of Islam.

In view of these objectives Pakistan had to develop close relations with the Islamic world. Moreover, the similarity of culture and civilization has also brought Pakistan closer to the Muslim world. The similarity of faith, culture and thinking has firmly attached Pakistan with the Muslim bloc. Pakistan, therefore, has sincerely endeavored from the very beginning of its independence to bring the Muslim Umma on one platform. Pakistan's relations with the Muslim nations are discussed below:

PAKISTAN AND AFGHANISTAN

The Islamic Republic of Afghanistan is a land locked and mountainous country located in south central Asia bordered by Pakistan in the south and Iran in the east. It occupies a territory of 251,773 sq. miles inhabited by a population numbering about 30 million as of the year 2010 with 3 million taking refuge in Pakistan and Iran. 24 % population is urban and obviously 76 % lives in villages. Afghanistan is a multi ethnic and multi lingual society reflecting its location astride trade and invasion routes between western , central and southern Asia. The majority of the population consists of Pashtuns and Tajiks. The pashtun is the largest group followed by Tajik, Hazara, Uzbek Turkman, Almark and Baloch. Pashto is spoken widely in the south, east and west of the country whereas 50 % francalingua of the country. Islam is the religion of 99 % of Afghanis and about 80 % belong to Hanafi law school while 19 % are shiites and follow Jafri law school. 1% practice other religions such as Sikhism and Hinduism.

Afghans mostly are a tribal society with different regions of the country having their own separate tradition. Pashtun culture dominates in the eastern and central region as well as in western Pakistan, which is an ancient style still in existence and pursued today. Tajiks Baloch and others are mainly influenced by Iranian culture.

The Government of Pakistan decided to develop diplomatic relations with Afghanistan in February 1948. Mr. I. I. Chundrigar was appointed the first Ambassador of Pakistan to Afghanistan. The Afghan Government sent Sardar Shah Wall Khan as their first Ambassador to Karachi. With the establishment of diplomatic relations between the two countries, it was hoped that friendly ties would he strengthened with time. Consequently, the prominent leaders of the two countries exchanged visits to each other's countries. Sardar Abdur Rab Nishtar, the Communication Minister led a delegation to Afghanistan to take part in the celebrations of Jashn-e-Azadi. Similarly, Mullah Shor Bazar, a prominent religious personality of Afghanistan, paid a visit to Pakistan in 1949.

Afghanistan initiated a hostile propaganda campaign against Pakistan through its Press and Radio immediately after independence. The main purpose of this anti-Pakistan propaganda was to compel Pakistan to accede to the demand of Pakhtoonistan. Afghanistan began this campaign on the behest of its two big allies, India and the former Soviet Union. Since then Afghanistan continuously adopted a hostile attitude against Pakistan and has been interfering in Pakistan's internal affairs. Pakistan's consulates in Qandhar and Jalalabad were raided in 1954. In 1949 the 'Faqir of Appy', instigated by the Afghan Government, instigated the tribal people to rise against Pakistan which nonetheless failed. A mob raided Pakistan's Embassy in Kabul on 30th March, 1955 when Pakistan announced the establishment of "One Unit." The hooligans destroyed the relevant record of the Embassy and set fire to the Embassy building. On this act of violence backed by the Afghan Government, Pakistan lodged its strong protest, which was arrogantly turned down by the Afghan Government. The diplomatic ties between the two countries were severed in 1959, which, however, were restored by the efforts of the late Shah of Iran in 1962.

The boundary line between Afghanistan and Pakistan was drawn in 1893, which is known as 'Durand Line'. It is the international boundary line between the two countries, which is 2,240 km long. The Durand Line was drawn by an agreement, which was signed by the Foreign Secretary of the Government of British India - Sir Mortimer Durand and Amir Abdur Rehman of the Government of Afghanistan.

The pact contained few provisions decided between the British Government and the Afghan Government. According to Article 11 of this pact the Afghan Government agreed not to interfere in the areas that formed part of the Indian Territory (now existing Pakistan) and situated on the other side of the Durand Line. Similarly, the British Government also agreed to accept Afghan hegemony over the areas falling within Afghanistan.

But after independence, the rulers and Presidents of Afghanistan refused to accept the Durand Line as the boundary between Pakistan and Afghanistan. Consequently the relations between the two countries were affected due to the dispute over the Durand Line. World leaders have recognized the Durand Line as the international boundary between the two countries. The British Prime Minister, Mr. Anthony Eden, in a statement on 1st March, 1956 recognized the Durand Line as the boundary between Pakistan and Afghanistan. Mr. Harold Macmillan, who succeeded Mr. Eden as the British Prime Minister also, accepted the Durand Line as being the boundary between the two countries. Similarly a number of other prominent leaders from the U.S.A. and ether countries have taken the Durand Line as an international boundary between Pakistan and Afghanistan.

However, efforts from both sides have been made from time to time to normalize the relations between the two neighboring countries. The world leaders have also tried to solve disputes and revive the broken relations between the two countries. President Jamal Abdul Nasser of Egypt on May 12th 1955 offered to bring rapprochement between the two countries, which Pakistan accepted. The United States of America and Saudi Arabia appealed to Pakistan not to sever its diplomatic relations with Afghanistan to which Pakistan readily agreed.

The leaders of the two countries exchanged visits in order to reconcile and develop friendly relations. In August 1956 the President of Pakistan, Sikander Mirza, paid an official visit to Afghanistan and held discussions with Afghan leaders in a friendly atmosphere. The Prime Minister of Afghanistan, Sardar Daud Khan, paid a visit to Pakistan in November 1959. Pakistan's Prime Minister Husain Shaheed Suharwardy toured Afghanistan in 1957.

The Afghan Ruler, Shah Zahir Shah, came to Pakistan in 1958 and held discussions with Mr. Feroz Khan Noon, the Prime Minister and Mr. Islander Mirza, the President of Pakistan. Mr. Z.A. Bhutto, Pakistan's Prime Minister paid a visit to Afghanistan in 1976. With the result of these tours of the leaders of two countries, the relations between the two nations improved and various pacts and agreements were agreed upon.

An agreement allowing trade passage to Afghanistan through Pakistan was concluded between the two countries in 1958. By this agreement it was decided that Pakistan would allow maximum facilities of transport, custom duties, and municipal tax, etc. to the Afghans as their goods passed through Pakistan. The Afghan Government, however, violated the agreement on several occasions. The Afghan Foreign Minister Prince Naeem continued leveling baseless accusations against Pakistan. He threatened if Pakistan did not resolve to solve the issue of Pakhtoonistan peacefully, Afghanistan would adopt other means. The Afghan Government declared '31st August' as 'Pakhtoonistan Day' and celebrated it condemning Pakistan.

Pakistan, due to the unfriendly attitude of the Afghan Government, was compelled to sever its diplomatic relations on September 6th, 1961. Pakistan requested Britain to look after its interests in Kabul, which the Afghan Government refused to accept. However, Pakistan allowed Afghanistan to carry on transporting its goods through Pakistan in spite of the closure of diplomatic relations. Diplomatic relations between Pakistan and Afghanistan were restored after talks held in Tehran on May 23rd, 1963. Both Pakistan and Afghanistan agreed to establish Embassies and also agreed to set up Consulates in each other's country in Jalalabad and Quetta.

Shah Zahir Shah, the Afghan ruler adopted a friendly attitude towards Pakistan. He pursued a liberal policy and expressed his desire of cultivating friendly relations with Pakistan. During 1965 War Zahir Shah did not interfere in the war and remained neutral. India and the former Soviet Union prompted him to attack Pakistan during 1965 war but he refused. President Ayub went to Kabul after the war and offered his thanks to Zahir Shah for keeping aloof from the war. Zahir Shah also paid a visit to Pakistan and was given a warm welcome.

Zahir Shah's Government was over-thrown by a military coup on July 7th, 1973 and Sardar Daud came into power. With Sardar Daud coming into power the Afghan policy towards Pakistan at once changed. Sardar Daud's Government followed a more hostile policy towards Pakistan. Mr. Z.A. Bhutto, the Prime Minister of Pakistan offered to hold talks to end differences. Pakistan immediately extended recognition to Afghan government in spite of her unfriendly attitude towards Pakistan.

The relations between Afghanistan and Pakistan continued to deteriorate. The Secretary- General of the O.I.C. Mr. Hasan Al Tehami offered his good offices to remove the misunderstandings between the two neighbors. He held discussions with Mr. Z.A. Bhutto and Sardar Daud. He stressed that the leaders of the two countries should develop friendly attitudes towards each other. Prime Minister Z.A. Bhutto took initiative and offered aid to the Afghan people who were hit by an earthquake.

Sardar Daud extended an invitation to Mr. Z.A. Bhutto to visit Afghanistan. During his visit to Afghanistan Mr. Z.A. Bhutto emphasized the need to develop closer ties between the two countries. He also extended an invitation to Sardar Daud for a visit to Pakistan, which was accepted by the Afghan President.

Sardar Daud came to Pakistan in August 1976, on an official tour. He exchanged views and expressed his desire of maintaining friendly relations with Pakistan. After these tours by the leaders, the relations between Pakistan and Afghanistan improved. However, Sardar Daud was assassinated and Noor Mohammad Tarakai was installed into power. Tarakai was also murdered when he desired to develop friendly relations with Pakistan. Hafeez Ullah Amin occupied the throne that too was killed when he extended an invitation to Pakistan's Foreign Minister to pay a visit to Afghanistan.

On December 27th, 1979 nearly 120,000 Russian troops entered Afghanistan. The Afghan people put up a resolute resistance to this blatant aggression. Babrak Karmal was appointed the Head of the Government. The Afghan Mujahideens took up arms against the aggressors for the defense of their land.

Pakistan extended maximum support to the Afghan Mujahideens by accommodating them in their country and training them for Guerilla warfare. Pakistan refused to recognize any Government formed under the umbrella of the Soviet troops. Afghan Air force, on several occasions, violated Pakistan Air space and heavily bombed Pakistani areas. However, the Soviet troops could not stand resistance of the Afghan people and had to pull out of Afghanistan according to Geneva Accord.

After Russian exodus USA left without forming a representative government in the country. After years of fighting between the different factions of Mujahadeens, Taliban took control of Kabul and established a fundamentalist Wahabi state. After the assassination of Ahmed Shah Masud, the leader of the moderate Islamic party, Taliban became the sole power, which let lose a reign of terror in the region; dismantled monuments valuable heritage, confined women in their homes and stopped them from attending schools. Not only that started spreading radicalism in tribal Pashtuns of Waziristan, Swat and former NWFP where they established parallel government depriving Pakistan its writ in the area.

USA, blaming Al-Qaeda and Taliban for 9/11 attack jumped in and after establishing bases in Afghanistan started fighting and invited Pakistan and her allies to help restore democratic regime getting rid of the fundamentalists. Taliban are resisting tooth and nail have continued guerilla attacks not only on US and UN troops but also targeted Pakistan and have caused huge losses of valuable lives and property of the country. Taliban have support from countries that have vested interest in the region. Hamid Karzai is playing a double game; has given concessions to India to establish consulates in the bordering areas of Pakistan that has accelerated attacks on Pakistan facilitating flow of arms and insurgents from there. The war that has now lasted over a decade has shattered economy of Pakistan and is contributing to the ever increasing American budget deficit. Although, elections have since been held twice and a president of her choice has been planted yet the government has failed to have support of the general public who occasionally give vent to their feelings of resentment, react and resort to violence. Pakistan is taking active part in resolving the issue and reaching a settlement to avoid further losses, giving end to purposeless unending conflict. Pakistan is also ready to rebuild war torn Afghanistan and affected tribal areas restoring peace and rehabilitating economy of the countries involved.

PAKISTAN AND BANGLADESH

Bangladesh has been an integral part of Pakistan till December 1971 when it was dismembered as the result of false propaganda against the then government and largely due to aggressive design of India against Pakistan's integrity and solidarity. Pakistan originally came into being with the joint efforts of Bengali and the people of North West Muslim majority areas of India now constituting Pakistan. Since independence of Pakistan, Bengalis have been actively participating in the development and welfare of Pakistan; Khawja Nazim-ud-din, served as the first president and Hussain Shaheed Suharwardy and Mohammad Ali Bogra as Prime Ministers of Pakistan. More than 50 % of Pakistan budget was allocated for East Pakistan. Over and above East Pakistan being an area frequented with natural hazards; floods and typhoons additional funds almost every year were given to help fight the hazards. Foreign aid received by Pakistan was equally divided for the development schemes of both the wings. Bangladesh these days is one of the poorest countries of the world with high rate of growth of population and limited resources at her disposal

Steps taken by Gen. Ayub Khan for the development and improving lot of the people of East Pakistan:

Provided new avenues of employment by encouraging industrialists like Adamjee Saigols and others to set up Industries in the eastern wing and stopped giving permission for new units except East Pakistan. A number of jute and cotton textile mills, paper mill and other units were thus set up during that period.
In order to reduce pressure of over population in the eastern wing, encouraged landless farmers from there, to settle on vacant lands in West Pakistan. He also encouraged inter wing marriages to develop a mixed culture and bring the people of both factions closer to each other.

East Pakistan comprised of about 54, 000 Square miles area with one of the highest densities of population in the world more than 15,000 persons to the sq. mile and as such could hardly meet food requirements of the people. Moreover, in order to allow Eastern wing to increase their area under jute, which was in great demand those days and a source of earning foreign exchange It was done like this that West Pakistan that grows superior qualities of Basmati rice and their staple food being wheat has sufficient surplus quantity for export. That superior variety has market all over the world particularly those days in Japan. In exchange instead of earning sterling Pakistan would import three times quantity of Irri rice from Japan which forms staple food of Bengalis to help meet their food requirements and to encourage the farmers there to cultivate jute instead of rice, because on a limited area if they cultivate rice for food cannot grow jute in large quantity.

People of both wings were primarily tied together due to common faith and religion of Islam. They were expected to cooperate with each other and work for the welfare of the poor and afflicted masses of both wings of the country as also emphasized by the founder of Pakistan on the eve of independence, "from this day you are not Punjabis, Balochis, Sindhis, Bengalis, Sunni or Shiites but Pakistani – birth of a new nation on the map of the world". He also asserted unity, faith and discipline in every walk of life. But in spite of his clear warning not to be divided, the enemies of Pakistan were able to misguide people of East Pakistan to demand a separate country on linguistic basis. India an erstwhile enemy of Pakistan who did not accept the partition of the sub-continent of India with open heart sportingly and, therefore, was always on the lookout for an opportunity to damaging Pakistan.

India made several attempts to create differences and divide the people to break the unity and strength of Pakistan of which some are numerated below:

In the first instance India tried to annex Eastern wing in 1949 when Ayub Khan was commanding East Pakistan Rifles there. India approached and asked him to let Indian forces enter East Pakistan and made a lucrative offer in exchange. India wanted to repeat her action that she did in case of Hyderabad and Junagarh states. Ayub Khan a great patriot and a soldier could never let that happen and after consultation with Liaqat Ali Khan, then Prime Minister of Pakistan accepted the offer and gave them a green signal. But as soon as the Indian forces crossed borders he surrounded and forced them to surrender. In this way the first attempt of India to dismember Pakistan could not succeed.

Second attempt was made in 1962 and a conspiracy for that was hatched in a border town in India known as Agar Talla with the connivance Bengali service men and Sheikh Mujeeb-ur-Rehman. According to the plan while Gen. Ayub Khan was on visit to East Pakistan he would be taken to inspect Karna Phulli paper mills located at Chittagong by boat. The boat to carry the President was fixed with deadly explosives. If the plan could be successful in that confusion Indian forces would have entered and annexed East Pakistan. Fortunately, Chinese intelligence informed Pakistan about the plan before hand and thus that attempt of India also failed. Due to political reasons defaulters could not be punished and while trial of Mujeeb-ur-Rehman was being done a large number of his supporters over ran the court and the trial judge, justice Rehman could hardly save his life. That unprecedented event encouraged the Sheikh further who accelerated his efforts to poison the nation.

India, however, did not stop her nefarious efforts and then used the weapon of propaganda and made a hectic campaign to poison Bengalis against Pakistan. Hindu teachers who were employed in the education department in large numbers carried out the propaganda campaign polluting the minds of their students. Also through newspapers and handouts every student had been sold the idea that Punjabis were eating the resources of Bengal and the foreign exchange earned by the export of jute was spent in West Pakistan.

Further, it was propagated that rice and other commodities of daily use in Punjab were available at much lower rates: price of one mound of rice was rupees fifty a mound in Punjab whereas its price in Bengal was rupees 250/- per mound. Although, it was a white lie and the price of the commodity had never been that low and rather was more than rupees 250/-. Such fantastic false statistics were published in the dailies to substantiate there point of view- but no Pakistani generalist or any government official ever bothered to refute and give a true picture to the masses.

Some under training officers from Lahore Civil Service Academy were on a visit to Multan (Punjab). One of my cousins who happened to be their colleague invited them to his house. His father being a land owner had constructed a big bungalow for the family on over two acres of land, some Bengali Officers included in the group, after having enjoyed a sumptuous meal and going round the house remarked, "We smell jute here." His father who heard them saying that sarcastically said, "My sons Multan is a cotton producing area and not of jute how do you smell jute here". In fact their remark was based on the rumors embedded in their minds that it was the foreign exchange earned by jute of East Pakistan, which was being spent lavishly in West Pakistan. It was the result of brain washing through false propaganda of Indian separatists. Why only Punjab and not other provinces, that were very much part of West Pakistan not targeted? Is another story- a dream of India that was thwarted by Mr. Zulfiqar Ali Bhutto through his diplomacy and planning?

Similarly Sheikh Mujeeb-ur-Rehman was on a visit to West Pakistan and he had also given such remarks after seeing Islamabad. A group of generalists questioned him, what will you eat if got separated from West Pakistan? His reply was jute. Another generalist asked what would you wear? His reply was again jute. Yet another generalist asked about the revenues. His answer was again jute. In short the minds of the entire Bengal was so much poisoned that they forgot all the sacrifices that Pakistan was making for them and could not see the realities on ground. One would have to admit that this weapon of India was right on the target and helped India emerge successful at long last in dismembering Pakistan in a brief war in 1971.

Indira Gandhi Prime Minister of India, before launching the assault in December 1971, had taken a hurricane tour of Europe and America. The purpose of the tour was to get approval of the world powers for her mission to relieve East Pakistanis who were subjected to atrocities at the hand of Pakistan Army dictators and a large number of Bengalis as a result had taken refuge in India and that was a great burden on India's economy. But Pakistan government never bothered to clarify her position and no such mission was sent to counter the move.

Gen. Tikka Khan was sent to East Pakistan in March 1971 to restore law and order there, which was created by Mukti Bahni and Awami League workers who were fully armed and had disrupted peace in that wing. Tikka Khan handled the situation by iron hands and restored law and order and made the Mukti Bahni to flee who were mostly Indians and were staying in Dacca university hostels. Tikka Khan having seen the attitude of most of the population after his successful operation had suggested to Gen. Yahya Khan to find a political solution to the problem as quickly as possible. But Yahya Khan did not pay much attention to his suggestion and remained in slumber.

If Yahya Khan had read the writing on the wall he should have handed over the charge of East Pakistan to Awami league who had swept elections there and of West Pakistan to leader of the winning Peoples party, when Mujib-ur-Rehman was not accepting his offer to come to Islamabad and take charge as Prime Minister of Pakistan. He was avoiding that because India had groomed him for the separation of the eastern wing and not to keep a united Pakistan. Ultimately which Yahya Khan had to do and should have done before facing all that humiliation at the hands of his rivals.

It was due mostly to the facts stated above that Eastern wing was separated after annexation by India and those who say that it was due to an adamant attitude of Zulfiqar Ali Bhutto who did not let the transfer of Power to Mujeeb-ur-Rehman leader of Awami league are mistaken. They also attribute tearing the resolution submitted by Poland in Security Council and his political slogan, "Idhar ham udher tum" responsible for the bifurcation, say so out of jealousy and closing their eyes from the historical facts stated above. The debacle, fall of Dacca, was the result of years of planning of Indian politicians to which army Generals, mostly in power, could not counter effectively. It was not a sudden phenomenon as some of the people particularly poisoned against Bhutto believe and propagate forgetting his valuable services and sacrifice for the country to have got released a hundred thousand POWs from India, given a unanimous constitution and above all made Pakistan invincible by making her a nuclear power at the cost of his rule and ultimately of his life. His daughter who has been the prime minister of the country twice and also his two sons have been murdered to keep Bhuttos away from holding power.

Pakistan accepted the division with open heart and recognized Bangladesh in 1974, and being a Muslim country has always supported her. The SAARC organization, initiated by Bangladesh President Zia-ur-Rehman, Pakistan willingly joined that and provides huge funds to eliminate poverty from her sister country Bangladesh. As such Pakistan enjoys cordial relations with Bangladesh any time.

PAK CHINA RELATIONS

China is Pakistan's immediate neighbor with a common border in the northeast of the country. Trade and cultural relations existed between the people of China and the region now constituting Pakistan from times immemorial. The ties between the two nations have grown and their mutual friendship has been tested through difficult times over the years. Pakistan supported its entry in UNO in 1950 while USA was opposed to that. Pakistan china relations got impetuous when boundary demarcation was settled amicably between them without any hassle during Gen. Ayub Khan's period through his foreign Minister Z.A. Bhutto. On the other hand dispute with India over demarcation resulted in Sino India war.

China's Support for Kashmir Issue:

China all along had been supporting Pakistan's point of view openly and in the Security Council. She having observed the adamant and unjust stand of India over the issue asked Pakistan to enter the Kashmir valley while she was engaging India on the other front. But the moment India came to know such designs of Pakistan immediately offered to settle Kashmir and other issues with Pakistan and also requested US to intervene. Pakistan instead of availing herself of the opportunity was taken in by India's fraudulent offer and consented to negotiate. A few sessions on the issue were held in Islamabad and New Delhi but as soon as the danger was over she again reverted to her old stand and parried further negotiations on the issue. In this way Pakistan lost a golden opportunity of settling the issue once for all which is hanging fire now for the last more than fifty years and has resulted in two bloody wars between the neighboring countries.

China and war with India - 1965

India imposed an undeclared war on Pakistan and crossed international border under the cover of darkness on September 6, 1965 with the intention of capturing Lahore the heart of Pakistan and advanced up to BRB canal in Lahore. In addition, launched a full- fledged armor attack on the Sialkot Chawinda front which was one of the biggest armor attack after World War II. Pakistan with its valor army and the support of the citizens crushed and halted the attacks on all the fronts and gave a befitting reply by occupying sizeable area including Khemkaran town in Ferozepur Punjab and her armies advanced on Kashmir front and were only a couple miles away from Jammu Katoha road the only connection and supply line of India to Kashmir. China also opened front with India to reduce her pressure on Pakistan.

India having been flabbergasted with unexpected resistance and high spirits of Pakistan knocked the door of Security Council and also literally went on the feet of US an ally of Pakistan to help affecting cease-fire. It was on the hot line that US asked Gen. Ayub Khan to accept India's offer of cease-fire while his foreign Minister Zulfiqar Ali through his historical address in the Security Council was busy convincing the members that Pakistan has been subjected to a blatant aggression by her five times bigger neighbor and we will now fight a thousand years for our rights and rights of the people of the valley of Kashmir which India is occupying illegally against the will of the people, in defiance of the verdicts of the Security Council, and has not given the right of self determination to the people of Kashmir. It was this speech in the Security Council that very much translated the sentiments and feelings of the masses that won their hearts and he emerged as one of the most favorite leaders of Pakistan after Quaid-e-Azam. Those who say that his popularity was due to his slogan of "Rooti Kapra Aur Makan" are highly mistaken and they say so out of jealousy and mislead the people. Such elements should bear in mind that masses of Pakistan are poor but not mean as to be lured by material resources. They love their country and honor those who are and have been sincere to their homeland. They are real patriots.

TASHKENT AND CHINA
After the cease-fire Pakistan was invited by Russia to come to Tashkent where she would mediate between the confronting parties. USA also persuaded Pakistan to accept the offer of mediation but China warned Pakistan not to go to Tashkent as Russia an ally and supporter of India would never favor her and it was a trap for her to thwart her success in the battle field. But Gen. Ayub Khan against China's advice went there and had to accept humiliating terms without a word about the settlement of Kashmir issue. He literally lost his popularity and the gains his valor army had earned on ground. It was these glaring political mistakes on the part of Gen. Ayub Khan, which led to his down fall and responsible for popularity of Zulfiqar Bhutto who was against accepting cease-fire without settlement of Kashmir issue and also opposed to Tashqand agreement imposed upon them by the Russian president.

CHINA AND 1971 WAR With India
When India committed aggression in East Pakistan in 1971 and Pakistan allies including US did not come to Pakistan's help and even refused arms and spare parts to equip her to counter the attack, it was China who offered all sorts of assistance and was prepared to open a front with India to divert her attention and to reduce pressure on Pakistan. If India had not declared cease-fire after the fall of Dacca China was prepared to play her

role as committed by opening front with India and replenishing Pakistan with combating materials to gain some ground at least on the West Pakistan fronts.

CONSTRUCTION OF SILK ROUTE

Construction of road linking China in a most difficult mountainous terrain is a remarkable feat of Chinese and Pakistan army EME core. It is one of the highest highways of the world. Its construction has further fastened the bonds of friendship of Pakistan with China. It has not only helped promoting trade between the two neighbors but also important from the point of view of defense of Pakistan.

China's friendship and devotion is with the simple people of Pakistan and not with personalities and that is why her relations with Pakistan have remained stable irrespective of change of Civil or Military governments in Pakistan.

PAK US RELATIONS

Pakistan came into existence on the basis of Islam and has, therefore, inclination towards countries that have religious base. Christ a holy and highly honored apostle of God is equally respected both by Christians and the Muslims. Then again, Muslims also respect and regard Injeel (Bible) as revealed book ratified in the holy Quran and its teachings are equally binding on Muslims. Because of this religious affinity Pakistan from the very beginning opted to look towards US rather than USSR an atheist state.

It was due to these considerations that Nawabzada Liaqat Ali Khan preferred to join the western bloc rather the Eastern. Not only that ignoring geographical factors entered into defense pacts; SEATO and CENTO designed against USSR an immediate neighbor and a world power, and the history shows that Pakistan had to pay a heavy price for that venture. Since then Pakistan has been a dependable ally of US in spite of threats and retaliation of USSR and cooperated with US throughout during its cold war.

There has, however, been some cold-shouldering on the part of US. Whereas USSR throughout helped India equip her with deadly weapons it was through unconditional vetoes of Russia that India could avoid its commitments and resolutions of UNO from holding plebiscite in the Valley of Kashmir. But US did not side with Pakistan in 1965 war when

India imposed an undeclared war and when Pakistan with its limited force and resources was able to not only stop the aggression but was also in a position to gain advances in the valley and on other borders as well, Pakistan was ordered to accept cease fire request of India unconditionally. Then again Pakistan was asked to go to Tashkent where Pakistan under threat was asked to withdraw her forces and revert to old positions without settlement of Kashmir or imposing any penalty on India to have initiated an undeclared war and having crossed an international border. Again in 1971 when India annexed East Pakistan US an ally of Pakistan never came to its help and rescue — instead remained an unconcerned spectator to the entire episode and did not force India to accept cease fire resolutions of UNO as she forcefully did in 1965 when India approached her for help.

For these reasons Pakistan had to revise its foreign policy and quitted SEATO and CENTO since those defense pacts failed to serve the purpose or ensured her security, and instead fostered her relations with China and patched up with USSR. However, Pakistan did not severe relations with US.

In 1979 when USSR occupied Afghanistan an important strategic area, USA again required help and assistance of Pakistan as China her first choice to confront USSR refused to do the job. It was with the undaunted support of Pakistan that not only helped exodus of USSR but also resulted in its collapse and disintegration. It was a remarkable feat on the part of Pakistan to have risked her security and helped USA who did not stand by her in the hour of need whenever she needed her help.

In the war of terror Pakistan has all along sided with US and it was largely due to the assistance of Pakistan that US could save her face to have successfully launched an operation in a most difficult terrain. Not only had that but Pakistan incurred annoyance of her reliable tribal folks in the interest of US alone. Tribal areas of Waziristan have always remained autonomous and even British that ruled the sub-continent for two hundred years never ventured to trample that area. Quaid-e-Azam also did not force them to remain under administrative control of Pakistan and extended them favors in recognition of their services to help fight for the rights of Kashmiri brothers in 1947. Although US has promised to remain firmly committed with Pakistan and help her resolve differences with India including the core issue of Kashmir but it is yet to be seen how far US goes to help settle the issue, on which India is not prepared to compromise easily.

Dr. Maqsood jafri chairman of Kashmir Dialogue Forum in a meeting held in New York on Jan. 15, 2011, with the senior officers of US department Washington D.C, talking on latest situation in Kashmir deplored attitude of US government time and again for non fulfillment of the promises to pressure India to resolve Kashmir problem and hold plebiscite under the auspices of united Nation committed by her in Security Counsel. In the first instance President Johnson during India China war in 1962 asked Pakistan not to attack India on Kashmir border in spite of encouragement from China and assured that the matter would be resolved amicably. Then again President Barack Obama in his election speech promised to appoint an envoy to sort out Kashmir problem with India but he also forgot the promise after elections. Mr. Jafri stressed that India is an aggressor and US should not lobby for India's becoming permanent member of U.N. Mr. Nasir Gilgati secretary general of the Kashmir dialogue forum asked the American officials to pressurize India to concede to the genuine demand of Kashmiris. Mr. Karen Roushkob, the adviser of Kashmir Dialogue Forum also participated.

Drone attacks by USA on North Waziristan are being launched since 2004. Whereas the USA justify their use to restrict and eliminate militancy in the region where many important Al-Qaeda and Taliban leaders, and fighters have been killed , the pro Taliban Islamic groups call it an undeclared war on Pakistan who blame the government as an ally for the killings, mostly civilians, school going children and innocent people. It is an unending war neither the militants are going to stop hostilities, suicide attacks-insurgency in Afghanistan on US troops and Pakistan, nor USA prepared to stop drone onslaught. A reasonable immediate solution of the problem is required to put an end to the war.

PAKISTAN AND INDIA

The two neighbors India and Pakistan that have much in common been browbeating for the last more than half a century and more often than not tempers went so high that resulted in bloody wars creating further bitterness. People of both the countries and so also their governments at long last have realized that solution of their problems lie in reconciliation and not confrontation. A good will has been created by certain friendly moves from both sides; revival of Cricket series that remained suspended for a long time, opening of rail and road connection not only between Lahore and New Delhi but also from Muzaffarabad to Sirinagar, Khokhra Par and Munabao are a good omen indicative of understanding between the estranged neighbors. Not only there exists a feeling of belonging amongst people on either side but also the super powers U.S.A and U.K besides other important nations are desirous of seeing the two important countries of south Asia coming closer to each other forgetting their bitterness of the past and to start afresh to participate in the elimination of terrorism and rehabilitation of peace and prosperity in the region.

Such favorable situations rarely occur when there is favorable environment at home as well as abroad; people of both conflicting nations and the world powers are desirous of solution of the problems faced by the people of both, for achieving lasting peace in the region that has attained great importance in the global politics. Unlike past decades there is only one super power and no rivals to create an obstacle in achieving the cherished goal. Time and tide wait for no one there is high time that all interested parties; people of both countries, their governments, and well wishers come forward and avail of the opportunity to turn this region into a model of peace and prosperity before it is too late and some rival force jumps in, to create bad blood and misunderstanding that has been a feature over times, and neutralize what has been achieved so far.

The SAARC leadership in their annual meetings persuaded the two neighbors to sit on the negotiating table to resolve all outstanding disputes including Kashmir. The past regime under the leadership of Gen. Parvez Musharraf had taken practical steps to resolve the issues by holding talks at Agra in 2000 and then again to bring the Indians on the core issue of Kashmir. A number of sessions on secretary levels have been held and during U.N. session at New York in October in year (2004) where both Indian prime minister Jag Mohan Singh and president of Pakistan Gen. Parvez Musharraf had met reiterated their resolution to discuss the issue of Kashmir in the forthcoming meetings of head of states of India and Pakistan as per schedule. World powers, the United States and then British Prime Minister Tony Blair were actively involved to bring about a settlement of the issue in the interest of a lasting peace in the region.

During the visit of Ms Condoleezza Rice had announced that US wanted to sell F 16s to India and Pakistan at that Jag Mohan Singh, then Indian Prime minister retorted, it would tantamount to initiating arm race and would annul the efforts of peace being made between the two reconciling countries. Such views of the Indian Prime Minister indicated a healthy change in the attitude and seriousness of India to resolve differences with Pakistan. Neither country wants to repeat the mistakes committed before and to turn the region into an arena of power politics. However, declaration of defense pact with US and collaboration in nuclear technology has naturally caused some concern in Pakistani circle, which may diminish if India continues to show flexibility and cooperation in the settlement of her disputes with Pakistan as committed by its leaders time and again. Ex-President of Pakistan Parvez Musharraf had shown some flexibility in a good gesture, and had asked the Indians to reciprocate, and reduce number of her troops in the valley and stop atrocities on Kashmiri people.

People of both India and Pakistan need clean water- necessities of life to live peacefully, which can be achieved by making sincere efforts to resolve their outstanding disputes with open heart and mind keeping into consideration humanitarian rather than religious or communal differences. We pray to God All Mighty to help maintaining the spirit of good will that has been generated between the two people - residing on either side India or Pakistan.

CHAPTER XXIII
MARTIAL LAW ADMINISTRATORS TURNED POLITICAL LEADERS

FIELD MARTIAL GEN. AYUB KHAN (1958-1969)

Politicians make mistakes and the generals never fail to cease the opportunity to intervene and take over with the assurance to restore democracy after putting things right and in the process avail themselves of benefits as the supreme authority of the country, only answerable to the God All Mighty. Pakistan, so far has seen four such phases and they have ruled the country for more years than the politicians. People of Pakistan also had been used to such changes and accepted them without much hassle.

President Sikander Mirza was under pressure of demand from the politicians in 1957 to hold elections under the constitution. In order to perpetuate his rule, and frustrate efforts of the politicians invited Gen Ayub Khan to impose Martial law and appointed him as CMLA. Ayub Khan instead of retaining him as President deported him and his wife to England and resumed full control of the Administration, abrogating the 1956 constitution. After taking over he took strict measures against, politicians, profiteers, adulterators, smugglers and imposed heavy fines against the defaulters. With the result prices of articles of daily use sharply lowered, adulterated food stuffs were thrown out in the drains and the shop keepers of the Anarkali Bazar Lahore got rid of the smuggled goods lest they should be caught and punished. These measures of Ayub Khan earned him wide appreciation of the General Public.

He then to keep the politicians quiet offered them the option of (ABDO) to withdraw from political activities for five years. Those agreed were exempted from any inquiry or investigation against their illegal assets. Most of the politicians accepted the offer and accepted Ayub Khan as head of the state. He took a number of steps to introduce reforms at various aspects of social and political life, which included land, educational and industrial reforms and B.D. system — an indigenous form of democracy. Ayub Khan instead of restoring parliamentary system introduced a new political system named Basic Democracies and promulgated the order 1959 to implement the same.

The first election of BDs was held in January 1960 in which 40,000 BD members were elected from each province that elected Ayub Khan as president. The BDs according to the constitutions of 1962 were to elect the president and the members of the provincial and National Assemblies. In the year 1964 such election were again held and Begum Fatima Jinnah was contesting election for the seat of president against Ayub Khan. As a large scale rigging, Ayub Khan was declared successful, before results from far-flung areas could be received and counted. It was largely the feat of bureaucrats who were helping themselves from both hands during his autocratic rule. Bengalis who almost entirely favored Begum Fatima Jinnah were particularly discouraged and the separatist movements got momentum. It was a golden opportunity for the General to acquit himself honorably to maintain spirit of unity thus generated.

1965 WAR AGIANST INDIA
India attacked Pakistan on Sep. 6, 1965, Ayub Khan handled the situation very competently; not only the attack of a much bigger force was halted but in a matter of few days Pakistani force got upper hand on the ground, air and in the seas. Pakistan not only made advancement in Kashmir but also conquered sizable area including Khemkaran town in Ferozepur, East Punjab. The whole nation was united and delighted chanted slogans in favor Gen. Ayub Khan in all nooks corners of the country that helped consolidate his autocratic rule.

AYUB KHAN'S DOWN FALL
In 1968 however, Ayub Khan had to resign under pressure of the politicians and large scale uprising against his rule primarily due to Tashqand declaration that demoralized the nation greatly. He tried his best to pacify the masses, called round table conference and accepted their demand of restoring parliamentary and direct election system but all in vain and he had to resign in 1969.

FAMILY LAWS
In order to give protection to the women folk he introduced family laws; Family Laws Ordinance was promulgated in 1961 through which polygamy was prohibited except under special circumstances as also emphasized in the holy Quran.

The Family Laws prescribed marriageable age for males and the female and maintenance allowance for the divorced women and her children.

A man wishing to divorce his wife shall have to go through union council and its reconciliatory process before the divorce was effective by law.

Family planning program was also introduced and supported to check high population growth. These family laws are still in practice and were much appreciated particularly by the women folk.

LAND REFORMS

Ayub Khan appointed Land reform commission in October 1958 to curtail land holdings of big land lords and to give ownership of the same to the sitting tenants. As against land reforms of 1971 by Zulfiqar Ali Bhutto that confiscated extra lands without compensation, Ayub Khan's reforms made the beneficiaries to pay the price on easy installments to the land lords. The minimum limit of land holding was also fixed 12.5 acres.

GEN. YAHYA KAHN (1968-1971)

In the wake of virulent agitation, Ayub Khan decided to step down and resigned on 25th March1969. General Yahya Khan took over and declared himself as Martial Law Administrator.

Yahya Khan abrogated the 1962 constitution, banned all political activities, dissolved the National and Provincial Assemblies, and dismissed the central and provincial cabinets declaring Martial Law throughout the country.

Yahya Khan, in his address to the nation declared that his sole objective was to protect the life; liberty and property of the people and to push the country back to sanity. Yahya Khan inherited disastrous conditions. He had to take a number of steps to put the country back on rails. He adopted following measures:

1. LEGAL FRAME WORK ORDER

When Yahya Khan took over charge of the country he promised to introduce civil rule at the earliest. In order to fulfill his promise for transfer of power he issued the legal Framework Order on 30th March, 1970. The LFO was meant to serve as a guide to future line of action with respect to transfer of power. It provided 313 seats for the National Assembly.

2. GENRAL ELECTIONS 1970

Yahya Khan ordered the general elections under the Legal Framework Order to fill 300 seats of the National Assembly, while thirteen seats were reserved for women; the political parties welcomed the decision and put up their candidates for the elections.

The Awami League under Sheikh Mujeeb-ur-Rehman issued its election manifesto based on his six point formula, which in other words aimed at separation from the center seeking provincial autonomy. But Yahya Khan did not permit Sheikh Mujeeb — Awami League to use six points as their election manifesto which he considered was against the solidarity of the country.

In West Pakistan, however, all the parties conducted their election campaigns under LFO peacefully. People's Party Slogan "food, shelter and roof", however, became readily popular particularly amongst the poor masses, which constitute more than 70% of the population. The educated class was attracted by his call for Islamic Socialism. Because of his appealing program People's Party swept the elections in West Pakistan beating hollow the long established Muslim League, Jamaat-e-Islami, and Awami National Party of Wali Khan in Peshawar.

Sh. Mujeeb-ur-Rehman erected his campaign on the basis of the right of the Bengalis. Awami league contested the election on Mujeeb's six points manifesto and heavily played up the grievances of the East Pakistanis and kept on telling them that West Pakistanis had usurped their rights. Other Bengali leaders like Maulana Bhashani, Dr. Kamal Hussian and Taj-ud-Din Ahmed added fuel to the fire with speeches and shoved the people of East Pakistan to the point of no return.

Polling was held on December 1970. The results of the elections were a stunning setback for other political parties; Jamaat-e-Islami, PML and NAP (Wali Group) had to face humiliating defeat. The Awami League secured 75.11% of total votes cast in East Pakistan. Nur-ul-Amin and Raja Tridev were the only candidates who won their seats in East Pakistan. In West Pakistan the PPP got more than 60 % of total votes and 82 seats out of 138 allocated to the western wing.

3. YAHYA, MUJIB AND BHUTTO

According to the legal Framework Order, the National Assembly was to frame the constitution in 120 days. The election results made it clear that the future of the country rested with three forces that had authority and importance i.e. the military, the PPP and the Awami League.

After winning the elections, Mujeeb had adopted a rigid line of action. He argued that as the people of East Pakistan had given their verdict in favor of his six points, therefore, he or anybody else could not amend the six points program.

On the other hand Z.A. Bhutto, PPP's Chairman had demanded due recognition for his party in the power set up. He declared that no constitution could be framed, nor could any Government in the center be set up without his party's co-operation. He said that both Awami League and PPP were two majority parties in West and East Pakistan.

Mujeeb was not prepared to share power with Bhutto. He adopted stubborn attitude. In fact Mujeeb acted as the Indian PM Mrs. Indira Gandhi and other High-ups in the Indian Foreign and Defense Ministries wanted him to do. Mujeeb was a separatist and had played an active role in the Aggartalla Conspiracy, which was aimed at dismembering Pakistan during Ayub's regime.

Bhutto went to Dhaka on January 20, 1970 and held talks with Mujeeb. The Awami League leadership adopted a determined stance on the Six Points program and refused to budge from their previous position. Having failed to pull Mujeeb down from his dictatorial position, Bhutto adopted a stern line of action on Six Points.

Yahya Khan convened NA session on March 3, 1971 at Islamabad. Bhutto demanded the postponement of the Assembly session and waving of 120 days limit for framing the constitution. Mujeeb insisted to hold NA session at Dacca. Bhutto forbade his party members to go to Dhaka to attend the NA session, when Mujeeb was not prepared to come to Islamabad for the NA session convened by Yahya Khan.

Bhutto's treats produced immediate effect and Yahya Khan postponed assembly session of March 1, 1971. The postponement surprised Mujeeb who had planned to emerge as "founding father" of Bangladesh in connivance with his Indian masters by declaring independence in the Parliament. The next date of NA session was fixed for March 25, 1971.

The Postponement of assembly session set ablaze the situation in East Pakistan. Mujeeb launched his civil disobedience movement on March 2, 1971. He demanded transfer of power as pre-condition to any negotiation and put forward his demands, which were as follows.

Immediate withdrawal of Martial Law

Immediate re-call of all military JKLT/barracks

An inquiry into the loss of life

Immediate transfer of power to the elected representatives

Immediate cessation of Military Build-ups and heavy inflow of military from West Pakistan

In reaction to Mujeeb's demands, Bhutto also demanded transfer of power to two assemblies: West and East Pakistan.

4. AWMI LEAGUE'S REVOLT

After issuing his demands Mujeeb did not wait for the government's response and permitted his workers to go on the rampage. There was wide-scale killing, looting and arson in East Pakistan from the first week of March 1971. The Awami League workers killed indiscriminately all those who did not agree with Six Points program. The non-Bengalis and Pro-Pakistanis were ruthlessly slaughtered. Some of the prominent Bengali Leaders like Maulana Farid Ahmed of Nizam-e-Islam party and Fazal-ul-Qadir Chaudhri of PML were made to suffer public humiliation and later on killed brutally for their support to Pakistan. Non-Bengalis who had settled in East Pakistan for business purposes and for their jobs were forced to surrender their belongings to Awami League workers.

The Awami League, in open defiance of the authorities, declared a unilateral withdrawal of Martial Law from East Pakistan. It also decided to proclaim independence and take-over Government on March 24, 1971. Yahya Khan ordered the military to move out and restore law and order. The Awami League was banned and a number of its prominent leaders including Mujeeb were arrested.

5. WAR OF 1971 WITH INDIA

With the launching of military action against Awami League, Civil War between the army and supporters of Pakistan and Awami League began.

The military action restored the authority of the Government. The rebels fled and crossed over to India. It mostly consisted of rebels and Indian personnel in white clothes. Gen. Tikka Khan was sent to help restoring law and order by helping the civil administration. He carried out the job and after restoring law and order suggested Gen. Yahya Khan to seek a political solution to avoid deterioration to which Yahya Khan did not give priority that provided India an opportunity to exploit and black mail Pakistan at international level. The massive influx of refugees into Indian Territory provided a pretext to India to exploit the issue and blackmail Pakistan on International level. Mrs. Indira Gandhi, then Indian PM claimed that with the coming of Pakistani refugees from East Pakistan, Indian economy had come under tremendous pressure. She demanded the return of the refugees to their homes but only if there was a government which they could trust. On June 3rd, 1971 Indian Defense Ministry declared, "We will not send these refugees to Yahya Khan's Pakistan but will only allow them to return to Sheikh Mujeeb's Bangladesh." On June 30th, 1971, two Indian agents pretending to be the Kashmiri freedom fighters hijacked an Indian plane to Lahore, *which* provided an excuse to India to ban all flights of Pakistani aircrafts over the Indian Territory thus cutting the airborne supply to East Pakistan.

6. INDIA-USSR DEFENSE PACT

As India had planned to attack Pakistan, she concluded a Defense Pact with the former USSR on 9th August, 1971. The main objective of this treaty was to seek protection from a Super power against any other country, which may have come to the side of Pakistan in the War. On 11th August, 1971 the Indian foreign minister informed the parliament that now on no country could stop India from taking unilateral action in East Pakistan. The Indian PM Mrs. Indira Gandhi demanded withdrawal of Pakistani troops from East Pakistan. On 17th August, 1971 Pakistan appealed to the UN Secretary-General to intervene and set up a committee of the Security Council in East Pakistan, which India did not agree.

In November 1971 Indian troops began crossing the border of East Pakistan and assisted Mukti Bahini to attack Pakistan army. The Indian army launched a massive offensive against Pakistan army on 21st Nov. 1971. On 3rd December, 1971 a full-scale war broke out on the West Pakistan-India border and Kashmir. On 16th December, 1971, East Pakistan fell to the Indian aggression. Dhaka was surrendered to the Indian troops and nearly 90,000 Pakistani troops were taken as POWs.

The fall of Dhaka was brought about through an International conspiracy in which India and USSR played a major role. The defeat of Pakistan in East Pakistan war of 1971 and the dismemberment of the country disgraced the Pakistan army. The army rule ended in disaster and Yahya had to step down making way for Z.A. Bhutto to take-over.

ZULFIQAR ALI BHUTTO (1971-1977)

After the fall of Dacca the whole nation was ceased with grief and dejection. Yahya Khan no more wanted to continue his office. In the first instance he asked the senior army Generals to take over the responsibility of running the affairs and later hand over the Administration to the elected representatives but the Generals refused. Yahya Khan then was left with no choice but to invite Zulfiqar Ali Bhutto the leader of majority party who had won maximum seats from West Pakistan. Bhutto was in New York where he had been sent to plead Pakistan's case that had fallen victim to a blatant Indian aggression. He accepted the offer and was called back from New York to assume the responsibilities as Martial law Administrator, as there was no constitution in force. He thus run the country for about two years as Martial Law Administrator-cum President of Pakistan and assumed Prime Minister's office after the introduction and approval of 1973 constitution.

Quad-e-Azam had built the newly born Pakistan with influx of homeless destitute men, women and children from across the border. The newborn state did not have resources to meet the challenge. Quaid-e-Azam courageously and with cooperation of his nation successfully surmounted the problems and in about a year's time made Pakistan a fort of Islam. In the same way Zulfiqar Ali Bhutto was given the task of rebuilding a dilapidated Pakistan without a penny in the treasury and about a hundred thousand personnel and civilians as prisoners of War and their impatient families crying to get their imprisoned relatives back.

Zulfiqar Ali Bhutto accepted the challenge and tracing the footsteps of father of the nation, faced the situation with intellect and fortitude. With the support of his people not only rebuilt and regained Pakistan's prestige- but made it an invincible, prosperous front line country of the world. It was his initiative and foresight that he gave priority to the development of Nuclear Technology in spite of resistance and threats from world powers and paucity of resources at his disposal. It was because of his that daring step that Pakistan is in a position to face a ten times bigger power. But for his initiative the position of Pakistan today would not be much different from Bangladesh-striven with poverty and no say in the world politics.

Those who blame Bhutto as hungry for power and hold him responsible for the catastrophe-separation of the eastern wing are saying so by keeping their eyes shut from the historical facts. Bhutto in fact emerged as a leader of the masses due to his role in 1965 war particularly because of his fiery speech, in Security Council, that reflected the sentiments of the common man. His opposition to a cease fire and then going to Tashqand and accepting humiliating terms raised his political stature which recognized and distinguished him as a top ranking leader. BBC in 1966 after 65 War had pointed out that there was the future president of Pakistan in Mr. Bhutto. Then again when Bhutto was in Sahiwal jail due to his differences with Ayub Khan for agitation against Tashqand declaration, Ayub Khan offered to withdraw in his favor and asked him to stop agitation on that issue-but Bhutto declined the offer saying that he would not accept that from a dictator but he would consider if it was given by the people. He got a clear mandate from the masses in 1970 elections when his new political party swept the elections in West Pakistan and after that Bhutto was justified in assuming responsibilities as head of the state and representative of the people of Pakistan and cannot be labeled as power hungry.

STEPS TO REHABLITATE ECONOMY

Zulfiqar All Bhutto after resumption took a hurricane tour of the Muslim countries and won their support and sympathies for Pakistan. He encouraged them to make investment in Pakistan. He also persuaded them to make recruitments from Pakistan for their expending projects and thus created job opportunities in oil rich countries. This initiative not only solved un-employment at home but a great deal in building foreign exchange reserves of the country. Then at home as well he created jobs for the educated unemployed youths by introducing youth volunteer program, which were unique in its nature. The departments were asked to assign them responsibilities and considered them as additional staff and make them regular as soon as a vacancy occurred. Stipend to these volunteers was paid from the exchequer. Hundreds and thousands of youths were thus benefited and got employed.

He introduced a number of reforms to relieve the common man from the exploitation of; industrialists, business tycoons and the bureaucrats. His policies that aimed at welfare of the downtrodden masses and independent stand in the world politics created enemies at home and abroad; particularly uniting the Muslim Umma and development of nuclear power.

ELECTION of 1977

US elections of 1976 resulted in replacement of Jimmy Carter in place of Johnson who had a stiff attitude towards Pakistan. Bhutto approached to meet him through Shah of Iran who conveyed him that he should get a fresh mandate from his people before that. Bhutto who enjoyed overwhelming support of his people, announced general elections about six months earlier than the due date to fulfill US president's condition to meet him.

Elections to the National Assembly were announced on March 7th and for Provincial on March 10. Because of great popularity of PPP no political party of even national status dared contesting elections alone. As such 9 parties joined to form an alliance named PNA and announced their manifesto "Nizam-e-Mustafa". Even then they were not hopeful of a victory against the most popular ruling party. They collected huge funds for the election campaign. All those who were unhappy with Bhutto's policies of Nationalization of Industries, Schools and colleges or reduction of land holdings and those opposed to his favor to laborers and poor masses donated generously to get rid of apparently Bhutto's regime – but factually Bhutto himself. They launched their election campaign half heartedly and as an eye wash and on the other hand concentrated on paralyzing and ultimately throwing over the government. Before elections, while election campaign was on I happen to meet one of the candidates of the PNA and enquired about prospects of his winning the seat. I was surprised to hear from him who admitted that the election campaign was a farce and instead they were planning to wage an agitation against the Government just after elections and their slogan would be "Dhandly" i.e. rigging.

Result was not much different from the result of 1970 elections when PPP had swept elections in West Pakistan securing more than 60 % seats in the National Assembly. In the 1977 elections PPP won 154 seats and the alliance of 9 parties could secure only 39.

RIGGING ALLEGATION IN 1977 ELECTION

As per planning the PNA leveled wild allegations of a large scale rigging the elections and boycotted Provincial Election, and demanded fresh elections for the National Seats. In order to pacify them Bhutto offered to withdraw from all the seats where in their opinion any rigging was done. Instead of coming to terms they kept on raising hue and cry and started agitation. Mosques were used for the purpose, hardly a score of scared persons mostly maulvis with flags of Muslim league in their hands would chant slogans in favor of PNA and their manifesto defying section 144 imposed by the administration and after a brief show scuffle with police, offered arrests of a few, and would disappear. The agitation had no comparison with those lodged by Muslim League before partition or even against Ayub Khan's government after Tashqand Resolution. But the news of the agitation with enhanced numbers was projected through media to force the government to kneel down or at least come on the negotiation table.

Saudi Arabia offered to mediate and the negotiations started and continued till the night of July 7th, 1977 when the army took over as had been planned by the opposition. While Bhutto was engaged in futile negotiations the conspirators carried on their plan of winning and paralyzing government agencies. A retired General Nawabzada Sher Ali, an active member of the opposition daily came to Aitchison College and sitting with the principal used his telephone for organizing the agitation, considering the place a safe haven to be detected by the intelligence if at all it was there. An employee of Intelligence agency known to me happened to meet me during those days. I enquired from him as to where be his intelligence? Our college telephone was being used for launching movement against the government? He told me to keep quiet as the entire intelligence had been taken over by PNA and the day when there was no one to agitate Intelligence people in civil clothes had to do the job. When Civil and Army intelligence had been made ineffective and the Government agencies had been purchased or won over there was hardly any chance for Bhutto to come out of the turmoil. The huge funds collected for the election campaign in fact were used to destabilize and ultimately overthrow a strong democratic regime — undoubtedly a shameful act on the part of those who under the cover of Nizam-e- Mustafa indulged into Hippocratic acts. Did ever Holy prophet (PBUH) indulged into such tactics to gain power or defeat his opponents?

INVOLVEMENT OF BHUTTO IN MURDER CASE

In the first instance General Zia and his associates wanted to involve Mr. Bhutto in a treason case but later changed their mind because of an earlier inquiry held by Justice Hamudur Rehman in that episode and instead reopened the murder case of Nawab Ahmad Raza Khan Qasuri who was alleged to have been killed on the orders of Zulfiqar Ali Bhutto because his son an MNA from Qasur used to argue a lot with him in the Assembly. Although the FIR lodged with the police had been disposed off after investigation and filed for lack of any evidence during Bhutto's regime yet the same was revived by maneuvering new evidence and witnesses on the assurance that no action would be taken against them, as they only wanted to pressurize and involve Mr. Bhutto and the surety was Chief of the Jamat-e-Islami Mian Tufail — But after implementing their plan awarded capital punishment to all the police officers, with the exception of Mr. Masood Mahmood who was allowed to leave the country and settle in USA. His two sons studying in Aitchison and other members of the family left the country before hand as pre condition to his confessional statement in the court. When the capital punishment was announced for the above stated witnesses their families rushed to Mian Tufail to remind him the promise. He contacted Gen Zia about that – but of no avail. Thus the rest four- five police officials, one of them S.P. Abbas, a neighbor, who was made to agree to record confessional statement on the false assurance of Jamat's chief and the administration before the court was also disposed off — to finish any evidence against the fabrication.

JUDICIO-POLITICAL MUDER!!

The story of proceedings in the court also exposed the designs of the government. In the first instance when the case was initiated in the Lahore High court Justice Zaki-ud-Din Pal set free Mr. Bhutto on bail considering it a weak case of the prosecution. But then the case was transferred to Justice Maulvi Mushtaq, who reared personal grudge with Bhutto, cancelled his bail and re-opened the trial in his court.

When the case was in its initial stages in the High Court a student who belonged to the industrialist family told that the decision to hang Mr. Bhutto had been made. He further disclosed that Justice Maulvi Mushtaq had agreed to award death punishment to Mr. Z.A.Bhutto on the condition that his judgment would not be changed at any stage; neither the Supreme Court nor the mercy appeal before the president. He further said that Zia-ul- Haq would replace President Ch. Fazal Elahi to do the needful. He related the story almost two years before it happened. We did not believe him — but later proved to be exactly the same as he had related.

While the case was being heard Judges on panel found to be divergent were removed or retired. Even then the decision of the death penalty of the Supreme Court was not unanimous. Home Secretary Punjab Mr. Khalid Mahmood wrote a four page differing note, pointing a legal snag, on the mercy appeal and recommended not to uphold the divided decision of the Supreme Court. All heads of states, including USA, Indian Prime Minister, Saudi Arabia who acted as mediator between PNA and Bhutto's

Government, so also the Muslim world appealed to spare his life and hand him over to them being chairman OIC if he was not needed there in Pakistan. Turkey also citing example of her own country to have executed their elected Prime minister, and was repenting, had warned Pakistan President not to repeat that mistake — but in spite of all that, the out of court decision of the group stated above was held. PNA could not eliminate Bhutto by ballot but could do that by bullet!

In the light of aforementioned circumstances; prejudiced Police Investigation, defective judicial procedure, retirement of judges during proceedings, divided judgment, reaction of the world and rejection by majority of the people at home and abroad clearly go to prove that it was a Judicio-Political Assassination when the "Justice Impaired". The Chief Justice Supreme Court justice Anwar-ul-Haq, that it was "Nazaria-e-Zaroorat" and Gen. Zia, the chief executive, termed it a political necessity. In the words of Allama Iqbal it was not politics — but CHANGAZI! (JUDA HO DIN SIASAT SE TAU REH JATI HAI CHANGAZI).

BHUTTO SENT TO THE GALLOWS ON JULY 4, 1979
In the eyes of the world a statesman of high caliber was sent to the gallows. It was not Mr. Bhutto but democracy in Pakistan and the hope of deprived masses, spokesman of the Muslim world who was quieted forever. The entire city of Lahore, heart of Pakistan was burning with large scale rioting and agitation when the news broke. Army squads had been posted from early morning on all streets and cross roads of the city, as the government was aware of the strong reaction of the public on a large scale — but failed to stop the mobs from burning Government vehicles and breaking street lights to give vent to their feelings of dejection, rejection, and anger over that brutal decision and action of Zia-ul-Haq and his associates to have hanged their elected president. The same lot that strangulated democracy accepted hegemony of the army is now clamoring to restore the same — having axed their own feet "Khud Karda Ra Ilaje Neist".

BHUTTO'S REFORMS:
ISLAMIZATION EFFORTS
INTRODUCTION OF ISLAMIC CONSTITUTION
Although his party won the elections on the Manifesto of Socialism and believed in secularism yet gave an Islamic Constitution to the country,

thus fulfilling the promise of Muslim League to bring the nation under the banner of Islam rather the manifesto of his party.

Declaration of Qadianis Non Muslims

Since there is a basic difference in the faiths of Qadianis and the Muslims; Qadianis believe in continuation of prophet hood and justify need of a Mujadid whereas Muslims believe in finality of prophet hood without any room for a Mujaddid when the message had been completed; "Akmalto Lakum Dino kum wa Atmamto Neimati wa Razito Lakum Islama Dina" (Holy Quran). Bhutto referred the matter to the Court who after hearing the arguments from both sides declared the Qadianis as Non Muslims. It was a great step on the part of his government to initiate and implement the decision, at the cost of his own vote bank, as Qadianis voted and would have always done that for Peoples party and not Jamat-e-Islami. What to talk of political party even a dictatorial regime invariably would have avoided such issues. It was a remarkable selfless feat of Z.A. Bhutto and his government to uphold Islam and Islamic values.

BETTING BANNED

Race Clubs were banned that held Horse racing with betting that earned substantial revenue to the government. Without caring for material gains his government banned and closed Race clubs and the land of Lahore Race club was handed over to Lahore Development authority who later converted that into a park. It was undoubtedly a bold step of his government and a service to Islam.

DEDUCTION OF ZAKAT

State Bank during Bhutto regime had suggested a reduction of two and a half percent in the interest rate to the depositors of Savings Account. Agreeing with the proposal and as the percentage was according to the figures of Zakat 2 and a ½ it was termed as Zakat fund which was only applicable to the Savings Accounts and the saving Schemes. Although the action as such was not that Islamic but the distribution of amount thus collected was allocated for the deserving poor and destitute people, as a welfare fund, which was of course a noble act on the part of the Government.

LIQUOR BANNED

The use of liquor and its sale was totally stopped and the wine shops were closed, in pursuance of Islamic Sharia although its sale and purchase yielded substantial revenue as excise duty to the Government As such no earlier government considering it a legacy of the British, ever thought of banning that, which Bhutto's regime did. However, there was some relaxation for Non- Muslims who could get that on obtaining permit from the Government.

NATIONALIZATION PROGRAM

Bhutto's Party had been voted in to implement its manifesto - Socialism and not Islam yet his Government to a great extent served the cause of Islam. His only step towards manifesto of the party was to bring change in the economic system- nationalization of industries. In January 1972 Government took over 31 industrial units. The industries included iron and steel, basic metals, heavy engineering, heavy electrical, motor vehicles, tractor plants, heavy and basic chemicals and petrochemicals. A Board of Industrial Management was set up under federal minister of production to manage the nationalized industries. The step was taken to put an end to sheer exploitation done by few industrialists and to ameliorate labor conditions.

The second phase of nationalization began in 1973 and was completed in *1976.* During this phase mainly the rice husking units, Sugar and edible oil industries were nationalized to stop hoarding. The private commercial Banks were also nationalized. Purpose behind the move was to benefit the labor and the common man who were being exploited by the Industrialists. They were making huge profits, avoiding taxes, and exploiting consumers.

Unfortunately, the program was inducted in haste and without any planning and the result was a chaos. Neither the new Management nor the labor knew how to run the business, tricks of the trade. The step proved to be a misfire. The government later realized their mistake and started denationalization beginning from small units like Rice husking, Oil and Sugar refining. In fact it was an initiative of Dr. Mubashar the Finance Minister and his socialist group and the fault of Mr. Bhutto was that he gave his approval without consulting the owners of the industrial units and financial experts who must have given a better advice to achieve the purpose; the amelioration of workers.

LAND REFORMS

The PPP regime announced land reforms on March 1, 1972. The land-holdings were restricted to 150 acres irrigated land in the first phase

(1972) and later to 100 acres in the second phase (1977). The land-holdings with respect to un-irrigated land were fixed at 300 acres in 1972 and 200 acres in 1977. Total ceiling after 1977 was fixed at 250 acres of irrigated land and 500 acres of un-irrigated land. A large number of landless tenants benefited from the reforms and also helped raising agriculture produce to usher an era of self sufficiency in food and industrial crops.

EDUCATIONAL REFORMS

Bhutto's regime laid great emphasis on making the education free and compulsory. The education policy was announced in March 1972. There was a two-phase program to accomplish the target of educational policy.

First phase was announced in Oct. 1972. During this phase education was made free and compulsory up to class eight.

Second phase was announced in Oct. 1974 and the education was made free and compulsory up to class ten.

New educational institutions/schools were to be opened to meet the requirement of compulsory and free education. All privately owned schools and institutions with the exception of Aitchison College Lahore were nationalized. Most of the schools were run on commercial grounds where teachers were being exploited; were paid low salaries and forced to sign on Government scales to cover the irregularity. Moreover, there was no security of jobs and their services could be terminated without any notice, invariably terminated before summer vacations. Nationalization of educational institutions helped a great deal in improving the financial position and working conditions of the teachers who also developed self confidence among them. There are black sheep everywhere and it is wrong to say that the teachers stopped exerting or became slack, which is not true and a blatant allegation on the teachers who have deserve respect that mould character of youths and groom a nation.

Opening of New Universities

Three new Universities at Saidu, Multan and Sukkur were set up and five new Boards of Intermediate and Secondary Education at Rawalpindi, Gujranwala, Bahawalpur, Saidu and Khairpur were

established. Engineering Colleges in Karachi, Jamshoro and Peshawar were upgraded to the Universities level.
A UGC was set-up.

LABOR REFORMS

Bhutto's regime introduced labor reforms in 1972-73 to pacify the labor force and to implement PPP's election manifesto that "Socialism is our economy". The labor reforms were as follows.

All the workers of the industrial concerns were given medical cover, compensation for injuries at work, compulsory group insurance and safeguards against arbitrary termination of service.

Under the Labor Laws Ordinance of 1975, steps were taken to check the undue formation of trade unions.

The Industrialists and factory owners were made responsible to bear the expenditures of the education of at least one child of every worker employed in their factory.

New rules were announced regarding the bonus, gratuity, leave compensation and retirement.

Social Security scheme was compulsorily applied to all the industries.

FOREIGN POLICY

When Mr. Bhutto took over the reins of the country, Pakistan's image had been badly tarnished due to its defeat in the war in 1971. In order to re-build Pakistan's image, Bhutto embarked upon the tour of friendly Muslim countries. Bhutto undertook tours of twenty-two countries and explained his foreign policy to all the nations he visited. He also visited China and former USSR, which were of great importance. Bhutto's reforms in domestic politics and his foreign policy of bilateral relationship made a healthy impact on the public opinion in the US. Consequently the ties of friendship between US and Pakistan were renewed and the US economic assistance became available.

The Second Summit Conference of the OIC held at Lahore in Feb. 1974. It was a great achievement under the leadership of Mr. Bhutto. It gave a tremendous boost to Pakistan's reputation on the International level. Bhutto emerged as an articulate statesman and elevated position amongst the world's statesmen and politicians. At the end of the Summit a Joint Communiqué known as "Lahore Declaration" was issued.

DEVELOPMENT OF NUCLEAR TECHNOLOGY

After the fall of Dacca and bifurcation Pakistan's capacity and capability was greatly reduced. The only way to strike a balance of power between the erstwhile rivals was to acquire a technology which could bring the two states at par or to accept hegemony of India for all times to come. Mr. Bhutto not only thought of it but also took practical steps in fulfilling that dream. He strived to collect funds to meet the expenses also in the first instance with the approval of US obtained Reprocessing plant from France. Later with indigenous technology and the fuel obtained as a bi-product defying objections of the world powers managed to give the country the most needed weapon of defense, for which he had to pay a heavy price; he not only got removed from the slot of Premiership but also removed physically from the world. If today Pakistan feels herself secure and enjoys respect in the region, owes greatly to Z.A. Bhutto's far sightedness and boldness.

GEN. ZIA-UL-HAQ (1977-1988)

At the end of Bhutto's government, Zia-ul-Haq takes over on July 5, 1977, as Martial Law Administrator (1977-1988)

Gen. Zia-ul-Haq got commission in the army in 1945. He held different command positions in the Pakistan army and was also sent on an assignment to Jordan. While he was posted in Multan Zulfiqar Ali Bhutto, then Prime Minister was visiting Nawab Sadiq Hussain Qureshi the chief Minister Punjab, who belonged to Multan, whom Zia-ul-Haq had requested to find an opportunity for him to see Mr. Bhutto whenever he happened to be in Multan. Nawab Sadiq thus arranged the same. Bhutto enquired Zia the purpose of his meeting to which he replied that he only wanted to pay his respects and showed great humility — instead of shaking hands went on his feet, which Bhutto did not appreciate. However, he got an impression about him, of a simple nonirritant officer. In 1976 when Bhutto had sensed some trouble with the Generals keeping in mind that impression appointed Zia –ul-Haq as chief of army staff ignoring a number of seniors raising him to a full General. Bhutto must have greatly repented his selection when the same humble man deposed him in 1977 and later in 1979 got him executed by implicating him in a murder case, which according to the prosecution was committed on his behest and had been filed after police investigation while he was in office.

IMORTTANT EVENTS OF ZIA'S RULE

1. Political Activities banned
Issued provincial constitutional Order (PCO) in March 1981; under that order it was declared that efforts will be made to restore democracy and representative institutions as early as possible, till then political activities will be banned.

2. Majlis-e-Shora (federal council) was nominated in December
1981. It was initially an advisory body that later on converted into a legislative forum by the president.

3. Elections for local bodies were held in 1983 on non-party basis.
The same on party basis were avoided because of popularity of the People's party.

4. Referendum to keep the slot of President was held to
perpetuate his authority as supreme power in 1984, the question that the voters were supposed to answer was "If you want an Islamic rule in accordance with Quran and Sunnah in the country?" and if the answer was Yes which meant that you voted for Zia-ul-Haq as president of Pakistan. The referendum was simply eyewash. Turnout on the polling stations was nominal, as most of the people and the political parties boycotted the futile exercise. However, Zia-ul-Haq thus secured his position.

GENERAL ELECTIONS 1985
After securing his position as President through that fake referendum he announced elections to the National and Provincial assemblies but again on non-party basis for the same reason i.e. because of the fear of the People's party sweeping the elections. The same were held in Feb. 1985. Muhammad Khan Junejo was nominated as Prime minister by Zia-ul-Haq.

JUNEJO GOVERNMENT DISSOLVED
There occurred some differences on the issue of conflict between some army personnel's and the civilians in Rawalpindi. During Zia's regime army considered it a supreme authority whereas Junejo government wanted to punish those who were found guilty and also on some other differences, Zia dissolved the civil government of Junejo using his power under 8th Amendment.

DE - ISLAMIZATION POLICIES OF ZIA-UL-HAQ

Unlike Zulfiqar Ali Bhutto Zia-ul-Haq came to power on the mandate of bringing Nizam-e- Mustafa i.e. implementation of Islamic law but on the other hand he took steps under pressure to save his skin against Islamic values and tradition.

Exemption of Zakat

Zia-ul-Haq relaxed the deduction of Zakat for Fiqah-e-Jafaria and others when they demonstrated against it in Islamabad in large numbers. Instead of referring the issue to a court of law or to the Islamic Counsel exempted it at his own for those who declare belonging to Fiqah Jaafria or Hanfia thus forfeiting the very purpose of the Institution that was meant to raise funds to help widows and the poor folk.

Bifurcation of Islamic Studies

Zia-ul-Haq again accepted the demand of the demonstrators at Islamabad to bifurcate teaching of Islamic studies. A separate course of studies was approved for Fiqah Jafaria, without referring it to a court of law or any Counsel of Ulemas or on a logical justification- when both Shia and Sunni believe in the same book and follow the tradition and Sunnet-e-Nabi there was hardly any need for the exercise that only encouraged sectarianism and division.

Patronization of Sectarian Extremist Groups

It was during Zia-ul-Haq's regime that extremist Organizations, Sipah Sahaba and Sipah Mohammad were established and started killing each other that resulted in extreme polarization and promoted sectarianism, which is neither in the interest of the state nor for maintaining unity of Islam. As a result there of besides loss of a number of Ulemas, Scholars, Government officers, places of worships of either sects have been targeted and daily prayers even cannot be held without police or armed guards.

Patronization of a party established on Linguistic basis (MQM)

He encouraged formation of the party on linguistic basis — an unconstitutional step to gain political benefits, to reduce vote bank of other parties popular in the province particularly Jamaat-e-Islami and the PPP.

Present government has taken some practical steps to defuse the tension and feelings of bitterness that had since been generated and has already banned the extremist parties to restore the spirit of unity and harmony among the two sects of Islam that existed before. Let us hope that sanity prevails and everyone realizes and makes effort to remove misunderstandings that are a result of ignorance and lack of knowledge of religion. An effort through this publication has been made to educate the readers about fundamentals of Islam, torchbearers of life in this world and the hereafter, which is the only effective way of healing the ailing nation inadvertently infected by the above stated wrong moves.

Gen. Parvez Musharraf President - Army Chief (1999 - 2008)

General Parvez Musharraf took over as Chief Executive (Martial Law Administrator) of the country deposing the Muslim League Government of Mian Nawaz Sharif in Nov. 1999 accusing him of charges of corruption, nepotism, high jacking his plane etc. Mian Nawaz Sharif and most of his family members were put under arrest but later sent to Saudi Arabia on an understanding (deal) that they would abstain from active politics for about ten years. Ms Bhutto was already in self-exile and thus Gen. Parvez Musharraf got an opportunity to induct a Government of his own choice assuming the slot of President and also the army chief. The parliament elected as a result of 2002 elections not only confirmed his nomination as President but also approved with a majority vote to retain the office of army chief as well.

General elections were to be held in Jan. 2008, and till then the electorate was supposed to remain in office. Zafrullah Khan Jamali was the first elected Prime Minister under that set up and later he was asked to resign to make room for Mr. Shaukat Aziz, a financial expert. A number of steps taken on his initiative bolstered the economy and raised the finances of the country. Besides financial betterment Pakistan's image in the global politics had also been enhanced. Pak-India relations had also improved considerably and there was a hope that the two neighbors would further come closer and developed understanding to live peacefully by resolving their conflicts with mutual faith including the longstanding core issue of Kashmir. Resolution of which would not only be helpful for building economies of the countries but also would raise the position and image of the leaders particularly Parvez Musharraf who had all along and whole-heartedly pursued Kashmir issue at various levels. He after consultation with his government and the Kashmiri leadership had given some practicable proposals leaving their stance of implementation of UN resolutions and now it was the turn of India to come forward with her response with an open mind to resolve the long standing bone of contention between two immediate neighbors. But as usual India so far has stuck to her guns and there seems little hope of a peaceful solution of the problem.

Catastrophe of October 8th, 2005 had been attended to capably by the government both through local and foreign help. The timely action could save hundreds of lives, and provided food, shelter and medical facilities to the affected that numbered in millions. The Government has also undertaken to reconstruct the towns and to also provide finances to the affected for repairs and reconstruction of their dilapidated/damaged dwellings to be able to restart their life.

Yet another most important and sensitive issue was the restoration of normalcy, on the western borders in collaboration with coalition forces. The region is the most difficult terrain inhabited by one of the bravest professional fighters that the Gen. had taken upon himself to tackle, extend control and introduce rule of law in tribal territories – remained autonomous regions; no one ever thought of touching the issue before – technically there cannot be a state within the state – but dualism had been allowed, most probably for some political considerations and even the Quaid-e- Azam ignored that for considerations that the people of the tribal areas instead of creating any concern had been helpful in the freedom struggle. Dualism in fact depicts weakness at the center. If the center is strong such issues do not emerge. Present situation in the areas demanded to straighten things and find a permanent solution to the problem once for all, which only a strong government like the one could handle and resolve the issue and implement single rule of law within the territorial limits of Pakistan. The goal ought to be achieved through persuasion and education as they are very much Pakistanis and love their country. The objective thus achieved would greatly help improving law and order situation in the region dispensing with safe havens for criminals.

He also effectively handled sectarian problem by banning the parties that under the banner of Islam were killing one another and attacking the mosques and places of religious sanctity of either faction so much so that even the prayers in the mosques were held under police protection. Through education and negotiations the situation had been controlled and the tension greatly reduced so also the incidences. Some of the hard liners have gone underground – continuation of the measures is required to uproot the menace-a manifestation of intolerance. Mosques, institutions and places of worship are meant to generate fear of God and purify souls, spread knowledge and turn out Iqbals, Muhammad Ali Jinnahs and not extremists, terrorists, and suicide bombers, somebody – the financers, government or the society has to ensure that.

As civil president he was doing well and things were moving smoothly. He had promised to hold free and fair elections in 2008 and to take off his uniform before that, which he did – but at the last leg of his tenure took some extra judicial steps; dismissed judiciary, introduced emergency, mishandled judges, lawyers, media men, unceremonious return of a former Prime Minister of the country, Mian Nawaz Sharif in August 2007. The unfortunate assassination of a very popular leader Benazir Bhutto chair person of the biggest political party of the country, who was invited to help restoring democracy, greatly deteriorated law and order situation in the country and lowered his image at home and abroad. So much so, that his confided ally US was also critical of his moves and had threatened to stop military aid until free and fair polls were held, which were held on Feb. 18, 2008 instead of Jan. 2008, due to assassination of Mohtarma Benazir Bhutto.

As a result, there of PPP emerged as party in majority in the National Assembly with Muslim League N securing second position, both the parties agreed on coalition and decided to share Government proportionately at the center and in the Punjab province. Mr. Yousuf Raza Gillani a senior MNA elect from Multan of PPP was sworn in as Prime Minister and the rest of the coalition Ministers were sworn in by President Musharraf, PML N nominees did that under protest by wearing black bandages on their shoulders. Governments in the provinces with mutual consensus have also been formed and taken oath of their respective portfolios. However, on the difference occurring due to delay in the restoration of judges as agreed upon earlier between the parties, Muslim league N has decided to sit on opposition benches in the center till such time the agreement is implemented in letter and spirit. In the mean time under pressure from the major political parties, PPP and PML N, President Parvez Musharraf had to resign on 8/18/08, who otherwise was threatened to face impeachment proceedings, which included a number of grievous charges leveled against him by the coalition parties. Mr. Asif Ali Zardari acting chairman of PPP was nominated by his party, and elected as the New President of Pakistan in the election held in September 2008.

BENAZIR BHUTTO (1953-2007)

Two times Prime Minister Chair person of the biggest political party founded by her father Zulfiqar Ali Bhutto was born in Larkana Sind on June 21, 1953. She received her early education at St. Mary's, Rawalpindi and Convent Jesus and Marry Murree hills, a resort 40 miles northeast of Rawalpindi when her father was a Minister in Ayub Khan's Government. Later, she got admission at Harvard USA from where she completed graduation, for her Masters she went to Oxford England and besides qualifying in Economics and Politics, chaired student union at the University.

She also accompanied her father to India in 1973, when he went to Simla to accord the historic "Simla Agreement". She thus had some grooming from her father, an eminent politician, originally a lawyer. She returned after completing her studies a few weeks before Gen. Zia-ul-Haq dismissed his Government through military coup July 5, 1977. While his two sons Mir Murtaza Bhutto and Shah Nawaz Bhutto were in Europe she along with her mother pursued the murder case instituted against her father and after about two years of court procedures he was executed on July 4, 1977. She along with her mother remained under house arrest and also confined in jail and later went to England where she stayed for about 7 years. She returned to Pakistan in 1986 and was accorded the warmest ever reception at Lahore airport by her party workers and well-wishers in million. The entire city of Lahore presented a festive look, men, women, children kept standing on either side of the road for hours to have a glimpse of their leader while she moved slowly standing on the top of a truck.

Her party then swept the elections held in 1988 and took over as Prime Minister of Pakistan. She said, although she was briefed by her father when she went to see him last time before his execution that it was her choice to settle in USA or Europe and live a peaceful life or to adopt a political career which undoubtedly would be exciting but challenging. She elected to choose the political career to complete the mission of her father and to avenge unjust assassination of her father and on assuming the slot as chief executive of her country, she remarked, "I have taken the revenge", and then by serving her people she would do the rest.

Although her government was dismissed just within 18 months of her taking oath she did not lose heart and again resumed the position within two years when the same president Ghulam Ishaq Khan dismissed her successor Mian Nawaz Sharif on similar charges. She again won the elections and took over as Prime Minister of the country in 1993. She was on her mission to ameliorate the lot of her deprived country men, created jobs and provided shelter but again she was not allowed to complete her tenure when her party president appointed by her Mr. Farooq Leghari using the same extra judicial order 58 2B dismissed her Government on unfounded corruption charges and also involving her spouse whom she wedded in 1987 in the murder case of her real brother. She faced the charges and her husband also remained in jail for more than 8 years but nothing could be established against either of them. She along with her 3 children and mother settled in Dubai, looked after the family and also the spouse facing trial in jail.

After ruling for more than 8 years as head of state, Parvez Musharraf desired to democratize the country and to revive the 1973 constitution but at the same time wanted to maintain his hegemony by retaining his position as President. According to 1973 constitution he could only be a figure head and not the executive head. He, therefore, before elections made necessary amendments through an ordinance including, Martial Law regulation 58 2 B, that vests in him the power to dismiss the elected parliament without assigning reasons not challengeable in any court to have an upper hand over the Prime Minister. In order to put his plan into practice he contacted prominent political parties; he met Benazir Bhutto in Dubai and made her the offer to withdraw pending cases against her, allow her to come back in Pakistan and carry election campaign to contact the masses. Benazir accepted the proposal with reservations particularly not agreeing to amendment in the constitution, the power to dismiss the government as she had twice been a victim to that weapon.

However, Benazir came back, most probably on the understanding not to keep the whip of Martial law regulation — but to consider balance of powers between President and the Prime Minister. Parvez Musharraf's party was not happy over the deal and her return to Pakistan; they were well aware of her popularity and had witnessed the scene when she returned after self exile in 1986. They knew once the episode is replayed would doom their political career or at least dwarf their stature in politics to the extent that their dream of becoming Prime Minister, would be doomed forever. Their party leadership had been expressing these views through the press to prejudice the authority to reconsider his point of view.

Benazir in the mean time decided to return, in spite of all the risks involved and landed at Karachi air port on October 18, 2007 and as expected once again was warmly received by teeming million. She was supposed to reach Mazar-e-Quaid-i-Azam from the airport a distance less than ten miles that normally should have been covered in about an hour but the crowd was so big and the entire rout was so much jammed with people that her motorcade was moving at a snail's speed and could cover half the distance in 5 – 6 hours when at a crossing at Shahrai Faisel suddenly lights went off and two huge blasts occurred on either side of Mohtarma's vehicle, killing about hundred and fifty; men, women and children and wounding over 500, some of them seriously.

Mohtarma and her party leaders remained safe, and were removed to Bilawal House Clifton. The incident grieved Ms Bhutto greatly in the first instance at the loss of innocent valuable lives and secondly not to have fulfilled her desire to meet and address her country men and women whom she wanted to meet and talk after a long time. The tragedy undoubtedly occurred due to lapse in security arrangements – the authorities were aware of the danger and had been receiving anonymous calls yet adequate protection to the leader could not be provided. Not only that half hearted inquiry and investigations were made and no attention was paid to the demand of PPP to probe the incident through some foreign agency. The attitude of the administration, inadequate security arrangements and earlier public statements - threats of some ruling party leaders, created doubts in the minds of the public.

However, in spite of the tragic incident and insufficient security arrangements, Benazir remained determined to continue her mission to meet the people to assure them that she had come to Pakistan to usher an era of peace and prosperity putting an end to oppression and suppression of the dictatorial rule to ensure them a better future. She was welcome every where she went, in Balochistan, Sind, N.W.F.P, Punjab and lastly when she was returning home after giving a sentimental speech at Liaqat Bagh Rawalpindi met with another fatal suicidal attack made by some unknown hired killers and thus she breathed her last on December 27, 2007 leaving a dejected lot of mourners in millions all over the country and her supporters abroad.

It was undoubtedly a great shock for the nation to have lost their leader at a time when a ray of hope was visible on the horizon. The assassination of Benazir has been condemned all over at home and abroad and has been admitted not only a national but an international- irreparable loss and the vacuum created by her departure would be difficult to fulfill as magnanimous intelligent, brave, devoted leaders of her caliber are seldom born. The crowds she attracted because of her beautiful flowery speeches reminded of the days of Quid-e-Azam and her father Zulfiqar Ali Bhutto. The reaction shown by general public, her lovers and followers at home and abroad speak of the degree of admiration she distinctly enjoyed by the people. Every eye was grieved and everyone expressed feelings of immense sorrow by holding programs through media and conveying messages of condolences to the grieved family and President Musharraf who also felt greatly sorry and announced three days national mourning to fly national flag at half mast.

Investigations at home and also through Scot Land Yard police have been conducted, one of the offenders has been arrested while others are still at large and declared proclaimed offenders but no clue of those behind the tragedy could be found. The new prime minister, Mr. Yousuf Raza Gillani has, however, declared that the investigation of the case would be held by UN Agency. After approval from the National Assembly the case has been referred to the agency, which has accepted the same and have ensued investigations of the tragedy.

It may be pointed out that it is not the first tragedy in the family; her father and two brothers have been martyred almost in a similar fashion that goes to prove that there exists a deep conspiracy against the family. Let us hope the culprits and the hands at their back are traced out so that such occurrences in future could be avoided — forestalled. As desired by Benazir Bhutto, elections have been held and her party as per her aspirations along with its allies has swept the elections defeating the ruling party with a wide margin and are in a position to dictate terms. Mr. Yousuf Raza Gillani has been unanimously elected as leader of the house in the national assembly and the remaining cabinet members have been sworn in. Bilawal Bhutto- Zardari son of Benazir Bhutto has been appointed as chair man of the party who is being represented by his father Asif Ali Zardari till such time Bilawal comes of age. He presently is a student at Oxford and after completion of his studies would return to Pakistan to participate in politics and head his party to complete the mission of his family mentioned by him in a press conference convened in London on Jan. 8, 2008.

CHAPTER XXV

MAJOR POLITICAL PARTIES OF PAKISTAN

There are two categories of political parties in Pakistan; parties of national level having supporters and membership in all the four provinces; Muslim League, Jamaat-e-Islami, PPP and MMA fall in the first category. On the other hand MQM, Jiye Sindh and ANP have representation in Sindh and NWFP respectively fall in the second category.

A political party has its own manifesto and program to attract followers but much depends on the leadership - its perception - foresight into future trends in politics - aspirations of the people. One, who can feel the pulse of the masses and takes initiative sets out to achieve the goal, wins following, emerges as the leader of the masses? History is full of such examples - of popular personalities all over the world.

Mohan Lal Gandhi after the fall of Muslim rule, domination and establishment of the British chalked out a program to get freedom from the British and assume control of the sub-continent. For the purpose, he organized Indian National Congress apparently to represent both Hindus and Muslims but mainly to advance the cause of his own community. Sir Syed Ahmed Khan who had also been associated with the Hindu leadership timely sensed their selfish designs and advised Muslims to keep away from Congress which was nothing but a trap for them and instead insisted on projecting their cause from a separate platform by organizing political party of their own.

MUSLIM LEAGUE was founded in 1906 - a political party having followers and support from all over the country that had come into existence to protect the rights of the Muslims of the sub-continent and to win a separate homeland for the Muslims. With the support of the masses and able leaders like Allama Iqbal and Mohammad Ali Jinnah it could be possible to achieve the objective. Muslims were successful to form a state for them in India. But after fulfillment of their cherished goal-creation of Pakistan the political party, Muslim League, could not maintain its image and status and fell apart into different groups at the hands of greedy politicians. Instead of a single united lot each leader assigned different names prefixing their own insignia; Jinnah League, Counsel League etc. and as such the party lost its importance and following.

So much so no single unit could ever win enough seats to be able to form a Government without seeking support of other parties except in 1997 when **PM L (N)** group swept the election securing 70% of the national seats. It was also possible by winning over the voters of other rightist parties to induce them to cast their votes to PML (N) otherwise it would go to the advantage of the rival party in a way it was also alliance of all the parties against PPP. Moreover due to murder of her brother, Murtaza Bhutto, involvement of Zardari, and herself in criminal cases, Benazir could not pay much attention to the election campaign and last but not least PPP voter did not come out and almost boycotted the election. However, in 2008 Nawaz League with its founders Mian Nawaz Sharif and his younger talented brother chairman of the party have again shown promise, securing 2nd position in the national assembly and the leading party in the Punjab province. This time the league participated as an ally of PPP formerly its erstwhile rival. Understanding between the two major parties of the country is welcomed by all and considered a prelude to a brighter future - an era of democratic stability and prosperity in the country.

PML (functional) is also called Paghara league as the name suggests Pir of Paghara is the chairman of the party and the party is primarily popular in Sind among followers of the reverend Pir who enjoys respect amongst politicians as well who seek advice and consult him whenever in trouble.

PML (Q) the party who was in power recently, had been carved from the PML (N) and other parties consisting of the rightists groups. Some opportunist members of PPP who won the election on PPP ticket using party vote bank joined the party bargaining - securing Ministries of their choice. The party under the umbrella of Gen. Parvez Musharraf completed its term but in the recent elections lost its position due to changed political scenario in the country; tussle with superior judiciary, assassination of Mohtarma Benazir Bhutto, added insurgency, crisis of power load shedding and flour shortage etc. greatly affected the image of the party which lost the elections miserably not winning enough seats to form its government neither in center and nor any of the four provinces. Its leadership accepting the results of the polls with open mind, decided to sit on the opposition benches, to strengthen democracy in the country.

JAMAT-I-ISLAMI (JI) is a well organized and established party founded by Maulana Abu Aala Maudoodi and presently headed by Qazi Hussain Ahmad. The party has its own manifesto and has following in all the provinces. The party is basically a religious party with restricted membership; to be a member of the party one has to be strictly observing Islamic way of life; saying five times prayers, keeping beard and in case of women covering their head and face all the time while in public etc. As such those Muslims who are no doubt believers and say prayers but have been influenced by western culture neither could get its membership nor have supported the party in large numbers. Hence the party throughout history of its existence could not form its Government at the National level. It was for the first time in 2003 that the party with the name of MMA could win sufficient seats to form its government in Balochistan and NWFP. Let us hope this trend is maintained and the party wins as many or more seats in the next elections. The party leadership elected to abstain from the general elections of 2008 due to differences with President Gen. Musharraf and did not expect a fair election as long as he was in power. Party's boycott however, was useful for N league that by using their vote bank could emerge as a single prominent party in Punjab.

PAKISTAN PEOPLE'S PARTY (PPP) was founded in 1967 by Late Zulfiqar Ali Bhutto s/o Shah Nawaz Bhutto, a feudal land lord of Sind, well educated and who was picked up by Gen. Ayub Khan, initially as Minister of power and later as Foreign Minister. His performance as the foreign Minister won him recognition both at home and abroad. It was through his good offices that Pakistan China relations were established and since then both countries have gained intimacy with the passage of time. His role in 1965 war with India, and particularly his speech in the Security Council, difference of opinion over Tashqand Resolution helped him emerge as one of the most liked and respected leaders of Pakistan; having thus gained fame and confidence of the people when he floated the party met with immediate success and enormous support of the masses. His party's sweeping poles in 1970 election was no surprise when the party emerged as a single majority party in the western wing.

Then again after assuming power after fall of Dacca as in the first instance as Martial Law Administrator, and then as elected Prime minister of Pakistan, did a lot to rehabilitate economy and prestige of the country; gave a workable Constitution to the country having approval of all the provinces, introduced reforms to benefit the common man and relieve the downtrodden poverty stricken population an opportunity to rise, participate in elections and have say in the government, which was unheard of before, being the privilege of Tisanes, Qazilbashs etc. alone. He made Pakistan strong and invincible, even after it was weakened due to bifurcation; his assassination through a fabricated case further venerated him and strengthened the party.

Like Nehru family that enjoys respect and recognition of the masses because of their sacrifices for the nation, Bhutto family has also place in the hearts of the people due to their sacrifices for Pakistan and democracy. It is for this reason that since its inception the party never needed support of other parties to contest elections. On the other hand even the combined opposition and alliance of all the parties could not defeat the party in the past.

PPP is a liberal party not opposed to Islam - but does not believe in coercion. Its membership is not restricted and its supporters come from all walks of life, spread all over the country irrespective of cast, creed, sect or status in the society. Vote bank of PPP is, therefore, solid unlike other parties that use local or provincial influence, religion or worst indulge in the politics of plots or other monetary attractions, buying I.D. cards of voters of the other party. The leadership does not need going from door to door for begging votes. The party is not divisible; whoso ever disassociated with the center, however, popular or capable lost his/her importance and failed to win support of the masses. Examples of Ghulam Mustafa Jatoi, Ghulam Mustafa Khar, Ghinwa Bhutto, Farooq Leghari, and many others are there before us. That goes to prove that Bhutto's daughter is the nucleus that plays a pivotal role in the party and this leadership will continue in her inheritance. Those who believe that by eliminating Benazir Bhutto they would weaken or finish the party are highly mistaken; the party will keep gaining strength after strength the more it is suppressed and the leadership persecuted. If at all democracy has to be allowed to flourish in the country all the parties must be given a fair chance to participate and lead the nation if the electorate repose confidence in them.

Factually there have been two major groups in the country; Muslim League, JI, the rightist and PPP the leftist group. That is why the rightist parties in the past formed alliances; PNA, IJI etc. for contesting elections, whereas PPP has been contesting the election alone, this shows the trend of the voters and the consequent popularity of the PPP. Mohtarma Benazir had been the chairperson of the party till her assassination on

December 28, 2007, led the party ably and kept it united against all odds and even after her death the party is going strong. Her spouse Asif Ali Zardari at present is looking after the party while his son Bilawal Bhutto named chairman, studying abroad comes of age and on finishing his studies would take over.

Benazir Nawaz Agreement:

Meeting between PPP and PML leadership had created confusion in the political circles as national politics since 1988, revolved around these two rival groups, so also tempers of voters remained charged against one another due to that. Should one assume that the meeting and resultant agreement between Mian and Benazir in London on May 21st, 2006 means end of the rivalry? A U turn in national politics that may change the whole scenario of political thinking in Pakistan. However, one should not be surprised at it, as the rivalry between the leadership was not on personal ground rather power oriented; the axis of power having been changed, shift of politics is a natural outcome. Gen. Parvez Musharraf is not a politician - rather a phase and PML Q is a mixture carved of different parties that may desert, the moment there is change of power and as such the only opposition, in case of complete accord between PPP and PML N, left would be JI and its auxiliaries; JUI etc. and some insignificant rightist parties. The alliance of the parties has shown promise and has resulted in clear victory of the parties both at the national and provincial level. Leadership of both parties has agreed to share the government, at center and the province of Punjab where they are in clear majority.

Muttahidda Qaumi Movement (MQM)

Historical Background:

It is a second cadre Party restricted to province of Sind. It was founded by Mr. Altaf Hussain a student leader in 1980s. Became spokesman of people who migrated from India after partition in large numbers settled in the urban areas of Sind, majority of them highly educated and as such could secure Government jobs and their sons and daughters got admissions in school and colleges without much hassle. Because of higher standard of education of the immigrants the local residents could not compete with them in securing jobs, admissions in the professional colleges on merit who started to bicker. The group also comprised of some Hindu population. India taking advantage of the situation tried to exploit the same like she did in Eastern wing.

Zulfiqar Ali Bhutto in order to put an end to that issue declared some concessions for rural inhabitants and fixed quota for them in Government jobs and admissions in professional colleges. This move caused concern among non Sindhi student community. Altaf Hussain a student at Karachi University used to be very vocal on that issue. Mr. Bhutto addressing the students at the University explained that he had given that relaxation to Sindhi students mostly hailing from rural areas for a limited period of 8 years, just to appease them and to avoid any exploitation by India, and further said that those denied admissions in Karachi and Hyderabad should go to Punjab and the Government besides ensuring admissions would offer scholarships to bear the expenses of their boarding lodging there. He also assured that the Government was going to open more medical colleges in Punjab for the purpose. The Indian threat in that way could be avoided but at home the issue was kept alive for political reasons by the opposition.

During Zia-ul-Haq regime Altaf Hussain who had been on the fore front was encouraged to exploit Mohajir Sindhi issue. In this way foundation of a political party with the name "MQM" came into existence. Initially funds were made available to establish and raise membership of the party by Gen. Zia ul Haq; youths, particularly the teenagers were given membership who had to give a bond that once members they would not be allowed to leave the party and obey the orders of the high command at all costs. They were armed with deadly weapons and given training to use them. The party in order to get prominence indulged into indiscriminate killing of innocent laborers to spread terror and thus through its armed members started collecting funds for the party. Torture cells were found existing when crack down during PPP regime was launched by Gen. Nasir Ullah Babar in 1992-93. Mr. Altaf Hussain who was alleged to be involved in some murder cases managed to flee to U.K. and got asylum there, while quite a number of his dangerous companions were either killed or arrested.

Thus the party did not have an august beginning and that is why labeled and known as a terrorist party. Even to-day name of Altaf Bhai is used for intimidation; young workers armed enter offices and business centers and exhort funds for the party, snatch purses from ladies and deprive them of their jewelry, and not only that wherever find food being cooked on the occasion of marriage or any function forcibly take away any quantity of cooked food in the name of Altaf Bhai. One of my cousins who had gone to Karachi, Rizvia from US on the marriage of an orphan relative girl, also came across such situation when he wanted to resist, snatching away the food before it was served to the guests, the people around stopped him from doing that, because of the terror associated with the party. They took away full cooked "degh" of biryani putting in their van. He was told that it was a thing of daily happening and no one ever dare reporting the matter to the police due to the fear generated in their minds about the party. I am sure that it was not being done at the instance of Altaf Hussain - but no doubt must be the side effect of arming the youth without exercising any check on them. The leaders, parents and the party, now in power, should take notice of such activities to relieve the innocent public of Karachi from such highhandedness. Controlling unlawful activities; terrorism, sectarianism is more important than beautification of the metropolis.

The party over the years has attained maturity and has been partner in the center with the ruling party and holds slot of governor in the province of Sind, and is slowly trying to establish its roots in the rest of the country. Mr. Altaf Hussain keeps contact with its supporters regularly through telephonic relays. The party which is now more responsible has been greatly helpful to the Government in resolving issues at all levels. Gen. Musharraf and the Prime Minister, Shaukat Aziz contacted and consulted Altaf Hussain whenever required. The party is well established and has potential to win a number of seats of the National and Provincial Assemblies that were before won by Jamaat-e-Islami or the PPP, and thus the purpose of its founders has been served to a great extent because the party had been mainly created to reduce vote bank of PPP rather than to attain the status of a national body. The party did not follow an agenda to enhance its scope/ status, with its leadership in exile its influence is confined to the urban areas of Sind, where the electorate enjoy majority. Due to the stigma of May 12, the party lost some face but due to constant telephonic contacts with its members the party in the recent elections 2008 has retained its seats in center and the province of Sind. However, with limited seats to its credit the party is not in a position to form a Government independently but has become a part of a coalition with the majority party PPP, to form a government in Sindh with Dr. Ishrat-ul-Ebad ullah retaining the governorship of the province.

Awami National Party (ANP)
In the North West Frontier Province, the anti-British activities of Khan Abdul Ghaffar Khan's "Khudai Khidmitgar' movement had created considerable political activism in the years before Partition. After independence, the National Awami Party (NAP), created in the 1950s on a

progressive, secular platform advocating social reform, continued to exercise a strong influence over NWFP politics, in opposition to the Muslim League. The politics of NAP was inherited in the 1980s by its successor, the Awami National Party (ANP), which under the leadership of Asfandyar Wali, the grandson of Ghaffar Khan, remains a major force in the NWFP today. However, the party has been accused recently of increased opportunism, particularly in the formation in 1997 of an alliance with the PML-N, a party which, in ideological terms, seems to be diametrically at odds with the more radical policies of the ANP. The party has been able to win sufficient seats, has formed a coalition Government with PPP in the province and a ministry in the center as a result of 2008 general elections. It can play a vital role to bring peace to the country in the present situation.

The MMA(Mutahida-Majlis-Ammal

Is comprised of several Islamic religious organizations: Jamiat Ulema-e-Islam or JUI's both factions — Maulana Fazlur Rehman and Maulana Samiul Haq, Jamiat Ulema-e-Pakistan or JUP, and Jamaat-e-Islami, as well as Shia group Tehrik-e-Islami, formerly known as the Tehrik-e-Nafaz-e-Fiqah-e-Jafaria TNFJ. The MMA is the ruling party in NWFP province. Other groups, such as the Ahl-e-hadeeth jamaat of Pakistan have at times been members of the coalition. Jamaat-e-Islami, which is the largest and most organized as well as the protagonist of the coalition, is popular with western-educated intellectuals and the Pakistani intellectuals as well as the clerics. Jamiat Ulema-e-Islam one of the more hardliners and traditional deobandi stream of thinking - with popular appeal amongst clerics and the Pakhtuns and Balochs of NWFP and Balochistan. Jamiat Ulema-e-Pakistan is a traditional Barelvi political party, which is more moderate in its thinking and is popular with traditional and folk Muslims in Pakistani villages in Sindh and Punjab.

Supporters of the MMA regard it as a legitimate "Islamic" political party, whereas opponents of the MMA criticize it, claiming it to be run by corrupt clerics and poor politicians. Opponents also dispute the idea that the MMA is "Islamic". They reject the idea that clerics have special status and are able to implement Islam on the people, and that "Islamic laws" are man-made rather than divine. Supporters, however, argue that clerics or ulema are the right people to implement orthodox Islam and the system of Islam in Pakistan.

Many Pakistanis are suspicious of the MMA, as the party, by virtue of its nature as a professedly religious Islamist party, openly states it desires the establishment of a theocracy, and does not believe in the Western notion of democracy. The MMA's definition of democracy which is identical to theocracy is unacceptable to its opponents.

The MMA benefited immensely from two factors in the general elections of 2002: the sidelining of major political parties as well as anti-American sentiment in Pakistani border provinces because of Afghan war in 2001. Since then, the MMA have been in power in 2 Pakistani provinces: NWFP and Balochistan. However, has lost ground in the 2008 elections partly because of boycott by the Jamaat and partly because of its partnership in the previous Government of Parvez Musharraf.

Pakistan Tehrik-e-Insaf (PTI)

Founded in 1996 by Imran Khan a cricketer turned politician. The party manifesto as the name suggests lays emphasis on rule of law and administration of justice. Primarily, it visualizes an Islamic republic that advocates tolerance, moderation aimed at political stability, social harmony and economic prosperity. Further enunciates that PTI is not only a political party but a broad based movement that embraces the interests of all Pakistanis who in spite of cultural and ethnic diversities blend into a society with common goals. The party undoubtedly has idealistic aspirations and it is yet to seen how it manages to achieve them.

Party founder chairman is Mr. Imran Khan who derived fame from his world class performance in international cricket. I happen to be personally associated with him as his teacher at Aitchison college from where he secured O level certificate and also showed passion for the game. I not only watched him but also played for the college team being cricket in-charge. When he announced and celebrated his retirement in 1986 from the national team, a BBC correspondent recorded my interview who asked questions about his student career both in academics and sports. It lasted for about 15 minutes which was displayed in media in England as well. Briefly, I declared him an average shy student, a promising sports man and differed with him on the decision of his retirement saying that I still see lot of cricket in him, which was later proved true and he returned to play for Pakistan and won the World Cup for Pakistan in 1992-93. The correspondent also asked about his joining politics, since he was being offered some position by Gen. Zia-ul-Haq like Sarfraz Nawaz who joined politics during PPP regime, and my reply was that I would not recommend him joining politics as cricket is a gentlemen's' game whereas politics is not, which did not suit his temperament and soft nature.

He is no doubt a successful social worker having completed a wonderful project of cancer hospital at Lahore doing great service to humanity and now charged with hat zeal has decided to jump into a career against his nature. I happened to attend one of his meeting at Atlanta Georgia in 2010, he seems to be determined to win sizable seats in the National and provincial assemblies in the forthcoming elections and assume as chief executive of the country one day to be able to give practical shape to his dreams. I also presented to him copy of my book "Geopolitical cultural study of Pakistan" and inscribed on it a verse from Allama Iqbal "Jahan main ho saki na qaim kabhi hakumt-e-ishq sitam ye hai keh mohabbat zamana saz nahin" I wish he can disprove that.

CHAPTER XXIV

MAP LANGUAGE OF GEOGRAPHY

Map is the representation of three-dimensional features of the earth on a flat surface so that it maintains shape and area as far as possible. If this representation is out of proportion then it may be a sketch and not a map like if the photograph of a man or women is not proportional to its features, it will be a cartoon not a picture. Photograph of an object- a human being or a building is a map as it proportionally transfers its image on a paper. A globe is very much a map of the world.

Maps are equally important in peace and war. All sorts of economic and strategic planning are first done on the ground. Buildings and roads are first planned on a map and then ground breaking is done. Maps display locations and patterns in geographic space. They are a sort of shorthand through which en-coded messages are transmitted to the reader. Maps compress a great deal of geographic information otherwise it could not have been possible to view global worldwide projects so easily and concisely. Map is the language of geography. If a photograph is worth thousands of words as is commonly believed — a map is worth a million. Map is a laboratory of geographers where they locate test and prove or reject their hypothesis.

Essentials of a map
Scale is an important requirement of a map. It depicts the distance on the map to the distance on the ground. It is also termed a ratio of map/ground. It is also stated as R.F., a representative fraction, which is displayed on the bottom of a map in words or fractions. A large-scale map will have small denominator and a small scale or an atlas map will have a bigger one.

Orientation
Each map must show the direction of north without that no location can be authentic. The direction of north can be determined by any of the features; grid lines, meridians or lines of longitudes or by a magnetic compass. There is however, slight variations in all these directions; the grid lines give the direction of grid north, lines of longitude or meridians point towards true north and the magnetic compass gives the direction of

magnetic north. All these directions are given on a survey sheet, which shows that there are three types of north:

(i)   Grid north
(ii) True north
(iii) Magnetic north

 Variation is also provided on the bottom of the map, which shows the difference in their directions at a given time, as the direction of magnetic north keeps on changing, some time it is to the west of true north and sometimes to the east indicating rate of variation as well.

Finding Direction of North

1. Grid north can be found by north south running red lines that point towards Grid north.

2. Magnetic north can be determined by the help of a magnetic compass any time as earth being a huge magnet; its north pole attracts South Pole of the needle, which will point towards north when the needle is allowed to oscillate freely.

3. True north: During the day time the true north can be found out by the direction of sun; In the morning if you stand with your face towards the sun, open your arms, to your left would be true north. At night, the direction of north can be found by observation of the pole star, which can be done with the help of pointers of a constellation called Ursa Major also named Great Bear — a group of seven stars prominent in the sky, third in dimension amongst the constellations, shaped like a plough/question mark. Its outer two stars called pointers, since they always point towards a distant star not very bright called Polaris. It remains almost at one position, whereas other stars, due to rotation of the earth, keep changing their position at different times during the night. Sailors mostly maintain their direction with the help of the Pole star at night. (The three norths are shown on the left hand bottom of the survey map and Ursa Major and its pointers alpha and beta in the celestial diagram produced below).

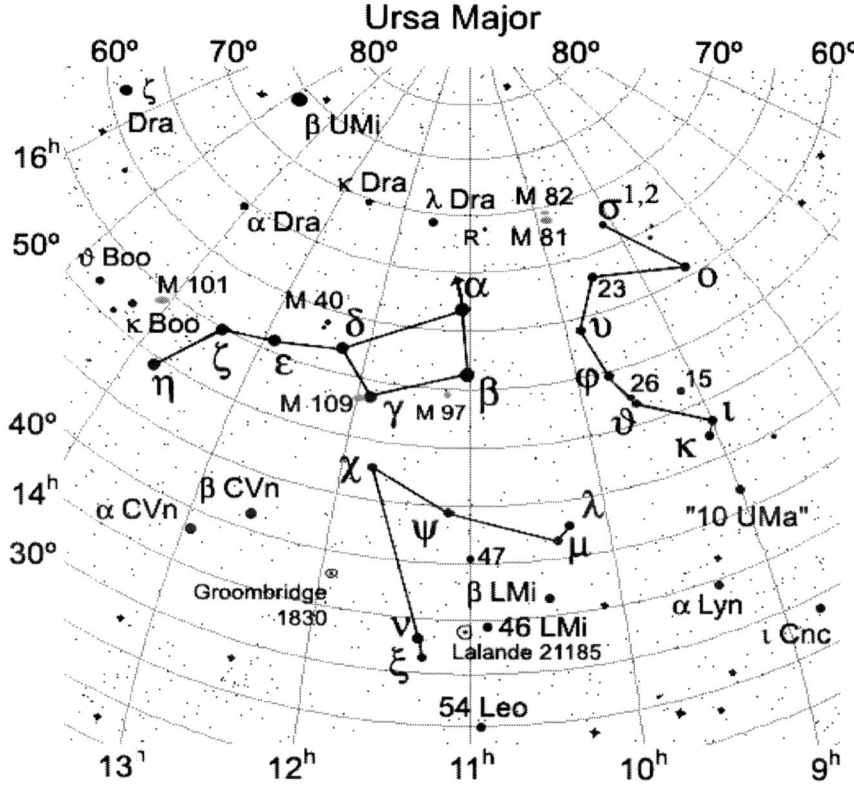

Figure 27: Ursa Major – indicator of the pole star
Note: Alpha, Beta are the two outer stars of Ursa Major the pointers

Map Projections

As we know that earth is round and a curved surface cannot be easily
transferred, without distortion, on a flat ground. The device of transferring
a curved surface on a plane is called map projection. There are different
types of projections. Polar locations can best be transferred by Polar or
Zenithal projections, for temperate regions; Europe USA, Conical
projections are more suited, whereas for Equatorial or tropical areas,
Cylindrical projections are used. The projections that maintain shape are
called orthographic, the ones that maintain area are known as equal area
projections. Some projections compromise and try to maintain shape and
area or direction in limited regions. Mercator's projection is a popular one
and commonly used for navigations charts that maintains direction and
shape but greatly distorts area, particularly away from the Equator.

Contour Lines

Contour lines are imaginary lines that join places with equal height above sea level and are shown by brown lines on the map, which depict unevenness or slope of land like hills, valleys, flat or plain areas on the same plane. The relative heights on atlas maps are shown by isopleths using different shades of colors on the maps. Hamlets, towns, cities and roads are marked by using different symbols.

MAP READING

Decoding the information given on the map utilizing the indicators provided in the form of symbols colors, stated on the margins is called map reading. Large-scale ordinance sheets prepared by Survey department for each area are available and can be utilized for acquiring proficiency in this field.

GPS

Global Positioning System consists of 21 satellites + (3 spares) that orbit earth on precisely predictable paths, broadcasting highly accurate time and location information. Although U.S. government owns the GPS but the information transmitted by the satellite is freely available to everyone around the world. All that is needed is a GPS receiver that costs less than 100 dollars that can relay longitude, latitude and height within 10 meters day or night in any part of the world. GPS has drastically increased the accuracy and efficiency in the collection of spatial data.

GIS

Geographic Information Systems and remote sensing (the system of collection of information about parts of Earth's surface by means of aerial photography or satellite imagery) is called GIS system. The photographs thus obtain after discarding overlapping, maps with greatest precision are produced which are known as Topographic maps. The GPS system in combination with GIS system has revolutionized map making and spatial analysis.

What Is GIS (Geographic Information System)?

GIS is a mapping software system that links information about places (location) with layers of information about the places (location). Unlike with a paper map, where "what you see is what you get," a GIS map can combine many different layers of information depending upon the purpose e.g. analyzing environmental damage, finding best location for a school.

To use a paper map, all you do is unfold it, and spread it out before you. It is a representation of cities and roads, mountains and rivers, railroads and political boundaries making use of the marginal information of the topographic sheet.

As on the paper map, a digital map created by GIS will have dots, or points, and also lines (arcs) and polygons that represent features on the map such as cities; lines that represent features such as roads; and small areas that represent features such as lakes.

The difference is that this information comes from a database and is shown only if the user chooses to see it. The database stores where the point is located, how long the road is, and even how many square miles a lake occupy.

Each piece of information in the map sits on a layer, and the users turn on or off the layers according to their needs. One layer could be made up of all the roads in an area while another could represent all the lakes in the same area. Yet another could represent all the cities.

Cartography

The drawing of maps and charts covering all stages from field survey to published map making is known as cartography. With the formation of The British Cartographic Society and the International Cartographic Association, cartography has officially been given a wider meaning and scope involving all types of political, physical and economic maps keeping into consideration all the elements, scale, direction and the suitability of map projection.

Types of Map Projections

Azimuthal Projection

If you imagine a piece of paper touching an illuminated globe at one point, the projection of the globe onto the paper would resemble an Azimuthal projection map. Azimuthal Projection maps are useful for viewing the polar regions of the world, because the poles usually appears near the center of the map, with longitudinal lines meeting at the poles and spreading away from each other as they move away from the poles. The Polar Regions are relatively free of distortion, but the distortion increases as the longitudinal lines move towards equatorial areas.

Conical Projection

If you imagine a paper cone placed over an illuminated globe, the projection on the cone would resemble a conic projection map. Such a map is relatively free of distortion in the middle latitude regions, and is useful for viewing countries that fall within those regions, such as some European countries, USA.

Cylindrical Projection

If you imagine a paper wrapped around an illuminated globe, the projection on to the paper is the cylindrical projection. The shape of the continents near the middle of the cylindrical

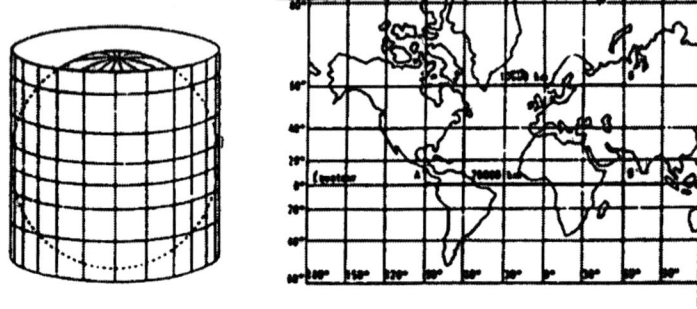

Figure 28: Cylindrical projection

projection would be relatively free of distortion but the region near the poles would be stretched out of proportions.

Topographic map

In addition to showing general locations and political boundaries, topographic maps depict the geography and special features of an area. This type of map offers   many advantages. For instance, most backpackers use topographic map to navigate through wilderness, planning their routs with obstacles and landmarks in mind. If they should get lost, they can find their bearings again by aligning their map and compass to a prominent feature observed nearby. A key on each map indicates the distance scales and special symbols (for features such as railroads, schools, airstrips and water towers) used to create it. Generally, the green on a topographic map indicates forest or vegetation, while the white indicate areas that are bare of growth. Series of brown lines indicate mountains and hills, showing elevations and relative slopes. Each line represents a specific unit of elevation; where the lines are very close together, the terrain is quite steep.

Drawing a Cross-Section

The map on top is a topographical map. The map's curving lines, or contours, are labeled. The number indicates how high the area is above sea level falling on the contour line. Below is a cross-section of the map on top. The x-axis of the cross-section corresponds to the line from A to B on the topographical map. The Y-axis is used with the x-axis to plot the height of each contour where it crosses the line AB. This creates a series of dots. By connecting the dots, a cross-section of the line of the landscape is created as drawn below: The tops of the hills are inter-visible.

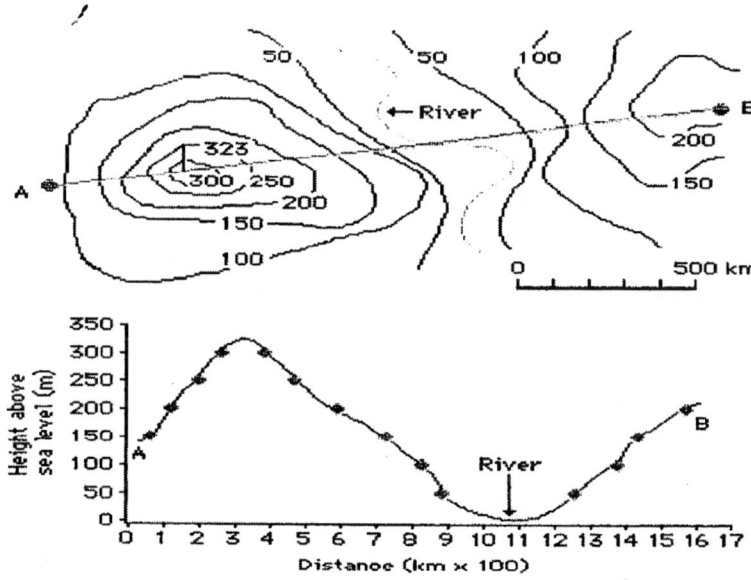

Figure 29: Cross section

- 415 -

SUMMARY

The present volume is an attempt to provide a reliable and informative work covering; geography, history, culture and religion (as perceived and interpreted by Allama Iqbal). It is a standard book for a common reader with ethnic and Islamic values. Efforts of Muslim scholars and devotees-Sufis and Saints who spread the light of Islam in this part of the world, coming all the way from far flung areas, setting personal examples, created deep rooted effects on the local bewildered population that helped them to behold and feel the truth - to adopt a way of life taught by His chosen reverenced apostles; from Adam to Prophet Mohammad peace is upon them. Besides description of geographical factors structure, relief, plains built by the Indus and its tributaries, loftiest mountains of the world, wonderful climates, vegetation, animals humans and their cultures, an independent approach to the history of the region and concerted efforts, struggle of leaders of India and Pakistan to gain freedom from the British rule has been made unfolding a number of mysteries, complexities of geopolitical nature.

The readers will find the experience not only informative but also exciting and exhilarating- would also help defusing religious, sectarian and regional rivalries and tensions between people belonging to the same soil and origin- the very purpose of undertaking the venture.
The book, therefore, should have a place in every house hold particularly Indians –Pakistanis and Bangladeshis having common historical, geographical and cultural background. Foreign policy and Pakistan's relations with Muslim world, neighbors and International organizations have also been discussed in detail emphasizing need for resolving differences amicably developing better understanding for the benefit and raising standard of living of their masses.

Comprehensive account of technique of map making and their interaction has been provided to help readers to acquaint them with this important skill of great importance in practical life during peace or war.

It would also serve as a textbook for students offering History, Geography and Culture of the region, particularly South Asia.

Author

Bibliography:

World Regions in Global contexts
By Sallie A. Marston, Paul L. Knox
University of Arizona

Holy Quran
Book of God

Khilafat-o-Malukiat
by Maulana Abul Aala Maudoodi

History of Islam
by Justice Ameer Ali.

Religions of India

Introduction to Pak Studies
By Prof. Ikram Rabbani, co-author

Geography of Pakistan
By Dr. K.U. Qureshi,
Ex Chairman Department of Geography,
University of the Punjab, Lahore.

CPSIA information can be obtained at www.ICGtesting.com
Printed in the USA
BVOW06s0754150813

328731BV00008B/168/P

9 781439 273265